CLEARLY
INVISIBLE
IN
PARIS

'This audacious and intimately crafted novel delves deep into the intricacies of belonging and acceptance, and at its heart, it radiates a joyous celebration of female friendships. A remarkable debut, this book is an absolute must-read.'
—**Twinkle Khanna**, Author

'Everyone has a story and, sometimes, these stories intertwine. Four fierce and flawed immigrant women in Paris become the friends you never knew you needed. Keenly observed and deeply felt, this is one hearty debut.'
—**Zoya Akhtar**, Film-maker

'Set against the enchanting backdrop of Paris, Koël Purie's *Clearly Invisible in Paris* immerses the reader in the captivating and eventful lives of four immigrant women, whose intertwined stories bring forth a searing examination of the complexities of identity, love and the pursuit of happiness. In this narrative, rooted in exploring the ideas of belonging and acceptance, the reader will find themselves moved by the immense resilience and endearing connections shared by the four protagonists. An entrancing debut.'
—**Dr Shashi Tharoor**, Member of Parliament and author

'This book is a triumph. It is fresh, fearless, intimate and intricate. It is layered equally with pain, absurdity, deeply lived experience and shallow vanities. It is a grudgingly extracted love letter to a high-maintenance city. Most of all, it is an ode to odd, enduring female friendships. Read it.'
—**Anuja Chauhan**, Author

'Vividly narrated and acutely observed.... The four immigrant women in the book make you wonder, *'Don't I know them? Weren't they friends and neighbours once?'* An insider–outsider novel that peers into the darkness of the City of Light. The Koël's call is loud and clear...'
—**Shobhaa De**, Author

'Koël Purie Rinchet's debut novel explores the delicate balance between identity, belonging and the pursuit of a meaningful life in the City of Light. Highly recommended.'

—**Vikas Swarup**, Author

'Grief is the fundamental reality of life. None of us escape it. But we all feel it in our own individual, and dare one say it, special way. It's difficult to believe that this is Koël's debut novel—so consummate is her storytelling. The characters of *Clearly Invisible in Paris* are all immigrants, going through their own pain, in a city that glitters on the surface with glamour and joy. They don't even know the others exist. And the pandemic, with the resultant lockdown, throws them all together. They manage their own individual grief and problems through the only way possible: through human relationships. Painful yet funny, irreverent yet inspiring, quirky yet deep, this book about friendships that defy logic and a life that—despite it all—must be lived is a must-read.'

—**Amish Tripathi**, Author

'A paean to Paris, full of laughter, wisdom, joy and heartbreak. This is a novel of intersecting identities, dislocation and survival that goes to the heart of the migrant experience, while never losing its terrific sense of fun.'

—**Aatish Taseer**, Author

CLEARLY INVISIBLE IN PARIS

KOËL PURIE RINCHET

RUPA

Published by
Rupa Publications India Pvt. Ltd 2023
7/16, Ansari Road, Daryaganj
New Delhi 110002

Sales centres:
Prayagraj Bengaluru Chennai
Hyderabad Jaipur Kathmandu
Kolkata Mumbai

Copyright © Koël Purie Rinchet 2023

This is a work of fiction. Names, characters, places and incidents are either the product of the author's imagination or are used fictitiously and any resemblance to any actual person, living or dead, events or locales is entirely coincidental.

While every effort has been made to trace copyright holders and obtain permission, this has not been possible in all cases; any omissions brought to our attention will be remedied in future editions.

All rights reserved.

No part of this publication may be reproduced, transmitted, or stored in a retrieval system, in any form or by any means, electronic, mechanical, photocopying, recording or otherwise, without the prior permission of the publisher.

P-ISBN: 978-93-5702-468-6
E-ISBN: 978-93-5702-464-8

First impression 2023

10 9 8 7 6 5 4 3 2 1

The moral right of the author has been asserted.

Printed in India

This book is sold subject to the condition that it shall not, by way of trade or otherwise, be lent, resold, hired out, or otherwise circulated, without the publisher's prior consent, in any form of binding or cover other than that in which it is published.

For my Tchoopsie,
you make me want to be better every day.

PART 1

Disobedient Organ

Chapter 1

The room was sombre. It had never seen the light the city was renowned for. The woman was half-sized, daring to live a full-sized life. She pulled up one panty after another over her two-euro leggings, her hands trembling like badly set jelly. Her face betrayed no emotion. It had forgotten how. She did not have the sisterhood of Number Thirty-Six to protect her yet, so she hummed a prayer to calm her hands and squeezed on two pairs of jeans over the five underpants she was wearing, followed by multiple pairs of socks. Each item of quarrelsome clothing felt like two hundred kilograms that afternoon.

Her chant became a soft song. Her voice was the sort that transports its listeners to a safe, sunshiny place, where life feels like a slow, barefoot walk on a white sand beach. Today her voice found perverse pleasure in taking her to a blind alley full of broken dreams and weeping banshees. Panic penetrated her pores. *No, no, not today, not now.* She forced herself to take a slow, long breath in, pushing the panic out, postponing it till she could allow herself the luxury to feel again. Life in dim rooms had taught her how, and this was not the time for such comforts.

A distant door slammed, making her jump. She froze, the hymn stuck in her throat. The sound of her heartbeat filled her head, bouncing off the walls of the bare closet she called a room. The sound grew louder and louder till her ears were about to explode with the noise of her own heart. How had she, Rosel Andal, apple of her father's eye, with a voice that summoned angels to earth, ended up here? Nothing was as it should be. She had to get out and she had to do it now. If only she could move.

Her overdressed jelly body felt nailed to the ground.

The sound of the key turning brought a benumbed Rosel back to life. The front door of the sprawling apartment, furnished like a love child of Tutankhamun and Versace, banged open. *Why had the Madame come back so soon? Hadn't she just left?* A young, flustered but chic woman, her head and neck covered with a Fendi hijab, walked in. 'Rosel. Ro-s-e-l. Where are you? Rosel?'

Rosel threw on her puffer jacket, zipping it all the way up to hide the multiple shirts she was wearing, and came out of her windowless chamber.

'Please get my red Jimmy Choos—you know the ones I bought at the airport, with the little diamanté straps. They're in my shoe closet or in the dressing room cupboard or check the one in the bathroom,' the Kuwaiti Madame ordered.

Rosel disappeared down the ornate corridor.

'These new Schuberry stilettos are biting me so badly, I should never have bought them,' the Kuwaiti said to the empty room. 'I'll never make it through the Christmas lunch wearing them. Imagine leaving early—they've booked a stripper! This might be the last bit of fun I'll be allowed before my husband arrives with his mother. He should've married her.'

Rosel returned with the red shoes and knelt down in front of the woman to change them.

'I paid two thousand seven hundred euros for these stupid Schuberrys, they could at least make them comfortable. Two thousand seven hundred euros! That's probably more than I pay you.'

Actually, that was more than triple of what Rosel was paid a month, on the months she did get paid.

'Can you hurry? I want to get a spot on the sofa in front with Sadia. I bet the stripper will choose Sadia to dance in front of. Yallah, Rosel, what's the matter?'

Rosel fiddled with the tiny buckle, breathing into her wobbly hands. Her fingers felt like soggy wooden clubs and she was beginning to overheat, her cheeks changing colour.

'Why are you wearing a winter jacket inside the house?' She didn't wait for Rosel's answer, instead going off on a tirade. 'You lot are all the same. My previous one never knew what to wear when either. What's the point of bringing you to Paris? All you know and feel is the cold. The City of Light! And you sit inside with a coat!'

Rosel built up the courage to ask once again for her passport—her Madame had pocketed it at Charles de Gaulle airport before the immigration stamp had even dried. The employer, who thought of herself as an owner, stared distastefully at the kneeling creature in front of her. Then, calmly, almost (but not quite) caringly, she said, 'Be grateful, Rosel, that I'm keeping your passport safe in a big city like Paris. If you lose it, what'll you do? Become a prostitute?'

Rosel meekly interjected, 'But Ma'am, I have no identity card at all.'

'And what exactly do you need an identity card for? Planning a boat trip down the Seine?' A genuine laugh escaped her twisted mouth and for a moment she looked almost-but-not-quite pretty. 'Where is it that you want to go? It's not like you leave this apartment without me.'

'Ma'am I just want to keep—'

'Let's discuss this later.' The Kuwaiti was done talking to the help. 'You are going to make me miss the stripper's entry.'

Rosel fell silent.

As her employer left and double-locked the door behind her, Rosel checked her underwear, caressing all the money she had in the world: four twenty-euro notes. She sang her song of praise again while neatly arranging the Schuberry shoes that had been left behind—a force of habit. Realizing what she was doing—what she had been doing for years—Rosel picked up the shoes and dropped them in the garbage on top of rotting hummus. Then she took a pot of tzatziki from the fridge and plopped the creamy substance on top of the Schuberrys with a vengeance that would've made Malcolm X proud. Her small and successful act of rebellion: a four-euro pot of tzatziki had destroyed two thousand seven hundred euros in less than twenty seconds. A perverted satisfaction travelled through her limbs, making her core tingle with power as she watched the stain spread across the satin stilettos.

She was ready now—if only her body would obey. Her heart beat with an unfamiliar enthusiasm, as if it was in clear sight of the finish line for a race she scarcely believed she had the right to run. Her life flashed past her: her son's little fingers, the bloated face of the husband that never was, the police shootings, the breeze on the salt dunes, sponge bathing obnoxious old men... *Stop this nonsense. This is not the end. And, if it is, better to choose it than have it chosen for you like everything else in your endless little life.*

Stop this. She took a deep breath.

Take the plunge.

Chapter 2

Not far from Rosel, twenty-five metres underground, Violet stepped off a train in her high-heeled boots. Something about the day felt urgent and made her uneasy. She checked her reflection in the shiny metal body of the departing metro. She was dressed in caramel-coloured suede pants that fit her like a second skin; her favourite knee-high, python leather Chloé boots; and a deep purple ostrich-feathered winter coat. Violet didn't care that she'd paid way too much for the coat. She felt spectacular in it. Her hair was slicked back into a ponytail so tight that her eyes looked like Catwoman's after an extreme blepharoplasty. She had a great figure with a tiny waist and wore no make-up. The last laser session had worked wonders on her stubble. In her opinion—which was the only one that mattered—she was a rather striking woman. *Why the discomfort today?* She walked through the long corridor to change trains, careful not to touch anything. It was not crowded, but a beefy young boy, part of a group of teenagers, shoved past her.

'*Sale pédé, homosexuel,*' he jeered, smirking to his friends and making a rude gesture with his finger and fist that left little to the imagination.

Over the years, Violet had taught herself to ignore such jibes. Today, however, it was the boy's turn to learn. She squared herself in front of the gabby juvenile. She was slender but, in her heels, almost a foot taller than him. Sighing into his face, she let him smell the spearmint and danger on her breath, eyeballing him just long enough to intimidate. He shuffled. She swallowed noisily, her Adam's apple incongruously bobbing up and down her delicate neck. She smiled and, in her acquired silky voice, corrected him, '*Je ne suis pas homosexuel. Je suis la femme dont tu rêves.*' Yes, you fucker, the woman you have pornographic dreams about.

Violet reached into her bag. He immediately covered his face, thinking she was going to mace him. She laughed, sniffed him, turned up her nose and chucked a Chanel deodorant at him saying, '*Utilse-le. Tu pues du cul.*'

Wiping her hands sensually on her suede pants, she winked at him and walked off before the boy could come up with a retort. Her body language was confident, nonchalant, but Violet's heart was playing basketball in her chest. Why couldn't this bothersome organ toe the line and stick to its job of pumping blood and keeping her alive? She couldn't bear it when it shouted out its presence, reminding her that her own existence was borrowed, invented and ephemeral. She needed no reminder of *that*, thank you very much.

She click-clacked her way down the tunnelled corridor. The geometrical Art Nouveau beauty of the tiles on the walls helped calm her. She kept her focus on their glossy white symmetry. Violet could do this route blindfolded—it was hardwired into her. There were days when she left her apartment and arrived at the club without remembering how she had got there. But today, nothing escaped her. Both the participant and audience of her own reality show, she had eyes for the minutest detail.

As usual, she smiled and tossed a coin at the busking geriatric swing band, the members of which lived by and for their music, performing underground day after day, like they were the closing act at the Carnegie Hall. They smiled back and started playing a funky rendition of Glen Miller's 'In the Mood'. She marched on, the music lifting her, making her lighter, until she heard the first strands of the operatic singing that haunted her every day. A plump girl with fuchsia smeared lips, stood strategically under a tiled archway, taking advantage of its hollow echo, and belted out the Purcell aria, 'O Let Me Weep'.

The marching footsteps of the crowd with the lugubrious singing, peppered with her own unarticulated longing, engulfed Violet in a bubble that felt at once light and suffocating. Her mind floated away, her body treaded in slow motion, wading through an ocean of music. She knew if she didn't do it today, she never would. So, with blind purpose, she moved away from the crowd and walked towards him, somehow sure—although not entirely certain—that he would be there.

Chapter 3

At that precise moment back above ground, Neera was running out of Number Thirty-Six, rue des Diablesse, in her oh-so-bourgeois west Paris neighbourhood.

Neera, the pen-wielding demolisher of lives, seen running barefoot in the Parisian snow! What would the bottle-blonde Mumbai ladies lunching at Bastian think of her now? Would they notice her lime green Issey Miyake skirt, dainty Zimbabwean emerald earrings, snug cashmere sweater and matching fur shrug? No, they would just focus on her bare feet. Even after all the years and miles, she despised those women, more than her father despised the summer flies stuck on his jalebi counter. She wanted to swat them, one by one, with an electric swatter! The pleasure she'd feel at watching them fry to death.

It was snowing lightly, and snow, like her, didn't belong in Paris. It would cover everything in its silvery splendour for five-and-a-half minutes and then the locals would rail against the sludge it left behind. She spotted the Mercedes that matched the details in the text she'd been sent.

She tapped the window, said *Bonjour, monsieur*—the full extent of her French, almost—and began to hand the tattooed driver fifty-euro notes. The driver, living up to the reputation of the city, instantly became agitated.

'*Montez dans la voiture, Madame,*' he protested.

'Sorry, I don't understand.'

The cold was travelling up her feet, setting into her spine. Pausing to put on shoes could've been the thing that changed her mind, and she was determined to finish what she'd set in motion that morning. Could he just take the money already?

'*Non, non, non. Madame, s'il vous plaît, entrez. Je ne peux pas le faire comme ça.*'

'Here, please take the money or speak English.'

The driver opened the passenger side door, signalling for her to get in.

'No, no, no, I have to go back upstairs, my husband is waiting.' Neera was hopelessly gesturing to make herself understood, not entirely sure how one mimed a waiting husband.

The driver slammed the door shut and started to drive away, but Neera ran behind the car, desperately holding onto the handle of the backseat door. He stopped and she reluctantly got in the back, relieved, at least, to have her feet off the slush.

The driver pulled out a credit card, slid it in the thin gap above the stereo and yanked the entire panel open. There was more weed in there than she had ever seen. The stench of it filled the car. Could she go to jail for this? How would she explain that to her waiting husband, or worse, her father, who'd spent his whole life waiting on her? Neera began to hyperventilate. The driver turned to look as she rolled down the window and stuck her head out, breathing in the cold to calm herself and ending up in a coughing fit, gasping for air.

The coughing made her feel about as calm as an illegal immigrant caught jumping a forbidden boundary wall. The tattooed driver-dealer, meanwhile, was handing her bag after bag of fragrant weed and she was handing them right back to him. It would have been infinitely funny had it not been truly terrifying for her and equally irritating for him.

From the day, way back in Mumbai, when she first got a taste for disconnecting from her mind, she made it a point to surround herself with convenient friends who were glad to score a bag of happiness for her. But this was Paris and Neera had no one to run her errands, or for that matter, anyone to be her friend, convenient or not. Even after five years of smoking the stuff, she had no idea how to go about doing the deal, how much anything cost, what the law was or how frightening it could all be. Still, like most things in her life, she was sure she could fake it till she figured it out. She wished she was high and not foreign. A recurring wish, she noted. Well, she was about to be a little more of the former. If only she could be a little less of the latter.

She tried once more in broken French to tell him she wanted just the one bag, but the driver refused to take the others back.

'*Ça c'est le minimum, Madame*,' he insisted in French, 'You *voulez* room service, non? *Alors, ça c'est le minimum. D'accord?*'

Neera understood the word 'minimum', and she had brought the money that the person on the phone had demanded.

'Yes, but I pay the minimum, I no want so much. I want one, un, une, ooonn, uno…' *What is the goddamned word?* 'I pay, I take ONE. QUIERO UNO. COMPRENDO?' *Okay, well done, that's not even French.* She handed him the sweaty roll of money she had in her hand.

'*Oui*,' he said, pocketing the two hundred and fifty euros. '*Voilà!*'

Success, she thought. Then he passed her five full bags.

Neera stared at the little green bags in her lap, wondering what to do, when the driver started to drive off, with her still seated in the back. She started screaming for her life. When he parked fifty metres ahead in an empty spot, she realized he was only trying to clear the way for a passing car. The driver turned around to stare at this looney lady, whom he had definitely had enough of. She tried to cover up the scream with, 'Haaay! Yay! Yaaaayeeee! Yaas, yes, yes, thank you.'

They were both desperate for her to get out of the car. She cursed herself for not carrying a bag or wearing a coat with pockets. She shoved the five bags, as discreetly as possible, into the front of her panty, got out of the dreaded car and stood barefoot in the sludge with a bulging crotch, which gave out a distinct aroma and looked decidedly aroused.

Chapter 4

Across town, a few arrondissements away, Dasha snubbed the cold—her father had taught her that it was nothing more than a number on a thermostat—and ran laps around a freezing warehouse in nothing but lingerie and pencil heels.

Seated at a table at the front in the grey, high-ceilinged room were a casting director, a producer and Benjamin, a lowly assistant with a video camera and the only one smiling at the unclad girl. All of them were wearing warm coats, jackets and scarves and still looking cold. Dasha ran past them again, half-naked. The casting director, who looked twenty years older than she actually was and wore far too much eyeshadow, spoke Franglais and shouted instructions at her to take longer, slower strides.

'Imagine *tu* jumping over the *rivières* and *montagnes. Comme une gazelle.* Long, long *jambes.* Floating,' she instructed. '*Plus haute, plus.* Higher, higher. More graceful. More, more. *En plus en plus*, that's it.' Then, without missing a beat, '*Arrête!* Stop! *Ça suffit.* Enough, thank you. *Fini.*'

Dasha stopped mid-stride. The recruiters began discussing lunch options, Dasha now seemingly invisible to them. She awkwardly started to collect her clothes.

Without looking up, the high priestess of eyeshadow said in a sugary tone, '*S'il te plait*, you *fini* dressing outside, *non? Et* tell *la* next girl *entrer.*'

Holding on to her clothes, she retreated into the comfort of her mind. Being an Insta-addict, Dasha had a knack for seeing the dreary and the cruel through filters—as many metaphorical filters as it took to shift the grainy harshness of a situation into a smooth, colour-enhanced, vignette-encased, palatable image, which often bore little resemblance to reality but garnered the highest number of imaginary likes and kept her heart from breaking into a million pieces. The mighty custodians of casting now sported cute dog ears and whiskers, and with each rainbow and bunny that tumbled out of their over-sized, unsuspecting, cartoon mouths, her smile grew wider. Inside her head, she remained the only one in control. She exhaled frost and pushed open the heavy iron door leading out.

'Hurry up,' Eyeshadow hollered, '*Vite! Vite, ma chérie!*'

Maybe it was the cold, or Eyeshadow's raspy interruption piercing through her filters, or maybe it was simply time. Dasha flipped around and leapt, gazelle-like in high heels, straight on to the casting director's table. Before any of them had time to react, she clicked an unbelievable selfie, standing on the table, still in her lingerie, with the terrible three looking up her long, bare legs, their mouths hanging wide open.

Professional suicide. She knew it, yet she laughed, laughed uncontrollably. It had been a long time coming, this laughter. It was unshared, but now that it was here, it filled the room and she couldn't stop. It was Osho or Bhagwan or somebody who had said in the documentary she had watched last night—'When you really laugh, for those few moments you are in a deep meditative state. Thinking stops. It is impossible to laugh and think together. You experience the power of consciousness.'

She was sure she was experiencing this power, whatever it was. Her clenched jaw released, her fear of failure faded, the strangers who controlled her destiny, sitting right in front of her, shrank and disappeared. Momentarily, everything was as it should be. Before the moment was snatched from her, she exited the room, still laughing.

Now that she had challenged the status quo and defied destiny with the same impertinence it had been showing her lately, she knew she'd be recompensed with the message she'd been waiting for. Fortune favours the bold, the brave are always rewarded and all that, right? She scanned her social media and her messaging apps with renewed optimism only to be slapped back into place. Nothing. Not a word since he had left. To add to her woes, she could hear destiny laughing at her, saying, 'Go on, ruin the few chances I send your way.'

No, I'm not done, far from it. I have enough fight in me. You don't get to win yet. Dasha always had to have the last word.

The cold outside reminded her of her father and this warmed her up. She would find him or make him find her. As hare-brained as Dasha's plans were, they invariably seemed to work, somersaulting her firmly onto her feet. Hadn't she managed to get someone to pay her to come live in Paris from her obscure town, a town that not one person she had met in France in the past eight months had heard of? Admittedly, in Paris, luck was playing a one-sided game of hide and seek—if she stopped seeking, the game would abruptly end.

Still, she had a plan. And a girl with a plan was better than one without. She was no more than one lucky break away. Soon she'd be on every magazine cover and billboard and TV commercial and cereal box and car launch and mega event there was in Europe. It would be impossible for him to not see her everywhere, and then he would be guilted or beguiled into calling her. It was a good plan. It was simply taking longer, much longer, than she had envisaged to get it off the ground. The lack of control over her future was unfair. Well, at least she could predict that the casting she'd just walked out of was not going to be her launch pad. She started laughing again.

Chapter 5

Crossing herself, Rosel inhaled courage, tied her shoelaces and opened the kitchen window. The promised rope dangled in front of her face, stupefying her. She'd half-hoped it wouldn't be there. *No turning back now.* Her friend Len must've risked a lot to hang that rope from the roof. With a double-locked door between them, the two had gone over the plan a million times. *Trust the plan.* It was Rosel's turn to defy danger. *Go on, grab the rope.*

Her hands were no longer shaky—or maybe they were. She couldn't tell. Rosel was no longer in her body as she swung on that lifeline to reach the open metal stairwell at the back of the building. Mustering strength that she had only a distant memory of, Rosel made her way down a narrow spiral staircase, leaving behind the unacceptable life she had come to accept.

Out on the street, she was overwhelmed by the people, the traffic, the signs, the Christmas lights and the melting slush everywhere. The euphoria of escape was gone. She was back in her body and didn't know what to do with it. Her mind ping-ponged, hitting the walls of her head. From the time she'd arrived in Paris two-and-a-half years ago, she had been out of the apartment a mere handful of times and never alone, except for that one time when her Madame had sent her lumbering home with all the shopping bags. The possibility of escape hadn't even entered her mind back then. Where would she go? What would she do? Paris was not her city. Was it anyone's?

She followed the directions scribbled by Len on a piece of paper, but was quickly disorientated and, she feared, lost.

Tentatively, she stopped people. 'Sir, which way is the street Jaampz Ay-lie-zee?'

No one had heard of this street. Pulling up their coat collars, hunching against the cold, they walked by.

'Excuse me please, could you show me the street Chumpes Aaleeysee?'

This was Paris, and if you couldn't say it right, they couldn't hear you and certainly didn't want to see you. She was near tears. Poor Rosel had managed to escape her prison tower, only to be defeated by pronunciation. Then, through her panic, she saw an exceptionally tall girl standing still amidst the rushing crowd, crying hysterically. Or was she laughing?

As Rosel walked towards that girl, she repeated the name of the street several times, until the laughing girl impatiently grabbed the paper and read aloud perfectly—*43, Champs Élysées*. She mocked her foreign-ness, conveniently forgetting that she herself was from elsewhere.

'You are *on* Champs Élysées, this is it, missy,' the girl said. 'Let's see. You need forty-three, this is hundred and seventeen; I'll walk with you, I'm going that way. Actually, I'll float with you like a gazelle. Jump, jump!' Dasha was about to start laughing again, when she caught the look of terror on Rosel's face. It was a look that she herself was intimately acquainted with. 'Come on then,' she said kindly instead.

Rosel followed, walking a little too close. Dasha eyed this miniature person, doll-like but not a dwarf, and wondered if the world was a luckier place from down there. Breaking through the heavy silence, she asked, 'So, where are you from?'

Rosel, the girl with no identity, didn't know how to answer this. 'Huh? Hello? *Coucou!* Earth calling. Where are you from?'

'I'm from here.'

'Yes, aren't we all,' shrugged Dasha. 'Now, if only we belonged.' Rosel was comforted by Dasha's presence and her English, even though she seemed a little more than completely nuts. A few minutes later, Len, Rosel's friend, rushed towards her.

'I thought you won't make it. Or chickened out. Or got lost,' she said hugging Rosel tightly.

'Yes, I was lost, completely lost, till someone told me that I was exactly where I needed to be.' She was too full of emotion to look up at Dasha.

'We all need someone like that,' said Len. 'Come on, let's go, we don't want to be seen.'

They were talking in Tagalog, and it took Dasha a moment to realize she couldn't understand them. Listening and speaking in foreign languages all day could do that to your brain: it pretended to comprehend more than it did. Or was it the other way around? Dasha thought of how children in a park made up complicated games to play on the spot without speaking a single syllable of the same language. And the 'grown-ups' couldn't even find their way home because of a few mispronounced vowels. She decided there and then that she was not interested in growing up.

Rosel thanked Dasha and walked away as fast as possible with Len. Dasha nodded, suppressing an urge to follow and force her way into their friendship.

Meanwhile, underground, another unordained meeting was taking place. Violet stopped and looked up. There he was, in the middle of the corridor, kneeling upright with a long, straight back, as if about to offer himself at the altar as some sacred sacrifice. He looked into the distance and held a sign close to his chest: 'J'AI FAIM'. *Aren't we all hungry,* she thought. The sea of people moving towards him was forced to part into two to continue. He was Moses. Violet had been bewitched by his presence before. In fact, she'd been bewitched every day for the last eight months. She stopped in front of him. He flinched. She looked directly into his piercing green eyes. He looked back at her. Time stood still.

The world rushed past. The mournful Purcell aria continued. He didn't know her, but she was sure he wanted to.

She signalled him to follow. Before the moment was lost, he carefully folded his sign, picked up the backpack he had been kneeling on, stood up and followed her out of the station. He was a towering presence. She walked silently ahead of him, leading him into a small café. There, she ordered two espressos and a croque monsieur.

They mapped each other with their eyes, sitting in silence. He was devastatingly handsome and, surprisingly, didn't smell bad. *How did he shave this neatly and keep himself clean while living on the street? Did he even live on the street? When was the last time someone kissed him? Hugged him?* She pushed these random thoughts out of her head. There was a stillness about him that she found reassuring and intriguing. She clocked the cuts on his arm as he rolled up his sleeves to eat. He caught her staring. She lowered her turtle-neck to reveal a long-hardened gash running all the way around, monstrously marking her otherwise flawless ebony skin. He nodded, identifying with her pain. She asked him his name.

'Raphaël,' his voice croaked, not having used it for days. Or was it years?

'*Comment?*' she asked.

Clearing his throat, he said more clearly, 'Raphaël.'

'*Enchanté*,' she said, extending her hand. 'Violet.'

To anyone watching, they looked like a couple on their first Tinder date—awkward and aroused.

Silence descended around them once more. She watched him eat. When he was done, she paid and they walked back to the metro together. He entered through the exit door without buying a ticket, took up his kneeling position once more, pulled out his handwritten sign and fixed his gaze. He didn't look at or say a word to Violet. No gratitude and certainly no expectation. Life on the street had taught him to insulate himself, not just from the cold but from kindness. She smiled, flicked her long ponytail and carried on. She felt centred, more at ease. And she knew she would see more of him, of Raa-phaa-ëlle.

Chapter 6

With the bags stuffed in her underwear, Neera began her bow-legged walk back to Number Thirty-Six, her skirt bulging like an erect penis, destroying the symmetry of Miyake's pleats. One bag was about to fall out, but she couldn't possibly stop on the street to rearrange it. This was her neighbourhood. They were all there—the *boulangère* with his big bay window, flaunting his assortment of artisanal *viennoiserie* and his contempt for those who ordered the wrong pastry at the wrong time of the day; the dry-cleaner who made it clear that she preferred chatting with her gang of delivery boys than attending to dirty clothes; and the Tunisian guy from the overpriced fruit shop who spent his day smoking over the perfect-looking peaches and strawberries, since all the penny-pinching, well-heeled residents chose the farmers' market across the street.

All of them insisted on greeting her every time she passed. This peculiarity of Paris—constantly saying 'hello' and 'goodbye' to everyone, only to render them invisible straight after—had always maddened her. What purpose did politesse serve when you had no intention of actually acknowledging a person or their needs? In Mumbai, you never bothered with salutations; you just cut to the chase, and no matter how hard you tried, you could never be invisible. There were always eyes on you and there was always someone more than ready to dive into your life and impose their assistance.

Though she was nothing more than a 'Bonjour!' to these vendors on most days, today, she was sure they'd notice her and her load. Would they care? She didn't want to find out. She limped, squirmed and managed to get inside her posh Haussmannian building and into the tiny Parisian lift that claimed it was for three people but could barely fit one. When she had first arrived at this apartment, she had happily mistaken the lift for a dumbwaiter, to be used for deliveries and other such modern-day delights. *What a tourist I was*, she thought laughing at her uninitiated self.

At first, she hadn't understood why a man with her husband's wealth had chosen this old building with creaky floors, where you could hear the water gurgling up the pipes and not opted for a soundproof penthouse in a snazzy high-rise. Little by little, she stumbled upon the reasons—Paris, a relatively low-rise city, had hardly any buildings over seven floors and the ones that existed were either in areas that she'd rather not be seen in or were ugly, low-ceilinged French renditions of 1970s functional architectural blocks, whose greying yellow façade looked older than the nineteenth-century white stone structure she lived in.

No glass skyscraper could compete with the way the city's celebrated light literally kissed and bounced off the smooth surface of her building. That same light entered her top-floor apartment in a hundred different ways depending on time of the day, and changed the mood of the space and its inhabitants. It was nothing short of a triumph. Haussmann had built these solid symmetrical apartment blocks, no higher than six floors, to be more efficient and less extravagant than their baroque predecessors. But Neera could not possibly call the giant gold door knocker—with its laurel motif on her building's wooden entrance that was wide and high enough to let in horse carriages—less than extravagant.

Once inside, the main lobby spilt into two. One section of the lobby led to a mahogany spiral staircase with its maroon carpet and stain-glass windows on each floor. In the past, these stairs had been the only way to access the floors, which meant that the second floor with its wraparound balcony was high enough to be considered the most prestigious of all floors, and the nobles scrambled to occupy it, leaving the ground floor for the merchants to live and sell their goods in. Above the second floor, the higher one climbed, the lower the value of the apartment went. With the introduction of the stick-thin lift, this social stratification turned on its head. The status of the ground floor remained unchanged: it either housed a *boulangerie, tabac* or hairdresser, or was occupied by those who wouldn't believe the number of zeroes in the asking price of the apartments just above their heads. Neera basked in the borrowed glory of being the proud owner of the most expensive apartment in the building.

The other section of the entrance lobby led to an internal courtyard around which the building formed a U-shape. The cobbled area, which had once been a resting place for the horses and carriages of Haussmann's time, now housed bicycles and garbage bins. All the apartments had windows that looked out onto this cobbled yard. Finding it too exposed, Neera rarely traversed it, except when she wanted to climb to the servants' floor. She was not being a memsahib by calling it that. This was a near-exact translation of *Chambres des bonnes*, and this floor could only be accessed by the back stairs on the far side of the courtyard because how gauche it'd be to grant the domestics the same entry as the nobility! It was all so intricate and, in many subtle ways, efficient. These stone blocks had more history and social etiquette built into their walls than Neera could hold in her head. Reason after reason validated her husband's choice, till one day, she found herself as in love with Number Thirty-Six as the man who'd brought her here.

As the lift doors were about to shut, the gawky young Eastern European girl who lived on the floor below ran in. The stench of the weed was overpowering. They rode in awkward silence. On the third floor, the girl moved further in to allow the folding doors to open inwards, rubbing against Neera and her skirt. Unintentional, unacknowledged, private touching in public spaces was part of life in Paris. The etiquette was to ignore it and carry on, no matter whose derriere was making friends with your tummy. This girl was obviously new.

'*Excusez-moi*, I didn't mean to shove you, this lift is impossible,' the young girl apologized, her accent untraceable. 'How can they make such luxurious buildings and then such silly lifts?'

'This building is more than a hundred and fifty years old,' Neera said flatly. 'In the absence of electricity and mechanics, I've no doubt the lazy ones were carried by their domestics. I suggest you get a servant.'

The girl laughed and turned to look at Neera. This slight movement dislodged one of the precariously placed packets, which slipped out of Neera's panty. She disregarded it, waiting for the girl to exit. Hiding her shock and amusement, Dasha picked up the stinky culprit and handed it to Neera. 'Your feet must be cold.'

'Ah, yes, they are. Thank you.'

Before the lift door closed, Dasha said, 'By the way, you are right about the lift. This building was built in 1861, during the expansion of Paris when Haussmann and Napoleon reimagined the entire city. Before that, it was a brothel outside the boundary of Paris and we'd have to be ladies of the night to live here. I mean, in case you were wondering.'

Neera watched the girl go, tickled despite herself.

Jean-Paul Allard, Neera's ageing husband, was warming his feet by the fire and turning a deaf ear to the much too serious Ludovic. Poor, loyal Ludo was only trying to do his job, just as he had been doing for the last twenty years. But how was he meant to find funding to complete this money-gobbling film when the stubborn producer kept dismissing his advice? There was no doubt he loved his talented boss, but right then, he was ready to throw him in the fire.

'Yes, I know I've gone over budget,' Jean-Paul said in his typical soft, unflustered manner. He had always thought of himself as wise and with age had come the additional belief that he was perpetually right. 'This is art, not banking. Seriously, Ludo, you want me to compromise on my vision—a vision that will impact generations to come—for the sake of two, maybe three thousand euros?'

'Jean-Paul, it is not two, three thousand, it is a question of eight hundred and fifty thousand euros, almost a million,' Ludovic was particularly perturbed because he knew the indefatigable filmmaker Allard was prone to getting his way and, in this case, he didn't see how he was to make that possible. 'Where do you expect me to raise this amount from? You refuse to cast any known face. You threw out Marc Maxime as director—'

'Please, Maxime has one foot in the grave and wants to make his swansong with my money.' Jean-Paul heard Neera enter the apartment and couldn't be happier for the distraction, not unaware that something about his wife's presence played havoc with the composure of his accountant friend. 'Neera, *ma choupinette*, come save me from the dreadful Ludo.'

Holding onto her crotch, Neera stuck her head into the triple-room salon with its five double French windows, original *moulure* on the ceiling and a fireplace designed to take one's breath away. Over the years, Neera had tastefully added bright Indian accents and artwork, making it a must-feature room for *AD, Elle Décoration, Maison et Moi, Haute & Hot* and *Lavish Living*. It did, however, amuse her to no end when the unnaturally tanned, wafer-thin, laxative-popping editors of these magazines, who claimed to be the last word in style since Marie Antoinette, fawned all over the 'authentic antique' handmade throws, rugs and cushions that she had bought for less than a few hundred rupees from the flea markets of Janpath and Colaba in India. Neera loved cheap street-side shopping even more now that it had gone from being a necessity to a choice. Jean-Paul often teased her that her eye for a priceless bargain was as good as his nose for fine wines, and thanks to her skill, they could continue to enjoy the benefits of his.

'Jannie, my love, give me a minute, I'm going to wash my hands, freshen up and join you,' said Neera lovingly. 'This slushy weather makes me feel dirty.'

Walking down the herringbone parquet corridor, she passed the room of her teenage stepson. Neera saw Eric as the enemy or, more precisely, as a rival for her husband's time. Why should she, still a head turner at forty-two, have to fight anyone, let alone a crater-faced fifteen-year-old, for an old man's affection? Eric's door was open and the lush beige carpet (definitely not from Colaba market) in his room was splattered with fresh mud stains. Forgetting about her loaded underwear, she walked right in ticking him off for the stains.

'Get out of my room!' Eric snorted, 'This is my home and has been my home long before it was yours.' Thanks to his fancy international school and all the Hollywood films he devoured, he spoke English with an American lilt. Or maybe his mother was American or Canadian. Neera couldn't remember what Jean-Paul had told her. She couldn't recall a name or if she'd even been given one. She knew the woman had been a small-time actress of some kind. She'd never met her and, if she could help it, never would. No one spoke about her, except when Eric was threatened with eviction, and that suited Neera just fine.

'That carpet is silk and cost a lot of money.'

'Yes, my Dad's money,' Eric gave back as good as he got. 'And what I choose to do with it is not your problem. So *chut!*'

'Don't you chut me, you ugly little runt!' He really brought out the worst in her. Moving closer to him, she said, 'Need help bursting that big pimple on your nose?'

The smell hit his nostrils. Neera saw him clock the bulge between her legs. Before he could put two and two together, she stormed out.

Neera knew that she hated Eric because his presence reminded her every day of her own childlessness, even though she had never wanted children. She still didn't want or need them. And yet, their lack had begun to gnaw at her. It was like a polar bear craving the desert—it made no sense, but that was Neera to a tee. She had FOMO for things that she was sure to her bones she didn't miss. She could have chosen to be maternal with her husband's child, but instead she had turned into a petulant child herself.

She sashayed up the elaborate stairs, down the long corridor, straight into her walk-in closet and shut the door. Sliding her skirt up, she contemplated the little green bags as they tumbled out. How could so much joy be contained in such a tiny bag? Clumsily rolling a joint, she climbed on top of her velvet pouf and smoked into the exhaust.

If only Jean-Paul could understand the solidity each inhale brought to her muddled mind, see how it crystallized her thoughts and cooled the fire that raged inside her. On it, she functioned effortlessly, with less angst. The world came to her slower, giving her space for a delayed reaction, resetting her into the person she aspired to be, a person people wanted to be around—a mellower version of her acerbic self. Alas, of all her many flaws, this was the sole one Jannie disapproved of. Thankfully, she'd insisted on separate dressing rooms when they had refurbished their duplex.

'In Paris? You want two walk-in closets? In Paris? People will think we are the Sultans of Brunei.' He had been genuinely aghast.

'Jannie, we have the space. We don't need a second guest room. No one visits us,' she'd said, cosying up to him. Her parents had made the trip once. Jean-Paul had gone out of his way to make them feel at home, their behaviour had been annoyingly impeccable and, yet, it had been the most uncomfortable fortnight of Neera's life. No one concerned was eager to repeat that experience any time soon.

'I could convert it into my screening room,' he had implored.

'It's not big enough. And even if it were, I'd never allow it. A screening room at home! You would never leave the apartment.'

She meant it. Her husband was already a 'quartier-man'—refusing to step beyond a two-mile radius—a syndrome that afflicted in particular the proud Parisians who were born here with no urge to cross a self-drawn invisible periphery. He went to extreme lengths to stay in his quartier, his neighbourhood, clinging to its familiarity like a security blanket. Not one to give up easily, however, Neera had dragged their designer, Ricky Garcia, into the argument.

'Ricky, you tell him. Shouldn't a home be designed to cater to the needs of those who live in it?'

'Jean-Paul, give the lady what she wants,' Ricky had pleaded on her behalf. 'Keep the undressing for under the silk sheets, *non*? I'm sure at sixty-four, you want to save this gorgeous wife of yours from the sight of your wrinkled *fesse*.'

'My buttocks are not wrinkled,' Jean-Paul had objected, good naturedly. 'Well at least, not the bits I can see.'

Squeezing his bottom, Neera had kissed him passionately and said, 'Jannie, I've had many a buttock but not one as wrinkled as yours, and you know I'm a sucker for novelty.'

They had all laughed, and that's how Neera had got her sanctuary—her own, rather large dressing room: something she could never have dreamed of growing up. Truth be told, the Neera she was back then would've died before having such a vulgar aspiration. What had *that* Neera, the super achiever of her crowded little hometown, aspired to? She was snapped out of her reverie by the beep of her phone. It was her latest app-matched lover.

So wyd tn?

It took her a minute to decode the text talk.

What do you accomplish in all the time you save by not typing full words?

LOL. C u tn?

She took a deep drag, rolled her eyes at herself and typed, OK, wondering if there was a shorter version of saying that.

Her eye fell on the business card that she had cut to make a filter.

> *Lucas Garnier*
> Master Chef and TV Personality

She recalled Lucas grabbing her arm at cocktail party the night before. He had whispered in her ear, 'Seriously, Neera, consider it. I can make it happen.'

She turned the card over. Scrawled at the back in his neat writing—*Call me, adventure awaits. XX.* Smiling at the memory, she crushed and hid the butt of her smoked joint into the card and binned it.

Neera had befriended Lucas two years ago when she'd smelt weed while coming out from the back of the restaurant at his opening night party. He had gallantly got her a small stash from one of his chefs and subsequently followed it up when he could, which was far from often. She hardly knew him, but she liked him. And whenever they met, they talked about her father's sweet shop, his unusual cooking techniques and the unique flavours only to be found in India. But Lucas's proposition had come out of left field. It made her uncomfortable. Besides, as far as she was concerned, it was a non-starter.

The Menthaline that she sprayed into her mouth was from a green, pocket-sized contraption that she had fallen in love with at the Macau airport on a work trip and now ordered in bulk online. The burst of mint bumped into her just-smoked joint's high, and together they woke her up from deep inside. Her languid, minty-fresh breath guided her steps down to the salon. The door to Eric's room, the only bedroom on the bottom floor, was still open, and he was engrossed in editing some new footage, wearing big, noise-cancelling headphones, dead to the world. Neera took his muddy boots from the foot of his bed and carried them to the guest toilet, decorated with Indian wallpaper and Venetian mirrors. She wet the dry mud-crusted soles in the sink, and then, wearing the boots on her hands like an enraged four-legged animal, crawled all over the apartment, leaving horrible mud stains all over the floor, furniture and up the walls, as far as she could reach. It was a crazed moment of sweet revenge. The fact that Eric hadn't really harmed or offended her was of no importance. She had survived—nay, *thrived*—this long by being an opportunist, not Mother Teresa. Those muddy boots were an opportunity. Satisfied with her handiwork, she silently and neatly placed the shoes back in his room.

Blissfully stoned, she joined her husband, who was stoking the fire and still arguing with Ludovic.

'Lola Ava Grâce may have won many awards but she is a baby,' explained Jean-Paul. 'She cannot tell me how to make my film. She has talent, Ludo, yes, I give you that. But if she wants to grow, she has to learn to take directions.'

'You hired her as a director, she won two Césars last year,' countered Ludovic. 'Let her direct.'

'Oh, Ludo, Lola will come around once she realizes how brilliant Jean-Paul and his ideas are,' Neera said, making Ludovic instantly feel like a traitor for suggesting differently. 'You'll see, they all do.'

She took Jean-Paul's hand and kissed the tips of his fingers tenderly. For all the men she had had (and all those who had had her), she had never had the urge to touch anyone as much as she needed to touch him. Stoned or not, she loved her old man, her Jannie, her saviour. Why should she have to share him? She wouldn't.

She casually asked him, 'Jannie, my love, can you please get my shawl from our room? I'm a bit chilly.'

She turned to Ludovic, who visibly stiffened finding himself left alone with a woman who, he was sure, was not above accusing him of having stolen his own skin. Neera merely poured him a fresh cup of ginseng tea, asked about his upcoming trip to Tel Aviv for the Christmas holidays and half listened to the answers. She was waiting. And then it came.

'If you are going to live like a pig, you better move back with your mother. THIS IS NOT ACCEPTABLE.' The treble in his voice reverberated like a hydraulic rock driller, cutting through the thick concrete walls of the double-height living room.

Hardly able to hide her delight, Neera asked a barely breathing Ludovic if he'd like a refill.

Chapter 7

Violet walked towards Manko. In no time at all, she had gone from an unnamed dogsbody working backstage to Queen Vee, the unmissable star attraction at the notoriously fun burlesque club. In the space of two hundred metres, her walk changed: the Violet of the metro station vanished, and she now embodied the diva people loved to hate. Confidence exuded from her every pore. She wished her father could see her now. Would he recognize the woman his son had become?

The son who had been born wrong, the son her father could not make right. Had her father been alive, he would have surely listed all that he'd done to bring his boy into Allah's realm. God could not fault him for lack of trying. Yet, the boy had defied the Divine and, instead of falling, was rising, which was an affront to the Almighty. Violet's dead father was, no doubt, squirming in his tightly wrapped funeral shroud, dying a million deaths deep under the earth.

Violet had a sudden pang of longing for her mother. She yearned for her wide, droopy bosom, more comfortable than any pillow; missed her dry, rough, paper-bag hands that always smelt of lime. *Vafi, my son, it is the best cleanser—you want me to bring germs of those sick people home?* She heard her voice in her head. *No, my mother, my yaay, I just want you to come home.* God, she even missed Senegal, the country that had given Violet her favourite living memories while also giving her an identity she couldn't live with.

She shimmied off the useless memories. She was in Paris now, and Paris had no place for Vafi and his woes. Here, she was the dazzling dancer Violet, and here, Violet had a boyfriend who could work miracles with a camera and loved the very air she breathed.

Benjamin the boyfriend, who was the same lowly video assistant at Dasha's jumping-gazelle-lingerie casting, was waiting for Violet outside Manko. He pulled her around the side of the building to the dingy fire exit, where they kissed, grinding against each other. Lowering himself onto his knees, he unzipped her suede pants and took Violet in his mouth. The dancer was thankful. Nothing worked better than an orgasm to bring her back into the present, making her feel that right here, right now, life is beautiful.

'Can you help me with my rent?' Benjamin asked her once they were done. 'I'm struggling this month.'

'I haven't been paid, Benjy,' she said firmly, knowing that she'd bail him out in the end.

'Okay, no rush, whenever you are,' he added earnestly.

'No.'

'No?'

'Yes, no. You need to sort your money out. I'm not playing sugar mama to you,' Violet said.

'How dare you? I'm not looking for a sugar mama. I'm your boyfriend; we are supposed to help each other. I'm looking for companionship, for love, for support.'

'Then ask me for love, for sex. Don't ask me for money,' she softened and kissed him, tasting herself in his salty mouth.

'Vee, you don't let me move in with you,' he said ruefully. 'I understand why and it's okay. Just lend me the money, you know I'll give it back. Come on, five hundred euros. I know you've got it.'

'I may have. But I may also have my eye on a vintage LV. Bags are a girl's best friend,' Violet sang this last bit out teasingly. Then she added bleakly, 'Benjy, seriously, stop working for free. Get that casting bitch to pay you what you are owed.'

The club was many hours away from opening. Violet, the showstopper, blew air kisses at the people busy setting up and cat-walked straight into the backstage dressing room. Soon, she would begin her three- to four-hour-long transformation. There was a picture stuck on her mirror of Goddess Kali, painted head-to-toe in blue. Actually, it was an old cut-out of Heidi Klum from *Voici* magazine dressed as Goddess Kali for a Halloween party. Violet was fascinated by how seriously Heidi took Halloween. Why would someone born with such perfect dimensions and flawless features revel in hiding behind a disguise? Had Violet been born Violet and not Vafi Dembélé, she may never have glued on one measly eyelash or donned a single disguise. And the irony of ironies was that 'Vafi' in Arabic meant 'complete'—a name chosen by her intellectual Muslim father that felt like a lifelong taunt as a boy. Did she feel more complete as Violet? Maybe not, but at least she looked fabulous.

She examined the six blue arms that would attach onto her bodice. They were big and awkward, and she'd have to go sideways to pass through the long, narrow backstage corridor that led to the main room of the club. Showtime was still many hours away. It'd be good to practise her new routine on the trapeze ring with the extra weight of the arms. 'Play track three and crank up the volume,' she said, handing the technician her flash drive.

An elaborate aerial rehearsal sequence followed in sync with a minimal staccato beat. It was almost meditative to watch. Even without the lights, costume or extras, Violet was sensational. The beat slowed down further, bleeding into a backing track set for her to sing over. She swung upside down from a trapeze ring and began singing her rendition of 'Just an Illusion'. Coming out of the mouth of a trans woman, the cheesy 1982 pop hit got a whole new meaning. Violet put her own slow, velvety twist to it, making it a ballad guaranteed to slosh around in your head for days on end.

'Vee, come down, I need to speak to you,' Nicolas Scalbert called out to Violet from below. He was the big manager of all small things that needed managing—from the private schedules of the dance girls at the burlesque club to the tantrums of wannabe models, the insatiable appetites of businessmen to the increasingly disobedient needle of his weighing scales. He bellowed, 'Queen Veeeee? Did you hear meeee?'

Startled out of the zen of her performance, she straightened herself and hollered back, 'Nicky boy, you know I love you, but fucking hell, open your eyes and show some respect. Let a lady finish her fucking song before interrupting her.'

'Apologies, My Queen,' said Nicolas in his playful, borderline sleazy manner. 'I merely and most humbly wanted to pass on a message from your admirer, Monsieur Baptiste de Beauchamp. He expects to see you after your act tonight. Apparently, he has many friends who can't wait to meet Your Royal Highness.'

To Violet, this was revolting rather than flattering. Had anyone been looking carefully, they would have seen a flash of horror cross her face, for she resembled the scared little boy she had been many lifetimes ago. Whenever she had felt hopeless as a child, her mother, who was an encyclopaedia of quotable aphorisms, would say, 'Life is like a book, my son. Some chapters are sad, some happy and some exciting. But if you never turn the page, you'll never know what the next chapter holds.'

Yes, and what about the chapters that never should have been written? Violet had ripped them out and shredded them, but how was she supposed to unread them? Unwrite them? Time had not healed her wounds. In fact, as she got older, she felt sorrier and more protective of her younger self. The horrors she had endured ought to have justified the horror she had inflicted. They hadn't—with time, the memories only became shriller, more embellished.

With a flick of her hair, she shook it off. 'Oh my dear messenger boy, please be so kind as to tell Monsieur Arsey Aristocrat that

I cannot wait. In fact, I'm wet with anticipation.'

Violet ordered the technician to play the track from the beginning, and a moment later, she was swinging upside down once again, trying to make sense of a world where strangers wanted to own her body while she wanted only to disown it.

Chapter 8

Across town, in a cramped Filipino café where she was picking carefully at a steaming bowl of rice and fish, Rosel sat surrounded by a group of men and women, all speaking superfast over each other in Tagalog. It was tough to keep up with the incessant babble of irrelevant advice they were dolling out to her. She listened patiently, knowing first hand that each of them needed to repeatedly relive their escape stories—the single bravest moment of their lives.

'I'm telling you, the Embassy knows the real story. They see hundreds of cases like this daily,' said a middle-aged lady with pencil thin eyebrows and orangish hair.

'My hands are still trembling,' said a visibly shaken Rosel.

'You've taken the hardest step already, you got out, so many don't,' encouraged Len. 'You go with me in the morning to the Embassy, tell them you lost your passport and they will help you. If not, we will seek out Mrs Rodriguez of Pinoy in Paris.'

'They know. The Embassy knows everything—the abuse, the cruel employers—but what can they do when all of us run after the Arabs for money?' expounded Orange Hair. 'Duterte says that we warn our women, "Don't go, be careful", but they still pack their bags, sell their house, a kidney or two and get on that one-way flight to hell!'

'France accepts you so fast, you'll see,' Len said, smiling at Rosel consolingly.

'It's a win-win. To our home country, we are a burden, to France, we are cheap and polite labour. Not like the rude, thieving Algerians!' concurred a man who had lived here for thirty-eight years. 'The heathen Africans have no Jesus, the Indians smell or are over smart and the French are always on strike, I say, praise Jesus we are Filipino—we get all their jobs.' He bulldozed through the few voices that objected to his xenophobic rant by becoming louder and louder. 'Make work your religion and you will be just fine, young lady.'

A girl talking into the headphones of her latest Galaxy tablet looked up to offer her two bits. 'Go get a job that will declare you. Then you can pay your taxes. No, I'm not talking to you, Mummy, you carry on telling me your story,' she said to the person on the phone and then, covering the mouthpiece of the headphone with her hand, she continued, 'See, you are *sans papiers*—a ghost, not legal. Without all the paperwork, you simply do not exist. Invisible, till the French attach a number to your name—a magic number that makes you instantly visible.'

'People are mad about this number, they kill for it,' said Uncle Xenophobe.

'No Uncle,' said the girl with the headphones, hijacking the conversation right back. 'They take two bottles of water, a piece of bread, a borrowed winter jacket and set off, in an over-packed, inflatable death tube the size of a mint that they know couldn't save a drowning fish,' she said without stopping for a breath, 'Most of them can't even swim and yet, they do it because the will to survive is the strongest human impulse of all. And do you know what the second strongest is?'

Rosel looked blankly at this girl, who spoke with the force and confidence of a river rushing to join the sea. She had never met a Filipina like her before. During her internship, when she was on the graveyard shift at the neonatal facility, Rosel had fed premature babies the size of a shoe from a bottle that had seemed impossibly big. It had amazed her how their tiny mouths had expanded beyond capacity to suck on the silicone teat. Even at age zero, their undeveloped brains knew that the nipple was life-giving. This fast-talking, gushing girl was right—survival was the primary impulse.

'Yes, Mummy, I'm here. I'm listening, what happened after Carlo refused to fix the roof, did you slap him?' River Girl said into her headphone. Then fixing her gaze on Rosel, she resumed, 'The second strongest emotion is—'

'Fear,' Orange Hair cut in.

'Hope. It's the hope that the very next moment will be better that makes us breathe, makes us want to live, despite the world nudging us to end it all,' continued River Girl. 'If fear was our guiding force, then we would've all jumped off the Eiffel Tower long ago.'

Rosel blinked in awe and fear. Surely it was not hope that she was feeling?

'In France, we are allowed to hope, encouraged to hope. It's definitely not fear that makes hundreds of people risk their lives every single day to come here. It's hope,' River Girl said with a contagious conviction.

'A hundred people daily? Oh, how your imagination runs wild!' quipped Orange Hair.

'Aunty, it's more than one hundred people that enter France without papers every day. That's an official fact.'

'Official fact is it? Did your police officer boyfriend tell you that?' Orange Hair teased.

This made River Girl blush.

'You see Rosel, our Madame here is sleeping with the enemy—an armed Frenchman,' explained Orange Hair.

They all laughed, including River Girl. The feeling of community was strong. It was a safe place to make fun of each other, or at least it seemed that way. Rosel knew from experience that the Pinoy grapevine was petty and malicious and made its way back to Manila in minutes or however fast the Wi-Fi connection was.

'Come on now, you're scaring Rosel. She hasn't even touched her food,' said Len. 'Eat your rice, before it gets cold.'

'Listen, France is great,' said River Girl. 'Because in spite of being illegal and invisible, you are somehow allowed to pay your taxes—it's some kind of loophole of fraternity and then, poof! You slowly go from being a ghost, to becoming a person.

'Now, the problem is, no one really wants to hire a ghost unless you can convince them that you won't steal or skin their babies and you'll willingly do all the menial things they won't do for a quarter of the price that they would have to pay to a complaining French person living off the state. *Then* you are home sweet home. All you have to do is will yourself to survive and be hopeful.'

Rosel swallowed a spoonful of rice under Len's watchful eye, wondering if 'hope' had made her make the biggest mistake of her life.

Chapter 9

Her five flatmates were thankfully out, so Dasha had the apartment to herself for a change. Or was it six girls now? The turnover in the seven months since she'd moved into this flat for models, which came with bunk beds from floor to ceiling and very little in the way of bare necessities, was too fast for her to keep track of. They came, they made it or burnt out and they moved on.

Dumping her bag on the Formica kitchen table, Dasha opened the favourites contact list on her phone and pressed on the tiny round photo of her father. *Please check the number you have dialled.* Her disappointed finger scrolled down the list to the pale picture of Andrei, her twin. She hit the FaceTime button with her thumb.

'How's Vyborg?' she asked in Russian.

'It snowed sunflowers, and you know when that happens, it gets so boiling hot that I have to make a trip to the moon to cool off,' Andrei smiled his impish smile, and it filled her with springtime sunshine. She loved him like a prized puppy—happily cleaning his shit, rationing cuddle time with others and expecting nothing other than endless drooling and eternal loyalty in return.

'I hope you didn't leave your transmogrifier there like you did the last time.'

'No, I held onto it for dear life! But I did find your cloud-maker on the way down.'

'Aaah, that's where I left it!' said Dasha, walking around the apartment. Clothes, underwear and make-up were sprawled all over the floor. 'Next time it snows sunflowers, climb on top of the mermaid tree and somersault straight into the diamond abyss.

You'll cool off in seconds.'

Talking in fantastical nonsense was the way the twins had always connected best. An outsider might think that they were talking in code. In fact, with the gibberish they spoke, most of their neighbours were sure that the twins worked for Putin's Secret Committee to spot deviators—the same organization that old man Nabatov's nephew's wife's third cousin's friend's father had had an unfortunate encounter with. This worked in the twins' favour. Everyone gave them a wide berth or went out of their way to show them their kindest and most useful side. In reality, the twins' gibberish was nothing more than a fun filter to escape their humdrum lives.

Dasha's phone beeped; Nicolas was trying to call. She had no desire to talk to her manager, the man who controlled her life. From the moment he had Insta-scouted her and paid for Dasha and her duffel bag full of dreams to come to Paris, he had assumed, without being asked, the role of a father figure and hustler. She knew he was going to blast her for the outburst she'd had at the casting that morning. Suddenly, remembering how rebellious and free she had felt, she opened Instagram and posted the picture of herself straddling the casting table in lingerie with the caption '#EATME!!!! #PussyRiot #winning #aboutthisafternoon #watchaLookinatloser?'. She also tagged the casting director and the production company, followed by every casting director she had heard of, every model she knew, all the so-called body-positive influencers and Brigette Macron. Then, like the errant teenager that she was, she ignored Nicolas's call. The chastising could wait.

She turned her attention back to Andrei. 'Andryusha, check out my Insta.' She told him all about her baffling moment of genius.

'Sis, I'm not sure I would use the word genius... Maybe hara-kiri would be more apt?'

'Is it not a genius photo?'

The expression of horror on Eyeshadow's face, framed between

Dasha's smooth endless legs, did indeed make for a brilliant picture.

'Fine, I give you that,' conceded Andrei. 'But at what cost?'

On cue, Nicolas flashed on Dasha's screen again.

'I guess I'm about to find out. Don't disconnect, Andryusha,' Dasha put Andrei on hold and braced herself for the berating of a lifetime.

Before Nicolas could get a word in, Dasha shrieked into the phone, 'Damn it, Nicolas I snapped, I know, I know. But they made me snap. It was *awful*. If you'd been there, heard them—'

'They're diabolical,' said Nicolas in an unexpected twist. 'And that Sandrine is vile, a total bitch, I don't know how she still gets hired to cast.'

'What?! You're not angry at me?'

'Someone had to do it,' laughed Nicolas. 'Now you'll probably be hailed as a goddess by all the models Sandrine's driven to anorexia, lunacy or worse. The good news is she's dying to change her image, so she might even cast you to prove she's not that stuck up,' he said conspiratorially. 'We'll see.'

Although Dasha hadn't bagged any big jobs yet and was far from conventionally pretty—more E.T. than Irina Shayk, with eyes set too far apart on an abnormally wide forehead, a narrow, pointy chin and an extra-long neck—she was a force of nature. And if there was one thing Nicolas knew, it was which giraffe to put his money on. Besides, in the interim, her fluency in English, quirky intelligence and general chattiness made her an ideal companion for men with money passing through Paris.

'So you're not putting me on the next flight to Russia?'

'No, chérie, I'm not.'

'Nicolas, you're the best! You'll see, I'm going to be the face of Chanel, no the face of Versace, no Gaultier—'

'Yes, you are, but for now can you slip into the dress I left in your room and be the "face of fun" for Kirk Dankworth?'

'Who?'

'You saw *Madame Fraud*, right? The director of the movie is in Paris and needs a no-pressure date. Join his table at Manko. 10 p.m.,' Nicolas instructed. 'And chérie, leave your phone and other recording devices behind, *s'il te plait*. There are no weapons allowed inside Manko.'

A much relieved Dasha switched back to her call with Andrei.

'I have some good news of my own,' said her twin. 'Although I'm not sure if it's good news or a pipe dream.'

'Spill. What is it?'

'I got my acceptance letter from LSE.'

'L-S-E? The London School of Economics?'

'The last I checked that's what it stood for.'

Dasha was jumping with joy. 'Oh, you clever, clever Andryusha! I wish, I could reach through the phone and hug you right now.'

'Sis, it's twenty-one thousand, five hundred and seventy pounds a year, and that's just the tuition. The living costs will be between eleven hundred and thirteen hundred pounds a month,' Andrei said, despondently.

'Accept the place, Andryusha, and a way will open up. You are going to London, we will make it happen—twin power,' she touched her palm to the screen at the same time as her twin did.

Dasha's mother grabbed the phone. 'My baby, I miss you.' She had no eyebrows or eyelashes and was wearing a headscarf to cover her bald head, but otherwise looked robust and positive.

'Mamushka, you look great.'

'And you look too thin. Are you skipping meals again?'

Dasha's younger sisters came running to the phone, they were breathless with excitement. Nadia, the baby of the family, held up an Instagram picture of Bella Hadid and Natalia Vodianova at a fashion party in LouLou outside the Louvre in Paris.

'Were you there?' asked Khristina, who, at fourteen, was almost as tall as Dasha. Unlike her model sister, however, she was big-boned and heavy-set. Yet, she too nursed dreams of walking down the fabled catwalks of Paris. 'What were you wearing to the party? Why haven't you posted any pictures? Is Bella beautiful up-close?'

'Is she friendly?' jumped in Nadia.

'Yes, yes, they are wonderful.' Not wanting to shatter her sisters' delusions of grandeur about her life, Dasha remained vague.

'I have to go, my loves. I'll send money soon,' Dasha promised, not knowing where she was going to find this elusive money from.

'You keep your money, my baby, we are fine,' said her mother. 'Eat something, okay?'

With a click of a button, the familiar comfort of her home disappeared, transporting her back to the messy cramped apartment. Alone.

Apart from her father, who was unreachable, and Andryusha, Dasha loved her own company the best. She'd never once been lonely or bored until she moved to Paris. But now that she was living in the chicest city in the world, it seemed to her that her life was either happening in the past with her family in Russia or in the future, also with her family, as an international icon. Her family, however, was far from perfect. In fact, some of her strongest childhood memories were of making plans with her twin on how to get away from the family and leave their poky home and pokier life, only to come back to Vyborg to buy the whole town outright. Back then, she hadn't known the stabbing pain of being an outsider, with no one there to fight your fights. Now, she missed her embarrassing family. They were *hers*. She belonged to them, and they'd take a punch in the face for her and happily give two back.

Dasha found a skimpy, elegant, royal blue cocktail dress hanging on the bunk bed. On its tag was scrawled, 'Manko. 10 p.m. Have fun. Nic X.'

She went back into the kitchen and opened the fridge. There was only a piece of Emmental cheese and half a bottle of Poliakov vodka. She took a big bite and poured herself a drink, before the front door clattered open. Three of the other models entered in a flurry. Snatching the bottle off her, they took swigs. Astrid, the only French model in the apartment, pulled out a stash of Christmas canapés she had stolen from her casting. Coming from a remote town called Ouch (that no one in the flat had even heard of, let alone could pronounce) and being perhaps the only plus-size French model in the world, Astrid was as much an alien in Paris as the rest of them.

Dasha flicked on the radio and 'Le lacs du Connemara', the iconic song by Michel Sardou, was picking up pace. Even if you'd never heard this anthem and didn't speak a syllable of French, you couldn't help but hum along. The song was a party-maker from its very first note, and the grimy kitchen had no choice but to turn into a dance floor. All the girls danced around, mouthing unfamiliar lyrics at the top of their voices. They were all new to Paris and to each other, and had less than zero interest in getting to know one another whilst cohabiting in this transient slingshot. They were here merely waiting for their turn to be catapulted to stardom or to be dropped in the doldrums.

At twenty, Astrid (whose perfect, delicate face sat defiantly on top of her meaty voluptuous body) was the oldest girl in the apartment and also the sweatiest. Halfway through the next song, her thumbs slid inside the top of her clammy waistband, lingering there as she bunched up and felt the damp Lycra of her leopard-print pants. Perhaps her fingers needed prep time to peel the yoga pants off her thighs like she did in one sensual motion. The freed layers of fat jiggled and then tumbled out sideways, doughy and dimpled, begging to be touched, especially the extraordinarily spongy bit just above the knee. Next, her tight, lacy top came off, permitting the four-inch rolls of her belly to stack neatly on top of each other, again tantalizing a hand to glide over the folds. With a practised flick of her fingers, Astrid unclipped her

40 FF bra, her globe-sized breasts shuddering with relief at being released. Her naked skin smelt of perspiration and confidence, challenging anyone to be more raw, more real, more irresistible. With dainty steps, she squeezed into the matchbox-sized shower cabinet, which, for some inexplicably French reason, needed to be accessed via the kitchen. Dasha took another swig of vodka, trying not to watch her as intently as she was.

Chapter 10

Neera downed her rather full glass of wine, paid, smiled at her date and walked out of the obscure bistro in Montmartre. He was younger than her usual: a harmless toy boy who taught capoeira. Or was it Krav Maga? She couldn't care less if he taught origami—he was fit, smelt soapy clean and couldn't wait to get into her pants, which was all she needed. She never bothered to commit any of their names to memory. They remained a profile, a photo, an emoji. She lit her joint and inhaled deeply. Monsieur Soapy Fit led her to a tunnel where a live fanfare band from Serbia was playing. A bunch of twenty- to thirty-year-olds, 'forever student' types, who thought of themselves as rebelliously retro, were showing off their modern jive and Charleston moves. They were wearing feathers and furs, silk gloves and bowler hats, shiny second-hand shoes and pearls, twirling and rubbing against their partners to keep warm.

Neera's phone rang. She told Jean-Paul she was on her way before dragging Soapy Fit to an isolated corner at the end of the tunnel, where there was a bonfire in a drum and the music could still be heard. She pulled up her skirt and pushed him down on his knees. He skilfully got to work with his tongue. It was the thrill of the forbidden that turned her on. The paradise she had lucked upon with her Jannie could blow up and she'd be the only one responsible for striking the match. The adrenaline was precisely what kept her addicted to the dating apps. She didn't need a therapist to tell her this. Self-destruction and she had been fuck-buddies for decades. Her groans of ecstasy drowned in the revelry.

Straightening her skirt, Neera patted Soapy Fit on his head

and walked up the stone steps alone. Jumping into a waiting taxi, she sprayed Menthaline into her mouth to wash out the germs and sins it harboured, ready to join her husband at Manko to help him woo an American director.

The burlesque club exuded a seediness that only the moneyed could afford. To those who were granted entry, the night promised repulsion and revelry in equal measure, each act more grotesque and fantastic than the previous one. Neera was surprised and uncomfortable to find that Eastern European or whatever she was—the one from her building—seated at their table. After air kissing her politely on both cheeks, Neera proceeded to leave her in obscurity by usurping the attention of Mr Dankworth. She was here to charm the director, the man with the film her husband wanted in on, and, as the dutiful wife, she wasted no time to achieve her mission. Jean-Paul looked on with fascination. His wife transformed into an intoxicating human magnet—gliding effortlessly through conversation about the future of cinema, the Venice Biennale, the pointlessness and yet the pervasiveness of virtual anxiety, the innate nature of humans to resist change, obvious ways to end the man-made crisis in Yemen, the best Baba au Rhum in Paris and the very viral and equally ridiculous bottle-cap challenge that was raising millions to fight alcohol addiction. She stroked her husband's thigh lovingly under the table.

For a while, Dankworth, like the rest of the table, seemed to find her irresistible.

Then, without warning, he interrupted Neera. Very softly, he said, 'My dear, you try too hard. Be yourself, not your repartee. Your act is a little annoying.' He had chosen the exact moment her husband had turned to offer the Eastern European girl the tapas to say this. Neither had heard what he'd said—Neera was unsure if even she had heard what she had heard.

'I don't understand what you mean,' a bewildered Neera

managed to say with a broad smile.

'Hmmm, I think you do, Neera,' Dankworth affirmed. 'And it's time you stopped,' he said, looking right into her, before turning to Dasha, who was lapping up the tapas and hors d'oeuvres. 'So, what was the highlight of your day, hungry lady?'

The effect of these words on Neera was devastating. Her charm was not only legendary but the armour she hid behind. With a few direct words, he had dismantled it and sent her hurtling down a dark void. She was like Sandra Bullock in that space movie, except Sandra had dealt with the natural, universal phenomenon of gravity, or the lack of it, while Neera's abyss was inside her being—entirely self-made and so heavy with gravity that nothing, not even light escaped: stars combusted inside and nothing came out. She thought she had mastered sidestepping this blackhole. He had not been rude. And yet, here she was, free-falling naked because he was right.

The lights went out. The cabaret was about to begin. Dasha used the opportunity discreetly to eat as many of the ham-and-cheese croquettes on the table as she could: food was a luxury for her, earlier because she wanted to be model-thin, and now mostly because she couldn't afford it, which had resulted in an abusive cycle of desire and regret. Dankworth asked her another question, but her mouth was too stuffed to respond. Luckily, the music got louder and a spotlight came on, revealing Violet with eight blue arms, perched like some great celestial bird on a trapeze ring. Neera watched Violet, entranced, a million thoughts racing through her head, unable to hold on to even one. The blue goddess turned directly to her, holding her gaze and singing Neera's whole life with her song. *Can she see through me too?*

Violet extended her blue hand as she swung low on her trapeze ring. Hovering above the table, she pulled Neera up onto the ring. For a moment, Neera swung gracefully alongside the goddess. She felt free, with her arms spread like an eagle. She fell backwards.

But now, upside down, her knees bent around the ring, she was gripping on for dear life. A soundless laugh escaped the wide-open mouths of the audience. In vain, Neera tried to reach one of the many arms, just millimetres out of reach. The upside-down swinging started gaining a frantic pace. The audience looked like a pack of ravenous wolves. She finally managed to grab an arm to pull her to safety—it was fake. The arm snapped, and Neera snapped too, to find herself seated between her husband and the American who had just shred her to size. Neera was totally disoriented. *Did that just happen?* Violet's singing continued from above.

Here for just a moment then you're gone
It's just an illusion, illusion, illusion

In unison, the older ones in the audience cooed, 'Ooh, ooh, aha.'

∫

Rosel kissed her eight-year-old son's photo and placed the treasured possession safely back inside her jacket pocket. She looked around Len's homely, Lilliputian room before undressing as carefully as she had got dressed earlier that morning. In the morning, she'd had a goal, a plan, a place she had to be. Every cell in her body had felt alive. Fearful, sure, but alive. But now that she had made it here, she felt like a plastic bag blowing aimlessly in the wind. She could not muster up the energy to think beyond. Rosel neatly folded and put each item of clothing inside the bag that Len handed her. Len then rolled out a thin mat for Rosel, which left no space in the room to move. *It was just as well*, Rosel thought, *that all my belongings fit into one Franprix paper bag.* She lay down and shut her eyes, thinking of the cramped home she'd shared with her twelve family members back in Dasol and how happy she had been.

Why had she been the one to leave? Her bones felt heavy

under her skin. At twenty-seven, she felt like the old women she had provided palliative care to during her medical training—all of them caught between desire for and dread of the inescapable end. She remembered how she had airily chattered away with the other girls in long queues, doing daily rounds of the international placement agencies, how optimistic she'd been that her life was going to change one day soon. And how wretched she'd felt when she had finally got the call. Saying goodbye to Danilo, her son, her heart, was the hardest thing she had ever done. At the airport, he was in her sister's arms. He was only four. She knew he would struggle to remember her and she would struggle to forget him.

Enough, thought Rosel. She hadn't escaped the Kuwaiti Cruella to drown in self-pity. She summoned an image of herself laughing with little Danilo, running breathlessly up the salt dunes near their home, half rolling and half falling all the way down. Tomorrow, her life would change. It had to. Humming a silent lullaby to herself—after all, no one else was going to do it for her—she shut her eyes and promptly fell asleep.

PART 2

Before the After

Chapter 1

Like a curious child barging in on her naked parents, only to regret it and never forget it, rays of light rushed through the gap in the curtain and caught Violet in the throes of an orgasm. Her ground floor apartment shared a wall with the lift and was a shrine to all things that sparkle, shimmer and steal the show, but being a zealous Konmari (long before the Guru of Tidy named and copyrighted the addiction to order), the small space possessed a zen discipline too.

A sequined gown on the linoleum floor reflected the rays, emitting a pink glow. She adjusted her pelvis to sink closer to pleasure. Her face was in full drag make-up. For Violet, sex, even with her boyfriend Benjamin, was a performance. And given that Manko had closed months ago, she needed to perform at any chance she could get.

On an animalistic level, sex with Benjy had always been great. But it smelt of her past, inevitably leaving her emotionally bereft rather than full. So, after years of practice, she had learnt to act her way to bliss. She performed how she wanted to feel till it wasn't possible to separate the imposed emotions from the real ones. With each rhythmic thrust, she went deeper into character. Often, she imagined she was running through verdant hills, like Maria at the beginning of *The Sound of Music*. An odd choice of escape, and sometimes the disapproving nuns made an appearance, but it mostly did the trick, and Maria's untainted joy became hers.

Perhaps, in another world, she and Benjy could've been friends or even brothers, but too much had happened now. Besides, she needed to dig into his flesh and for him to be in hers to validate their existence and quench a whole host of other needy... things neither of them had names for. They understood each other on a base and basic level. Once they had crossed the carnal line, on a monumentally lonely night in a crowded camp under a festering tunnel, they didn't know how to go back.

Their union was not shallow and never had been. Lately, she'd had to remind herself of that. But who had saved who? Did it matter now? Would they have made it out of walking and working the tracks of La Petite Ceinture if they hadn't met? The rodents breeding on that long-disused train track, which ran like a belt around the periphery of Paris, were considered inherently Parisian, while nightwalkers like Violet and Benjy were the scum infesting society. The hope-sucking neighbourhood of Barbès was not one she had imagined possible in the Western world, but she'd settled for living—if it could even be called that—in the dangerous, dehumanizing stink-bowl as punishment for running away from Senegal. The night she'd rescued Benjy from being beaten to death in the tunnels of Barbès, she had saved herself too. He still had stars in his eyes despite them being swollen and pulpy. And his will to live had allowed her to dream of a better life once again.

Over the last decade, they'd helped each other to consciously forget the smells and threats of Barbès. Yet, there were moments when a memory would come back with such force and detail that she felt she was living it again. A random whiff of urine mixed with the fragrance of goat meat cooking slowly; a particular pitch of a quiet voice pledging violence; a certain combination of rain and wet socks. And then there was the flashback she loathed the most, brought on by the weight and texture of a cold, solid steel object in her hand. She wished she could lose these muscle memories. They crippled her, making her feel like a criminal, even though deep down she knew *she* was the victim. Benjy thrust deeper, making her sigh and bringing her back to the act of sex.

It wasn't just history that held Benjy and her together. They shared an honesty, an almost-hideous nakedness of souls, even if she did wear a disguise to bed. Did she love him? She wasn't sure. He was part of her, and she certainly didn't love every part of herself. She disentangled herself and jumped into the shower, letting her make-up run down her face.

There were taped lines on the ground indicating where you needed to stand on the road outside the Office Français de l'Immigration et de l'Intégration, as if a metre's distance would keep everyone safe. Several years ago, putting distance—an ocean, in fact—between her and imminent death had saved Violet, so she obeyed. Strangely, today, just like that day long ago, she was masquerading as a *he* to fulfil legal obligations. Blank name-tag stickers were distributed. With great deliberation, Violet spelt out V-A-F-I. It was not only the fact that the name carried baggage—handling a pen made Violet tremble and shake. The written word and she had long parted ways. An omitted prefix to indicate her gender had altered the course of her life. Two measly letters, or rather the absence of them, on an official form had categorized her incorrectly, dictating how she must identify and who she was meant to be. Words and names had hurt her more than any stick or stone ever had. She was grateful for the obligatory mask. Her long hair was hidden under a black bandana, her cargo pants and oversized collared shirt disguised her feminine form and her dainty manicure was concealed under rubber gloves (thankfully à la mode in corona season). She was pleased to see that her new friends, one exceptionally tall with an extra long neck and the other equally short with a doll face, walked past to join the line without even recognizing her.

This French civics course was another compulsory step that had to be taken by uncivilized outsiders like them, eager to become European insiders. There were still hundreds of administrative ladders and snakes to vanquish before France would welcome them as her own, but the newly founded ladies' squad of Number Thirty-Six—the unlikeliest of friends—had decided together that it was worth it. They would go the whole way. After all, the pandemic had revealed to the world that your passport was not just a piece of paper but the value of your life. And the passports they already held valued them at less than the price of the paper the documents were written on. The clear solution was to become French.

Inside the fluorescently lit hall, every alternate chair was turned upside down. There was free coffee at least, which a masked helper was pouring out, refusing to let anyone else touch the pot. The helper's entire nose was peeking out of the mask, and he couldn't stop scratching it. No one pointed out that this was like wearing a condom on your thumb and then wondering how you caught an STD.

No one noticed as Dasha slid several packets of biscuits into her bag. Old habits died hard. Thanks to Violet introducing her to a certain lucrative area of e-commerce, food was no longer a luxury for Dasha. Still, her relationship with food was ruinous—she was like a street dog around free grub. Rosel raised her perfectly shaped eyebrow at Dasha, and then found a place to sit, careful to avoid eye contact with the gang of Filipinas. They glared and muttered among themselves, trying hard to place this woman occupying the body of a child. For almost half a year now, Rosel had managed to remain incognito. But in this classroom, she was too visible—if it wasn't for the girls of Number Thirty-Six, she would've run fast enough to become invisible.

Sometimes she fantasized about going back in time. Would she have done things differently? Yes, if for no other reason than to not wake up in the dead of night imagining Len and the police barging into her room. The pandemic had been protecting her, and with each round of stricter lockdown rules, her nightmares had retreated. She was genuinely sorry about what she had done to Len, who, by the grace of God, had not caught up with her. Mercifully, she was not in this class either. She needed to make amends with Len, for she had been nothing but kind to Rosel. The rest, some of whom she recognized, were not her concern. Yet, she had become theirs. She could hear them mumbling menacingly about her fancy shoes, her plucked eyebrows (Violet had insisted on tweezing them again last night) and her surprising fluency in French, thanks to little Toto. One day, she was sure she wouldn't care. Today, however, was not that day.

The instructor opened a lone window and asked everyone to take turns to briefly introduce themselves in French. It was only 9 a.m. on a beautiful Monday morning in July of 2020, but exhaustion was written all over his face, as if he'd been working twenty-four hours a day, seven days a week on an endless loop. The truth, though, was that this was his first proper day back at work after ninety-six days of sitting at home and getting paid for doing nothing. He would retire in less than two years and he was still doing the job he'd got when he was twenty-four. Hardly surprising, given that there was not one ambitious bone in his body.

Pre-confinement, he couldn't wait to fast-forward to his retirement when he would finally be free. Not that he wanted to do anything with that freedom. Travelling, reading, eating out or even gardening inspired nothing in him. He was French—freedom in itself was aspiration enough. Now that confinement had given him an immersive preview of his retired life, he was irritated. He hadn't worked his way up to owning a garden or a balcony or a patch in the sun, and his wife of thirty-five years was permanently busy with the three Gs—grandchildren, groceries and gossip—to notice his growing frustration. Without the obligation of having to step out for work, retirement would be no different from confinement, except that he would have chosen it. In short, he was no longer sure of his choices.

'Okay so I'm... Je m'appelle Darya Smirnova. Je suis Russe... Russie?' Dasha was introducing herself in broken French.

At that moment, Neera burst in, clearly quite late and in a flurry of chaos. She was still annoyed that her wealth and status could not circumvent this mandated nonsense of a class. It was not easy to become French, even if you were married to one of France's treasures. Righting a turned-over chair, she plonked herself next to Violet, oblivious to the instructor's dirty stare. The big movie-star sunglasses were back on her face. Had she been up all night? Had she been ranting again? This had to stop. Violet reached out and patted her improbable friend's hand. What she really wanted to do was slap her hard across her face, dislodge the heavy-duty glasses she used as shields and tell Neera to pull herself together.

All three of them—Violet, Dasha and Rosel—had taken turns sitting up entire nights with Neera as she smoked and fumed. High as a kite, she told the same stories on repeat. How and why these women's lives had collided was beyond explanation. Each had been an individual planet revolving around the same sun, and each had reconciled to being impacted by the ball of fire in different ways. Then, suddenly, some baffling force of quantum physics had distorted their routes, making their lives collide and entangle.

If they hadn't left everything behind to come to Paris, and if Paris hadn't come to a standstill, would their lives ever have fused like this? Let's not forget that formerly, they occupied separate social spheres that overlapped only transactionally. Back home—'home' indicating different continents—it would be entirely understandable if the four women didn't notice each other's existence, even if they lived in the same building, as they did now. No one would blame them; they had nothing in common.

In Paris, however, they were all foreign, fighting to fit in. And wasn't that commonality enough? In the quantum realm of itty-bitty things, that was more than enough. The burst pipe, the flood and the food that followed had, for sure, played its part in bringing these women together (though Dasha, even after her online escapades, could hardly be called a woman—she was still just a child struggling with her sexuality and abandonment).

Dasha continued, '*Je suis* model, what is the word—*mannequin*? *Je suis mannequin.*' As if on cue, her mobile rang. The instructor watched gobsmacked as Dasha, instead of switching it off shamefacedly, answered it. He was convinced he ought to be teaching politesse and cultural etiquette in modern society rather than these bookish, outdated courses on civic sense mandated by the State. But he was too tired to go up against a system that prided itself on being erudite and unchangeable, and too old to get into a fight with the uncouth, often scary youth. So, he waited till this curious-looking Russian finished her call, hurriedly placed her notebook and pen in her bag and rushed out, saying something about a casting call she finally, finally, *finally* managed to get, how this was going to change her life and how she didn't need to be here anymore, so goodbye and good luck to all you good people. Before he had time to even process what she said and translate it into French in his head, the Russian giraffe of a girl was clicking a selfie with her elbow on his shoulder and the rest of the class in the background.

Her exit changed the energy of the class as a unit. It was as if a proton had been removed from an atom, making it unstable, which was the only possible explanation for why Neera said all that she did and why the Filipinas did what they did.

Chapter 2

'*Je m'appelle* Neera. Like Lira with an N. You know Lira: the non-existent currency?' Neera didn't bother to stand up or remove her sunglasses. 'The rhyme is perfect, as I should no longer exist either, in fact if—'

The instructor interrupted, '*Êtes-vous mariée ou célibataire?*' The poor man had no way of knowing that a routine question about Neera's marital status would trigger an interminable monologue.

Violet sought out Rosel's eye and they exchanged a knowing look of panic, both of them now sitting ambulance-ready at the edge of their plastic chairs. Over the last two months, Neera's grief had defied all rationale. She had assumed the role of a Bollywood tragedy queen out to destroy herself, taking whoever she could down with her, only to prove to everyone watching (except to herself) that she was truly indestructible.

It was barely two weeks ago while Violet was airing out her studio that she saw Neera silently swaying upside down outside her apartment window. She was so serene and calm that no one on the street noticed a woman suspended from the fifth-floor, not that there were many people outside save the Tunisian fruit seller, who was finally busy selling fruit now that the farmers' market was shut. How long had she been dangling like that? Once Violet comprehended what she was seeing, she didn't wait for the lift. She legged it, taking two or three stairs per stride. Rosel walked in seconds after her. Together, they gradually pulled up the five hundred-thread-count sheet, wrapped like a lifeline around Neera's ankle. They should've called the *pompier* or the ambulance or some professional, but instead they went into emergency mode, not stopping to think what would happen if the sheet came undone while hauling Neera up. Once Neera was lying safely on the bed, with her head resting on the said sheet of salvation, she started laughing hysterically, a genuine guttural laugh that showed no sign of stopping. The other two didn't join in. The laughter eventually subsided and she offered an explanation that only made sense in *The World According to Neera*.

Apparently, after consuming a handful of ineffective painkillers, Neera had bundled herself tightly in a sheet—she had read somewhere that inconsolable babies felt comforted in swaddling cloths because they mimicked the womb. One end of her sheet had still been annoyingly tied to the vertical post of her four-poster bed, where the random Scandinavian lover from the night before, a Japanophile and self-taught master of some erotic spiritual art form called 'Shibari', had tied it in an impossible-to-open knot. As he had been binding her, he'd said, 'You're about to lose your ego to serenity at the knife-edge of danger.' The bondage, the sex, his presence had only made her feel more alone and she had shooed away the almost-lover before he had even come. Then, she'd used the free end of the sheet to wrap herself in it, curled up tightly in a swaddle and waited in foetal position for the promised consolation of not being born yet.

When she had no longer been able to tolerate the pain in her heart, she had wanted to throw it out of the window and, since it was inside her chest, logically she'd have to throw herself out with it. So, in her woozy state, enmeshed in her sheet, she'd managed to stand up on her four-poster bed next to the south-facing window and had leapt over. The sheet had unravelled around her like something out of an aerial acrobatic act as she'd plummeted down. Her right foot, however, had got entangled in the sheet, while the other end had remained firmly tied to her bed.

Voilà! The pain in her heart had stopped the minute fear, along with its buddy adrenaline, had rushed in. Focussed on survival, it had beat a thousand times faster and no longer hurt. But somehow fear hadn't scared her, so she had swung soundlessly, serenely, till someone, or death, rescued her. Some combination of the Shibari thing and the swaddling sheet had done the trick.

'Monsieur, I am not single. I am not married,' answered Neera, 'I am simply alone. And let me tell you, not a second passes where I wish I was not.'

The voice in the instructor's head knew he needed to cut her short and move on. Encouraging a lonely immigrant, no matter how glamourous, to share her story had proven dangerous time and time again. But he was bored and the atom in the room had already been rendered volatile, so he went with the flow, asking her to continue.

'Let me ask you, Monsieur: does your saviour, the God you believe in, the One who guides you out of hell, have a face, a form, a smell?' Neera didn't wait for him to answer, which was just as well because he wasn't quite following her. 'Mine does. My "One" has a name: Jean-Paul Allard. His smell: an unwashed pillowcase soaked in seawater, musty and salty, yet so familiar and comforting.'

Violet and Rosel had never heard about Jean-Paul's smell, although every other detail had echoed off Neera's walls and burrowed in their ears.

Neera continued, 'Of course, at first I didn't know who Jean-Paul was. In India, French celebrities carry such little weight. But I felt his eyes burn my flesh when we first—'

'Jean-Paul Allard? *Le producteur de cinéma?*' interrupted the instructor. The only words he had fully deciphered were 'saviour' and the name of his favourite film-maker. 'Monsieur Allard, *l'homme célèbre est votre mari...* It iz your uzband?'

The instructor couldn't believe he was in touching distance of the wife of the man who had made the 1987 teenage cult classic *Ces Crocodile dans Ta Tête* (*Those Crocodiles in Your Head*). He had watched it a gazillion times. In fact, he had rewound his favourite scenes till the VHS tape had worn thin and static lines had started appearing on his screen. Even today, he could blindly re-enact the everlasting scene where Jacques talks to his reflection in the lake and Sonia overhears it, is overcome with bitterness and hurls herself into the crocodile-infested lake. No one made pure cinema like that anymore—that's why he didn't watch films or TV now. It absolutely was not, as his wife often complained, because he was no longer interested in engaging with anything in life.

'*Oui*, Monsieur, the same Jean-Paul.' Now there was no stopping Neera. She spoke with the intensity and speed of a TGV train on pandemic rescue duty. 'He was on a recce trip in Rajasthan for his magnum opus, a love story between a French nuclear scientist and an Indian ghost. He wanted to see and be part of a genuine Indian wedding. The Beymanis—you know, the First Family of India—the ones that own everything? You've heard of them, right?'

The class looked on blankly.

'Anyway, they were happy to welcome a producer-director of Jean-Paul's calibre to their daughter's big fat wedding. And I was of course there, too. This was *my* gang.'

Well, it wasn't her gang, per se, because one had to be born into it and she was from a small town with no inheritance, unless you counted a tiny local sweet shop. But ever since moving to Mumbai, she made it her life's mission to infiltrate the crème de la crème of society. And she succeeded. But due to her growing infamy of late—hosting orgies, revealing secrets, unmarried, confident and, worst of all, not from Mumbai—her invitation to the wedding was iffy. So once the invite was safely in her hand, Neera vowed that through the course of the festivities she'd redeem her reputation and herself. She should have known there is no redemption for the wicked—only rapture.

Her mother forced her to dream bigger and taught her to despise their small life in the banana city of Jalgaon (not very far from Mumbai geographically, but a million miles away in every other sense). As a child, she was pushed to enrol in every imaginable activity, including accent and etiquette lessons. Always a people pleaser, and wanting to please her parents most of all, Neera did it all obediently and diligently. She excelled in school too. Her real passion, however, was devouring books and helping her father make his sweet Indian delicacies (with a local twist of banana). Her mother, a junior-school maths teacher, discouraged this by ensuring there was no time left in Neera's day to hang around the sweet shop.

When Neera graduated from university with honours in English, her mother found her an internship with the unsparing newspaper, *The Mumbai Mercury* (popularly known as the TMM). In no time, Neera was transferred to the society pages, which the TMM commonly used as secret missiles aimed at unsuspecting socialites. Her assured-yet-unpretentious manner only enhanced the fact that she was pretty, witty, supremely well read and ready to follow the lead. Exploiting her enthusiasm, the output editor at the TMM pushed Neera to hotel-hop to cover one glamourous non-event after another. Coming from the town of Jalgaon, she posed no threat to the Modern Memsahibs of Mumbai. Armed with her humble need to please, she quickly found her way in as everyone's best friend, confidante or lover. Being in her company made the less wise, poorly read and mega rich feel commended, cultured and cheery. So, she climbed up the TMM ladder at lightning speed and, soon enough, wangled her own weekly column.

With the high life came parties, sex and drugs, and, for the first time in her life, she didn't have the suffocating love of her parents. Neera was at liberty to think her own thoughts. She should have felt free. Well, in her defence, it's not easy to shake off the imprint of your parents from your viscera, no matter how much you despise them—and Neera *loved* her parents (or at least her father). So she found herself caught in a vortex of guilt, pleasure and repugnance, her predicament only made worse by her acute awareness that this adolescent behaviour had arrived a decade too late and lasted a decade too long. And still, she pushed her mien to the limit.

Nothing she wrote or did was taboo. She slept with married politicians, tripped on acid with young actors and, on one occasion, successfully scored a protected white tiger for a nouveau riche non-resident Indian to take to Shanghai as a pet. The more venomous and personal her column became, the more the public lapped it up. With her popularity came the hatred of those she betrayed (and worse, of those she ignored). Secure in the knowledge that they feared her too—either because they had darker secrets to conceal or they couldn't bear to be relegated to irrelevance—she knew they wouldn't dare unfriend her, just like she also knew they considered her a ruthless girl from the provinces with no class. They weren't wrong: Neera was aware of where she came from and what she'd become. She perverted her parents' honest ambition for her into something ugly and hated herself for it.

Rosel and Violet sighed with relief in the knowledge that she did not feel obliged to tell the classroom this part of the story—a story they themselves could vomit verbatim.

'The wedding was at the Udaipur Lake Palace, which, if you don't know it, is a fairy-tale setting,' Neera continued. 'Israeli bouncers slipped a magnetic security bracelet on each guest.

Hillary Clinton sat on the family table alongside Priyanka Chopra and Nick Jonas, Beyoncé entertained the guests and Jean-Paul made a beeline for me,' Neera stopped to take a deep breath, luxuriating in the memory.

Till date, she was not sure what it was that had made her Jannie walk up with two flutes of champagne and introduce himself. After all, the wedding was overflowing with brainy, blue-blooded beauties. When they discussed it later, he had said it was a fleeting look on her face of being far, far away whilst animatedly chatting that caught his eye. His head was full of the script about the ghost when he saw a live wire of a person who was a phantasm—somehow so alive and yet barely present.

'Do you believe in ghosts?' was his opener.

'Only of the people I've killed. They haunt me sometimes.' And with that answer she sealed their fate.

Neera moved to the front of the class, which, by now, had lost any interest they may have had in French civics and were collectively willing this strange creature with an uneven buzz cut, resembling a hurriedly mowed lawn, to never stop telling this enchanted tale from another world. It was a miracle how such impassioned words were escaping her tense face and tightly held mouth. If you looked very closely, you would have seen each pent-up syllable prying open the prison of her lips to be released into the world. And once the prison break was set in motion, the words began to pour out in an unstoppable mass exodus.

This was an audience she neither knew nor cared about. Who needed a therapist? She preferred the eager ears of strangers. All she wanted was to be heard and not be told what to do. For this lot, she and her shame were nothing more than an anecdote they could repeat to great effect. So they soaked in her words, along with her fierce features—recently made fiercer by the incompetently razored hair—and her fragility, which Neera no longer had the energy to hide. All missed details were translated and urgently whispered by those who had a better command over English. The instructor got only a gist of what was being said, but it was enough for him not to go back to teaching the course. Only Violet and Rosel had their heads in their hands, knowing that this was not going to end well.

'Can you imagine the bitches, stuck with their cheating husbands, glaring at me as I danced the tango with a dashing French stranger?'

Once again, Neera was grateful that her assertive mother had signed her up for every available dance, music and personality-building class. Jean-Paul tangoed like a beast, and Neera more than kept up. The packed dance floor made a small clearing as drunken aunties, dripping in rubies and sapphires the size of golf balls, cheered on the sexy dancing couple. A sharply dressed white man was still a gold-class status symbol for the Indians, no matter how high and mighty they themselves were.

Neera and Jean-Paul were on fire, electricity emanating from their spins, spreading waves of desire through the dancing crowd and those watching them. It brought out the best and the worst.

The husbands Neera had slept with ruminated on the memory of fluid flowing down her legs—for the girl could orgasm and it had been sheer joy to pleasure her! Even the wives who disliked her felt something hot stir in their groins, making them grab and rub against their long-ignored husbands. A gilded corner of the endless dance floor transformed into a fully clothed, PG-13 orgy. Everyone involved circled and twirled, partners were exchanged, tango turned into thrust-your-pelvis-and-gracelessly-gyrate bhangra. Collective want went up and up and up, till a feeling of communal ecstasy washed over all of them. Neera swirled and ended up with an ex-lover, who conveniently forgot that he had been thrusting against his coquettish wife just seconds before and, with a sense of nostalgia, stuck his tongue inside the fire starter's mouth. It was a wonderful kiss down memory lane, even for Neera, who reciprocated with equal fervour. Shame that the wife turned to smile at her husband right at that moment. Bigger shame that she happened to be a close relative of the groom. Even bigger shame that she grabbed a bottle of Dom Pérignon from a passing server and brought it down on Neera's head.

Everything went into slow motion. Neera hit the ground with a thud. The gash on her head bled onto her face. A few excruciating beats of silence followed. The aunties in brocade saris gasped. All eyes were on the fallen woman. Moments later, she was helped onto her feet by Jean-Paul, who held her hand tightly and deftly weaved her through the crowds. The wedding was too big a beast to stop for longer than a sigh, and with the next song, the disrupters had been forgotten and the revelries continued with renewed momentum.

Like renegades breaking free, Neera and Jean-Paul broke into a run as they neared the exit of the Lake Palace, jumping into the first boat in a row of ornate boats waiting at the dock to ferry guests to and from the wedding. The traditionally dressed boatman welcomed the two with a toothy smile and rowed them dutifully across the Udaipur lake. This had already become the most memorable night of his life, first, because he'd had a ringside, or rather a lakeside, view of the wedding of the century and then, because his prayers had been answered. All the boatmen on duty had prayed to Lord Vishnu to be given a chance of ferrying a famous actor or actress. Without doubt, Shah Rukh Khan was on top of any wish list. When Shah Rukh, better known as King Khan, had been ushered into his boat (*his boat! Oh, such luck!*), the butterflies in his gut broke free and flew around his head, making him dizzy with happiness.

The larger-than-life actor was slight and slim in real life. Whilst on the boat, the actor had chain-smoked two cigarettes, remarked on the beauty of the city, then casually asked the boatman if he had kids and genuinely laughed when the star-struck fan had mouthed a famous line from his film, 'Agar kisi cheez ko dil se chaaho, toh puri kayanat usey tumse milane ki koshish mein lag jaati hai.' King Khan had laughed and agreed, 'Yes, my friend, the universe does conspire to help all those who wish with a pure heart.'

At that given moment, the dialogue had felt true—the universe *had* conspired to give the humble boatman exactly what he had wished for with his whole heart. Shah Rukh never got tired of his fans—the love they gave him was purer than any he had known—and as he had stepped off the boat, he had shaken the local fan's hand with a disarming warmth. A hand, the boatman had been sure, he was never going to wash. Earlier that day, when the boatman had stood in line to have his turban tied and change into the shiny gold uniform designed especially for the occasion, he had been made to check-in his phone. There was a gag order on pictures. He had known that his wife would be disappointed not to have documented proof of this midnight meeting that was guaranteed to make them royalty in their locality. He had not cared. Every detail and smell of the eight-and-a-half-minute encounter with King Khan had already been etched in his memory.

Now, for the second time that night, the butterflies in the boatman's gut flipped and somersaulted, threatening to break out of his skin. Yet, he respectfully rowed on. The lady with the bleeding head leaned into the man with zebra hair, kissed him on his fingertips and made her way up his arm, collar bone, neck and chin, to finally find his lips, slide her tongue over his and feast on him with an appetite that the boatman hadn't even seen in any Hollywood film, where actors locked lips in all sorts of ways.

'Once he had taken my hand in his, I knew I was never going to let it go. An energy stream flowed through me. For the first time, I felt one with the world, with creation itself. It was like the great creator was openly speaking to me, forgiving me,' Neera said to her beguiled audience, taking off her sunglasses for the first time. 'From the boat, we jumped straight into a taxi to the hotel and then to the airport—or did we go to the clinic first? The details are fuzzy—all I knew was that Jean-Paul could see through me; it was like he was directly talking to the person I'd forgotten I was. Peace washed over me. I no longer had any concept of body, time or space. The next thing I knew, we were getting off the plane at Charles de Gaulle, my fingers still entwined in his. His lips caressed my ear as he whispered that I was everything he had been searching for his entire life.'

None of this was a lie, but all truth can be subjective. It's possible that Neera had been light-headed and seeing stars because of the untreated injury on her head and the copious amount of champagne and ganja she had devoured. It's equally possible that the director in Jean-Paul had been looking for a ghost to fall in love with and, across a starry lake in a fortified palace, he had found the most haunted person he could. Neera had not been interested in explanations, and they had both agreed to not deconstruct only to destroy the celestial love they had both been sure they felt. The civics class—which by this point, was listening with the intensity of teenagers raging with hormones, desperate to be punched by tragic love or multiple orgasms—felt it too. They didn't, however, expect the story to take the dark turn it was about to.

'A snake can shed its skin but it can never change its colour. I am the most venomous snake, the ultimate poisoner.' Neera's face contorted with discomfort, nonetheless her words continued to pour out. 'He saved me. How many people get to make a stab at a second life within their lifetime? My Jannie gave me a new life. And what did I do? Demolish his. Ruin everything. I ask myself what did I do it for? Hubris? Fleeting madness?' By now, Neera was almost wailing. 'No, it's because I have a black heart and can't bear to be happy or see anyone else happy. In fact, happiness and I have been mortal enemies for decades. Nobody can save me from myself, not even the goddamn universe!' She scanned the room for objects she could use against herself.

Rosel and Violet stiffened. They knew it was coming. If the floodgates opened, it could take hours, even days, to bring the torrential self-loathing under control.

The instructor had begun to fidget. He didn't need to understand the words to sense the approaching typhoon and this was where he drew the line—if only he knew how. Confrontation made him want to hide. The fact that he had neither been promoted nor had he asked to be in over forty years was proof that he was a sucker for status quo. His throat was dry and his palms were clammy. He ached for the endless ennui of confinement. This foreign lady, meanwhile, was about to start crying or get violent, and he didn't want to be in charge when either happened.

Someone, let's call it Universe, must've heard him, for at that exact moment, a very loud siren went off on his mobile. He didn't remember setting his alarm. It was midday and this was his chance to avert another unruly electron from running amok.

'*Excusez-moi, on va arreter ici. C'est dejuner,*' the instructor's voice halted Neera's shipwreck. He felt authoritative announcing the lunch break, although it was an hour too early. For once, he had taken matters into his own hands and cleverly cut short the melodramatic monologue without conflict.

Thank you, Universe.

Chapter 3

Across the Seine, on Kahlil Wolf's shop floor on Avenue George V, Dasha was holding her headshot in her hand like she was in a prison line-up. Casting for the first post-pandemic fashion week was underway, and a makeshift catwalk for the auditions had been created between the chaos of mood boards and hanger rails with numbered clothes. Tediously self-important busybodies wore surgical gloves and masks that made a political point with a clever slogan, or a style statement with a strategically placed body part, or claimed to solve homelessness by donating three per cent of the price of the mask.

No one dared tell them that they were taking themselves and their jobs a lot more seriously than they ought to. After all, the virus had knocked them off all essential-services lists, demoting them to the bottom of the non-essentials lists. Hairdressers before fashion stylists, lymphatic drainage detox before personalized bespoke shopping, gourmet picnics in the park before fashion shows and, without a doubt, Uniqlo breathe-easy organic pants before indigenously-dyed, you-can-not-eat-dinner-for-a-week, fitted bodycon skirts that must only be lightly dry cleaned. Even if you did buy the skirt because you deserved retail therapy, you could only wear it to the gourmet picnic in the park, as there was nowhere else to go in this age of social distancing.

It bugged Dasha that the French defended haute couture as art, giving it pride of place in society. It was true that she was desperate to be part of this insular industry, but only to serve a higher personal purpose. High fashion, for her, could never be art. It derives its worth from exclusive ownership designed to inspire envy, while art in all its truer forms saves you from the mundane by inspiring your imagination. Once experienced, a painting, a monument or a film belongs to everyone simultaneously, regardless of ownership. Art has the ability—nay, the duty—to transport the onlooker to another reality. Art can put you into the shoes of someone else, experiencing something else, in some place you've never heard of. Art can also hold a mirror to your own tedious existence by showing you someone experiencing exactly what you are, making you feel less alone and more connected. Haute couture and the realm it inhabits merely outline the world you can't afford to belong to. For too long, these designers and their minions have weaved allure by being inaccessible and unaffordable. Now, overnight, they had become unnecessary. To survive, they were going to fight tooth and nail (or needle and thread) against the growing sentiment that fashion had lost all meaning.

Fashion is the biggest industry in France. And even if it isn't, it is what separates the pedigreed from the plebs, and every country needs its own royalty. Egalitarianism is a wonderful concept as long as all evolved societies cultivate an unconstrained tier of first among equals. What would France be without envy for the wives and chateaus of Bernard and Antoine Arnault? Or the generosity of art patrons like the Pinaults? An invisible virus may have brought the world to its knees, but it certainly was not going to be allowed to dislodge such noble bastions of privilege. Their paid personnel scrambled around attempting to erase the last six months and return to normal. This was a normal where the moneyed were free to fly around the globe in their twelve-seater ozone-depleters; where they felt superior sitting on uncomfortable benches—as long as it was the front row, it didn't matter—ensconced inside packed spaces, to watch seemingly androgynous human hangers sashay up and down runways, exhibiting garments that they would then be obliged to buy for a price that could potentially solve child hunger; a garment they'd wear, perhaps, once for fifty-seven minutes and expect to be reposted on social media fifty-seven thousand times.

Today, none of this concerned Dasha. She focussed on strutting her tush without emotion, just the way Nicolas had taught her to. The blander she was, the greater chance she had of being cast. On the phone, he had reminded her to be efficient—the game was to catch as many open auditions as she could. If one designer didn't want her, she had to say thanks and run to the next. It was a successful system: it left no time to stop and think about how crushing this process was.

'It's the kind of ugly that works these days,' the stylist pleaded with the Lebanese designer. Neither lowered their voice nor took their eyes off Dasha, who was standing in front of them as still as a statue in her heels.

'I dress Angelina, Nicole, Penelope, Marion… My dresses are for princesses! Can we just have an old-fashioned beauty, please?' Kahlil said in his heavily accented English. 'This is not the time to reinvent a brand. We need to remind my clients how gorgeous they feel in my clothes. I want to get them out of their tracksuit bottoms and wrap them in embroidered magic. And I cannot do that if they think they are going to look like E.T. in a dress.'

Dasha had been called E.T. before but had never actually seen the film till a few weeks ago. It was an American kids' classic from her parent's communist childhood, and thanks to the ban on Hollywood films, her parents could lip-sync all of Raj Kapoor's Hindi songs but had no idea who Clint Eastwood or Harrison Ford were. During confinement, she and Astrid had cosied up on her single bed, an iPad strategically placed on a pillow, and bawled their eyes out as Elliot tried to revive E.T. Dasha had loved the film and not just because her head had been resting against Astrid's ample breasts and Astrid's pudgy fingers had been twisting their way through her hair. In fact, she had watched it a few times on her own after.

The film was proof that love could transcend the boundaries of country, colour, culture, shape, planetary origin, maybe even gender. She couldn't quite see the resemblance—but anyway, she had no objection to being called a lovable alien if it got her the job.

'I think she's got something, but you're the boss, Kally,' the stylist said, and seeing the look on her boss's face, called out, 'Next!'

Dasha grabbed her bag, forgot to say thank you, pulled up Google Maps and ran to Ralph & Russo down the road.

After four rejections, she was beginning to feel deflated. One of the designers had stopped her and sent her on her way before she'd even had a chance to walk towards him. She still had the money she had earned with Astrid, through Violet, and Covid-19 had deferred her brother's life in London, so she didn't really need the job to survive. But she still wanted it. She wondered if her mother had ever had the extravagance of choosing between want and need. It's true, she had come to admire her mother for all the ways she had turned her life around when her father had upped and left with that British tourist. Still, her mother's life was not one she wanted for herself.

Dasha was only thirteen when her father came home in the middle of the afternoon to pack a suitcase. He announced he was leaving for Liverpool with a man he had met while giving him a regular guided tour of the Swedish castle in Vyborg. He told his kids he was ready to stop living a lie. So, with all the love he could muster, he kissed each of his children as if it was the last time he ever would (and so far, it had been). Dasha felt his absence like a knife through her heart. Secretly, she blamed her fat mother for not making more of herself, for not holding on to her husband. Her fat mother, who hadn't always been fat, cried for forty-eight hours straight. Then, she picked herself up, found a job at the local paper factory and never mentioned, and forbade anyone else from mentioning, her husband again. Their neighbours wondered where he went and speculated that Putin's Secret Committee to spot deviators surely had something to do with it. No one guessed that it was humiliation that kept the family tight-lipped about his disappearance. Yet, even without his name on her lips, Dasha would forever be daddy's girl.

For weeks and months after he left, she roamed the streets looking for a clue, not knowing who she was anymore. By leaving—leaving the way he had—he took her with him. She would ask the old castle, the harbour, the library—*who am I?* They knew even less than her, now that the teller of their stories had started a new one. So, who was this girl he left behind? Nothing more than a girl left behind. When her twin tried to bring her back to herself, she was unable to hear him. His voice seemed to come from continents away, though he had his hands on her shoulders, propping her up.

'Are you listening, Sis?' he said. 'You can't keep doing this.'

How could Andrei's voice have been so far away when she could feel his breath on her? But her ears, her head, her being were filled with the sound of another voice: a voice that came from inside her and yet didn't belong to her. No, it certainly didn't belong to her. The voice had left, and somehow it was all she could hear. This voice was one that she knew better than her own. The first voice she had heard coming into this world, forty-one minutes before Andryusha. Perhaps that's why her twin couldn't comprehend her need, her emptiness. Andrei's first sounds had been Dasha's cries filling the sanitized room, mixed with welcome cheers and the sound of Papochka's delight. *His* delight had been all that welcomed her into the world. Now, it was gone.

On one such day when she skipped school in search of a sign or a coded message she was sure her father would have left her, she paused at the harbour. Her fatigued body felt like the long-abandoned barge in front of her that belonged in another country's waters was stuck and could no longer be moved. But, of course, if a powerful international organization willed it, the immovable barge would find its way home, or, if the barge was Roman Abramovich's billion-dollar yacht, a special canal would be constructed to sail it home. She knew in that moment that she had to stop looking for her father and make him find her. She would be the one to leave the clues, the coded messages. By leaving her, he'd made her find who she needed to be: either a barge every power wanted a piece of or *Eclipse*—an oligarch's boat.

Suddenly, her home and her life started feeling pokier than ever, and her plans and dreams became larger than ever. Though she respected how strong her mother became through this humiliation, the very fact that she didn't want to end up like her mother became Dasha's driving force.

Dasha walked to the banks of the Seine and chose the most spectacular domed building across the river. Going by the sandstone façade, the decorative mouldings, the floor-to-ceiling windows and the swirly, black grill framing the balconies, she guessed it had probably been built by Baron Haussmann, who was an official in Napoleon the Third's court but was, more accurately, a demolisher.

More than the symmetrical boulevards and the exquisite buildings, she marvelled at the audacity of Georges-Eugène Haussmann to turn the most coveted city in Europe upside down and rebuild it. Imagine the confidence such a challenge takes. It took him seventeen years to gut the city, and by the time he'd finished, he was as reviled by the Parisians of his time as he was now revered by the Parisians of Dasha's time. Her father often said that though everyone knew the old must die for the new to be born, people still can't help but mourn and hold on to the dead. The greatest cities, in his opinion, saw the greatest change and the greatest resistance to that change. When the Eiffel Tower was built, they called it a monstrosity that even the 'uncouth Americans' would reject and wanted it torn down. Her interactions with the French helped Dasha conclude that this was exactly what made the

City of Light uniquely stubborn and unwelcoming—their aversion to the adage 'change is the only constant'.

She inherited her aptitude for cultural trivia from her absconding father. Lately, she had become an aficionado of lifestyle minutiae and surprised herself by retaining information she had barely browsed through, when she couldn't remember a single lesson drilled into her at school. Her true school had been the weekly excursions around the medieval town she'd grown up in with her history-obsessed father. Even now, when she dissected the historic buildings of Paris, she found his voice inside her.

Focussing on the top-floor apartment, which boasted an exceptionally large balcony with potted red geraniums, she conjured up an image of herself reclining on a Corbusier lounge chair inside its grand salon. Astrid was there too, searching for their kittens who were hiding behind the extravagant Louis XVI jacquard curtains flowing lavishly to the floor. Her twin, meanwhile, was stoking the fire in the baroque marble fireplace and making a not-so-funny joke about inviting a shirtless Putin and his horse for tea along with Macron and his old mare. A maid in uniform brought in hot herbal tea and flaking mille-feuilles. Her mother called them all to sit on the Boca Do Lobo dining table under the Baccarat crystal chandelier. Insta voyeurism had become her university for all things plush, and never had there been a keener student. Dasha's aspiration smelt of *verveine* leaves, cats, firewood and family. There was little doubt in her head that one day, this was going to be her life.

Suffused with the aroma of her future, she pushed aside her impractical ego and got back on the saddle of that degrading casting horse.

Chapter 4

The mud outside the civics class tasted of her own betrayal. Rosel didn't dare make a sound. She spat out the dirt, wiped her face, stood up and dusted off her clothes. But River Girl, whose real name was Julie, was not done yet. She pushed Rosel down again, sat astride her little body and started to rub her face in the mud all over again. *Where the hell is everybody?* Lunch break was over. The girls of Number Thirty-Six were supposed to be here. *Where is Violet?* Rosel could have done with her help right at that moment.

And now that she was actually watching Rosel's humiliation, Len, in whose name this was being done and who'd been specially called to seize her moment of revenge, couldn't take it anymore. 'That's enough, let her go. We're not in kindergarten.'

Rosel's shame wouldn't allow her to look Len in the eye. It was Len who had discovered that Rosel was being treated like a slave by her employer. She cleaned the apartment next door twice a week and, one day, a misplaced delivery had made Len ring the Kuwaiti's doorbell. It had taken a long time for Rosel to answer. She'd had a light blue Gillette shaver in her hand and had been shaving the back and private parts of her employer. Len, who had simply been happy to find another Filipina working in the building, had tried to strike up a conversation. But Rosel had looked at her with eyes that had long lost their light and remained as wet and silent as a stone underwater. From deep inside the apartment, Len had heard the Kuwaiti shriek.

'How long can it take to open the door? I'm freezing. Do I have to get dressed and come out?'

Len could see from Rosel's terrified face that this had been a loaded threat. The following week, however, Len had waited till she had been sure Rosel was home alone to knock on the door. Rosel had been too scared to let Len in, but over the course of several months, they had exchanged fast and furious whispers in the doorway. At first, it had been comfort enough to chat in Tagalog to a friendly person. Plus, Len had let her use her phone to video call her son in Dasol. When the Madame had started double locking the front door every time she left the apartment, Rosel had realized that her situation was an exception and not a norm. She had wanted out. With Len's encouragement, a plan had started taking shape. So, five months later, runaway Rosel had found herself sleeping on Len's floor. After a few weeks of queueing and begging, the embassy had issued her a temporary passport—a new lease of life. Holding this paper had made her delirious with a freedom she thought she'd never taste again after Kuwaiti Cruella had locked away her passport.

The day her lover, Ferdie, and her older brother had been shot by Duterte's men on suspicion of drug peddling, her life had taken a curiously dark turn. When she had told Ferdie that she was pregnant with his child, he'd been over the moon. Those had been the happiest days of their lives, spent dreaming and planning the future they could neither wait for nor afford. He had assured her that with the consignments he had coming and with her on the cusp of becoming a nurse at the local hospital, they would move into their own little shack and, in no time, fill it with little ones. Money had always been scarce, yet somehow, her brother had managed to pay the required fee for Rosel to intern at a nearby hospital. No one had thought it was bizarre that you had to pay to work. It was just the way it was. If you wanted to move out of poverty in the Philippines, you paid to do white collar work. The two families had already been close and they'd agreed on a small wedding before Rosel started showing.

Before the wedding had come the news of the raid. Eleven boys had been shot dead in broad daylight by the police. Shot dead! Finished. End of story. She had imagined the bullet entering Ferdie's solid body, which had, in fact, not been solid at all, but 60 per cent fluid, with organs floating around. A bullet travels at a speed of 900 miles per hour. If your body is solid wood, the damage can be contained. In nursing school, she had learnt that it is not the bullet itself that kills but the destruction it causes when it enters the body, bursting blood vessels, exploding organs, like Arnie, the Terminator, annihilating everything in its path: bone, muscle, tissue, skin.

Rosel had been among the chosen few to observe the dissection of a freshly procured cadaver. What with the growing number of unclaimed dead bodies, there had been no shortage of fresh human corpses to practice on. Hail the war on drugs (also known as the President's license to kill—a president she and Ferdie had proudly voted for, ironically)! Standing on a stool she'd been allowed to bring in, she had scrutinized the body on the operating table. The dead boy, who'd had no mourners, had been shot in his groin. The entry wound hadn't looked big at all. But when the residents had cut him up, his organs had been pulverized, as if someone had run a steamroller over them. The velocity of the bullet had caused a one-time hydrostatic shock, leading to an internal explosion. 'This could be one possible cause of death,' the professor had explained. Before she could hear the rest, Rosel had been called out to change an old man's diaper.

Where had the bullet entered her Ferdie? At what speed? It had not been the bullet itself that had killed him. Yet he had died all the same. Shot dead! Those two words had hit her ear, pulverizing her life as she had known it.

The following weeks and months had been her worst. The families could not afford the undertaker's bill, which had been more than their annual earnings. So, like the majority of poor families who didn't want their deceased to end up in mass graves or on cold operating tables for students to experiment with, they had made a deal with the funeral director. They would take the bodies home, and he would come every week to inject them with formaldehyde and other preservatives to stave off decay till the kin had gathered enough money to pay for a proper Catholic funeral. The bodies had been placed in makeshift coffins fashioned out of crates and left in the alleyway outside their tin and wood huts. Rosel had spent the days with the other women in her family inviting passing men to play a game of cards near the coffins. It was tradition that the money gambled was donated towards the funeral fund. Listening to Rosel sing while they were dealt hand after hand had been the real draw. For a few blissful minutes, the players had piggybacked on her voice to forget where they lived and who they were.

The endless wake had made her hate Jesus. And yet, the only comfort she had found had been in His prayer. Religion is a double-edged sword for the penniless—the expensive rituals and diktats suck on every last centime they don't have while simultaneously filling them with the faith that they are part of His grand plan. It gives them a sense of belonging, keeping them from jumping off the nearest church spire.

Watching her lover and brother puffed up in their boxes as life grew inside her, had seemed like a morbid joke. Rosel had wanted out. She had applied for a domestic-worker job abroad, which had not been at all straightforward in a town where everyone was crawling to the fastest exit. Her family, who could not help with tickets and agent fees, had encouraged her all the same. It had taken more than four years for her to find an employer who had been willing to pay for the flight, visa and living costs. At first, it had felt like Jesus was finally blessing her. That is, until she realized that to her employer in Kuwait, an 'all-rounder' had translated into 'slave for life'.

'Enough,' Len said, pulling Julie off Rosel. 'I don't want you to hurt her, I just want... I just want...' She didn't know what she wanted, only that she wanted something. It had taken Len a long time to connect the dots after Rosel had gone AWOL. Even then, she wasn't sure what the whole picture was. How had Rosel gotten away with it? And what did 'it' entail exactly? All she knew was that, after all that she had given, she was owed something. 'I want my money back,' was all Len could come up with.

'With interest,' Julie added viciously. 'And money for using your phone and money for the days she slept on your floor and ate your rice and the money she earned in your job.' If Julie was not going to be allowed to draw blood, then she was damn well going to get every centime she could from this double-crossing whore.

It must have been delirium or the bitter taste of slavery still fresh in her mouth that made Rosel steal Len's wallet and work permit on the eve of Len's big job interview. Rosel's plan was not a very clever one. In fact, it was heavily flawed. She'd come up with it on the metro after being refused yet another job because she didn't have papers. She sweetly borrowed an unsuspecting student's phone to send Len a message. Posing as the potential employer's husband, she typed that the job interview scheduled for the next day was cancelled because they were moving out of Paris for personal reasons. The next day, Rosel showed up for the interview as Len. From experience, she knew that to western people, all Southeast Asian girls looked the same and were interchangeable. Plus, she chose to wear a mask, even though back then only the most cautious people were wearing them.

Madame Decoste was skinny, cold and her English was to the point. She wore an expression of defeat and constipation— truth be told, with three kids under ten, a dog who needed to be walked come hail or high water, a high-powered communications job at Hermès, an irritation of a husband and a bursting social calendar, it had been months since she'd had time for a full bowel movement. After arguing bitterly with her husband for five nights and five days, she had eventually worn him down: he had agreed that they could hire a live-in nanny. She'd spat on his suggestion of perhaps cutting down the time they spent away from the kids, away from the apartment they'd spent a year renovating, importing tiles from Portugal and furniture from Cambodia. She had known he'd let it go since he knew she never needed his permission for anything anyway—it was just easier for everyone to have him fully on board than silently sulking. So, before the day had been out and before he'd had the chance to change his mind, she had set out to find one.

Everyone in France—everyone in the world—knew that there were no better domestic workers than the Filipinos. The third one she interviewed said she would do everything and claimed to be a trained nurse and good with dogs—bingo! And obviously she knew what to do with kids: she had an eight-year-old son who she hadn't seen in four years. *How could a mother survive such separation?* On second thought, if someone asked Colette Decoste that question at that very moment, she might have admitted that she could do without ever seeing her kids again.

She hired Len, who, in reality was Rosel, on the spot; told her to move in that weekend; and quietly dreamed of the leisurely poo she was going to have on Monday morning.

'Let's go to the ATM now and you pay Len,' Julie ordered. 'Len, how much does she owe you?'

'I don't have a bank account still.' This made Julie charge at Rosel again, till she said, 'I can give cash.'

'Cash?' sneered Julie. 'Of course, you can. Your kind only deals in cash, you slut. Give Len five hundred euros right now and then we'll see.'

Rosel carefully counted out one hundred and sixty-five euros.

It was all she had on her. She was due to be paid next week, she could give the rest then. She had only taken—okay, stolen—ten euros from Len. Well, that and the job. It had always been her intention to pay Len back for her kindness and thereby to absolve her own treachery. But the nationwide confinement, not to mention the absurd personal drama that had followed, had complicated her modus operandi.

Madame Decoste had wanted her to confine with them. After all, they had enough space, and the kids loved Rosel, who had, by that point, gotten used to being called Len and being paid in cash. Then, without warning, the Madame had made her pack her bags, moved her to a room across the river and given her a bonus. One day, Rosel intended to tell them her real name. Then she'd be able to claim her earnings openly and stop waking up in a cold sweat having dreamed that a murderous Len was in her room. But every day felt too soon. After years of sinking, she had been standing with both feet firmly planted on solid ground—no longer teetering on one tired foot at the edge of a storm, lugging the weight of her emptiness. The unbearable noise in her head had been hushed by the sound of laughing children and there was no way she was going to allow herself to drown again due to the dubious details of her identity.

However, in spite of her prayers, hard work and deceit, she'd been caught up in a tsunami. Had she known the turbulence she had been about to unleash, she would *not* have gone into the children's room that night. The littlest one had had a nightmare again—this time about a witch and a tomato—and couldn't put himself back to sleep. Madame Decoste's rules had been clear: after lights-out at 8 p.m., the kids were neither to be seen nor heard. No going in to comfort them, no matter what. They had to learn to solve their problems by themselves or wait till the morning. Calling Maman or coming to her room at night was forbidden unless it was a real emergency—fire, blood or robbery. She herself had slept with earplugs for almost ten years. Her philosophy was simple: Without sleep, she was irritable and unhappy. And everyone knew that a happy mother made a happy home. Except she was never home and Rosel had never really seen her happy.

Chapter 5

Rosel had held the job for less than a month when she was asked to accompany the Decostes on their annual ski vacation to Val d'Isère in mid-February. Meanwhile, somewhere closer to her country of birth, a virus was making its invisible way towards them. The family chalet was old, overheated and had a clear view of the French Alps. Rosel had fallen in love with snow, or the idea of snow, after watching a badly dubbed version of *Doctor Zhivago* with Ferdie in a video-parlour a lifetime ago.

He'd queued for close to an hour to get them prime seats right up front knowing his pixie love wouldn't be able to see a thing with a chair in front of her, even if he had ensured it remained unoccupied. She had squeezed his hand to suppress a loud cry that was threatening to escape as Lara was tricked into leaving her lover and sent off into the snow. The film is a thesis on impossible love—a sonnet written in snow. Impossible love, Rosel was well acquainted with. But she had never experienced snow in its full, natural glory till that fateful February. White, soft, cold and powerful—all the things she wasn't. And yet she felt inexplicably drawn to it.

On their first night in the chalet, once she was sure everyone was fast asleep, she sneaked out to stand alone at the front door and stare at the shimmering blanket covering the earth. The smallness of her own being became one with the vastness of the white. To think, the same God created both of them! It was an honour to be part of this magnificence. Nature was so complete and foreboding—she couldn't tell if it filled her or drained her. Hot tears rolled down her eyes as her breath froze in the night air. The elation mingled with icy fear that ran down her spine was the same feeling as when she'd first set eyes on her newborn Danilo. She had been petrified and bare, and yet had felt so complete, having just created life.

Unbeknownst to her, Olivier, her Madame's husband, was watching her from his first-floor bedroom window. The creak of the front door opening had woken him up and he'd gotten out of bed to check. Seeing Rosel in Colette's threadbare hand-me-down T-shirt that hung on her like a nightgown made him strangely uncomfortable. But he didn't want to startle her or interrupt whatever she was doing. While he'd hardly had any occasion to interact with the nanny, he had no reason to not trust her.

Yet he couldn't stop peering down at her from his bedroom window. He saw her put her tiny foot in the snow, which sent a chill up her spine and made her smile. He found himself smiling. She bent down and put her cheek on the snow before standing up again. She stood there for a long time, shivering and crying. He had to fight the urge to run down with the plaid blanket lying on the armchair next to him, wrap her up, hug her tight and rub her small delicate body down till she melted into his warmth. Olivier blinked the ridiculous thought away, patted down the beginning of an erection and got into bed next to his dead-woman-sleeping wife.

The weekend before their trip, Colette Decoste piled them all, poodle included, into her SUV and drove to Decathlon to kit out the kids and Rosel for the ski holiday. Luckily, the Madame could buy everything from the kids' section—their nanny fitted into clothes for ten- to twelve-year olds and her foot size was barely thirty-four. This made the kids roar with laughter. As they moved to the shop floor near the shoe rack, holding their bellies, pulling out baby boots and handing it to their miniature nanny, the dog did his bit to help by biting and slobbering on the shoes.

It wasn't till Rosel started laughing too that Colette burst a fuse.

'*Arrête les enfants!* Enough,' she hissed through clenched teeth. 'Len, you are supposed to be minding them, not encouraging them to behave like wild hyenas.'

Seeing Rosel's cheeks burn with shame, the kids prised a boot out of Milo the poodle's mouth and fell silent instantly. They were good kids and instinctively understood that laughing with abandon would have to be another one of those things they only did in secret with Rosel.

In the space of a month, Rosel became a mother, playmate, cook, comforter, organizer and keeper of secrets for all three kids. Her singing and endless capacity for play were what they loved best, and they just about tolerated her cooking, which made everything taste doughy and the same. They weren't always sure, for instance, if they had just bitten into chicken à la crème or cauliflower cheese, but they never complained because meal times had become mini town-hall meetings, where the minutest detail of their day was dissected and discussed. Before this, no one had ever been interested in hearing about when, how many times and with whom they had played Dragons and Vampires at school that day, or in memorizing the ever-changing list, ranked in order of preference from one to twenty-two, of new best friends. For Rosel, it was sustenance for her starved soul. The kids, meanwhile, were delighted that she wanted daily updates about the gigantic snail they had found in the schoolyard. Everything was more fun with their itsy-bitsy nanny, who made a game out of even the most routine activity.

They would sing all the way walking home from school. It didn't matter that Rosel hadn't heard any of the songs before, she hummed along and harmonized with an *ooh-aah-ooh* or a *la-la-la* or a word she'd picked up phonetically, and with the addition of her voice, the song would suddenly take a new dimension and become immediately memorable. Hiding behind the game of songs, she sang out her sorrow, and it brought much pleasure to the three siblings and their school buddies. Had Simon Cowell been passing, he would have signed her on the spot and instantly copyrighted her haunting version of the mediocre pop song of the day.

Blanche, the nine-year-old, was obsessed with the current singing sensations, Louane and Vianney, both of whom were young, beautiful, French and sang songs of random, everyday joy. On school mornings, Blanche would wake earlier than necessary to write the words of her current favourite song. At breakfast, she would proudly present the sheet of paper, her perfect cursive letters hanging like pearls. It was understood that Rosel had to learn the lyrics so that they could sing them together on the way back from school.

Rosel had so much love to give but, for so long, had no one left to receive it—love that belonged to Ferdie, to her brother, to her parents and to her little Danilo. Since leaving the comfort and scarcity of her life in Dasol, like a mountaineer battling weather and altitude on an Everest climb, her only focus had been survival. Everything else—whether good, bad, happy or sad—had been blocked from entering her mind. As long as her employer would send money home, however sporadically, she would continue to inch up the mountain. Years later, she was still nowhere near the summit, but Rosel was thankful that the effort had, at least, numbed her heart. The first thing she pushed out of her life was love, in the hope that doing so would harden her. She should've known: love is defiant. It slyly stayed put, like a silent seed waiting for someone to water it.

The laughter of the Decoste children flooded her heart and the parched seed had sprouted, making their home feel like spring in January. For once, they weren't being told to behave properly or differently from how they were. No one was shushing them; screaming at them for letting Milo climb on the sofa; telling them to grow up, to go to their room or to pick up their socks. She hung onto every word they said, delighted in every smile they smiled. With her, they could run around being the kids they were without worrying about volume and manners. And with them, Rosel's life didn't feel like an advancing avalanche she was trying to outrun.

Trudging up the bunny slope in the *parc à luge* with baby Toto and his sledge for the twentieth time that morning, Rosel marvelled at her pink and grey snow boots. They were new, brand new—no one had been done with them or outgrown them. They'd been chosen from a rack by the kids, they had lickably clean soles and a fresh unworn smell. She had tried them on, then they'd been paid for in the shop and now they were hers. And, no matter how long she had stood with her feet in the snow, they hadn't got wet! She was the proud owner of new shoes, of waterproof shoes, of snow-proof shoes that kept her toes toasty. They were hers, hers alone, and once she was done with them (as if!), *she* would be the one to hand them down. What more could she ask for? Rosel inhaled bountiful alpine air and exhaled years of paucity.

While Blanche and Augustin were deposited at the ski school for the whole day by their parents, Rosel spent the next ten days of that February hanging out with four-year-old Thomas in the snow park. The parents, meanwhile, spent the day high up on the slopes, skiing, drinking and catching up with friends from Paris and Italy. Colette and Olivier were a popular couple, easy to hang out with, even easier on the eyes and forever up for fun. Some days, Rosel's phone (a phone that came with the job) would ring and Madame Decoste would instruct her to pick up the older kids from ski school, bathe and feed them and herself and not wait up. On those nights, the delinquent parents would tiptoe into the chalet late, as Rosel lay in bed, smiling to herself, waiting to secretly share a loved-up couple's drunken gaiety.

Invariably, all she heard through the walls was vicious arguing in hushed tones. The French in those heated conversations was too fast and too low for Rosel to make head or tail of. Like the kids, she wished she too could believe that everything was fine—that that was just how *maman et papa* talk. But, irritatingly, her child-sized body didn't come with a child's mind, and so she knew better: this little utopia that she had conned her way into was about to auto-combust, and there was nothing she could do save going up in flames with it. Actually, this was not at all the turn her story was going to take—but Rosel's convictions were coloured by her continuous encounters with catastrophe.

On one such night, Thomas woke up and was calling for his maman, who, by this time, tired of quietly yelling at her husband, had put her ear plugs in and passed out. Rosel was well aware of Madame's golden rule, but the boy had been crying for close to an hour and she could not bear it anymore. Blanche and Augustin were so exhausted from the relentless ski lessons that they would sleep right through anything, but little Toto's cries made her feel wretched. If Rosel and her family hadn't been near starving, she never would have left her baby boy. Every night, she would have pulled him close to feel his sticky breath on her and sung him the sweetest songs of sleep. She would have given anything to be the one to wipe away all his tears. What sort of mother could sleep soundly through the wails of her youngest child? And why did these rich French people have not one, but three or four children, when they couldn't even tolerate being in the same space with them for more than a few hours at a time?

The bedsprings creaked as Rosel climbed out of her narrow single bed and crept into the children's room. Seeing her, Thomas, cute little Toto, held out his arms and she picked him up in one swoop, wrapping her small frame around the boy. The embrace brought equal comfort to both and would've remained yet another secret between them if they weren't being privately watched.

Once again, Olivier felt his member rise as he stood in the darkness watching the nanny cradling his youngest son in her lap, singing a barely audible song of comfort. This time, however, the stirring was more than lust. He wanted to sneak in softly and put his arms around both of them, completing the family picture he always thought he'd have.

Except she was not his family, and this was not the picture his wife would ever paint or allow him to. Suddenly, he felt the weight of his unarticulated family ideal bearing down on him. Colette had convinced him that children became brats with this kind of late-night tenderness or, for that matter, any unessential tenderness at any hour of any day. If you wanted them to be autonomous achievers, they had to cry it out—and it was best they did it silently and invisibly, behind heavily closed doors. And Olivier had bought into it. After all, they'd both been brought up with iron fists and they had turned out fine—or, as his wife would say, more than fine.

But were they fine? He couldn't remember the last time he had voiced an opinion, other than to offer treatment or diagnosis to his patients. In fact, he couldn't remember the last time he'd cared enough about anything to even have an opinion. Some might go as far as to call him spineless. He would prefer to use the word non-reactive, not that that made him sound any better.

His wife was a one-track ball-breaker who had been running to win, no matter what the race was, since before he knew her. In her twenties, she had already been earning more than her exacting father ever had—a goal she had fostered from the age of fourteen, on the day he had shown public disappointment and mocked her in front of aunts, uncles and cousins for scoring five out of twenty in her economics class. The sole lesson she had come away with had been that a parent's ridicule is the most potent driving force. By marrying Dr Decoste, she had gained class and good genes, for he was a high-cheeked, chiselled specimen and, everyone agreed, he was ageing better than a Malbec. While he didn't have the coveted *de* particle in his name—his aristocratic mother had married a man whose mother had also not been able to pass on the two-letter particle she had been born with—for all practical purposes, the family had enough blue blood for him to be invited to all the exclusive Rallye dances and grow up quasi-aristo. In any case, Colette's success at Hermès more than made up for the absence of *de* or *de la*.

After a few early hiccups in their marriage, they had been in complete sync about the direction their life should take. When asked, he would say, with a seasoned glint in his eyes, she wears the pants and if he wants to get in them at night, he knows better than to contradict her.

They bought and renovated the dilapidated chalet right on the piste next to the ski lifts in Val d'Isère, where little Thomas had been conceived, five years ago; they went for a family holiday abroad twice a year; he walked to work, she drove a Porsche Cayenne and she had three well-presented, exquisitely mannered children who loved her very much, and he was almost certain she loved them. Yet, it was now instantly clear to him as he watched a relative stranger rock his own flesh and blood back to sleep that these were his kids too and that he didn't love his wife. If he was being honest, he had fallen out of love with her on their wedding day—a day that had been all about her. That in itself had been a non-issue: he had known wedding days are almost always about the bride, but it had been the way she had treated him, as if he had been some annoying, out-of-place prop that had refused to remain where she had wanted it.

It's true, he feared her anger, which could erupt without warning like a volcano, spewing lava for days—weeks—on end. One minute they would be talking about the weather and how rainy it was going to be that week, and the next minute she was accusing him of raining negativity in her life and how he was always bringing her down rather than building her up. For his own sanity, he had learnt to wait it out and not engage, but that only seemed to enrage her further. Yet, once the eruption ended, the air felt clear and pleasant. What she destroyed in her rage, she repaired by being the most fun, liveliest person in the room. Her loyalty, too, was legendary. If you were on her team, then she was guaranteed to bite off any hand before it scratched you. The question remained: what would save you from her near complete inability to tolerate anyone she suspected of being a sluggish fool?

It was equally true, though, that he admired and encouraged her unwavering focus and ambition, and it was undisputable that no one could be as obsessed, as hardworking as his wife—that she achieved everything she set her mind to. Her ability to see the larger picture was unmatched, the trajectory of her triumphs awe-inspiring. But as a person, Colette was rotten. There was no other word—rotten. Yes, he finally said it, 'Rotten.'

The sound of her employer's voice startled Rosel. She had thought she was alone with the children and he had thought he said the word in his mind. They held each other's gaze awkwardly. A million thoughts raced through Rosel's head about how she had broken the rule, how he was going to berate her or worse, get the Madame and fire her on the spot. Instead, he looked down with a sheepish smile and whispered, 'Thank you, Len. Do get some rest. Good night.' And with that, he was gone.

Chapter 6

The next morning, Rosel helped the kids rush through breakfast like every other day. Though baby Toto had easily fallen back asleep, Rosel had spent the night tossing and turning, wondering what the morning would bring. Colette was dressed in her thermal inners and ski socks, sipping her hot water and lemon at the table of the open-plan kitchen. She stroked the carved wood of the table with her hand, remembering the day Olivier and she had received the shipment from India.

Neera, their friend Jean-Paul's charming new wife, had helped connect them to Vikramjeet Rathod, a furniture designer in Jaipur who refashioned tables from intricately carved wood-panelled doors found in the medieval palaces of Rajasthan. Colette was particularly fond of this table. It signified her ascent to a class of art patrons, people who commissioned objects of desire and beauty from around the world. And Colette liked Neera, who had a sharp, calculating mind not so different from her own. They lived not far from each other, the Allards in the 16th arrondissement and the Decostes just across the Seine in the 7th, which made socializing that much easier. They met for dinner or drinks at least four or five times last year, which, by Parisian standards, was far too often.

All those years ago, when Jean-Paul was making his docu-fiction about the encounter between Jean-Louis Dumas and Jane Birkin, a twenty-something-year-old Colette was sent from Hermès to help him. Jean-Paul was the first adult in her life to treat her as an equal, which made her come clean about actually being sent by her boss to ensure that nothing unflattering, which could be blown out of proportion by the raging animal activists, would make the final edit. They surprised each other by striking up an implausible friendship. Of course, this was before Colette's babies and Jean-Paul's Neera. On several occasions, the pair, both chain-smokers back then, walked and talked along the Seine after she finished work. She would lay bare the full spectrum of her ambition, basking in his fatherly advice—something she never got from her own father, who was still very much alive and disparaging of his daughter. Jean-Paul would listen without judgment to this compelling coquette who wanted to leapfrog to the top of the world. He observed and stored her no-nonsense character traits for use as and when his oeuvre might require. Jean-Paul, meanwhile, was going through a draining divorce, which made him feel tired and old. He was glad to be enthused by a person whose entire life lay ahead of her, who had never met his wife and who had nothing to gain by taking sides.

A few years later, when she was six-months pregnant with Thomas—gosh, it had already been five years!—she and Olivier were one of nine people invited to the *mairie* in the 16th to witness Jean-Paul exchange vows with a dusky Indian lady with haunting eyes—or were they haunted eyes? It was a wonderfully warm and windy autumn Sunday. There was so much love and laughter in the air; it felt like the falling leaves were spraying fairy dust on them all. She remembered holding Olivier's moisturized and manicured hand and giving him a wet kiss on the side of the neck just as he liked. That night, she had got on all fours, letting her swollen belly hang free as her husband entered her from behind. If you get the position right (not always easy), pregnancy sex can be as dramatic as the moment in the finale of Beethoven's Fifth Symphony, when the music suddenly shifts from minor to major, from soft to loud, darkness bleeding into light.

The memory made her heart race. If they weren't running late, she might even have locked herself in the bathroom and put the shower faucet to good use for a few minutes. She was efficient, all she needed were a few minutes. Suddenly, Colette missed her marriage and her husband, although he had been right there, sleeping next to her for over fourteen years. When had she first started ignoring him and his needs? She wished she could put her finger on the exact moment when things began to get ugly, for if she knew the cause or the turning point, she was trained to fix it. She was a professional problem-solver.

Was the problem that her marriage—okay, *their* marriage—was past its best before date? Or was it her pointed ambition? Or was it the fact that Dr Olivier Decoste hadn't amounted to the man she thought she was marrying? Whatever it was, every problem came with a solution. She was going to solve it. This endless bickering had to stop. Most likely she'd make Internal Communications Director for the group before summer, and she could do with Olivier's support and some peace at home. She made up her mind: she would cancel the dinner plans they had with Leo and Antonio. Instead, she would go with Olivier to the Blizzard Hotel for a cosy wine-soaked, apéro dinner in front of the fireplace.

Many moons ago, they had stayed at the Blizzard for a romantic getaway. Luxury back then had still been new to them. The understated decadence of the hotel—all alpine chic with faux fur rugs on the floor and real deer heads, taxidermied and mounted on the walls—had blown their minds. After dinner, they'd sat in the bathroom on a worn leather armchair abutting a sleek black-slate bathtub. This bathroom that had come with its own little fireplace. They had made love in that tub. But how? She could no longer comprehend the mechanics of underwater sex.

The clock on the oven flashed 8.13 a.m. She would call Leo at nine to cancel, and then the hotel after to make a booking.

'Augustin, please can you go wake your father? We'll be late and I know he'll want muesli before leaving.' It irritated her that he could never just have a coffee and be done with it like everyone else she knew. The fuzzy feeling she had for her husband a moment ago had lasted no more than three-and-a-half seconds. 'Aug, are you listening? Leave that croissant and go wake him.'

Olivier came in, kissed his children on the top of their heads and, for the first time in a long time, lingered and smelt their scents. His kids. Did they know he would take a bullet for them? Did *he* know for certain that he'd take a bullet for them? Of course, he would. They were his. He helped create them. Augustin was the spitting image of him—dark bushy eyebrows, sand-coloured eyes, the same full bow-shaped lips and a nose that sloped to one side. Just enough asymmetry to make their perfect faces more believable. And Blanche had his dimples. Not any old dimples— *his* dimples.

'Who wants to take the big gondola and the funicular to the other side and go dog-sledding with papa?' he asked.

'Don't tease them like that, honey,' said Colette in a clipped voice. 'Blanche, who's the girl from ski school you wanted to invite for a playdate and dinner? If Len is okay with it, we could do it tomorrow.' She didn't care, of course, if Len was okay with it. She was simply making small talk with her daughter.

'Please don't interrupt me like that, honey,' said Olivier, shocking himself more than anyone else with his tone. Well, at least he had their attention now. 'Are we going dog sledding or not?'

The kids didn't look as enthusiastic as he had hoped. He tried again. 'Maybe the sled guy will let us pet the dogs after. We will have to be careful, you know, as they are big dogs—huskies. I think usually there are eight or nine dogs that pull a sled.'

'Olivier, what are you doing?'

'Maman can come too,' he continued, cutting off his wife.

'And Len,' squealed Thomas, delighted.

'Of course, if she wants,' he replied casually, certain that no one noticed the blood rushing to his cheeks.

'Youpeee!' said Thomas and Blanche in unison.

'Do you think we will be allowed to hold the reins?' asked Augustin. 'I want to drive the sled myself. I can, I'm almost eight. I'll be careful. I promise. Please, please can I drive?'

'Maybe,' responded Olivier. 'If you are super gentle and ask politely, I think they might allow it.'

'Oh yeah. Youpee! Youpee! Youpee!' All three kids were high-fiving happily.

Now this was the level of enthusiasm Olivier had been expecting. His children so happy and him the sole cause of that happiness! This felt good. Nay, it felt right. From now on, this was how life was going to be.

'Okay, that's enough everyone,' Colette's sharp voice cut through the clamour. 'Finish your breakfast. We will be late for ski school.' Why did she have to be the bad one? At that moment, she hated Olivier for putting her in this position. Someone had to be the adult here, but why always her? 'I'm sure we can organize sledding next year properly and not last minute like this. We could go for a full-day picnic. Today, it's not going to happen. You have to be in ski school and we have Amélie and Paf waiting on the piste for us.'

'But why can't we do a full day picnic *today*?' asked Blanche. 'Len could make us some sandwiches and we bought meringue and mint syrup yesterday. Oh, and I think we also have some *fougasse* leftover.'

Rosel busied herself with the washing up, avoiding eye contact and wishing she was invisible.

'That's a great idea,' agreed Olivier. 'Len, would you mind?' His cheeks were burning again.

She gave the slightest nod without looking up, scrubbing hard to clean the non-existent grease.

'Can I talk to you in the bedroom please?' demanded Colette, who had by now forgotten all about fixing her marriage and was seething at her husband's unfathomable behaviour.

The children rushed around, packing little treats and toys into their rucksacks. Thomas zipped his bag, leaving just enough space for the head of Lappie, his little bunny to stick out. He kissed Lappie, pulled the zip tight so it wouldn't fall back in and put the bag on his back, ready to head out. Blanche took her new mandala colouring book and agreed to put Augustin's unfinished Tintin comic in her bag, as he wanted to be unencumbered and free to drive.

'Len, shall I help you with the sandwiches?' asked Blanche. 'I know what everyone likes.'

'BeeBee, let's wait to see what your parents decide. Okay?' said Rosel, wishing that she could leave immediately and spend the day with Thomas, just like every other day, on the bunny slope. Of course, she was curious about dog sledding and would have loved to try it, but not at the cost of the not-so-hushed screaming match that was in full swing above their heads.

Rosel wanted to sweep up the kids and escape. But where would she go? What would they eat? She looked out of the kitchen window, mulling over the possibility. Outside, the snow was falling gently in huge flakes and, for the first time, she clearly saw their patterned, hexagonal shape—delicate and complex, melting into the waiting snow, losing their individual form to become one with the endless white.

'Alright kids, are we ready, steady, go?' Olivier had obviously won the match, if there was such a thing as a winner in a losing game. 'Len, please could you pack lunch? Make whatever's easiest.' This was the beginning of a new era for him. Colette could sulk all she wanted, they were going sledding with or without her and they were going to have the best day of the trip. 'Len, you should come too. Just make sure you dress extra warm. When the dogs run fast, it can get very cold. I mean, they'll probably give blankets but it's better to be prepared, *non*?'

Colette did end up going with them. The kids ignored her foul mood, even when their triumphant father leaned across the gondola to kiss her ticklish ear. Instead of laughing, she bristled, swatting him away like a wasp. He caught Rosel's eye watching them for a moment before she looked away.

When they arrived, they were told all the sledges had been booked weeks in advance, no amount of begging or bribing was going to get the Decostes and their *nounou* on one and no, they were sorry, there was no petting these dogs. They were on duty.

'It's peak season, kids, we should have booked. Which is why I said let's book for next year,' this twist put Colette back in the game and this time she was determined to come out tops, even though she knew that the biggest losers, either way, were her own kids. The look of defeat on Olivier's face cheered her to her bones. If she could, she swore she would have resisted gloating. 'Your father tried. He forgets spontaneity requires meticulous planning.'

'What is meticulous?' asked Augustin.

'It means paying attention to small details,' the dark cloud over her mood speedily sailed away, but unlike the sun, her cheerfulness warmed no one but herself. 'I, for instance, am a meticulous person. Papa isn't. I consider all the tiny little details before making promises. Your father doesn't.'

Rosel could see her Madame was building up to a fight. She felt sorry for the kids and even sorrier for her embarrassed Sir, whose eyes she had been self-consciously avoiding as best as she could.

'Look, there's an empty picnic bench there,' Rosel said, trying to salvage the situation. 'Madame, shall we go get it?'

'Great idea, Len,' said Olivier, clinging onto her words like a lifeline. 'We could still build the biggest snowman—the snow is fresh and soft here. Perfect for building and perfect for battle,' he said, throwing a snowball at Augustin.

'*Ouais!* Super.'

'*Très* cool.'

The kids were easy enough to please, and for that, Olivier was truly grateful to Colette. Under the guise of not spoiling them, she deprived them of so much that they expected almost nothing and made do with everything.

'No, no, no, if we head back now, then you can still make the afternoon session of ski school,' countered Colette. 'We can eat our sandwiches in the gondola.'

Big tears fell from Thomas's eyes. What had begun the night before as Olivier had watched the elf-sized nounou dry his son's tears had culminated once again with the tears of his youngest.

This was the beginning of the end: he was sure his only choice now was to race to get to the finish line, to the end point of this lost game named marriage. It made him feel like he was retching on an empty stomach. Not the marriage, but the fact that there would no longer be one or that there hadn't been one for years. To stop himself from vomiting his own guts out, he sat down in the snow and started pretending to make snowballs.

At that point, it would be fair to say that Rosel had no idea of the role of catalyst she had played in this story, and how her character was about to go from supporting part to protagonist.

∿

Julie snatched the crisp notes from Rosel's hand and snarled at her, shoving past her as she exited the courtyard of the immigration office building with the real Len. Rosel dusted herself off. Her face felt raw on one side, probably grazed. She put her mask on and walked back into the French civics course. There, she spotted Violet looking over Neera's arm, carefully copying her answers. The instructor announced, '*C'est l'heure!*' And with that the students put down their pens.

The exam was already over. Rosel had missed it, and no amount of pleading was going to make the instructor let her sit for it. It had been the longest first day back in the history of mankind—or at least in the short dull history of the instructor—and he was ready to crawl back into his garden-less, balcony-less, one-and-a-half bedroom apartment and call it a day. So, without further ado, he did just that.

Chapter 7

In a hot, airless stairwell, lit only by the fluorescent light of cell phone screens, Dasha sat trapped among twenty other human hangers. They all looked alike, boys and girls. Or maybe it was the sameness of their scent—a base note of desperation, cleverly camouflaged by a top note of eagerness with just a teaser of energy, all tied together by a middle note of courage. The French language, Dasha thought, was spot on for using the word 'mannequin' for models. She really did feel like a manufactured plastic dummy, whose arms, legs and body could be adjusted and readjusted at the proprietor's will to attract the passing eye.

Have they forgotten us? It had already been over two hours since the last girl had been called in. The steel fire door was the only exit or entry to the stairwell, and it refused to open from the side they were on. Every five to seven minutes, an impatient hopeful would rise from the grimy concrete step on which they were sitting to try their luck opening the unyielding door. The fact that they couldn't find phone network in this confined corner enhanced their sense of abandonment and compounded their exasperation.

But being treated like cattle came with the territory. All aspiring models quickly got used to being herded around or hastily fled the industry. The difference was that there wasn't a single animal in the world of livestock that wasn't tagged, tattooed and valued by its owner. This motley crew, though, didn't yet belong to anyone. They were an unwanted pile of nuisance that someone might eventually sift through to find a potential golden goose.

Before walking into any casting, each of them would persuade themselves that *this* would be their moment, the turning point that would split their life into a before and after. A few of them would spend their lives awaiting that moment, most would give up and one, maybe two, would be transformed into that elusive cash cow.

The hours ticked away. Dasha busied herself discreetly taking photos: the cold metal door jammed shut; masked faces anxiously huddled together; close up of fingers tapping futilely on phone screens; the growing collection of cigarette butts; footprints on discarded masks on the floor; a boy stretching his back in a modified downward dog; a top-angle shot of the trash on the stairwell; a selfie against the exposed brick wall with a postage stamp–sized window... A window! She could smell network.

Before anyone else could understand what was happening, the girl with the giraffe legs was balancing on top of the back of Bendy Boy, who had obligingly moved his downward dog so that he was conveniently in line with the window. Typing out the multiple hashtags—#saveusfromLURE #Houseof LUREIsAPrison #LockedAndForgotten #TreatUsBetter #Helpthe HumanHangers—and inserting the exact location pin took no longer than a few seconds. She pressed share. Then, stretching her arms high above her head, Dasha went live. The bird's-eye view the phone captured of the scores of masked, emaciated models trapped in a narrow, crumbling, grey, spiral tower looked a gazillion times more intense than even the biggest exaggerator among them would have ever claimed. And yet, from then on, this augmented image was how they would all remember it. A classic case of virtual reality rewriting real life.

It took twenty-nine minutes after Dasha posted on Insta for the House of Lure casting bosses to push open the heavy door. Before relief could wash over the deflated captives, one of the Lure lot shouted, 'You are all free to go. We apologize for the inconvenience. The casting has taken longer than we anticipated.'

A blatant lie. In truth, to comply with social distancing norms, they'd limited the number of people who could wait inside the studio and had all but forgotten about the models they had asked to wait outside—obviously not *outside* outside, as that would have caused a commotion in the courtyard and the neighbours would have complained, and they needed all the socially responsible, community-minded, public-generated PR they could get. So, they'd ushered the models in to wait on the stairs at the back of their building, out of sight and earshot of the neighbours. What they hadn't known was that the door only had one-way access. In fact, till that afternoon, they hadn't known what was behind that heavy-duty door. The discovery of the stairway had provided nothing more than a momentary solution to an unending global problem—overcrowding.

'We're very sorry. The casting is done and all of you need to leave please. Thank you for coming, House of Lure appreciates it. Everyone out,' said another authoritative person, herding them all out of the building. 'Please be mindful of the neighbours and leave as silently as you can.'

'That's not fair. *Pas juste.* Come on. You have to allow us to audition,' objected one of the hangers.

Others joined in half-heartedly. 'We've already waited and wasted half a day for our turn.'

'Give us our turn.'

'Why did you keep us here for five hours if you didn't even want to give us a chance?'

'I missed Gucci to be here.'

'We're people too.'

The objections died out as feebly as they had been given life. All of them were so exhausted that if someone had actually stopped and offered them an audition, they would have rolled over and played dead. There wasn't a single one among them, Dasha included, who wasn't dying to get home and rip the infernal, compulsory mask off. So, they pretended to protest and kept walking out of the exit. If only they'd been able to check their dead phones that instant and seen the virtual rage Dasha's feed was arousing, they might have decided to stay and push through to see if this was indeed *that* moment when their lives got propelled into the 'after'.

'Okay, move along everyone, except @I_Spy_Me—you stay, please,' said an important sounding voice with a musical accent that most likely wasn't French—the sort of voice that could bring a room full of fighting bulldogs to order.

Dasha froze in her tracks.

'Is @I_Spy_Me here?' asked the woman with the important voice, before turning to her assistant. 'What is her real name? Does she have one?'

'Darya Smirnova, please make yourself known to us,' shouted the assistant on her boss's behalf.

Chapter 8

Years on, Dasha would still find it ironic that the big moment she had prayed for, planned and played out in her mind in the minutest detail, down to the colour of the lip gloss she'd be wearing, crept up so meanderingly on her that she scarcely noticed its arrival. After she revealed herself to Ms Bulldog Boss, she was led into the studio, and what followed was a blur of instructions and fittings. A male voice behind her said, 'Bravo! Bravo! You are quite the piece of work, young girl. You know how to make us sit up and take notice.' The sarcasm in his voice cut through all language barriers.

'You mean my Insta feed?'

'Of course, what else?' came the incredulous response from Important Boss-lady, who really wasn't the boss of anyone except her assistant. In fact, she was pretty low down the Lure hierarchy, but the top cats liked her because she was more efficient than any of the other executives, and it was universally, albeit unofficially, agreed that her main job was to protect their creative minds from the dreadful drudgery of marketing, admin and trolls. She'd become a human shield, reporting to them things that they were grateful to have no understanding of or knowledge about. 'You, Signorina Smeer-nova, lit a small fire on social media. Now, understand this: House of Lure is too big to burn with it. Nevertheless, we don't like embers flying around.' Her confidence and command over words—a key part of her bulldog persona—was a skill that she had mastered over the years.

'Besides, we like your feed. You are *loufoque*. How do you say in English—zany? Wacky? It's what we need right now to shift the conversation and bring people back in. Lucky you. Enjoy your two minutes of fame. Use it well, be clever, work harder than anyone in the room and you may just push it to Five. Minutes. Of. Fame,' she suggested, slowly shaping her words for maximum effect.

Dasha was struggling to keep up. She was being moved around from one makeshift station to another as hair, make-up and tailoring experts poked, prodded and measured her. Her head felt cloudy. These were all new conversations from new people coming right at her, and she was catching less than half of it. The masks weren't helping. She needed to see their full faces, like they were seeing hers. No, like they were scrutinizing hers. She tried to focus by biting down hard on her tongue.

'Am I going to walk for Lure?' Dasha's innocence was so genuine that no one assumed she was being cocky or stupid.

'Oh, you're cute,' said the couturier sticking pins on the aubergine-coloured, stiff, silk deconstructed gown that Dasha couldn't remember having changed into. 'Yes, you are going to walk for Lure, although it might end up being virtual this year. This should suit you and your followers just fine, *non*?'

This reminded Ms Bulldog to demand of her assistant, 'Sylvie, when will we know whether the mairie granted us permission to hold the event on rue Saint-Honoré or not?' Sylvie had no answer to give, so her boss continued, 'No one can bear these online events anymore. It's too much, they all look the same. People need to get out of their houses. These garments are works of art, their purpose is to inspire wonderment, and wonderment is a big word and a bigger emotion—it certainly cannot be felt through a screen. The clothes need to be seen by the naked eye, the impact felt by actual humans.

'Everyone is sick of switching on their laptops from the comfort of their sofas, sipping home-made cocktails, wearing red lipstick to glam up their pyjamas. It's not enough. I hate these "made-for-TV" awards and red-carpet events. We've been through so much isolation and misery. We need beauty and chitter-chatter. We need *contact*. Human contact. We must marvel at splendour together, not be locked away alone to live a life where we are not even living.'

Over the good few minutes she'd been ranting for, her speech had become rather impassioned. The French in the room forgave her: Italians were prone to such histrionics. And also, she was excellent at her job.

It was all unfolding so quickly that the exhausted Dasha wished for matchsticks to keep her eyes open so she wouldn't fall asleep as she stepped into her dream. From the far end of the room, she spotted Bella Hadid walking towards her. Now they were chatting like old friends: yes, her and *the* Bella. The supermodel said something about walking into the new world together. Dasha made a joke and Bella laughed loudly. How kind and humble was this mega celebrity? Dasha looked around the room to orient herself.

Champagne was chilling in strategically placed silver ice buckets. On a low glass table, there were lines of white powder. Dasha knew that coke was rampant in the industry, but she never imagined it would be displayed this openly. Maybe it wasn't being 'openly' flaunted—Dasha was an insider now, part of the club. From now on, she would be privy to the secret lives of these glittering, glamourous demigoddesses. She pulled out her phone to cast this moment to memory. The Ibiza lounge mix doubled in volume and everyone swayed softly. The whole thing felt like an intimate cocktail party that everyone who was anyone wanted an invitation to. And here she was, nattering with the star attraction, the one and only Bella Hadid! She had arrived, and the world ought to know it this instant.

'You can't post anything from here without my prior permission, you understand? We will share our social media strategy, which obviously you will be a big part of. For now, your contract has a ban—' Ms Italian Tamer of Dogs couldn't finish her sentence before the couturier's pin accidentally pricked Dasha's neck as she fell backwards without warning. Dasha felt her head hit something cold and hard.

When she came around, masked helpers were forcing ice from the champagne bucket into her mouth, with cold water dripping from her hair onto her face. How long had she been out? Five seconds? Five minutes? Had she missed her moment?

'When is the last time you ate or drank something, young lady?' asked the Italian in a low, gentle voice. There was genuine concern written on her face, for she believed you couldn't be a tamer without being a carer first, which made her even more of a keeper for Lure.

Dasha couldn't remember if she had actually eaten the stolen biscuits from the French civics course, which now seemed a few light years away. She knew for sure that she had skipped breakfast, as she had been running late as usual, and that dinner the night before had been a few glasses of vodka and olives while Astrid had polished the leftover curry Neera had given them. She didn't mention any of this to the lady. Passing out had worked like kicking a jammed appliance, the hard knock rewiring her brain back into functioning.

'There was no water or drinks in the staircase. I didn't know we'd be locked in for so long without a break,' she answered with shrewd naivety. 'I had planned to eat straight after the Lure casting. I'm so sorry this has never happened to me before, it must have been the heat in that airless corner we were stuck in. I feel fine, perfectly fine. I'm only seventeen and in great health. It's the most exciting day of my life, it probably went to my head. I just need a sip of water.'

Sylvie, the assistant, placed a tray with sugary tea and pâtisseries on the low table. This wasn't the first model to pass out and Sylvie was certain it wouldn't be the last. The tea was tepid and the sad-looking pastries tasted stale. It felt like a poor woman's echo of her daydream from earlier. But it didn't matter. She was being served in Lure by Lure and the insignia on the tray, cups and plates bore witness to her fantasy becoming reality. Wait a minute, was it the other way around? Had she turned reality into fantasy?

Now that her head was no longer fuzzy, the lines of coke on the table revealed themselves to be thin white strips of masking tape, being used to label the dresses with the names of the models. There was no music, and with all the high-stakes backstage commotion—made much more dire with the question of survival looming over their heads—the atmosphere was more tetchy 'don't want to be here' than 'cocktail party everyone wants in on'. Stealing a look at the far end of the room, she confirmed her fear: Bella Hadid, was, in fact, a mere first-timer like Dasha. A fine-looking one, with a nose that young girls would beg their surgeons to copy if she ever became famous. But she was not Bella. Dasha returned the first-timer's smile with a nod, forced herself to stop staring at her, downed the tea, gobbled the pastries, walked back to the couturier, armed with a flurry of apologies and once again began the first chapter of her dream. This time, with eyes wide open.

Chapter 9

'Why were you copying my answers?'

'I was not,' replied Violet, suddenly cagey. 'Why would I copy your answers? It's not like you were listening to what that poor instructor was trying to teach. And you don't know anything about how France works. You've never needed money from the government, filed your own taxes or used free hospital care. When that pipe burst, you didn't even know what the number for emergency was.'

'It's not 911?' asked Neera, surprised at Violet's outburst.

'No, it's not. And I did not cheat from *you* of all people.'

Neera hadn't been particularly interested in the answer, till Violet's guilty-as-charged defensive response. In fact, Neera hadn't been interested in anything of late. Yet, here she was, curious, burning to get to the bottom of whatever Violet was hiding. Curiosity was not a killer—*au contraire*, it was bringing this cat back to life. She could feel the questions bubbling inside her. Years of professional practice in digging out dirt had taught her that going in directly with a shovel is likely either to splatter mud on your face or break your shovel by hitting a rock. You have to come at it from the sides with an archaeologist's delicate tools, traipse around and loosen the soil first. Then, once the tough top layer has been slackened, you push persistently, gently going deeper and deeper till, eventually, the earth willingly yields.

'I'm glad we both passed,' Neera said, changing tactics. 'With my level of French, I thought I wouldn't understand a thing.'

'Your French is getting better by the day, *chérie*. Ever since you met me, you've learnt to greet and shoo away the French in

French. What more do you need?' teased Violet, softening and linking her arm with Neera's as they walked out of the immigration office building. 'Honestly, I don't know what you were doing in Paris for five years before you met me.'

'Exactly, what on earth was I doing? Not speaking French and then complaining to everyone that the French don't speak to me,' she said.

They both laughed. Since her daily dose of drama had already been expunged from her system in the civics course, Neera felt calmer, which allowed Violet to release the tension in her hunched shoulders and exhale, till the next explosion anyhow. Except, there wasn't going to be another one. Without an active minefield, the work of filling of the holes left behind could begin, in theory at least. But in reality, when you've stuffed your insides with gunpowder for so long, there are bound to be withdrawals and relapses. For the moment, however, the two reposed in the ceasefire.

Rosel had rushed off to the metro without saying bye properly. She'd looked upset and understandably so—she would have to apply for and sit for this dreaded exam again. She said something about being on time to cook dinner for the kids and cleaning for the family or coming clean to the family. Either way, the other two didn't react. She'd been promising for months to tell her boss—who was now either her lover or wanting to become her lover or didn't want her as a lover anymore—and she had never built up to it. They weren't even sure if, by boss and lover, she meant the husband or the wife. Rosel often used 'she' instead of 'he', because in Tagalog they used a gender-neutral pronoun 'siya', so it was a forgivable Filipino mistake. And to confuse matters further, Rosel was the worst raconteur. Unlike Neera, who had an astonishing ability to articulate every emotion she felt and spin it into a spellbinding blanket that you wanted to wrap yourself in, Rosel's recounting was like a jigsaw puzzle assembled from different boxes with missing pieces.

They bitched out Rosel and the ridiculous situation she had dug herself into as they aimlessly wandered off to soak in the best part of the day, the time when the temperature had finally fallen to a bearable level. These long summer days had been a revelation to Neera, who came from a country where it was dark at 6.30 p.m., winter or summer. Even nature seemed partial to the West.

Paris was having an Indian summer—only minus air-conditioning. It was excruciating. Houses and buildings had become furnaces. Homes didn't even come with ceiling fans. She found it weird that these Frenchies lived for the heat, while in India, generations sweated away, not for a rightful place under the sun but for a respectable one under the direct draft of artificially cooled air.

Any time the sun was out, so were the French, regardless of the hour or the day of the week. And, remarkably, they were unapologetic about it. *Flânerie*, which Neera understood to mean strolling aimlessly to enjoy life, was a beloved Parisian pastime. They took in the sun like a national right. The civics course instructor had forgotten to teach the fourth tenet to the French motto of Liberty, Equality and Fraternity. No, it isn't secularism, it is Leisure with a capital L. The Indians live to work while the French work to live. Pleasure is sacrosanct.

No one in France seemed to think it odd that they were always between holidays or living for the weekends, which in sunny weeks could start as early as 5 p.m. on a Tuesday. Neera couldn't think of another country that shut down in its entirety for a whole month in the summer, so that people could go on holiday. What was even more shocking to her was that the French never hid the fact that they were on vacation or playing in the park with kids or in the middle of dinner with friends or, as Indians liked to say, 'partaking in pleasure'. Here, work dutifully waited for working hours. The motto in India was work, work,

work and make sure everyone sees you do it. It was the only way to save your soul and grant yourself that holiday, which, naturally, you were obliged to hide from the world.

'Vee, what do you like the most about France?' asked Neera casually.

Where was this coming from and, more worryingly, where was it going? By now, Violet knew Neera well enough to know that she only ever asked for another's opinion to serve some greater scheme brewing in her head.

'Who said I like France?'

'Come on, you moved here when you were sweet sixteen or something and you've lived here for what—twenty years, now?'

'No need to give a girl's age away,' Violet said with a fake laugh, trying to sidestep the trap.

'I think about how different Mumbai is to Paris, sometimes. What I left behind and who I was there. Do you ever think of going back home to Senegal?' Neera was skilled. The question dripped genuine empathy.

'No. There's nothing back there for me,' Violet replied, feeling a lump rise in her throat.

'Same for me. This is my only home now.'

'Except it will never be home,' Violet said this with such finality that they both fell silent.

The streets by the canal were full and joyous with Parisians playing the new favourite game in town, The Return of the Confined—Part I, which entailed devouring the outdoor time they had lost in lockdown with a vengeance. There would be many sequels to this franchise, but this first remained the most memorable. The two walked along, letting their thoughts carry them. They aimed to become French at the end of this administrative mountain. Yet, would they ever be considered Parisians? Did this city claim not-so-extraordinary citizens as its own? What made someone feel at home? *The strong, muscled arm of my tall friend linked in mine*, thought Neera. *This feels like home.*

'I love you, *mon amie*.' Neera hadn't meant to say this, it just fell out of her mouth.

'I know,' said Violet, pressing her friend closer. 'My mother used to say, "Home is nothing but two arms holding you tight when you are at your worst." She was full of these nuggets. I miss her. I miss her jiggly arms.'

'I never miss my mother. Why don't you bring your mother here?'

'She died a couple of years after I left,' said Violet.

Neera was at a loss. How did she not know this? They walked on in awkward silence, thinking about Violet's dead mother in their own ways.

Undeterred by mortal events, the day continued to be glorious. The green leaves of the chestnut trees, the blue of the late evening sky—the very colours Violet's mother always chose as fabric for her custom-made *boubou* and matching turban. The blue and green represented peace and health, neither of which had blessed her mother's life, although nobody would've guessed it from the way she went about town gossiping, laughing and spreading joy, her crisp turban tied in a grand knot, bright pink lipstick perfectly applied to match her hand fan. In her previous life as mama's boy, Violet had often sat under her mother's tent-like skirt with a cauldron filled with scented hot coals to perfume her boubou. With polygamy shadowing marital security, the women of Saint-Louis were forever competing to be the most elegant, most desirable and seldom left home without first infusing their robes with sweet incense. Violet could spend all day watching those ladies fluttering their eyelashes and pouting, trying to keep or trap a man that was not worth the rouge on their cheeks. 'I'm sorry about your mother,' said Neera, piercing through Violet's nostalgia. 'I didn't know.' More silence. 'How?'

'It doesn't matter.'

'That's a weird answer. Of course it matters.'

'What's your problem today, Neera? Why are you snooping?' Violet snapped, unlinking her arm from Neera's.

'You know every disgusting detail about my life and I know nothing about yours.'

'That's because you are so full of yourself that there's no space for anyone else to fit in. If the conversation doesn't involve you talking or people talking about you, you switch off.'

That was not fair. Neera was a good listener. Okay, maybe of late, or since the time that they had met, which had only been a few months but felt like many lives ago, she had been a bit self-obsessed. Surely, they understood why. She had to be allowed this self-centrism. It stopped her from being suicidal—and wasn't she becoming a little more cheerful by the day? Perhaps not cheerful enough. These new women in her life had become her whole world and it was important to appreciate them if she didn't want them to abandon her. And she most certainly didn't.

'You are right, Vee. I'm going to do a better job of being a friend.'

Violet rolled her eyes.

'This is a thorny point in my life. I know you know that. It will pass.' Then, with as much compassion as Neera could muster, she asked with a smile, 'Tell me about your mother. What was she like?'

'Fuck off, Neera.' Violet had had enough of Neera's bullshit for one day. Of course, she got that Neera was suffering. Weren't they all? She had to stop monopolizing sorrow. The others needed their share too.

'What did I say, Vee?' Neera was genuinely flummoxed. 'If you ask me, I'll tell you my mother transferred all her unrealized ambitions on me. Making me tremendously talented and driven, till I realized I had no dreams of my own.'

'Oh, I'm crying for you. What a tough life.'

How had the conversation soured to this point? All Neera had wanted to know was why Violet felt the need to cheat from a person who hardly spoke French when she herself was fluent in all things French. She didn't care at all if Violet had cheated. She just wanted to know why.

'I can't deal with you and your questions right now,' said Violet, walking away. 'Anyway, I have somewhere to be.'

Neera stood there like a bruised apple—bypassed. Perhaps Violet was overly sensitive today because it was that time of the month for her. Neera's own PMS-related mood swings had become stratospheric with age. Like clockwork, an irritable alien entered her body the day before her period, its only mission to pull dark clouds around anything sunny. *Hang on, did Violet get periods?* Of course she didn't. Neera felt dumb. She had never thought to ask Violet anything about her transition or anything about anything to do with her life at all.

In these last few months, Neera had simply talked and talked, till no unspoken words remained inside her. This was going to change starting now. No more vomiting her story into any available ear. The embarrassing episode from earlier that day, she promised herself, was her last. From that moment on, she was going to be as good a listener as she had been a talker.

Suddenly, she craved the compassionate cloud of a joint, under whose brume she could listen till there were no more stories left to hear. High, she was present mentally and physically without actually having to be present emotionally. She engaged without being invested. It was a comfortable place. A womb.

No, no more escapes. No hiding behind a happy haze. She was going to listen like her Jannie had listened to her, delighting in every uttered phrase as if it was an event in itself. Violet was going to get the friend she deserved, a friend who paid attention.

Stone-cold sober (and not stoned), Neera was going to become the best receptacle of woes for all three girls. So she went home, fully ready, alert and waiting for Violet and her stories.

Then, she lit a joint. An obese one.

Chapter 10

He wasn't there. Violet started to panic. She hoped he hadn't been picked up by the police again. During confinement, he had been first fined by the authorities for being on the streets, then moved to an unoccupied hotel along with the other homeless people they had rounded up. It had been a better place than any of them had been inside in a long while. They each had their own bed, running water, a toilet with an unbroken seat and a working flush, and two germ-free meals a day.

Yet Raphaël had lasted just three nights there before escaping to take up residence in a forsaken bus stop near the forest of Bois de Boulogne. Walled spaces and he did not share a happy relationship, evidently.

Violet had assumed he'd been put in some kind of shelter for the lockdown. Then she'd stumbled upon him camping at the bus stop on her one legally permitted outing per day. The entrance to the woods was just within the one-mile radius she was allowed to traverse from her home. Those had been inexplicable days: you could hear birds—not just those awful pigeons—chirping in Paris, the spring sky was a hyper-natural indigo and everyone felt they had been forcefully cast in the global remake of the film *Contagion*. No one had known back then that real life was going to take a one-and-a-half-hour commercial film with a happy ending and turn it into a sci-fi horror series where the credits refused to roll. The critics would pan it as excruciatingly lengthy, misinformed, terribly researched, poorly scripted with far too many reprises and scarcely believable twists, filled with ridiculous self-sabotaging leaders, all hinging on a silly suspicion that a peckish man, thousands of miles away, ate a bat he shouldn't have.

So finding Raphaël in her neighbourhood in a world that had been pitching a script that wouldn't get greenlit by any channel or platform due to plausibility issues had not felt strange at all to Violet. She'd tried to offer him a mattress on her studio floor despite not being entirely sure how Benjy would react. But Raphaël had refused, continuing to camp out at the deserted bus stop. After that, her daily outings had taken on the higher purpose of checking on him. He always had enough food, left for him by the rich bourgeoisie from the neighbourhood who wanted to feel like they were doing their part in the war. They had already gotten to know each other a little, after the first time she had bought him a toasty and before President Macron had channelled his inner Winston Churchill to declare, 'We are at war', and then locked the country down.

In the pre-war world, Raphaël had often walked out of the metro with her. She had bought him food and they had talked—not a lot, though, for neither wanted to relive the horrors of their lives and because being in the other's silence was comfort enough. She knew this much: he had not been able to finish school or hold onto a job, and a short while after his mother died, he had left home. He thought of begging as his profession. It was, after all, legal in France. There was something peculiar or extraordinary about him, and Violet was still undecided as to which it was. Though he was a big, beautiful man with moss-coloured eyes that you could drown in, Violet never lusted after him. He simply brought out the best version of her, making her love who *she* was around him. Something bigger than herself had called upon her to connect with and help this man. And now, she couldn't find him anywhere.

The bus stop had been cleaned out after the first confinement, leaving no trace of him. Somehow, she felt like she was failing her mother. He had to be found. She ran through the woods, thankful to be wearing sneakers today. The prostitutes, risking more than the virus, were already lurking between the trees in their G-strings, open coats and heels. Yet he was nowhere. She didn't want to check the metro—she hadn't used public transport since the virus had arrived, as she hadn't had anywhere to go. Besides, the entire universe had entered her home through her little screen and the metro was a germ pool. *Desperate times call for desperate measures*, she thought, and legged it down the stairs, careful not to touch anything.

And there he was, back to work, kneeling upright, holding his hunger sign. There were no crowds being separated by his presence today. The station was empty. At first, it disturbed her that he didn't recognize her. Then she remembered that she was dressed in a version of herself from a time before she knew him— or, for that matter, before she knew herself.

'Can you believe my father only knew me as a boy?' she said, as they bit into the hot Nutella crêpes she had bought them near Jardin des Tuileries. The sun was still out, and now that she had found Raphaël, the day felt like a blessing. 'He might have died sooner, had he seen me like this,' she snorted.

'A long time ago,' he said, 'my mother died. I think.'

She was used to his non sequiturs.

'Mine too,' she continued. 'She was my partner. In more ways than my father could bear.'

He said nothing and then, 'It was not my father's fault.'

'I wish I could say that about mine. I want to forgive him and myself. I don't know how, nor if he or I deserve it,' she said sadly, before changing the subject. 'Mothers are miracles, they see your truth before you do.'

The gentle, unhurried way Raphaël turned and looked at her felt like he was seeing her through her mother's eyes. Or maybe that's the way his mother had looked at him. He, too, must've loved his mother, the way young Vafi had adored his. Poor little Vafi Dembélé, Violet thought, feeling distress for the boy she had once been, caught between fear of his unfaltering father and shame for being too weak to protect his mother.

Had his father always been reactionary? The students he taught at the prestigious Senegal Gilbert Brenner University in Saint-Louis thought of him as a rockstar, and not only because he was built like one. His paper on the science of faith had been much read, dissected and re-read. His students would hang around and wait for him after his lectures on the social science of religion, hoping to pick his brain as he walked home. Many a time, they would be invited in, their discussions carrying on well into the night.

Vafi was least interested in their talk of reclaiming the true essence of the teachings of the Sunnah and most intimidated by their alpha presence. Yet he welcomed these nights, for it was only on nights like these that his mother would sneak him out of the house to join the regular roadside musical soirées.

Music ran in his mother's blood. Her family were griots, like troubadours in France—storytellers and musicians who could trace their lineage to medieval times. A tradition frowned upon by a society that was, paradoxically, becoming increasingly traditional. Not a day went by that his scholarly Sunni father didn't taunt his mother for it. So, their rendezvous had to be a mother–son secret.

On one such night, however, the father came out to find them. The tempo of the drum beat was high, and his mother was in the centre of the group of singers, her hips keeping pace with the beat without her feet moving at all. Vafi was trying hard to copy her when he caught sight of the fire in his approaching father's eyes. He froze.

Surprisingly, his father was a vision of humility, apologizing for interrupting the festivities and sweetly pardoning himself for taking his family home for dinner. The community had great respect for Senior Professor Dembélé and humbly requested him to join them the next time he had time in his busy, important life.

He didn't even wait to close the front door, before he picked up the steel stool and threw it directly at her face. Next, he went at her with his belt. When that didn't satisfy him, he shoved her down and started choking and punching her alternatively. She was a big woman and could have overpowered him, but the will was missing. Vafi hid inside his airless cupboard all night, too scared to so much as cry, despising himself.

'Come, my baby Vafi, its wake-up time.' His bruised and cheerful mother was stroking his face with the kind of love that only a mother can give. 'You don't want to be late for school again.' She was already in her white lab coat ready for work.

'It's better you stay home today,' said the professor from behind his newspaper. 'I don't want your colleagues from SaniAid nosing around here asking me about your face.'

'They won't, as long as I show up today,' she countered softly. 'The government has organized a big immunization drive in the shanty with our SaniAid doctors today. We need all hands on deck to set up the booths and the screen for the film. If I'm not there, someone will come here asking.'

He grunted.

'I'll tell them I was cleaning the top shelves when all the heavy utensils fell on me. Again.'

He grunted some more.

'Vafi will help me cover it up. He's such a good painter.'

The professor ignored her, which was consent enough.

Handing her son his uniform she whispered, 'We are showing *The Sound of Music* at the shanty today. I know it's your favourite. You can come straight after school.'

Film screenings as bait for vaccination had been his mother's genius idea. Her colleagues would help her load the rented projector onto an old Tempo matador that now had a tuk-tuk engine. The kids would run behind the vehicle as it entered the village shanty and eagerly pull the white sheet across the uneven red brick wall. Anyone with a medical plaster on their arm proving they'd just been inoculated could enter the open-air cinema, grab a seat on the mud floor, wait for the sun to set and escape to a foreign land. Vafi, as the son of his mother, got to sit in the VIP section on a chair on such evenings. No matter what the the film was, the makeshift hall was invariably packed with kids and adults for the miracle it offered.

'You want to bring a friend today?' she asked.

Eleven-year-old Vafi couldn't look at his mother, and he certainly didn't want to look at his father, a man of words who lived by violence.

For as long as he could remember, Vafi had been witness to this morning-after ritual. By the time he had been four, he had taught himself not to be winded by a punch to the gut and how to curl up into a ball when being kicked. At first, he believed it was the way of the world till the day he didn't, which was altogether worse because he didn't know what to do about it till the day he did.

All these years later, even as Violet, she could taste shame. It was not the reason Vafi forgot how to read and write. That came three years later, was wickeder in every way possible and made her culpable for life. These moments, however, were the little stepping stones that Vafi walked on to get there.

It was that bewitching hour, when it's almost but not quite dark. Raphaël's quiet presence allowed her to disappear into herself. He never asked anything of her and allowed her to give herself in a way that brought her closer to her yaay, her mother. Imagine if she had to explain this to Neera or any of the other girls. Where would she begin? *Oh, I cheated from you because I don't know how to shape my words anymore. I don't mean metaphorically— I actually haven't held a pen for anything, apart from signing my name, since I was fourteen.* But this story was long and boring and had no happy end. It was best left untold.

PART 3

Tap of Plenty

Chapter 1

The photographers' flashing lights were blinding her. When was the last time she'd been on a red carpet? They were not interested in her per se: the cameras were pointed at her date, Lucas Garnier. He removed his mask and smiled obligingly. She'd be surprised if they knew her name. They would caption her as 'Widow of the late avant-garde film-maker, Jean-Paul Allard'. The thought of the caption sent a crippling cramp through her chest. Neera had learnt to recognize it as her 'pain-body', accept it as a fact and not succumb to it. She wasn't sure if this is what Eckhart Tolle actually meant in his online mindfulness class, but it's what she understood and it was helping her heal. Jannie was gone or, as Eckhart would say, no longer present in physical form. Either way, his death was a fact: it was an 'is'. Jean-Paul Allard *is* dead. And you can't fight with the is-ness of any situation.

Lucas and she were on a date but they were definitely not dating. He was, however, purposely being ambiguous with the paps, who were shouting to know their status. He had recently entered a serious relationship and was keen to keep it out of the press for as long as he could. Neera didn't give a damn what rumours he fuelled—she knew he'd had his share of loss and agony when Miss GiGi, one of Jannie's all-time favourite jazz singers, had carelessly and rather publicly dumped him via Twitter and then he had gone and shattered his body in a skiing accident a few days later. The incidents had reportedly been unconnected. If Neera had thought that a little far-fetched at the time, she had serious doubts now that she was spending more time with him. Getting to know him better was also helping validate another one of her new discoveries—that the more you suffered, the more chances you had of being saved.

From Buddha to Jesus to Eckhart, all men pursuing enlightenment—the women must've been too busy getting on with life, Neera assumed, to sit under trees chasing Nirvana—emphasized the necessity of suffering in order to access the transcendental dimension. She wouldn't exactly call herself, or the starred and scarred chef Lucas Garnier, enlightened. Still, after what each of them had been through, they'd both experienced a change in their essence and, sometimes (and those were glorious moments), they were able to detach from worldly want and material desire. Yet, here they were, posing on a carpet that was the incarnation of capitalist consumption in a commercial world. She reined in her mind before it spiralled into intellectual masturbation about the evils of haute couture. Champagne socialism wasn't her style, and she could hardly be a dissenter when she herself was dressed head to toe in Lure Privé in honour of the show. Besides, she was here to support her girlfriends and witness them living their dream.

The stars must have aligned on the night of the civics exam a few weeks ago—what else could explain the synchronicities of that night? Dasha had got cast in her dream job, followed by Violet getting a call from sleazy old Nicolas saying House of Lure had been looking for someone to choreograph an aerial spectacle for their show with a postmodern twist. Rosel, meanwhile, had finally confessed that she was Rosel and, instead of kicking her out, the Decostes had practically consecrated her. And as for Neera, well, she had finally picked up the phone and called Lucas.

It wasn't as simple as punching numbers on a keypad. To begin with, Neera didn't have his number anymore. She'd ripped up and smoked his card long ago, as she had no intention of taking him up on his offer to cook and even less of appearing on his TV show.

On the said night of serendipity, after waiting an interminable time for Violet to come home, Neera took the lift down to the entrance lobby, walked out of her building from the back door on the side of the lift to the internal courtyard and then climbed the filthy, winding service staircase all the way to the sixth floor to knock on Rosel's little servant quarters. Most of the nine-square-metre rooms on this top floor were occupied by students or young people living off their first salaries in this unaffordable city.

Paris was not known to be consistently generous. To some, she revealed her wonders; others had wonder sucked out of them. Neera panted up the stairs. *Number Thirty-Six is an allegory of the city*, she thought. It offered different versions of life lived under the same roof and was judiciously built to not grant every inhabitant the same access. She stopped at the top to catch her breath. This part of the building was as stifling and grimy as her apartment was luminous and cheerful. The rotating laser light from the top of the Eiffel Tower filtered in through the slanting windows on the roof, but no amount of neck craning would get you a glimpse of the famed metal tower that Neera could see so clearly from her own bedroom, bathroom and kitchen. Not for the first time in her life, she saw it as unfair that those who did the heavy lifting (such as climb six steep flights of stairs) got nothing more than shortness of breath as reward.

She thought of the Amazon workers, Uber drivers and FedEx delivery men who were risking their lives during the pandemic to make hers easier, feed their own families, keep the economy on its feet and, most importantly, add millions of dollars to the pockets of their billionaire bosses. These same grateful bosses shared videos of confining themselves to palatial country homes to help flatten the curve while graciously refusing to pay for the sick leaves of the very employees they sent out to work in unsafe, squalid conditions. None of this was new, of course, and Paris was by no means the only city in the world with such working conditions. Neera looked around the carpet-less, parquet-less, damp corridor and wondered how miraculous it was that societies sustained—no, bourgeoned—on the rival forces of insufficiency and surfeit.

Once upon a time, she could have accessed the top floor via the service door at the back of her own apartment and saved herself the trek—all the apartments in her building came with this door that connected them to the service stairs and the servants' floor on top. In the days of the nobility, domestic staff would use this access to creep in and out of the main apartment without disturbing their masters. Now, the access was one way—those with rooms on the topmost floor couldn't enter this side of the building or use the lift. Neera's apartment, occupying two entire floors, was the biggest of the lot and came with two such service doors. Yet, she climbed the winding servants' stairs, for she had long shut and entombed that portal of doom. The last time it had been opened was when she had let a scrawny student, clanking suitcases on each arm, pass through her pristine apartment to use the lift on her privileged side of the building.

Anyone with a place to go had fled Paris minutes after the first confinement had been announced. No one had known much about the virus back then or how an uninvited, invisible entity had been about to wreck the world. All they had known was that another menacing, undetected foreigner, impatient to feed on and destroy the Western world, had to be expelled.

Neera had heard the clatter and banging coming from the service stairs on the other side of the door and had peeped through the keyhole to find a waif-like girl perilously lugging two big bags down the narrow spiral staircase. She had been rushing to make it to the train station to go back to her parents' home in the mountains before all means of transport were brought to a halt. Normally, Neera would have looked away. This would not have been her problem. But, suffice to say, these had not been normal times. The waif had thanked her distractedly, entirely missing the enormity of Neera's gesture. The depth of her gratitude had been more suitable for thanking a waitress who was showing you to a table than for a woman who had literally let a complete stranger traverse her very private space in the middle of a war, where no one had been certain who the enemy was.

The squeaky sound of the broken wheel on the student's suitcase had been one Neera was unable to forget. She would often wake in the night covering her ears, trying to escape the attack of screeching luggage. This aberrant moment of charity had cost her *everything*. And that service door was never going to be used again, regardless of how many steps she had to climb.

Rosel was not in either. Neera made her way back down, walked through the cobbled courtyard and into the main lobby again. She knocked on Violet's studio next to the lift on the ground floor. Then, she stopped on the third floor, only to be told by one of the models that they had no idea who Dasha was and whoever she was, she wasn't in anyway.

After rolling and smoking her third joint of the day and going up and down knocking on the girls' doors for the nth time, she pulled down the projection screen that Jannie had finally been allowed to install in a corner of the triple salon and slumped down on the couch. If she hadn't been stoned, the mass disappearance of her friends would've irritated her immensely, especially since she was now so keen to demonstrate how interested she was in their little lives and how eager she was to hear every one of their tedious stories. Each puff made her more stoic. *Ah well, their loss*, she placated herself, and settled on a channel to watch.

Back in her parents' home in Jalgaon, it had been a cherished Sunday ritual to rent video tapes—*or had it already been LaserDiscs in those days?*—and curl up next to her confectioner father to watch American cookery shows. They would watch in awe as a middle-aged Indian aunty, Madhur Jaffery, showed white people the flavours of India. They would learn about French cooking from Jeff Smith in *The Frugal Gourmet* and how to roast a picture-perfect chicken from Martha Stewart. This simple pleasure had been among her sweetest and most uncomplicated childhood memories. Throughout her years in Mumbai, she had binged watched *MasterChef Australia* and *Nigella Bites* as a sure-shot stress buster.

On the projector in front of her, Lucas Garnier, that most affable pâtissier, was slicing into a conical piece of edible art, a replica of Mount Fuji made of nougatine and black sesame chocolate, with meringue mousse cementing it altogether. She held her breath in anticipation. Steaming blood orange and yuzu confiture oozed out in a you-have-to-see-it-to-believe simulation of erupting lava. The plate itself was covered with a sheet of dark-green mochi paste and decorated with wild red berries, grey-and-white chocolate dust and caramelized nuts, all painstakingly scattered to resemble a volcanic mountain spurting molten ember and ash. The hot flowing liquid circled the plate without destroying its design. Her dad would have applauded.

Back in the day, the father and daughter had often dreamed of their own cooking show about desserts. Obviously, others on the trendsetting side of the globe had been salivating about the same thing. There had been a barrage of binge-worthy and probably obesity-inducing baking shows on American TV—*Ace of Cakes, The Ultimate Cake Off, Cupcake Wars...* It was a pity, they had all been broadcast only after she'd moved out of home. French TV programmes had entirely bypassed US-obsessed India, else she and her father would have been addicts despite the language barrier.

Lucas's TV show, *Le Grand Gourmand*, was marvellous in every way. She imagined her father taking notes and then getting riled up by how nougatine was a rip-off of the Indian *chikki*, which was also made with caramelized sugar and nuts and, without a drop of doubt, had existed long before the Frenchmen had left their caves.

Now, tit for tat, he would be entitled to use Lucas's glazing technique on his banana laddus to make them look like shimmering crystal balls. He'd add a surprise burst of mango ganache with a dash of green chili in the middle of his laddu, using only unripe mango to balance the sweetness. Then, he would shush himself and Neera to focus on a participant delicately bringing out a mould of chocolate petals from the fridge. He would fold his hands in prayer and bring them up to his lips, concentrating so hard as if he himself was about to pour the caramel on the freshly made white chocolate petals; if the temperature wasn't exactly right, the petal would crack or the caramel would harden too quickly. He would often say, 'Cooking in general is all about practice and experiments. But mind you, Neera, desserts are a precise science that require sturdy hands attached to a patient person.'

Daddy wouldn't have let her miss a single episode, for watching Lucas counsel and judge budding pâtissiers would've brought untold pleasure to the duo.

Before she had time to talk herself out of it, she found herself plugging in and scrolling through her dead husband's phone. She dialled directly from Jannie's phone, which, in retrospect, must've been creepy for Lucas—all of France, after all, knew the disease had taken one of their finest talents years too soon. But if receiving a call from a dead film-maker had freaked Lucas out, he didn't let on. Instead, he offered his genuine condolences and was frankly thrilled at the idea of a possible collaboration with Neera. So, that very week, they met in the kitchen of his temporarily closed restaurant, Chez Garnier.

'That is the first time I'm tasting a… ludoux… loodoo… sorry, I forget, what is the name again?' asked Lucas as he bit into the small spherical sweet that Neera and he had just made.

'Laddu,' answered Neera. 'Rhyme it with—' She couldn't think of a single word that sounded the same in English or French.

'It's too sweet... But the texture makes you want to come back for more,' he said polishing off the crumbling ball.

'As a child, I used to eat ten, maybe twelve in one go. My mother had to literally snatch them from me, warning me that fat girls never go far in life,' she said, laughing. 'This one is traditional gram flour with a dash of coconut and pistachio. But what I'd *really* like to do is use French dessert techniques with Indian ingredients and make something at once authentic and appealing to both palates. I want to use molecular cooking and take it to the next level. Create a whole new genre with unexpected combinations.' Her enthusiasm was infectious. 'It's an acquired taste of course—it'll need clever marketing to attract first-timers. But once they attain it, they open themselves up to a whole world of possible tastes. There are no limits, Lucas!'

'It seems like you've given this more thought than you'd like to admit.'

'I haven't!'

He smiled without making eye contact. 'Okay.'

A few days later, they created a crustless tamarind-Camembert cheesecake, garnished with saffron and jaggery. Lucas had never come across or used jaggery, which he learnt was a crude, dark sugar, almost like hardened molasses, common in Indian cooking. Again, it was too sweet for his French palate. And yet, the way it melted on his tongue, countering the acidity of the tamarind while complementing the creaminess of the Camembert... It felt divine.

'Neera, I have to say your timing could not have been better,' said Lucas as they dug into yet another creation. 'You know that all shooting for *Le Grand Gourmand* had to be suspended due to a Covid-positive case, and we didn't like what we had shot anyway. And in any case, the old format in this new world doesn't make much sense. This pause has given us time to rethink and rework what to do for the new season. Say yes, and I will find something you are comfortable with.'

When she nodded, he cheekily added, 'We have a great team of hair and make-up artists, I'm sure they'll find a solution to that missing hair of yours.'

And now, just a couple of weeks later, here they were, accompanying each other to the open-air, Covid-safe Lure spectacle at the corner of rue Saint-Honoré and rue Cambon.

Chapter 2

Meanwhile, backstage, Violet was gripping Raphaël's hands, looking into his emerald eyes and asking him to take slow, deep breaths. Every floor of the five-storey shop was being used for backstage chaos, from costume to make-up to press to holding onto male models who wanted to make a last-minute run for it. Violet, like the other dancers, was dressed in couture rags— long strings and straps intended to flow down as performers dangled and danced from the scaffolding above the catwalk and audience. The dancers called out for her to join them for a warm up. She had bigger fish to fry than loosening her muscles.

'You are not going anywhere,' pleaded Violet. 'You can do this. You *have* to do this.'

Raphaël simply blinked back at her, not understanding her words or why she was holding onto him.

'All you have to do is follow these girls out of the shop entrance, walk around the block on that shiny, mirrored platform and come right back in. Just like you did in the rehearsal,' she said trying to keep the panic out of her voice. 'I will be there throughout, right above your head. Just look up if you feel nervous. Okay?'

Raphaël's hair had been teased and tousled with such precision that every seemingly unruly strand was exactly as out of place as it was meant to be. His skin had been darkened to a tropical tan, making his miraculous eyes pop intensely. They had dressed him in a flowing silver silk trench coat, under which he was wearing an ash-grey, asymmetrical, double-breasted jacket and an off-white ruffled shirt that looked like it was made of gauze. The charcoal-coloured, jodhpur-style cut-off pants had a flap over them that gave the illusion of being a wrap-around skirt and the fingerless gloves and bulky floor-length scarf completed the beggar-chic look or whatever it was the House of Lure was aiming for. He looked good. The kind of good that made teenage girls, menopausal women and everyone in between sticky with libidinous desire.

'Go. I have to go,' Raphaël repeated. 'Outside. I have to go outside. Violet, I have to go. Violet, I have to.' He looked terrified, disoriented, like a lost child who had woken up from a nightmare only to find himself in the middle of a highway with speeding trucks coming right at him.

'Okay. Okay,' said Violet, trying to find a way to solve the situation she had put him in. The ringing bell warned her that she had less than fifteen minutes to do it. 'I'll come out with you, we will have a smoke, get some fresh air, come back in, finish the show, and then you and I will go get something nice to eat. Okay?'

She was still holding his hands, but Raphaël was so far away that her voice was not reaching him. A minion came with a lint roller and, without asking or saying a word to either of them, started sanctimoniously rolling it on Raphaël's trench coat. It was all that was needed to push him over the edge. He bolted out of the fire exit, muttering, 'I've gotta go, I've gotta go, I've gotta go,' his flowing silver trench adding to the unfolding farce.

All the minions' walkie-talkies were suddenly ablaze. *The male finale has run away, still dressed in runway clothes!* Violet stood there as the world around her exploded. What had she done? This was the opposite of the triumph she had pictured for herself and her beggar friend, whose life she had planned to change tonight. Hadn't she successfully convinced Lure that by giving a chance to a bona fide homeless hunk, they could steer the conversation away from the sinking relevance of fashion and focus it on how fashion bigwigs can use their clout to do good? It had been so simple and, in today's time, hardly that radical.

Any hesitation Ms Dog Tamer might have harboured in bringing this idea to her top brass had floated away with one look at the drool-worthy specimen Violet had presented to her. Yes, she had agreed, those malachite eyes would do the trick nicely. The sullen press and the fickle fashion bloggers would all hanker for an audience with him. And, in exchange, Lure would control the narrative.

The final go-ahead to cast Raphaël came quickly from the top. He fit perfectly with the theme of the show—New World, New Rules—which, on the catwalk, was being interpreted as 'bring out the rebels, the crazies and the unexpected'. Violet, Dasha and Raphaël ticked all the boxes in their own nonconformist ways. Jackets and T-shirts sported hand-embroidered, jewel-encrusted slogans: 'U Be U', 'I Do Me', 'New Not Normal', 'Safe, Never Distant' and 'Unexpect-Me'.

The House of Lure was going to do not-normal like no one had done before. The show was ambitious, designed to shock you out of your lockdown lethargy. It was time to rethink fashion, and Lure was going to help you do it. Violet had hand-picked five other aerial performers (Ms Dog Tamer had insisted on transgender dancers—'The weirder the better,' she had emphasized. Any offence at being called weird was overlooked. This was not the season to get stuck on nomenclature and semantics).

The choreography Vee came up with was a gravity-defying marvel. A special scaffolding with loops, ropes and hooks was constructed. The dancing divas draped themselves like rubber dolls on eight-metre-high poles and made death-defying sequences look like poetry in motion. In the end, it was an ode to the era-defining martial arts film *Crouching Tiger, Hidden Dragon* in the flesh, without visual effects, green screens, stuntmen or safety harnesses. What Violet kept to herself was that it was all inspired by the dangling image of a wild new friend. Each time the dancers mastered an impossible act, Violet upped the ante and pushed them one step further. The two weeks or so of rehearsals were arduous and utterly rewarding.

It went without saying that they were all happy to be back at work after months of uncertainty. What they hadn't expected, however, was Violet getting their adrenaline pumping at max levels. They danced like their lives depended on it—and not just because hanging at that height, one wrong move could literally bridge the gap between life and death.

These were blissful days: the sky was a perpetual blue, a warm breeze teased, tickled and disappeared on repeat while the sun delighted in its own radiance. Violet gleamed too. The light within her was finally allowed to be switched on. She was unanimously affirmed the Queen of Composition. She could do no wrong, which made it easy enough for her to propose a professional beggar as a finale act. And it was not unthinkable for the proposal to be accepted with appreciation.

'It will get you off the streets,' Violet rejoiced after she had official approval for the plan. 'You can't beg forever, you know that, right?'

Raphaël did not react. If Violet stopped to listen to his silence, maybe she would've heard him. But she was too busy playing a good Samaritan. It made her so happy to be aiding someone who wasn't her. Her yaay, who had given her life working to help those who couldn't help themselves, would have been so proud.

'Forever has no end. No end is good. It's good, Violet,' Raphaël said, long after it was possible to work out what he was referring to.

'Yes,' Violet said, not bothering to ask what he meant. 'I will come get you from the metro at nine tomorrow and they will fit you and tell you what to do. This is going to be the best fun.'

'My mother was fun,' he said without a beat. 'I like fun.' And that, as far as Violet was concerned, settled it.

'Me too,' she agreed.

They walked in silence for a while, till he eventually spoke. 'Making fun of someone is not good. It's terrible.'

She pulled down her mask and kissed him goodbye on both cheeks, knowing it was prohibited by law in this period of death by touch. She couldn't care less—illegality and she went back a long way. Besides, she was a woman on a mission.

In a matter of seconds, the men and most of the women at the House of Lure were hankering after the mute beggar-showstopper the choreographer had brought in. An aura of mystery adorned him. He did everything he was told to do with minimal engagement and maximum eye contact. In fact, the penetrating way he looked at anyone speaking to him was a bit too intense. Those instructing and directing him were often forced to look away, blushing and giggling like schoolgirls whose crush had just spoken to them for the first time. When they thought back on that evening, it dawned on them that his intense gaze had probably just been a blank stare.

'So, Vee, this is your guy? Your bus-stop man?' whispered Dasha, as they stood near the coffee kiosk on the day of the tech rehearsal. 'I had pictured him older, smellier, uglier... He's beautiful.'

'Yes, he is,' agreed Violet, swelling with pride, as if she herself was the sculptor who chipped away at him to make those strong, clean lines.

The two friends loitered about, openly watching him. They had nothing better to do. The technical rehearsal involved a lot of waiting and hanging around for the models, the performers and anybody who wasn't in overalls or holding a clipboard and speaking urgently into a walkie-talkie.

It was a complicated show to light, and everything was taking longer than necessary due to the strict (sometimes nonsensical) sanitary measures they had to follow. But this was Dasha's first show, and no amount of handwashing was going to water down her excitement. The cherry on top of her gateau was being part of the same show as Violet, who, during the confinement, had become a kind of godmother to her. She was careful never to articulate this because the one time she had mentioned it, Vee had reacted rather unpleasantly.

'I am no one's mother. Even if my body allowed me to, I will never be a mother, okay!' she had exploded. 'And as for god, I don't believe in any god. My father was killed because of god. The irony is, if there was a god, with all the saintly goodness in his heart, he would've agreed that my father had it coming.'

This was the only time Dasha had seen Violet rage like this and she was not stupid enough to stir up the hornet's nest twice, especially not that of a queen hornet, whose nest had become Dasha's home.

Violet was who Dasha wanted to be when she grew up. She dripped fabulousness, grabbed attention and had confidently defied the odds to become the extraordinary woman she now was. She wore her inner strength on the outside like a medal of honour. What came as a surprise was her kindness and patience, all wrapped in the softest and most genuinely sympathetic demeanour.

Getting cast in the show, and with Paris opening up once more, Dasha got to spend less and less time in Violet's studio apartment experimenting with Astrid and the computer. Gosh, the things she had been exposed to and how much she had experienced in those three short months! Maybe the reason she hadn't shared all the details with her twin, Andrei, was because she hadn't yet digested it all. Instead of feeling exploited, she felt empowered, which didn't make any sense. She needed to sit down and rationalize it to herself before she could describe it to anyone else.

It wasn't because she was ashamed. Absolutely not. In fact, it made her feel free in her own body. She was finally beginning to understand the difference between confidence and self-acceptance, a difference so subtle that it had to be experienced, not explained.

For Andrei, it would never be necessary to separate the two. He was born knowing who he was. It was the first time she had chosen not to tell her twin something, and it sat like a lump at the bottom of her neck, in the gap between her collar bones, refusing to move up and come out of her mouth. Before it grew further, she had to spit out the knot. But where would she begin?

Chapter 3

Was the afternoon of the burst faucet and the subsequent flood on Neera's floor the first time Dasha spoke to Violet? It was almost April; the year 2020 was disappearing in plain sight. The building had been empty for days. All the other models in her apartment, including Astrid, had run home. Only one had gone to shack up with a new-found lover/benefactor, who had been more than happy to pay for company to wait out the virus with. Dasha feared arriving home empty-handed far more than the arrival of any unseen virus. Her tongue and lips refused to form the words to ask her cancer-surviving mother for help to get home. Andrei understood and Nicolas was kind enough to let her stay on while he claimed compensation from the government.

In the abandoned kitchen, she found half a pack of flour, an assortment of dry pasta, three cans of tuna, a bag of frozen peas, a giant unopened box of American Girl Scout peanut butter and chocolate cookies, a multipack of diet shakes and several tins of baked beans—*left behind by the Brit model no doubt, who else ate that tasty crap?* It would have been prudent to ration the supplies, but how could she when she had no idea of what time frame she was working within? No one had offered an end date for the crisis. So she did the thing she had become a pro at since her father's departure: she ate like a bird and distracted herself from hunger by making content for her growing online persona.

She now had forty-seven thousand, three hundred and fifty-one followers on Insta, mostly thanks to her table-top gazelle act. One of those followers was Benjamin, who had the privilege of witnessing Dasha's performance in the flesh. He Insta-messaged her that same day—Bravo I was in the room at your casting. The boy with the video camera, that's me. I think you are delightful and brave. If you are willing and able, I'd love to do a photo shoot with you.

Dasha liked nothing better in the world than to be in front of a camera. 'When? Where? I'll be there,' she agreed in a flash.

When it emerged he wasn't going to pay her, she was conveniently not able to find a suitable time. But now that she had nothing but time, they were already on their third virtual collaboration.

It started with Benjy getting Dasha to place her phone camera at a certain low angle and ended with chairs, stools, plates, hairdryer, hangers, towels, ironing board and other dreary household objects hanging off her three-tiered bunk bed. He wanted her to topple the bed down so that it would be horizontal on the floor, but the room wasn't big enough. It got stuck halfway down, which worked even better for the post-apocalyptic picture he had in mind. On his cue, she threw the softer items up in the air and crouched down for the camera. He made her find lamps and extension cords and directed the lighting, framing and expressions virtually, creating an optical illusion where she looked like a miniature person being attacked by domestic items. The result was stupendous and the comments instantly galvanized them into a team. They captioned the series 'Home Sweet Home'.

On the afternoon of the flood, her phone was clipped onto a tripod and placed on the landing at the bottom of the fourth-floor stairs of Number Thirty-Six. Taking advantage of the uninhabited corridors, Dasha was in her birthday suit, playing hide and seek with the beams of light bursting through the stained-glass window on that floor's staircase.

'Don't worry, just move freely. We won't use the ones where you can see nipple or bush,' Benjy's voice boomed on the speaker phone. He had no way of knowing that this was Violet's building—he'd never made it past the ground floor where she lived and he often crashed at.

Dasha hadn't seen or heard anyone in days. There was no sign of life. No one was in. If they were, they were lost in themselves and their devices. If she died or got sick, how long would it be before anyone found out? How long would it take for her family, the only people she spoke to everyday, to sound the alarm? And who would they call? The thought sent a chill down her spine: she was living all alone in this grand, one-hundred-and-sixty-year-old building. Then, a thrill went through her body as she realized she was running naked all alone through this grand, one-hundred-and-sixty-year-old building.

'I think this series should be called "The sun is alone too, but it still shines",' Dasha shouted as she ran up the stairs again.

'No, no, too long. A better title is "Be the light" or "Be your sun". What do you think?'

'I like "Sun-kissed",' she said, moving in and out of the shadows, turning different parts of her body to the blasting beams that made her solitude seem even starker.

'Don't move, don't move,' Benjy screeched excitedly. 'The light is catching you just right. Turn half a point to your left. Yes, yes, that's it. Now, don't move a muscle. You are going to love this, it looks like light is coming out of your you know what,' he giggled naughtily, like a kid leafing through his father's *Playboy* collection.

Although Violet was his girlfriend, girls didn't ignite any spark between his legs. If asked about his orientation, he would say he sought out beauty, a trait his artist mother instilled in him. She had been obsessed with surrounding herself only with fine-looking objects and finer-looking people—difficult when you are poor and impossible when you don't have imagination for the beauty you seek. So, when his single mother had been propositioned by an Italian antique collector with a pointed roman nose and a strong chin, she had bounced, leaving her unsightly offspring to their own devices. Her idea of beauty had been so literal, so narrow that her two sons had never made the cut.

The younger one looked like his face was caving in at the centre, as if a magnetic force was pulling in his lips, cheeks and eyes while his chin and forehead jutted out to complete the concave look. The face would have worked, like Quentin Tarantino's or Jay Leno's, were it not for the unfortunate inclusion of an exceptionally big nose. And Benjamin looked like an awful version of a young Adam Driver without the fame, charisma or broad shoulders. Thankfully, unlike his mother, he was not repelled by outer ugliness and found the oddest faces and objects attractive. Luckily, he was also as talented as Adam Driver, and he knew it. All he needed was a chance.

He shouted directions, clicking through the phone.

'Can I move now? Did you get it?'

'Yup, sending it now.'

Dasha ran to her phone and squealed with delight, '"Immaculate Conception"! That's what we need to call it. The way the sun is shining out of my pussy, it looks like Jesus himself is about to be born.'

Benjy laughed. Dasha joined him. They shared the same sense of humour. She couldn't wait to meet him IRL. What a laugh they would share!

'Benjy, I love this filter you've used. Will you send me a link for it please?' she asked. Suddenly, felt something wet under her feet. A gentle cascade was making its way down the stairs.

'What's going on?' Benjy asked.

'I'm not sure,' she replied. 'I'm going to investigate. If you don't hear from me in twenty-four hours, please come find me or call the police.'

'Stop being so dramatic. And I don't even know where you live.'
'I'm texting you the address,' she said rather seriously. Tapping her screen shut, she pulled on her dressing gown and ran up.

Chapter 4

It'd been three days since Jannie had been taken to hospital. Neera had not been allowed to visit—she hadn't even been permitted to ride on the ambulance with him. Sporadic updates about his condition were all she was given. Yet she didn't fall apart. It was normal life she couldn't cope with. In an emergency, she thrived.

She called Olivier and pushed him to call his doctor colleagues at the Hôpital Européen Georges-Pompidou and ensure that Jean-Paul was getting the very best care. She wanted hourly updates, but settled for twice a day. Then she called Ludovic to check if all matters of business were in order and told him to mount substantial pressure on the hospital's administration too. Jean-Paul's PR, meanwhile, was instructed to do whatever it took to keep the matter out of the press till he was back home. She informed her stepson, Eric, who'd been visiting his mother in Toronto when the frontiers had closed. Surprisingly, bound together by love for the same man, they'd had their first civilized conversation. Some might even say it had bordered on affectionate.

When she finally told her parents about Jannie being in the ICU, their worry sped through the weak Wi-Fi signal, hitting her bang in the middle of her chest. It was the only time she allowed herself a few tears.

She quickly pulled herself together, took to reading every scrap written about the damned virus and kept a close eye on the rising numbers, checking the figures every couple of hours. She busied herself with organizing and sanitizing and refused to smoke, scared that it might make her mind wander and land on how he had been infected. The answer terrified her, for it would confirm her own culpability. Jean-Paul, the only person to have navigated the unbridgeable gap between Neera's delight and dismay at being alive, was now fighting for his life because of her.

'He's off the ventilator,' said Olivier down the phone. 'They're keeping him in the ICU for the time being, but I think the worst has passed.'

'Can I visit him?' asked Neera.

'You know you can't, Neera,' he sighed. 'When he's out of the ICU, you can FaceTime him. I'll organize that, okay?'

'Okay,' she conceded.

'Now, listen to me, if you have so much as a cough or any loss of taste, you have to get tested. You will call me immediately if you have any symptoms. This is not optional. Okay?'

'Okay,' she said, too indebted to argue and hung up.

Olivier and Colette were the only friends of Jannie Neera could endure. They were the happy exceptions to the cliché she had sadly found to be true: Paris would be a wonderful city without the Parisians. For starters, the couple had actual things to share beyond a long list of complaints. In addition, they were young, eager and wanted to inhale the globe, along with all the exhilarating experiences it had on offer—or at least Colette wanted to. They had met only a handful of times, which was a pity but was apparently the chic thing to do. Imagine the shame of being available all the time in The City of Aloof!

When the four of them did get together, they talked over each other and laughed a lot. From the beastly way Olivier looked at his wife when she wasn't looking, Neera could sense without being told that their marriage wasn't as idyllic as Colette would like the world to believe. Then again, what marriage ever was?

They had last met for dinner at Balagan—an Israeli restaurant that had been on Neera's list forever—just a few weeks before Jean-Paul was driven away in a van with blaring sirens. With lockdown looming, the meal had taken on a twisted 'last-supper' significance, the place adding to the heightened air by living up to its name, which meant hullabaloo in Hebrew. The service had been terrific and the delicious looking servers, who seemed to be having a party of their own, had hollered *mazel tov* and *l'chaim* and had danced to their table with dinner.

The Decostes had been full of stories from their ski holiday and had insisted that Jean-Paul and Neera join them next year.

'Now that we have Len,' Colette had said, 'We are so free that we only wish the ski lift would open earlier and the bars would close later.'

'She's wonderful, a tiny little thing full of smiles. Works harder than anyone. We're lucky to have her,' Olivier had added. 'I mean for the kids. They simply love her. She's got endless patience and sings like a nightingale—no, like Whitney. Yes, she has a voice like Whitney Houston, if you can believe that. The other day I heard—'

'Do you ski, Neera?' Colette had cut in, putting a stop to her husband gushing over their domestic worker.

Olivier had mentioned their new nanny a few more times over the course of dinner. So, when Colette had called Jannie a couple of weeks after the dinner to ask if she could rent his unused *chambre de bonne* for their live-in nanny—the reason being that it was no longer feasible for her to stay overnight with them—Neera and her husband had assumed Olivier had been hitting on the nanny in confinement. They'd had a good giggle about it. That had been exactly eleven days before Jannie had gone into hospital, since their legs had nuzzled as they lay reading on opposite ends of their long sofa.

Thanks to the neatly drawn class divide, this kind of infatuation towards a domestic worker would rarely be acknowledged in the India she knew. Sexual atrocities towards a domestic worker were not uncommon, but public relationships were far less so. In egalitarian France, however, who knew what was considered acceptable? At that moment, she didn't care who or what Olivier was banging—she was just grateful to have a Parisian friend, a friend who was a doctor, a doctor who cared deeply about the well-being of her husband, a husband she couldn't conceive being without.

The news that Jannie, after three chancy nights on the ventilator, was turning the corner had greatly lifted her spirits. She changed out of her three-day-old kaftan, slipped on a robe, ran a bath, made herself a mint tea and switched on her laptop to lap up the latest morsels about corona. Knowledge was power, after all, and the more she educated herself, the more useful she could be to the situation at hand. She found herself thanking the mother she couldn't stand for instilling this discipline and desire to arm herself with information.

What she found online was an ocean of ignorance, along with a horrifying mine of conspiracy theories. No one knew anything, yet everyone felt compelled to share the nothingness of their knowing. She felt her jaw tighten and her body tense up. This virtual window she was looking through had very real repercussions on her physical being.

People are such idiots, she thought. Those in power were expounding beliefs that went against common sense. Why make statements that they knew they would be forced to retract in the coming months? When President Macron addressed the nation to claim that scientists had dismissed the need for anybody except the frontline workers to wear masks, the war became real for her, for throughout history, leaders had covered up war shortages with illogical lies.

It was befitting that her generation should face an enemy

to civilization that wasn't wielding guns and tanks or sporting military insignia in a foreign language but an enemy that came out of the breath of the person closest to them. Her generation of forty-year-olds were still trying to sort out who they were, why they were on Earth and what place they occupied in the hierarchy of adults because their own parents were refusing to take a bow while their kids were already basking in spotlights of their own making. It was hard to find room at the top when, at sixty plus, boomers still commanded respect, made applause-worthy decisions, found new love, travelled to must-see, impossible-to-reach parts of the world and, most annoyingly, knew all along who they were or, worse, found the question redundant.

The millennials had found and re-found their purpose. Gen Z (and whatever alphabet came after) found it offensive and detrimental to their mental health to live under the man-made construct that humans need to have purpose. They rejected the premise outright for being flawed and un-woke. While her generation, aptly termed Gen X, with 'x' denoting a yet to be discovered value—played deferential copycats. In their own nonchalant way, these later generations lived at a slower pace, understood the sweetness of delayed gratification and publicly cared more about the bigger questions, such as how to save the planet, and not the smaller ones of why they were on the planet. They didn't ask to be on the planet, certainly not on the dying one they inherited. And to this end, most of them would not be bringing any new humans into the world. It was simply too cruel for all parties involved. For them, this invisible war was proof of nature raging against Gen X.

So engrossed was Neera in her reading and postulating that it wasn't till Dasha was furiously and incessantly ringing her doorbell that she pulled herself out of the cyber well to notice the water.

She ran up to her bathroom, where the forgotten bathtub was overflowing and the tap was stuck. Running back down, she opened her front door to let her forever-present and always-unwelcome neighbour in. Together they tried to unplug the tub and turn the water off.

'Do you have a tool box?' asked Dasha.

'Of course I don't,' snapped Neera at the undernourished, underdressed girl, as if she was personally responsible for this plumbing disaster and not a person twisting a towel over the tap, trying to help. 'And even if the apartment has one, do I look like the person who'd know where it is or what to do with it?'

'I'm sorry, I didn't mean to insult you,' said Dasha, not sure why she felt obliged to apologize to this hostile lady.

'Is the guardian downstairs?' asked Neera. Not that the guardian, the person who got paid to live on the premises in exchange for its cleanliness and maintenance, was skilled at anything except punctually missing the delivery man and muddling up the post.

'I'm sorry, I haven't heard or seen anyone in the building for days,' said Dasha. 'Let's call the emergency.'

'No!' shrieked Neera. 'And deny a dying person limited lifesaving resources that have been stretched to breaking point? Absolutely not. We are going to figure this out ourselves.' With that said, she dialled Len.

Neera assumed the housekeeper, who'd moved in upstairs a few days ago, would know exactly what to do with a plumbing catastrophe. *After all, it was a working-class skill.*

A baffled Rosel, who hadn't fully understood what 'bring a spanner' meant, said, 'Yes, of course, Madame Allard. I will be down in a minute.'

Chapter 5

Confinement for Rosel was better, much better, unimaginably better than any freedom she had previously known. The kids were home all day and all she had to do was make sure they stuck to their side of the apartment till dinner time, so that Madame Colette could work like a maniac in peace. Whichever child's turn it was to walk the dog with the nanny had to first finish his or her chores and schoolwork. The other two were in charge of choosing and setting up the game they would all play on Rosel's return, with karaoke being a hot favourite. The days felt like an endless extension of a holiday where the flight home from the sunny beach kept getting cancelled due to bad weather conditions on the other side.

One evening, in the early days of this marvellous confinement, as Rosel was standing on the balls of her feet, cooking something that resembled dinner, Olivier came into the kitchen and opened a bottle of wine.

Being a general practitioner, he wasn't on the frontline. Yet, instead of feeling emasculated for not contributing, he secretly felt like a war hero for seeing the few patients he did face to face at his practice a few doors away. To be fair, his phone hadn't stopped ringing and he did what he could to comfort and advise the panicked callers remotely. It didn't once cross his mind, however, that he should volunteer to help in one of the understaffed hospitals across Paris, all of them close to collapse.

He wasn't a man who could be accused of having noble intentions or, even if he occasionally had them, he lacked the resolve to see one through. In the Alps, he had fully intended to call it quits on his marriage, but now that he was back in Paris, it seemed like such a bother. Luckily, the prospect of the world coming to an end had saved him from his own lack of tenacity. This was the time, he told himself, to be stoic and stay home.

'What are you cooking there, Len? Smells great,' he said, lying through his teeth.

'Sir, it's onion fried rice, lemon butter fish and beans in garlic,' Rosel replied. Her menus always sounded more appetizing than they tasted.

'Glass of wine?' Olivier offered.

Rosel was entirely unsure what the correct answer to such an offer was. She had drunk home-made *tubâ*, a kind of coconut wine, a few times and enjoyed the effect. Then again, when she'd done so, she'd been with Ferdie, the love of her life, with whom she would enjoy counting the coconuts on the trees if she had to.

Olivier poured her a glass. 'Here, just a little. You work too hard and it's no fun drinking alone.' Then, he clinked his glass against hers and waited for her to take a sip, which she awkwardly did. 'It's a 2009 Margaux. A good year for Bordeaux. Amazing, right?'

Again, Rosel didn't know how to respond, so she went about setting the table in the kitchen. Swirling his wine in the glass, Olivier walked closer to her under the pretext of helping her with the table mats.

'No, Sir, the Stormfly plate is for Blanche, that's her favourite dragon. The Tintin one is for Augustin,' said Rosel, swapping the plates around.

'You really spoil the children,' Olivier said, patting her little shoulder and gulping his Margaux.

'They are great kids, Sir,' Rosel responded with a broad smile. How could she talk about the source of her joy without smiling?

'You have a son, right? How old is he?'

'Danilo is eight years old, Sir. He'll be nine in June.'

'Show me a picture, Len. I'd love to see your baby.' Olivier was not sure if he'd meant to, but he'd sounded quite lecherous. 'You must have a photo, show me,' he insisted.

Instead of taking the phone she was handing him, he peered at it from behind, towering over her small frame, pressing closer than he needed to.

'Oh, look at his cool undercut! He's a bit of a dude,' he said leaning in closer. 'Don't let Aug or Toto see that; they'll want the same haircut. I'm not ready to have such little hipsters giving me competition. I'd like to remain the stud of the house for a few years still, Len, you know what I mean?' he winked. Then, to hide his sleaziness, he neighed and snorted through the nose, 'I'm such a stallion, neighhh, neighhh, bhrrrr.' *What on earth am I doing?* He had to stop. He laughed, trying to conceal his embarrassment, the laugh came out as a horse's snort and several similar snorts followed. He held his nose, swallowed to stop this bray and then gulped down some more of the Margaux, which he knew should be sipped, not quaffed. These things didn't matter in lockdown—nothing mattered when the world as you knew it no longer existed. He had every right to be unfettered. The tannins sloshed in his mouth and hit the back of his throat, reminding him he was not in fact a horse but a suave stud of a man.

He knew he was making her uncomfortable—he was so close she would be able to smell his wine-infused breath—but he didn't want to stop. He liked playing with danger when he knew that he himself was in none. Flirting was his thing. What was the point of looking the way he did if he didn't put it to good use? Okay, it wasn't always harmless. Sometimes, he'd had a little consensual feel up while dancing or a lingering peck on the lips under the guise of being tipsy. But 'consensual' was the operative word and he was aware that it didn't apply in this case.

Now that he thought about it, his past flirtations had been entirely reactive. He had never initiated anything. It was the ladies who would brush up against him or ask him to check their pulse or whisper steamy secrets when their respective spouses would be out of earshot, their lips grazing his earlobes. Yes, he was a reactive flirt. And now he was an active pervert, too. Why couldn't he just stop? He didn't care to find out.

'So, how did you meet the father of your son?' he asked, moving closer and lowering his voice to a purr. 'Was it love at first sight?'

'The clapping has started,' said Colette from the door, startling them both.

How long had she been standing there?

Everyone dropped everything they were doing and rushed to the balcony to add their little clap of gratitude to the sacrosanct 8 p.m. applause for frontline workers.

'Bravo! Bravo! Braaaaaaavooooo!' cheered the kids, trying to drown out the sound of the applauding neighbours.

The days were getting noticeably longer and this nightly routine had become charged with emotion. The Decostes and their nanny applauded with all their hearts. Colette hugged her husband and children, feeling more connected to them than she had in years—the power of collective crisis! The moment was hallowed.

Parisians found themselves waving at strangers across the road and awkwardly acknowledging, for the first time, those they had been living alongside for years. Tears were shed, music played. Finally, Paris had become a community. Every eager applauder was aware that this moment was fleeting—this feeling of inseparability would end the minute the virus left the air they were breathing. In that, however, they were wrong. It left long before the bug did.

'I'll take Milo out for his night walk today, Len,' said Colette after they'd finished their barely edible meal. 'Will you get the kids to bed on time please? They've been having too many late nights and then they're cranky in the morning.'

'But maman, we love your stories,' protested Blanche. 'Ah *oui*, can we have the one about us escaping the farting Titakamoon again,' said Augustin. 'Please, maman, nobody tells stories like you do.'

So this had happened, believe it or not. Now that the government had put an official stop to their social lives, Colette had started tucking the kids into bed at night and discovered that she was an absurdly skilled storyteller. Her imagination was like her ambition—it knew no bounds. Once she started a tale, she was as invested and immersed in it as she was in image branding and corporate strategy. And her kids were an animatedly attentive audience, running behind every word as she took them on adventures through dark forests, where sunlight was forbidden to enter and you had to wait till nightfall for the stars to guide the way. They swam after her through fluorescent pink, polluted oceans, where mermaids had lost their love for water and jet-black sharks devoured plastic, till the oceans turned blue-green again.

Her three munchkins—yes, in those moments, she thought of them as munchkins because they were nothing except munchkins snuggled next to her as she weaved magic around them—featured heavily in all the stories, either as underdogs who find courage to fight the vomiting, farting monsters, or as bullies who realize the follies of their way and are given superpowers to be used uniquely against other bullies, or as explorers and inventors who save the world with their discoveries.

It alarmed her how much this precious hour replenished her. The more love she took, the more they had to give. Discovering this tap of plenty shook her belief system—the system that had governed her parenting both as its receiver and giver. How had she miscalculated, no, entirely flouted, the huge benefits of this small investment of time? She would've been toast at work if she'd made a similar error of judgment there. Parenting, it struck her, was so forgiving.

'I want the one about the dolphins in the clouds who come to save the little boy stuck on the frozen waterfall,' pouted Thomas. 'That is my favouritest.'

'There's no such word,' said Augustin.

'Maman says, if you can think it then it can be possible,' said Thomas. 'And I'm not just thinking it, I'm saying it. So, shay.' He stuck his thumb under his chin, flicked it at his brother and repeated, 'Shay.'

'It doesn't quite apply to words, Toto,' said Colette.

'Why not?'

'I'm not sure,' said Colette and got up to fetch the dog's leash. 'I need a walk to find a solution to a problem. You kids better be in dreamland by the time I return.'

'Just tell us one quick story and then you can go,' said Augustin. Seeing that his mother was not about to budge, he offered, 'Okay, two brand new, extra-long ones tomorrow, plus cuddle time? Say yes, or we're not going to bed till you're back.'

'Okay, okay, yes,' she agreed, thinking that if that boy of hers didn't become an acquisitions officer at a cut-throat company then he was wasting his talent.

Apart from dog walkers and a rule-breaking jogger, the streets were desolate. After buying a packet of Davidoff Beige from the tabac, Colette chain-smoked three. After all these years, the smoke hit the back of her throat, making her cough and giving her a virginal head rush.

She bent down to scoop up the dog's poo and was instantly sure that she couldn't do this three times a day every day. She needed Len, and so did the dog and her kids—but she was not going to allow her husband to need the nanny, too.

'Salut, Jean-Paul. I hope it's not too late to call you,' she said into her phone.

'Colette, *mon chérie*, for you I'm available day and night.'

'Is your *chambre de bonne* still available to rent?'

'Are you finally kicking Olivier out?' Jean-Paul laughed.

'I wish,' she said. 'It's for Len, our nanny. It's too much to have her in the apartment all the time, especially since I'm working from home and we have no dinner parties to go to.'

'You know, I could get used to this confinement, with Neera all to myself, no pressure to go out,' said Jean-Paul. 'And yes, of course, you can rent the service room. Be warned, it's quite small, but we just had a new cooker installed.'

'It'll be perfect. Thank you, my dear,' said Colette. 'Give my love to Neera, will you?'

All problems came with a solution and she was a master solver. Len could walk across the bridge to Number Thirty-Six, rue des Diablesse every morning and evening—no need to stay late and cook dinner. *Great plan*. Olivier could cook—he always said he loved it, or they could manage with Picard, which, of course, remained open or no parent would be able to work. The chances of her husband being left unsupervised with the nanny would be reduced to the bare minimum. *Yes, a great plan*.

It was about time she regarded her marriage like she regarded the age-old practices, set in stone, at her archaic workplace. Hermès prided itself on being an old-fashioned institution that steered clear of mass production, but in truth, it was more like an antiquated beast that everyone pretended to revere because they were nothing without it. She'd made the organization contribute efficiently to its own brand value by exploiting and not liquidating its traditional values. The key to her success was early recognition of the fact that compromise and covert individual autonomy within a rigid framework were the only ways forward, much like her marriage.

'Len, I have some great news,' she announced on her return, making sure her husband's ears were pricked before continuing. 'I found you your own little apartment. Well, not quite an apartment. It's a small, cute room on the other side of the river, above where our friends Jean-Paul and Neera live. It's very comfortably furnished, has a mini kitchenette and high-speed Internet, so you can finally have your nights to yourself. Talk to your family back home or watch films in Tagalog or whatever it is you want to do.'

'I'll still work for you, Madame?' asked Rosel nervously.

'Of course, you will, Len,' assured Colette, 'We can't do without you. None of us can,' and handed her an envelope of money. 'This is just a little something to help you set up your place,' she said, smiling at her husband, her partner, who was going to pull his weight from now on to save the beast they had both built. She was not going to wreck this home or allow anyone else to do it—not now that she had noticed that her children lived here.

Whatever dread Rosel had of staying alone or being abandoned was overshadowed by her relief of not having to kiss the boss to keep a job she had obtained under shady circumstances.

'Thank you, Madame,' said Rosel. And she meant it.

Chapter 6

Back in Neera's bathroom, three clueless women were now standing with soaked feet, contemplating a tap that refused to stop running. Over the sound of the water, they heard knocking, growing louder like an ominous drum broadcasting doom, before Violet burst in. Rosel's first thought was whether all women on this side of the building hang around half-naked in silk dressing gowns.

In spite of her long, false nails and her dainty demeanour, Violet managed to turn the tap off, tapping into the strength she'd built hanging off trapeze rings.

'You have got to be the most glamorous plumber in the world,' Neera said, giving her an unexpected bear hug.

'Madame, I can clean up here if you tell me where your mop is,' said Rosel.

'I'm Dasha,' said the aspiring model, shaking hands with the rest of them. 'I live on the third floor.'

'I know who you are,' said Violet. 'My boyfriend called to tell me there was a flood in my building and that it would be best not to leave a skinny Russian to fix it.'

Without missing a beat, Dasha exclaimed, 'Benjamin is *your* boyfriend? No way. And we live in the same building. Oh man, oh man, that is freaking crazy!'

Violet, who was wearing a red lace teddy under her robe and had done her face like Kim Kardashian gone overboard, was amused. 'I'm Violet,' she said. 'But you, young naked girl, can call me Queen Vee.' She then turned to Rosel. 'And you are?'

'I'm Rosel Andal. I live on the *top* top floor, the service floor just under the roof.'

'I thought your name was Len,' butted in Neera.

Rosel went pale. She was caught so entirely off-guard that she couldn't think of a single lie to cover up the truth she'd accidentally spilled.

'Madame, please don't tell them,' she managed to say, fighting back tears.

'Tell who?' asked Neera, not entirely keeping up with what was going on.

'Madame and Sir Decoste, Madame. Please don't tell them,' she begged.

'I don't think they'd care what you choose to call yourself,' said Neera dismissively. 'So, what is it? Len? Rosel? Madonna?'

'Hey, don't I know you from somewhere?' asked Dasha, racking her brain for a clue. Surely if she'd met this cute little button at a casting, she would have remembered.

Then suddenly, Rosel realized why Dasha looked so familiar. Months ago, on the day of her escape, the first kindness on the harsh streets of Paris had come from this tall girl. Rosel had shown unforeseen courage that day and it was about time she did it again.

'Well yes, it's a long story,' began Rosel. 'I asked you for directions to—'

'Shall we clean up here first?', by which Neera meant Len/Rosel/whoever she was should deal with the flood before launching into the saga of her name. 'Since it's Sunday, I've cooked biryani, and it's not a dish you eat alone,' by which she meant: I invite you all to join me.

It took more than an hour to get the apartment and the stairway dry and clean. Neera went about removing the home-made dough that sealed the clay pot in which the biryani had been cooking for hours. The coalescing of the ingredients took place secretly, undercover, and no matter how many times she had flawlessly prepared this layered dish, this moment of reveal made her hold her breath.

Aaah! she thought as she inhaled. Each grain of rice was smothered in spices and cooked to perfection. As Neera served, the fragrance of cardamom, cinnamon, mutton and ghee filled their nostrils, making her guests ravenous. Sunday biryani was a family tradition that she revisited after moving to Paris with Jannie. She wanted to share the dishes engraved into her soul by her father. So, once a week, her little mixed family, including Eric, would sit around the oval kitchen table to eat. Jannie would say each bite made him travel to her home and understand better who she was. Even Eric was tolerable on Sundays and, between mouthfuls, would share details of the latest video installation he would be working on. On one occasion, Neera had even written the text to go with his video clip. Biryani brought people together. And on that evening of the pseudo-flood, it once again accomplished what it was created for.

'I've gone easy on the spice quotient,' said Neera, 'But you can add yoghurt if it's too hot to handle.' This was her way of thanking them for their timely aid. She didn't mention that their presence was momentarily distracting her from Jannie's absence.

The four of them sat around the long rosewood dining table and dug in, filling their bellies and spilling their secrets.

'You can never judge a book by its cover. No one can guess by looking at baby-faced little you that you were capable of jumping out of a prison window. That's a heroic story,' said Neera, looking at Rosel with admiration in her eyes. 'I won't tell Colette and Olivier if you promise to come clean to them yourself.'

'Madame, I just need some time and I will,' Rosel promised.

'I think you can drop the Madame and call her Neera, no? This is France and she's not even your employer,' Violet said.

France or not, Neera liked to be addressed in accordance with her privileged status. Yet, in the spirit of the meal, she made a big concession. 'Sure, you can call me Neera.' Now that they had forced their way into becoming her equals, she shared her own dark secret about letting in the girl who had infected her husband.

'So the student tested positive?' asked Dasha. 'Is she okay?'

'How do I know if she's okay? I don't care if she's okay or not!' barked Neera. 'She's not my concern. My husband is. And thankfully, he's going to be fine.'

'I'm sorry,' said Dasha. *There she was*, she thought, *apologizing all over again to this rude woman who had just served them the most divine dish she had ever eaten*. 'But then how do you know the student infected Monsieur Allard if you don't know whether she had the virus or not?'

'Ugh, stop being rational. There are some things you just know,' she said. 'We haven't stepped out at all since the beginning of March. Jannie is no spring chicken, and I didn't want to take any chances. Even before the confinement was announced, I cancelled the cleaner and immediately stopped seeing all my lovers. So who else could it be?'

'You have lovers?' asked an incredulous Dasha.

'Oh, my darling, one day you'll understand. Lovers *save* marriages,' said Neera, a rare twinkle in her eyes. 'The love of my life is Jannie, I'm his, and that's the only thing that matters.' She pulled out her little stash of happiness and, while passing around a joint that no one felt they had the right to refuse, went into graphic detail about her sex life.

The long and short of it was that she went out of her way to satisfy her old man, seeking pleasure in his pleasure and finding her own outside their bedroom, where young lovers went out of their way to satiate her carnal needs. It kept the magic alive, she explained. Discretion was the key. Jannie never asked and she never told because these encounters were akin to having a mani-pedi to look and feel good. Nothing more.

It was only after the 8 p.m. applause could be heard that

they broke up their serendipitous soirée. It was to be the first of many. After all, for months, they would have nowhere to be and no one to see, save each other.

Chapter 7

On their way out of Neera's palatial apartment, not wanting to be alone with empty bunk beds, a somewhat high Dasha followed Violet into her studio. This tiny treasure trove of all things glittery was the cleverest use of space that she'd ever seen.

'How long have you been seeing Benjy?' asked Dasha.

'Since you were still hanging on your mother's tit, young girl,' Violet replied with a smile. 'And how long have *you* been video calling my boyfriend naked?'

'Queen Vee, it's not like that at all,' stammered Dasha. 'We don't even know each other, we've never met, we are just…making photographs together.'

'Uh-huh?' Violet raised her heavily pencilled eyebrow.

'I'm not interested in him and he's not interested in me in that way and we only talk work and plan shoots and it's the first time I took my clothes off Queen Vee and it was—'

'Relax. I'm pulling your leg. And you don't have to call me Queen Vee,' said Violet. 'Your innocence is adorable. I can see what Benjy sees in you.'

Violet's computer beeped and turned on, startling Dasha. Violet had all but forgotten what she had been in the midst of when a flustered Benjamin had called and told her about the flood.

'You can stay and watch or you can leave,' said Violet, touching up her make-up and taking off her robe. 'But what you are about to witness, my dear, will change your unsullied mind and you won't be able to un-see what you see. So, choose well.'

'I'd like to stay, please,' came her response without a pause. When she thought about it later, perhaps the marijuana had played it's part in her smooth initiation into sleaze. But she had no regrets.

'Alright, you have to play invisible,' instructed Violet, whose movements suddenly gained a languid sensuality. 'Sit on this chair on the side so you can see but don't come in front of the camera. Okay?'

A man with pale greenish skin popped up on the screen. He looked annoyed.

'I've been trying you all day,' he grumbled.

'My prince, good things come to those who wait,' teased Violet, in a voice that could melt glaciers. 'And I'm going to show you more than a good time... But first, you take your clothes off and let my thirsty eyes feast on your big jewel. You're making mama's mouth hungry. Oh yeah, oh, there it is. I want to wrap my tongue around it. Put your hands on that beautiful dick and stroke it to for me, my prince. Now gently squeeze your balls with the other hand, ooh yes, like that. Harder, like that, exactly like that,' she purred, arching her body and fingering her nipples, leaning into the screen.

And that's how the evening unfolded, one call to the next, with breaks just long enough for a rum shot in between. Violet was an enchantress like no other. She jiggled her breasts and contorted her taut dancer's body into positions on the bed that didn't seem possible. Her red teddy stayed on, although she slipped and slid it seductively to reveal different body parts on demand. Dasha was scared to blink in case she missed a move, a single breath. It was only after several calls that she noticed the black satin sheets. She had a sudden urge to touch them.

'Whose hand is that?' demanded the pimply boy on Violet's screen.

'Nobody.'

'What do you mean, nobody? Of course, it's somebody and I want to see. Or I won't call in or pay next time.'

'Ooh la la, my boy is becoming a man! Grrrr. I'm creaming

myself,' said Violet. She was too much of a diva to be bullied by some zitty teenager.

Before Violet could stop her, Dasha stepped into frame.

'Hi, it's me, Xenia,' she said, waving at the screen.

Violet never knew if it was intentional, or an inadvertent consequence of Dasha's wave but her robe flew open revealing her still developing body to the camera.

'Wow,' was the only response the boy on the other side could manage.

Imitating what she had intently observed for the last however many hours, Dasha took centre stage on the satin sheets. She was performing for the camera. The lust-struck boy watching was incidental.

Over the coming nights, Dasha touched herself in ways that she had never been touched, and it made her burst in ecstasy. Meanwhile, Violet was careful to screen the clients, ensuring her accidental protégé got only the most docile ones. And when Astrid sneaked back into a sealed Paris via unmonitored dirt roads, having irreconcilably fallen out with her parents in confinement, she joined Dasha and Violet for their trysts with turds. The girls paid no heed to the men on the other side; the screen protected them, allowing them to focus on themselves and the money. Astrid's bounteous tyres and curves were in high demand, as were Dasha's mosquito-bite breasts, and soon, the two young models were rolling in it and with each other. The first time they had touched one another had been for the camera, but subsequently, it was only ever for themselves, regardless of whether the camera was on or not.

∽

The Lure spectacle was running more than thirty minutes late, but Neera didn't mind. She had so much to discuss with Lucas about her debut on his show (he still hadn't built up to telling her that it would most likely be a cameo). None of the other invitees seemed fussed about the delay either: being part of the reconvened glitterati was already a treat. They were happy to revel in their own lipsticks, heels and handbags.

The lights dimmed and spotlights came on, revealing bodies suspended above their heads. Violet was the first to roll down a rope dramatically, stopping inches above the audience. Each move was met with a group gasp. It was nothing like what anyone had seen before and all the more miraculous because their collective brains had become born-again virgins as far as a live performance, or live anything, with real people within touching distance, was concerned.

Neera clapped and cheered the loudest the two times Dasha walked past. On the ramp, Dasha was a discovery, her odd looks and odder energy sucking in every eyeball, making her unmissable. Neera saw her omnipresent neighbour, who, thus far, had been nothing more than an uninvited plus-one, in a completely different light. She'd have to rethink how she treated her.

Months of isolated misery came to an end with the show. There were those in the audience for whom it even symbolized winning the war. Some shed tears. Others cheered and whistled. Everyone stood up. And the show got a twelve-minute standing ovation.

The show was barely over and Neera's phone had ten missed calls from Violet. *What was going on?* She called back.

'You were outstanding, my friend,' said Neera. 'I'm bursting with pride. Just sensational, Vee.'

'He ran away, Neera, he ran away,' Violet sobbed into the phone.

Neera had never heard Violet cry. 'Who?'

'Raphaël, the man who was going to save me,' Violet tried to explain, but she couldn't find the words. 'Where are you? I need you. Are you still at the venue? I'm coming to find you.'

'Uhmmm... Yes, I am. But I'm kind of tied up.' Violet's neediness repulsed Neera.

'Okay, I'll see you back at home, in an hour?' pleaded Violet. And she never pleaded. Never. At least not since she'd been forced into escaping Senegal. 'I'm losing my mind here.'

'I won't be home for many hours, I need to go sort out stuff for my grand debut with Lucas.' This was far from the truth, as Lucas was going home to join his girlfriend, and all the details for his show were being planned by producers, who weren't quite sure how to include Neera. 'I'm so sorry, Vee. I'll catch you when I can. Okay? It's a busy time for me right now. Oh, and well done for tonight. Big kiss.' And with that, she hung up on the person who hadn't left her side when she had been slipping off the planet.

PART 4

The Runaways

Chapter 1

Slumped on the floor like a disowned dog, Dasha leaned her head against Violet's door. She couldn't understand why the door, and the life that lay on the other side of it, had shut her out. Instead of celebrating the success of the show together, Dasha felt she was being punished for a crime she was yet to discover she had committed. It was the affliction of adolescence that made it inconceivable to her that she wasn't somehow at the centre—or for that matter, the cause—of this unfolding drama. Not yet eighteen and her life was already repeating itself. Why did the adults she loved the most abandon her?

As far back as she could remember, every Saturday, before the sun broke the spell the night had swaddled them in, her father would sneak into the room she shared with her siblings, stroke her face, push away the stray hair and whisper, 'Come, my heart, my *kroshka*, it's time.'

He would help her into her hat, boots and gloves and out they would walk into the darkness, all bundled up and holding hands. Maybe it was a trick of memory, but she recalled that it would always be dark and cold. Or maybe she recollected correctly and it would mostly be a winter jaunt because summer Saturdays were swarming with tourists whom her father was obliged to beguile for money. Andrei had long been excused from these ritual excursions. He had preferred to wrap himself in sleep, traverse his meandering dreams and play the captive audience when his twin retold a highly embellished version of what she had learnt earlier that day with their Papochka.

The cobbled streets, medieval cathedrals and Nordic-style houses with coloured roofs in their small port town all had stories of Swedish, Finnish and Russian conquests. Her father would shine his torch on a monument or body of water and begin an action-packed account of its history. The cold had never bothered him, and she had never known anything else. The little sips of laced coffee he offered her from his thermos would fill her with warmth so golden, she could swear she'd swallowed the sun.

One such morning, they stood in waist-deep snow and he told her about the Winter War that had broken out between Russia and Sweden during the Second World War. Soldiers from both sides, submerged in snow, in temperatures falling to minus forty degrees, had fought for months to gain control of Vyborg. Her Papochka wanted her to feel as proud of their historical hometown as he was. And in those moments, as he immersed her in unforgiving wars or talked her through one of the largest naval battles in history that took place on the very shore they stood on, she was proud—not just of a town she couldn't wait to get out of but also of her father, who filled her with wonder and curiosity. Did he miss the town he had been so enamoured by? And did he miss her, the daughter he had industriously educated in the wee hours of winter mornings—the daughter he had so easily left behind, unannounced, on a summer afternoon?

Suddenly, Dasha was filled with rage. The kind of rage that must have pumped through the blood of the White and Red Guards alike, keeping them warm as they fought under merciless conditions to control a town she couldn't hate more. How *dare* her father forsake his family the way he had without any explanation? No address, no number and no real reason. And, if her mother was to be believed, he'd left them with no money either. What was so urgent or secret that he couldn't take his kids with him? Or at least call them once the urgency and secrecy had passed? Nothing remained secret or urgent forever.

She would've understood and forgiven everything, if he'd just loved them enough to explain. Four years on, her breath still caught if she saw an unknown number flash on her phone, willing it to be her father, hoping that, somehow, he had found her and was waiting around the corner to ask for her forgiveness. Then, like a lost puppy reunited with its owner, she would run towards him and slobber all over the stories of his new life, of his chosen family, far away from his old family. There would be nothing to forgive because by finding her, she would know that he loved her, longed for her, as much as she did for him.

Her commitment to post hourly updates on Insta begun right after his departure. It was her way to let him see her or, more accurately, let him see a version of her life that would either entice him to contact her or let him know that she didn't need him, that she, in fact, had an excellent life without him. She ranked every tiny event by its posting potential and developed an uncanny ability to transform the most mundane moment into a magical one, paying little heed to the number of laws she broke or the locals she enraged. The imaginary escapes that she wandered through with Andrei fired her creativity. And with a little help from free-trial filters, she created images that made you want to jump right on top of the roof she was sliding down or squeeze the snowflakes or ride on the mast of the icebreaker on top of which she was posing.

Wanting her father to know that she was not her mother, she starved herself till her bones jutted out. To remain à la mode, she scoured English fashion magazines at the library in the town centre, then groomed and primed herself, making the most of her unique, pre-pubescent, bony face. She sewed together rags and fur to make chic jackets, dyed her hair platinum with cheap ammonia, and got her ever ready sisters to shoot elaborate portraits of her at all the freezing sites that she and her father had ever explored. And when even this was not enough to make him connect or comment, she decided that fame was her only recourse: at fifteen, Dasha had shot up to just over six feet, and with her height had grown the dream of superstardom. Encouraged by the little local notoriety she was gaining, her family believed she had the face, the attitude and the grit to endure—that one day, she would be the brightest star to have been born in Vyborg. Not that she had much competition for that title. Between them, they managed to save a little money to send her to Moscow in search of a modelling agency. But then her mother—whom Dasha had finally begun to treasure and who herself had begun to blossom like a lotus through the muck—was diagnosed with breast cancer. The money had to be used for surgery.

Dasha, however, was not born to give up. She filtered out her mother's illness and went on a rampage with her pictures on social media, tagging every single potential agent or employer. In the end, Nicolas scouted her, flew her over to Paris, gave her a menial allowance coupled with a spot on a bunk bed and bound her with a typically exploitative modelling contract, where he would take sixty per cent, plus expenses, of any job she landed. To think that it all started because she wanted to win back the man she loved!

And here she was again, abandoned by Violet, whom she loved and who had become family. *No, I'm not going to let history repeat itself.*

Dasha's bum felt sore. It had only been a few hours, but she was sure radishes were sprouting out of her bottom and lush green moss was covering her skin. She adjusted herself and banged her head on that silent, unrelenting door again as she slumped against it.

'Vee, I know you are in there. I heard you flush earlier,' pleaded Dasha. 'Tell me what I've done and I'll leave you alone.'

Silence.

'I'm not leaving. If I starve to death, which by the way I am, it will be on you.'

More silence.

'This doormat is rough and I'm dying to pee. Come on Vee. Talk to me! If this is about me going out for a drink with the other dancers and models, I'm sorry. I should've waited for you. I know that now. It was such a big moment for me, I got carried away and didn't stop to think. It will never happen again.'

Her bladder was bursting, her head was pounding and the inside of her mouth felt like the doormat she was sitting on. She had overdone it last night.

It was the first night that the city truly belonged to her. She went from being an uncastable alien to a bona fide Parisian ramp model, hand-picked by the gods of fashion to walk on a shiny stairway to stardom. The pearly gates of Paris flew open—what was she supposed to do? Wash her face, pack her bag and go home?

No, she danced and drank the night away—and this time not because some travelling businessman was paying her to do it but because she was the one buying the rounds. Then, rounds were bought for her (it didn't matter that the House of Lure was most likely going to pay her in clothes and not cash). At an indecently enjoyable hour, one of the backstage handlers suggested they carry on bar hopping to Quai d'Austerlitz in the 13th arrondissement. Apparently, *les guinguettes*—open-air watering holes favoured by party-goers in the eighteenth century—along the Seine were all the rage again. They all piled into taxis sans debate; it was a night where all suggestions were acted upon, including playing tongue tennis with the said handler on the backseat of the taxi.

Deep down, the revellers feared that this was time they were snatching from the jaws of the pandemic, that there was no telling when the beast would wake, hungrier than ever, and make them scramble for the safety of sanitized spaces, solo. So they took their chance while they could and partied like it was 2019 again. At some point, the stragglers finally had their fill and scrambled out of a club on top of a boat that never sailed. Dasha shielded her eyes from the mocking sun. She couldn't remember what she'd done with her left shoe and why it wasn't on her foot. Upon returning home, she knocked on Violet's door, wanting to fill her in over breakfast before passing out. But Violet wasn't in and had probably forgotten her phone because Dasha heard it ringing on the other side of the door when she dialled it. Sleep summoned Dasha and she obeyed, and by the time she opened her eyes, the ugly, ceramic, owl-shaped clock on the wall opposite her bunk bed told her it was four-thirty in the afternoon.

Hungover, tired and abandoned, she banged on the merciless door again with the back of her head. Her phone said it was almost seven. She furiously dialled Benjamin.

'Calm down,' said Benjy. 'She must be sleeping.'

'Of course she's not! I can hear her moving around,' cried Dasha. 'You have to come now. Where are you? How long will you take?'

'Relax, Dasha,' he said. 'She's probably with one of her clients. I'm not coming now.' He knew better than to interfere when Violet needed space.

It was the principal reason he hadn't pushed to live with her. For all her clamour and spectacle, the diva needed silence and non-being every so often to work through the din in her mind. Everyone did, of course, but Violet's silence was absolute, like that of the gods: the silent gods, who made themselves that much more powerful by not uttering a word to the mothers who prayed to them, night and day, to save their starving, malnourished kids. Once, when he had tried to break through a particularly prolonged bout of Violet's silence, she had quoted her mother at him. It went something like—*He who does not understand your silence will never understand your words.* And with that, Benjamin had shut up till she had been ready to play his luscious lippy ladylove again.

'What do you mean you are not coming now? Don't you care about—'

'You were a knockout on the ramp last night,' he cut her off. 'I have a few amazing shots, although I was a bit far and the lights were a bit low. There are one or two I know you will be crazy for, once I've worked on them.'

'Really? Send them to me,' said Dasha, forgetting about Violet momentarily. 'It was a super slick show, no?'

'Yes, it was,' said Benjy. 'What happened to that homeless friend of Vee's? Wasn't he supposed to walk at the end? I was excited to finally see him.' Violet had been talking about him non-stop. Getting him off the streets had brought her untold joy, which had made Benjamin grateful for the beggar's existence. His girlfriend deserved every chance to be happy.

The alarm bells that went off in Dasha's head were so loud that she was afraid the *pompiers* would rush in brandishing their fire hoses any minute. How could she have forgotten about the runway runaway? How self-absorbed and selfish was she?

Yes, the show went on as it must. And yes, Violet and her dancers were breathtaking as they were born to be. But no, Raphaël was not found, and the look that Dasha caught on Violet's face as she was hauled up onto the scaffolding was of a woman who had just been told that she had accidentally run over and killed her only child. It made the hair on the back of Dasha's long neck stand on end; luckily, the very next moment, she was herded into the wings, and the loud banshee-like wail that came from the choral sisters to open the show made it impossible for her to think.

Maestra Maria Bellin's orchestral composition was sinister

and eerie. The singers puffed, wheezed and made sounds that didn't belong to a human. They spanned octaves, hitting notes that Dasha scarcely thought possible. The music sounded like lost souls sighing in agony. Dasha looked up. One by one, the dancers unfurled from a great height, almost caressing the hair of the seated audience, before hauling themselves up just as efficiently as they had plummeted down. She was the third model to walk. Her strides felt longer and lighter than usual, like the full stretch of a galloping racehorse, slowed to funeral pace. The industrial fans, concealed on the side of the ramp, blew open her aubergine coloured dress in a way that made her feel like Wonder Woman.

A quick dab-and-check backstage and she went back on. She could have walked that ramp a million times. The euphoria of the never-ending applause (that ended too soon) was pure heroin. Everyone was flying high: for an enchanted moment, they all became the person they wished they were.

'You all did me proud,' exclaimed Ms Dog Tamer after the show, spreading her arms out in a big gesture. '*Fantastico! Meraviglioso!* This is what the world missed. This is what they needed. And the House of Lure, not without a little help from each one of you, just gave it to them. Did you see their smiling faces?' She brought her hands together and started clapping; others joined in. It soon turned into an echo of the intoxicating applause they had all flown on outside. 'Now, girls, don't forget to return every piece of clothing and accessory before signing out,' she announced, and just like that, it was back to business. 'We've already lost expensive merchandise to the streets tonight. I don't want any additions to that. Thank you.'

If Dasha's head wasn't floating in the clouds and if her body wasn't gliding alongside, she might have caught Ms Dog Tamer looking directly at Violet while saying that last line. And she might have even caught them exchange angry words. If she hadn't felt the urgency to FaceTime Andrei there and then, she probably would've seen Violet speeding out of her costume and out of the venue. Alas! She missed it all.

'He left,' Dasha screeched into the phone, 'And no one found him. Or no one had time to look. Raphaël ran away and then I ran away too. It's not *she* who's abandoning me.' Dasha started knocking on Violet's door with a renewed fervour, powered by the light shed on the situation. 'I'm sorry, Vee, I'm so sorry. Open up and we can go look for him. I will find him for you! Open up and I will help you! We can do this.'
 'What do you mean he ran away?' asked Benjy. 'Was he at the show?'
 'Yes, yes. He was all dressed up and looking drop-dead gorge, he was there like a minute before the show and then he went all crazy or something and ran out. I don't know... Can you *Please. Just. Come. Here?*'

Chapter 2

Why hadn't she carried her little pleasure-pouch with her? She couldn't possibly go home to get it and risk bumping into a disintegrating Violet. Walking the streets alone, all spruced up and sober, was no fun at all. High, Neera could watch paint dry and be entertained. At least the streets on this side of town were not splattered with faeces. Dodging dog droppings was one of the first things she had mastered after arriving in Paris. The number of dogs in her neighbourhood, which Neera called chi chi boo boo for all its bourgeois affectations, was ridiculous. And all the owners had, most definitely, signed a secret treaty that it was some invisible person's job to pick up after their four-legged darlings. The affluent areas, it struck Neera, were the dirtiest in Paris. Everyone was too damned entitled to clean.

One time, her Jannie had sharply scolded an old, elegantly dressed biddy who had been turning a blind eye to the crapping of her yapping chihuahua. Apologizing, she'd creaked down to scoop up the cause of his scorn. But the crackle of her dry, fragile bones had made both Neera and Jannie turn purple with embarrassment for telling her off. Later, they had placated themselves with the argument that there is an age appropriate for everything and those who couldn't bend for their beasts should not be legally allowed to have any. They never, however, told off another *caca*-criminal again.

Were the streets of Mumbai this filthy? She couldn't say. The only place she—or anyone from her social standing, really—had ever walked was either on private driveways and treadmills or in privately cleaned lawns. It's true, she hadn't always belonged to this strata of society. Those early days of taking rickshaws, trains and buses in Mumbai were nothing but soft-focussed flashbacks to her now. It was so easy to move up in life and then fondly reminisce about how you got there from your delicately scented, air-conditioned tower without the faintest memory of the smell, heat and distress of the process. Anyway, other than the garbage, Paris was a walker's delight. It was wonderful that she could walk everywhere in this urban jungle. If only she could find somewhere she needed to be tonight...

It was not the first time in this city that Neera had nowhere to go. Sure, she had a social life and knew plenty of people—they all ticked a tightly segregated functional box. Her let's-have-a-coffee friend. Her meet-at-a-museum friend. The I-need-some-local-advice friend. Gossip-and-window-shopping friend and try-the-new-CrossFit-class friend. Trending-restaurant-dinner-date-couple friend. Well, at least she wouldn't be needing the last one any more. That box had been buried. Jannie had been her only all-weather-everything-except-getting-stoned-together friend. She smiled at how he ticked all her boxes.

That was the first time she'd thought of him without a stabbing pain in her chest. *Is that it? Am I over the death of the love of my life?* She waited. No pain, no sadness. She was one cold, heartless bitch. Sorry Eckhart, she knew she was supposed to be more mindful of the words she used to speak about herself. Right now, though, all she wanted was for her heart to bleed.

But what did that even mean? Wasn't the heart always bleeding? Its job was to push blood into the body. If it was beating, then it meant blood was flowing out of it, into her veins; in spite of her best efforts, her heart hadn't yet learnt to stop. Her head flooded with these nonsensical, ludicrous thoughts. Without her magic cigarettes, on lovely, lonely nights like these, her brain behaved like a caged hamster trying to outrun his burning metal wheel. If she couldn't smoke herself to a more functional rhythm, she needed to get off that wheel by finding something to distract herself with.

She longed to be officially confined again so she wouldn't be faced with the predicament of having to create a social life out of boxes. She pulled out her trusty rectangle and swiped right on a dozen potentials, waiting to be swiped back. Maybe she could call a dealer. Dressed the way she was tonight? Maybe not.

`Evr   hd   ur   brns   fckd   on   a   péniche?` her phone flashed.

Maybe she'd missed the memo that foregoing vowels was a prerequisite for this app. What did 'brns' stand for? Buns? Brains? Bum? Bush? Was it a new-gen word or a concept she was unfamiliar with? Was it a typo, if the vowel-allergic could be credited with such a mistake?

Between two large oval skylights in a wood-panelled room on the boat were two mirrors, designed like portholes and strategically angled to capture the bed and its occupiers. Neera caught the reflection of her own eye and the back of a perfectly shaped blonde head between her legs. Her Lure ensemble lay discarded in a heap on the floor, the only clutter in this temple of minimalism.

The péniche was on the smaller side, but the Seine glimmered through its large rectangular windows, illuminating the straight clean lines of the interior. The blonde Brit tasting her, who lived on this boat, had repainted everything, including the floorboards, a pristine white. The monochromatic furniture was simple in form, functional and looked expensive. The only colours permitted were those of nature being let in through the windows and the bamboo he had planted all around his terrace deck. He worked as a global sustainability manager for some European cement company, loved his job and was the most positive person Neera had ever had inside her. She'd been with him once or twice before, but this was the first time she had met him on his houseboat or noticed how tanned he was. He was also kind and came with an extra dry brand of English wit. At another time, in another place, she might have fallen for him. But, right now, she couldn't remember what had made her come here.

His tongue and fingers were taking slow expert turns exploring her. Technically they were hitting the right spot and seemed to be enjoying themselves, but there was no reaching her tonight. She watched herself watching herself for a while. The gel on her short hair had lost its potency, making her hair unevenly spiky again, and she looked even more tired than she felt. She gently pushed his head away. He wiped his mouth on the back of his hand, kissed her belly and came to lie next to her.

'My boat's not rocking your boat,' he said cheesily.

'Have you got something to drink, Dan?'

'It's Dave, and yes, I do,' he replied without taking the least bit of offense. 'G&T, vodka, tequila, champagne and blinding white orgasms—all freely available for room service tonight, Madame.'

'A double vodka will do me just fine, Dan... Dave.' She watched him walk towards a concealed cabinet, without bothering to conceal his very erect penis. 'Actually, do you mind just bringing the bottle and some ice please?'

Neither did they end up having sex, nor did she take him in her mouth, nor loan him her hand to relieve his throbbing blood rush. But he didn't complain and continued to lie next to her, comfortably flashing his discomfort. She traced the tips of her fingers along his penis and thought of her husband—of his impeccably formed organ; how the girth exactly fit in her mouth as if a Japanese artisan had measured and custom-made them to dovetail.

Dave explained how Zero Mass Water, made of sunlight and air, could solve the world's water shortage. They lay there naked: she with the memory of her husband, he with the excitement of the cutting-age technology; she drank from the bottle, he crunched the ice in his mouth and kissed her; the next thing she knew, he was carrying two white cups of lemongrass soy chai and a bowl of watermelon sprinkled with pistachio, acai and goji berries. He had showered but was still naked. She looked up at the round mirrors: she was soiled and still naked.

Neera stayed on the boat sunbathing till the day dissolved into night and it seemed pointless to make her way home. He talked about the clear miracle of tiny forests in urban spaces, and she drank her way through all the clear liquor in his hidden closets.

'Do you need to charge your phone?' he asked, handing her a T-shirt made of the softest, ethically sourced, organic cotton.

'No,' she said too quickly. 'I need to unplug from the world for a minute and your péniche seems like the perfect place. Do you mind?' Her words came out slurry, which surprised her more than him.

He answered by kissing her in a way that couldn't be more welcoming, making her kiss him back with all of her, till she had to pull away to throw up all over his white armchair.

Dave forced a few pieces of pumpernickel bread and vegetable broth into her before tucking her in. When she woke up, she was surrounded by primeval whites and clean smells all over again.

'I'm in a Zoom conference,' Dave mouthed from a pull-out desk she hadn't noticed the previous day. He muted himself, switched off the camera and crawled up to her. He was naked under his smart linen shirt—underwear seemed pointless when working from home. He lightly nibbled on her neck, took in her scent. 'I put a fresh towel for you in the bathroom. I'll be done in ten–fifteen minutes, then maybe we can go for a walk and grab some lunch.' He returned to his conference about the benefits of co-processing and how to make waste the main source of energy.

How long had Neera been asleep? Why was Dan, no Dave— *his name was Dave, damn it*—tolerating her? She wasn't going to question it as long as he didn't make her go home: a home that was filled with the presence of her needy friend and the absence of her Jannie, whom she could smell as if he was lying next to her. She closed her eyes to inhale his musty familiarity and lay a little longer in the bed of this benevolent bohemian eco-warrior. She felt like her body weighed ten tons and had been cut open from the jugular notch to her uterus without morphine.

The pain was back and it was rendering her immobile. With great determination, she moved to lie on her side, curling herself into a foetal position, imagining her dead husband's arms cradling her, pulling her closer as he spooned her from behind. She tucked her cold feet between his knees, resting her neck on his bicep as his arm wrapped around her shoulder. His breath tickled her ear and when she turned to kiss him, his full head of hair flopped rakishly to one side.

Every cell in her body felt the lack of him. Five years had not been enough. They were nowhere near enough. They were wrong, those wise old proverb writers—it was better to have never known love like this than to have had it wrenched from her. She wished she had never met him. Now that he was gone, she could see all the invisible holes he had filled. Now, without him, she was so full of his void that she was going to burst and overflow.

Chapter 3

To be dismissed because she was not technically an adult was even more infuriating than being locked out. What exactly had Vee meant? Her words looped in Dasha's head. *Honey, it's not about you. I'm just very, very angry at myself. I need to be surrounded by adults who can understand.* Adults who can understand. Adults. Not about you. Very, very angry. Adults.

When Dasha had tried to object, Violet had cut across her. 'I don't have the energy to explain and I don't want to drag innocent you into my mess. Okay, my baby?'

Dasha understood being ditched better than most. More importantly, she was the only one who cared enough to be here—didn't that count for something? Where were the adults? Where exactly were Violet's 'grown-up' friends when she needed them, huh? Neera refused to answer her phone, which wasn't new. She had never once answered Dasha's calls or spoken to her apart from asking her to pass the salt or stop being so naïve. Rosel had been sent somewhere out of Paris to look after someone's ageing parent who was resolutely refusing to die or some such thing. One was never sure of what Rosel was up to, partly because Rosel's idea of conversation was listening and partly because she mumbled and muttered half-baked information when she did speak. And Benjamin? He was the worst of them all.

He had only showed up because Dasha had begged him to. And then when Violet had finally let them in, he'd had the nerve to ask her to step out. What kind of boyfriend was he anyway, when he needed to be told by a 'child' that his girlfriend was falling apart? Why couldn't she go with them wherever they were going?

She didn't want the keys to Violet's apartment. She wanted her.

Adjusting a lilac-coloured bee-hive wig that would've made Amy Winehouse's hair look limp, Dasha moped around her favourite indoor space, opening and closing drawers, unsure what to do with herself. She opened the little cabinet above Violet's sink and discovered a pharmacy.

There were Estrace pills, Féminité patches and Profem, which looked like gummy bears but claimed to be pure progesterone, promising change. Then, there was a row of testosterone blockers—Blend MHB féminiseur, Elevate and Changes Gel Modifier. The final shelf had bottles lined up in ascending height, the labels on them leaving little to the imagination—BustMaxx (dissolvable tablets), ProCurves Plus cream, Lady Skin, Transfume eau de Parfum, Vitamin D for feminine hair, Vitamin C, Omega-3, Keratin hair enhancer, Collagen Exxxtra polish... All the jars and bottles seemed most definitely contraband, undoubtedly expensive but procured from some dodgy dealer on the Internet.

Some of the pink and rainbow-coloured tubes, with descriptions like 'male to female spray', seemed even more juvenile than she had been accused of being. There were very few things in life that made Dasha, the overconfident oddball, uncomfortable, but this cabinet was one of them. Maybe it was because her prying had spelled out in bold letters something she'd pretended not to read.

The fact that Violet had been born male and had become female made her the wondrous creation she was, and as far as Dasha was concerned, she was akin to the force that governed the universe itself—a universe where nothing meant anything without duality. Yin and yang wasn't merely a concept where light existed only because of darkness or winter had no meaning without summer, its very heart was governed by opposition; Violet *embodied* it better than most—the inseparability of contradiction by being an amalgamation of both male and female energies. It is what made Dasha believe that you couldn't be good without simultaneously being bad, you couldn't be happy if you weren't sad and you needed to be cruel to have kindness. The essential necessity of these opposing forces made existence possible. And it also made it easier to explain her devoted father's desertion. It had never occurred to her that Violet perhaps didn't want this duality; that by becoming Violet, she had rejected it.

She was not ignorant, and yet, she'd never thought to consider Violet's daily dilemma of having to supplement her body to be the gender and person she was and not the sex she was born with. Coming face to face with proof that her idol was not a totally natural phenomenon but a calculated creation from a cupboard full of randomly sourced pills made her want to smash the cabinet. How dare that cabinet challenge her perspective? Those bottles and pills were openly mocking Dasha. They—the adults—were right. She was nothing more than a stupid naïve child and better left behind. She ran out of the apartment so fast that she didn't see the duffel bag on the floor and tripped over it, only to be caught by a skinny girl dragging a suitcase with a broken wheel.

'Pardon, pardon, I shouldn't have left my bag there.'

'It's not your fault,' said Dasha, 'I wasn't looking.' Then seeing the girl's oversized bags, she asked, 'Are you coming or going?'

'I'm coming,' she answered. 'I just got back from my parents' because they're finally opening the university again. I live on the *top* top floor and—'

'You are the girl who infected Monsieur Allard,' screeched Dasha.

'Excuse me?'

'Do you have corona? I mean *did* you have corona? Did you have any symptoms, like loss of taste or fever or anything? Did you get tested?'

The girl was taken aback by the interrogation.

Blocking her way, Dasha persisted. 'Please simply tell me:

did you test positive or not? I need to know if you had Covid.'

Cornered and wide-eyed, the girl managed to answer, 'No. Not that I know of. I'm fine. Can I enter now?'

'Sorry, so sorry,' Dasha said, realizing how crazy she must sound. 'Let me help you.' Then, as an afterthought, she asked, 'When you left this building, did you use the lift via the fifth floor?' Dasha was sure as hell not going to help lug two heavy bags up a hundred flights of stairs if she was barking up the wrong tree.

'I guess I did, but I'm not sure what that's got to do with you,' said the perplexed girl.

Dasha smiled, threw the strap of the overstuffed duffel bag around her shoulders. 'Come on, then. You are just the girl I was looking to help.'

༄

Benjamin held Violet's hand, which felt shaky and small today. She guided him through all the usual spots where she and Raphaël met. This was the third day of their search and Violet was dwindling by the day. She squeezed Benjy's palm. The touch of his skin reassured her, repeating silently that he's got her, that he was not going to allow her to slip away.

From the moment he had forced his way into her studio, he had worked to remind Violet of who she was, who she had fought hard to become and how she was the ultimate queen of courage. Friends with history are memory-keepers, and the best ones know which cards to hold up and when, which memories need reiteration, which ones can be discarded and the occurrence of which ones must be denied as mere mirages.

Dasha had watched helplessly as Benjy had jolted Vee into action. He had been like a mother coaxing their child to step back and not jump off the roof of the Montparnasse Tower—he had instinctively know when to cosset and when to chastise. She could've never imagined this side to a man she'd regarded as invertebrate creampuff. After all, how could she have guessed that, as a boy, he'd learnt to mother himself and his younger brother because the person meant to fill that role had been repulsed by them?

Violet spotted him near the play area with swings at the far end of Jardins du Trocadéro. Raphaël was bending down, shirtless, shampooing his hair under what looked like a Wallace fountain. She looked away. Her gaze felt like an invasion on his private ablutions and her nerves were making it hard to breathe.

She focussed on a piece of trivia Dasha had imparted: more than a hundred-and-fifty years ago, when Napoleon was captured and Paris was ruled for a few months by a group of wrangling revolutionary citizens, a philanthropic foreigner—who was nonetheless Parisian at heart—named Richard Wallace built these green wrought-iron drinking water monuments all over the city. Water became so scarce and expensive back then that the poor preferred to drink and give their children alcohol, which was cheaper. Dasha had said, 'When I become rich and famous, my act of compassion for this crazy city will be to build wine fountains and vodka taps for the poor. At least then poverty and the cold will become more bearable.' Violet had certified it as an ingenious Smirnova scheme.

This Wallace fountain, if it was that, now had a bulky soap dispenser of the same shade of green attached to its side—a Covid measure the mairie had undertaken to ensure the French made friends with hygiene. Her friend from the street had never been hygienically challenged and the suds sliding down his bare back were proof.

She cleared her throat. 'That's him,' she said softly to Benjy, her voice drowned under the squeals of the kids running with no purpose other than joy.

The two of them waited, out of sight, till he was dry and dressed again.

Benjy let go of her hand and gently nudged her forward. Violet stood in front of Raphaël. He stopped gathering his things and looked at her. Time stopped, just as it had the first time. She looked into his incredible eyes, the colour of her father's cherished Islamic flag. Children rushed by. He didn't move and she didn't dare either.

'*Salut*,' Violet said.

'*Salut*,' he replied as if talking to a stranger. Maybe she had reduced herself to one.

'Are you okay?' she asked. 'I shouldn't have...' She wasn't sure how to complete that sentence. 'I'm sorry. It doesn't cover how I feel or how I made you feel, but it's all I have.'

He stood for a long time, looking at her blankly. She thought she could hear the cogs of his brains working, hopefully, trying to lift the fog and breach the divide.

'It is what you have,' he said at last. 'I have this bag. It is what I have.' He neatly folded his damp towel along with his shampoo and toothbrush into a plastic bag, placed it inside his rucksack, looked around to check he hadn't left anything and said, '*Merci, bonne journée*,' as if someone had just given him some loose change, and walked out of the park.

Benjamin saw from a distance what Violet had missed up close. Raphaël didn't owe anyone for the few things he owned. He was a person who wanted to be seen and not be shown, who lived in a world that confused him. He was as attracted to and intrigued by this upright man as his girlfriend was, but he knew that the only way to be with such a man was to walk along his path without wanting to change it. Wordlessly, he took the hand of his stupefied girlfriend and led her home.

Chapter 4

The gold gleamed off Pheme, the goddess of gossip, as she restrained Pegasus. Perched on her high column, her trumpet announced to the city and to Neera in particular—*Your secrets are never safe with me, I, who live for rumour and babble, hear all and tell all.* They stopped in the middle of the world's most unapologetically ornate bridge, Pont Alexandre III, with all its statues and angels looking down at them. Neera felt queasy. The cherub astride a sea monster pointed his trident at her and smirked. Pegasus flapped his wings violently.

'What's going on?' asked Dave, offering her some water.

'I think I drank too much and ate too little last night again.'

'No, what's really going on?' he persisted. 'I know self-destruction when I see it. Been there, bought the T-shirt and vowed never to go back or to let a drunk Indian with quirky hair get stuck there.'

Neera snorted a smile. 'It seems I bought a one-way ticket to Wreckville and then lost my wallet.'

'There's plenty who'll give you a free ride home,' he said with a sympathetic smile. 'All you have to do is stick your thumb out.' He took her hand, folded her fingers into a fist, leaving her thumb sticking out and extended her arm like a hitchhiker as passers-by looked on. His intention had been to make her laugh, but instead she crumpled to the ground, collapsing right in the middle of the bridge in a flood of tears.

∽

Dressed in Jean-Paul's favourite papaya and sangria-coloured wrap-dress, her long hair carefully tied up in a messy topknot (just the way he liked it), Neera waited in front of her fully charged phone. The hospital had informed her, via Olivier, that he'd be out of critical care and ready to call sometime after the doctors had done their morning rounds. She was so grateful that her Jannie was famous and loved—she'd been hearing horror stories of ordinary sick Parisians having to wait for hours to get a ventilator and hundreds being told to stay home until they really couldn't breathe. Inadvertently, she found herself chanting the Gāyātri Mantra, a prayer of thanks to the Divine Creator, the only Hindu prayer she could remember from her childhood. Her mother had made her recite it every night before going to bed.

The last time she had recited it had been for Jannie when they had travelled down to the south. On an evening walking tour through a chateau in the medieval city of Carcassonne, they had stumbled upon a Caucasian couple performing it within the sky-scraping, Roman-built fortress walls. The pale man, wearing an Indian kurta–pyjama, had been strumming a sitar and chanting his own entrancing version of the Gāyātri Mantra. Meanwhile, the girl, sporting giant butterfly wings with flashing LED lights, had been going through some deeply ridiculous dance moves that could be attributed neither to the East nor the West and had required, possibly, less than zero skill. The effect had been hypnotic, and Neera, like everyone else watching, had found it impossible to pull away. Afterwards, her husband had asked for an in-depth explanation and translation of the sacred Vedic words.

That had been a few years ago now. Jannie had taken her on a three-week road trip from Paris to the south to discover France. She had never set foot in his country before running off with him. In fact, apart from short work trips to London, Dubai and Macau, she hadn't travelled out of India much at all. She knew the world and its great cities through her reading. She could navigate the streets and avenues of New York thanks to *The Fountainhead*; Russia had been brought alive to her through *Anna Karenina*;

Tales of the City had made her long for San Francisco; *Memoirs of a Geisha* had given her a scent of Kyoto and she had lived the life of a peasant in northern China reading *The Garlic Ballads*. But travelling with her husband, who seemed to be getting younger with every mile they put between themselves and Paris, was better than the best book she had read.

On a holiday, he was the opposite of a quartier-man— hungry for every experience, eager to be enthralled, keen to learn something new every day. Outside of his Paris hole, he behaved like an inquisitive bear cub who knew his time out of hibernation was limited. It's not that he hibernated in Paris; it was fairer to say that he had an invisible periphery surrounding his home that he refused to cross unless pressured, and that was because he was self-sufficient, having stocked his den with all that he needed. Now that she was travelling with him, Neera could see how he foraged and stored creative sustenance like a bear eating all day and night to bulk up before settling down for a long winter rest.

It bugged her that she couldn't remember whether it was on that repeat trip to Bordeaux or on their honeymoon that they discussed death. Every other detail from that king of nights was etched in her memory.

They were sitting on the wisteria-hemmed terrace of the double Michelin-star restaurant at the hotel, overlooking the vineyards in all their rustic glory. Wayward grape vines crept and climbed along the wooden pillars of the canopy to consort with the lavender-hued flowers. Neera felt like they had time-travelled directly into a Pissarro painting. Her Jannie toasted her with a big glass of the locally grown Château Smith Haut Lafitte, Grand Cru Classé from the Graves vineyard. Its leathery chocolate texture lingered on her tongue, and she felt worthy of that toast, of that hundred-and-eighty-euro bottle. She felt worthy of creation itself, proud and humbled to be part of its grandeur.

Life was pumping through them both, making them hot with desire for everything the world had created—and for each other, of course. They felt so alive that they spoke about death, how they would welcome it as part of life when it came and the details of the rituals they each wanted.

Neera wanted to be put through an electric crematorium or an incinerator, not because she was Hindu but because she was fire itself. He wanted to donate all his functioning organs to whoever would have them and then have whatever was left embalmed and preserved. They were making it up, of course, as they made their way through the bottle. She wanted him to scatter her ashes in a green patch of his choosing and then plant a clementine tree on top, so when he ate the fruit, she would become part of him. She also wanted to suggest that he smoke some of her ash in a big fat chillum—but it sounded too Keith Richards and she was more Mick Jagger, if anything, so she let it go.

Jean-Paul wanted her to keep one or both of his clavicles because the collarbone was an ideal-sized bone with a natural curve that made it easy to hold. If it was too creepy for her to keep in her handbag, she could have it framed and pretend it was a Palaeolithic relic when the hoity-toity lifestyle editors came around. They laughed so hard that the stuffy maître d'hôtel had the gall to tell them to keep it down. They took their unfinished second bottle to the room and made slow, fairy-tale-like love to celebrate living, dying and laughing together.

Hotel Caudalie, with its restaurants, its vinotherapy spa, its poetic rooms and its heated pool with art installed on the tiles at the bottom, was a definite repeat. And the Allards had done just that on their road trip. So, was the death talk on the first trip or the second? She made a mental note to ask Jannie—his superpower was information retention. He could cite Voltaire, Victor Hugo or some nothing Neera had said on the plane ride from India to France word for word. He often used Hugo's words to push away Neera's self-loathing and doubt—*The greatest happiness of life is the conviction that we are loved—loved for ourselves, or rather, loved in spite of ourselves.* Yes, her husband saw who she was and loved her so deeply that she, at last, stopped wanting to better herself as her well-intentioned mother had taught her to. His love was enough for her to begin to love herself just the way she was.

The phone hadn't rung and she was still chanting.

It was fitting that the only prayer she knew was the ode to Gāyātri, the Divine Mother. Neera's mother used to tell a mythological story she loved listening to: the story of how the Divine Mother, in the form of Savitri, outwitted the god of death to bring her dead husband back to life. *Why all these thoughts of death?* She reapplied her lipstick using her phone as a mirror. It rang.

'Olivier, hi. Can I call you back please? I can't talk now, I'm expecting Jean-Paul's call any minute.'

At first, she didn't understand his words. *Jean-Paul passed away this morning.* She didn't understand. Jannie was going to call. She was waiting. She had to hang up on Olivier. She was wearing his favourite dress. They were going to chat. He owed her that. For all these thoughts and talk of death, it hadn't once crossed her mind that he was going to die. Or perhaps it had and she had hustled it away till she could discuss it with him first. She was waiting for him to call. He had to tell her on which trip they had talked about their last rites.

'Breathing complications,' she repeated. 'Yes, uh-huh, yes. I see.' No, she didn't see. Where was the rewind button? The delete button? The phone was going to flash *My Jannie*, not *Dr Olivier Decoste*. She was the only one to call him Jannie, a nickname which came from *'jaan'*, a Hindi endearment that literally meant 'life'. *My Jannie, my life*. He loved this dress. He loved her hair, all neatly messy. If she hung up, he would call.

Chapter 5

In the Philippines, Andal was a rich person's name. So how had *she* ended up with it? Rosel looked around her narrow grey room on the top floor under the roof, the closeness of the walls making her feel cosy rather than cramped. It helped that she was small—more than that, she had never occupied too much space in the world. When Dasha stood in the middle of the room, she could stick her head out of the sloping window on the ceiling without standing on her toes. As neat and organized as Violet was, Rosel knew that this room couldn't contain her personality. And Neera, despite being slight, would simply refuse to go through the door.

For Rosel, the room was large enough to house all her biggest desires. It was a room that dared her to imagine living with her son one day. She was careful not to entertain the thought too often, for she needed to survive, but, on some nights, when she lay in bed, looking up at the slanted window, humming a timeless tune, she would allow herself the luxury to dream. River Girl, aka Julie, had been right—hope was indeed an irresistible emotion.

This room had given her the three women, and without Len—or access to anyone else from the Philippines in this foreign land—they were all the friends she had. The three had given her the confidence, push, ultimatum or whatever it was that made her own her truth.

Besides, Paris was slowly opening up. Len and Julie had already caught up with Rosel and her face, and could show up any day at the Decoste household armed with Rosel's lies. In the Philippines, she'd be handed to the authorities, and she dreaded to think what her fate would be in Kuwait, a country where she had stood for hours on end, on more occasions than she cared to remember, holding shopping bags, not being allowed to sit in the restaurant as her employer finished her long, leisurely ladies' lunch.

Her second act of bravery needed her to be more courageous than her escape—she had had nothing to lose then, no dreams would've shattered and died if she'd been caught jumping out of the kitchen window. Now, at stake was the love of three of the sweetest kids, a family that allowed her to sit and eat with them, monthly money to send home and a room packed with possibilities.

Rosel steeled herself as her boss slipped out of the children's room that climactic night back in July.

'Len, what are you still doing here?' asked Madame Decoste, adjusting her eyes to the light. 'I thought I told you I'd put the kids to sleep and you can wash up and go.' Colette was irritated. She didn't relish the idea of the nanny having unmonitored free time around her husband—or rather her husband being unmonitored when the nanny was free.

'Madame, I need to talk to you about something, if you have the time,' Rosel said submissively, her confidence ebbing with every syllable.

Colette seethed soundlessly. Had her incorrigible husband hit on this poor pygmy again? The housekeeper stays to cook dinner for *one night* and Olivier's already at it. Just when she thought things were getting better between them. They'd been chatting and sharing and smiling and been making love at odd hours of the day. They had become a team again. Why must he always barf all over her plans? Red-hot fury started to bubble inside her. This time she would kill him with her bare hands.

'Sir, please could you join also?' requested Rosel.

Colette clenched her teeth, wishing she had a bone to gnaw on like Milo in the corner.

Olivier put down his book and came into the kitchen. 'What's up, Len?'

'I'm not Len,' whispered Rosel.

As Rosel explained the circumstance and details of her treachery, Colette visibly relaxed and smiled at her innocent husband before realizing it was not the appropriate response to the nanny's confession. With effort, she twisted her face into a false grimace, which was hard to sustain because the bubbles of fury had burst into a rain of relief. Her husband looked confusedly at Rosel. He was always slow on the uptake, but this was not the time to be annoyed at his IQ. He was not dallying with the domestic worker: this was a good thing! The domestic worker was not who she said she was: this was a bad thing. Not the catastrophe she had expected but not pleasant either.

'This is awful. I'm in shock,' said Olivier. 'What you did is unforgivable.'

'I know, Sir.' Rosel's face felt bruised from the bashing she had received from Julie earlier that day outside the French immigration and integration office. It had knocked some reality back into her. Her happily ever after was a fib and something she had to remedy before living another day. She had rushed off without talking to Violet or Neera. Rosel knew she needed the momentum of shame and anger to propel her into confessing.

'I didn't know what to do. There are so many people depending on me, Sir. And I had no money to send them. I wanted Danilo to continue school, it was impossible to get a job as Rosel, and I didn't think my plan would work but then Madame hired me,' she didn't dare stop for a breath in case the pause made them call the police, 'What I did was wrong and you and Madame and the kids have been so kind and I was going to tell you on the first day itself, but I got scared. Your family became home to me and—'

'This is fraud and completely unacceptable,' said Olivier, his voice trembling with anger.

'Yes, Sir. I cheated you but I'm not a cheat. I've never done something like this and never will again. I was only thinking of my son: I really wanted to have a chance at earning, of giving him a life,' said Rosel. Truth is the ultimate power and now that it was on her side, she felt less and less scared. If they sent her to jail, so be it.

'Okay, everyone calm down for a second. I need to think,' said Colette, marvelling at the might of this meek midget. For all her determination and drive, would Colette have risen to the challenge of feeding a dozen desperate kin? She couldn't so much as remember the last time she had been kind to her sick father. Yes, for her kids, she would slay monsters or, more likely, tell whatever lies that needed to be told.

Additionally, it would be insincere to claim she hadn't misrepresented herself or her company to get ahead at work. Didn't everyone who wanted to advance do it? This very morning, she had vulgarly hyped and oversold what was possible to her Dubai clients. She would do the same or more to the Chinese tomorrow. It was for survival—they were the only ones spending on fashion in this diseased market. The end justified the means and all that, she thought. And, more pertinently, Olivier was not seducing the nanny.

'"Rosela"—that's how you pronounce your name, right?' asked Colette but didn't wait for the answer. 'Go home. Let Olivier and me talk this through, then we'll take it from there.'

'Thank you, Madame. And I am very, very sorry.'

Then, remembering that she had to be up early to attend a conference with the Chinese and knowing her husband would ask her a hundred maddening questions of where everything was if he was left in charge, Colette added, 'Rosela, can you come in the morning at the usual time to feed and take the kids to school? We will talk after, okay?'

'Yes, Madame. Goodnight,' said Rosel, and left to spend a sleepless night, not knowing if it would be her last, in the narrow room of hope.

It was not until two terrifying days after Rosel's confession that Colette finally had time to deal with her domestic situation. Olivier and she had discussed it in bed—or rather she had told Olivier that this was not the time to make a destitute woman jobless. Anyway, now that they had confined together, Rosel was part of their unit, their responsibility. And hadn't she proved herself to be an unexpected godsend in dealing with Neera's loss?

Five-and-a-half months later, Colette still couldn't bring herself to say that her precious Jean-Paul was dead. She blamed it on the fact that he, a jewel in France's creative crown, didn't get a suitable send-off. If she'd got a chance to say a proper goodbye to her friend, her mentor, her chosen father, she might have felt differently and been able to come to terms with his demise.

The funeral, if it could even be called that, brought more grief than consolation. Olivier and devoted Ludovic tried their best, but the virus was so frightening back then that no one was willing to budge or push. Only six direct relatives of the deceased were allowed, including the spouse. Jean-Paul had one sister living somewhere near Grenoble and poor Eric was stuck in Toronto. The hospital wanted the infected remains disposed of quickly. Olivier managed to get the hospital and burial ground to overlook the fact they were not blood relations—that was the only concession made.

On that horrible day, they ticked the 'compelling family reason' box on their digital self-attestation form to be allowed outside. Jean-Paul's body had been bagged, zipped, disinfected, rebagged and placed in an airtight box before they arrived.

There was to be no ritual washing or mortuary make-up and definitely no kissing a cold, rubbery cheek. The workers of the funeral home were in makeshift protective gear and everyone else had to maintain a two-metre distance from the box and from each other. When Colette saw Neera step out of the taxi, holding on to some tall black person of indeterminate sex, she broke all the rules and ran to hug her. Neera looked ghostlier than ever and her body felt limp and lifeless in Colette's embrace.

'Can I not see him before they lower him?' were the only words that came out of her mouth. Salty tears of shame streamed down Olivier's face as he shook his head in response. He couldn't bring himself to say no.

Beyond them, a priest in a black bandana-style mask and cleaning gloves, along with the funeral director, were present to lay the celebrated son of France to rest. The stripped-down service was live-streamed, so that Eric and the world could virtually attend. The director read out tweets of condolences, one from the President himself. A short prayer was said and, in twenty unbearably brief minutes, Jean-Paul was returned to the earth.

Colette suggested she'd take care of a memorial service at her church, which was open and would permit a small group of mourners. Neera had no response, so Colette decided to bring it up again when things were more normal.

Frankly, it was Colette who needed the service. Rituals helped people grieve. Unless you grieve, you can't heal. It would be healing to say the Lord's name together in remembrance of the beloved one they'd all lost and bear testimony to each other's sorrow. It would bring comfort to be with a group that loved him as much as she did and look lovingly at his framed photo by the altar. She wanted to sit on the hard bench next to Neera, hold her hand and weep listening to his eulogies. The only way to bid goodbye to a person who was no longer there was by commiserating with the people he left behind. It felt essential to remember him en masse to move on.

Colette's hurt couldn't compare to Neera's. She was aware of that and, in any case, the endless demands of her job, her housebound kids and her fragile marriage were welcome distractions. And what did Neera have? A swanky vacant duplex full of her dead husband that she was trapped in, back then by legal decree, for twenty-three hours a day.

Colette made it a point to call her daily, till one day Neera simply stopped answering. She had offered to lend Neera Milo for company, but the latter thanked her and declined. With no other options left, the nanny—Len, Rosela, whatever her name was—had been ordered to check on Neera before she came to work and was sent home early each day to do the same. She was instructed to force her way into spending Saturday and Sunday with Neera under the pretext of cleaning the apartment. Colette couldn't have possibly known that the two had already become well acquainted and that every minute not spent at the Decoste home was now spent helping Violet put out fires ignited by Neera—sometimes quite literally.

That was that—the decision was made. Rosela/Len would be shown good old Christian mercy and was to stay. If for nothing else but to reward the guts it had taken her to confess the way she had. As penance, however, she'd be sent to look after the dying father Colette wished dead. Two birds, one stone—this is how you solve a problem. Hermès was lucky to have her.

'Her name is Rosel,' was all Olivier had had to say.

To Rosel, it sounded like the words were coming from Mother Mary herself.

'Do not judge, and you will not be judged. Do not condemn, and you will not be condemned. Forgive, and you will be forgiven,' incanted Colette, before adding, 'Do not dare double-cross me or my family again or you will see hell on earth itself.'

'Never, Madame, never. I swear on the Holy Spirit and on my son's life,' cried Rosel, bending her tiny body so low that Colette thought the nanny was prostrating herself in prayer to her. And, honestly, she didn't mind being hailed as the redeemer.

Chapter 6

That night, Rosel heaved the tall metal cabinet from the corner of her room to the top of her bed, climbed up on it, stuck her head out of the slit on the ceiling, and sang to the night sky: 'I am Rosel Andal. I am poor but I own a rich person's name. My room is small but my dreams are big. Small room, big dreams. My room, my dreams. Dreeeaammss. I don't own my room, but I own my dreams. Big dreams. Dreeeaammss!' The words came easily, and on and on her song went.

The stars must've been pleased because she swore she heard them serenade her in return.

'Will you shine for me?' she sang back.

This time, it was the sky that answered back in a baritone. 'If I make it to see another night, I'll ensure they do.'

'You promise?'

Then, a hand reached through her window. She grabbed it and it heaved her up.

The hand was attached to a young black man, straddling the narrow rectangular chimney on the slanting roof. He budged back, making room for her in front of him.

'Oh!' Rosel gasped, 'You can see the Eiffel Tower from here!'

'That you can,' said the man, whose name was Victor, but who felt utterly defeated by life tonight.

They sat in silence, astride one of the brick chimneys that gave the city its unique skyline, looking at the metalled marvel, till Rosel asked, 'Do you sit here often?'

'Only when I'm thinking of jumping off.' He was not being facetious.

Being trapped in a small, damp box with an even smaller hole to look out of, with nothing to do and nowhere to go had brought him to this moment, with this sentiment, on this chimney. But as he had taken what he had believed would be his last long breath in, he had heard an angel sing. The voice had pulled out his heart, held it in its hands and had taken it to the well of hope, dipping it again and again, till hope spread through the length of his limbs, making him forget why he'd climbed onto the chimney. It was at that moment that Rosel had heard the sky speak.

Five months ago, Victor didn't have time to pee, rushing between his management course across town, waitering job in the brasserie down the road and his internship in La Défense. Back then, the grey box he called home was a welcome refuge to rest his exhausted body for a few hours, shower and be out again.

The course had since gone online. He never had Wi-Fi and now with the brasserie shut and the internship cancelled, he had no money to pay for 4G data on his phone and was about to run out of money for food. His room morphed into a coffin, threatening to trap and bury him alive. Tonight, his plan was to outwit the murderous cubicle and end it before the walls closed in on him. Instead, he found himself sitting on a chimney on top of the world with his singing saviour.

'This must be the best view of Paris,' said Rosel. 'All these days and nights, and I didn't know it was right above my head. This room just keeps on giving. Thank you for showing this to me.'

Victor said nothing. This was the first person Rosel had met in Paris who spoke less than her.

Suddenly, a million bulbs, like twinkling diamonds, began to sparkle up and down the tower in front of them. They did that every hour, on the hour, each day after dark. If this wasn't magic, she wasn't sure what was. She felt compelled once again to fill the silence the quiet boy left. 'What'll stop you from making that jump?'

Not all problems come with easy solutions. This one, in that moment, did. Rosel left her mobile with Victor every morning before going to work and brought him leftovers from Neera every evening before taking back her phone. And this simple nothing, for the time being, postponed his plans of a grand leap.

Rosel could never have imagined that the night she reclaimed her own name to become Rosel again, life would come full circle for her in the way it did. For that was also the night she channelled the real Len by helping a distressed stranger to return to life in his box-like room, just like she'd been helped to escape hers.

Many happy nights later, there was a knock on the door. No one ever knocked on Rosel's door.

'Where have you been?' demanded Dasha, barging in.

'I thought I told you. Madame Colette sent me to look after her father, in Sa-Klow.'

'Where?' asked Dasha, never having heard the name before.

'Sa-Klow, it's some place close to Paris. West, I think. I take a bus from the beginning of the forest of Bois de Boulogne.'

Dasha pulled out Google Maps, and after much deciphering and deducing, she found the suburb of Saint-Cloud.

'Rosel we really have to work on your pronunciation. It's Saan, with a long nasal sound, Clue like in a riddle or quiz—clue, k-l-oo not kl-oh. Get it?'

'Not really, but I'm fine the way I am,' said Rosel, surprising herself with her ever-growing confidence. 'You know we would've never met if I wasn't lost in pronunciation,' added Rosel, oblivious to the cleverness of her turn of phrase.

'What were you doing in Saint-Cloud? Is her father dying?' asked Dasha.

'No, I think that's the problem,' Rosel answered, uncharacteristically chatty after having spent five days with a man who only barked complaints in French. 'He's very old and everyone wants him to die or move into a care home, and he's refusing to do either. I went to relieve the wife for a few days, who's become a prisoner or a jailer—I don't think there's a difference because, in any case, she can barely step out till he's gone.'

'That sounds terrible,' said Dasha, who was far too young and protected to understand the inevitability of death.

'It's not so bad. I've had lots of practice of having plates thrown at me and of changing old people's diapers before I left the Philippines.'

'Eww. Do you want to come down and use my proper shower?' offered Dasha.

Rosel laughed and brought her fingers under Dasha's nose. 'No, I quite like the lingering smell of an old man's caca on my hands,' she teased. It was so easy to be silly with the girl who had pointed her in the right direction at the onset of her new life. Really, Dasha and the three kids were the only ones Rosel felt this spontaneous with.

'How was your show?' asked Rosel.

It'd been less than a week ago, and yet life had turned topsy-turvy.

'The best moment of my entire existence. I was fantastic—I mean the *show* was fantastic. Violet's dance was electric.'

'I'm so happy for you both,' said Rosel with a smile.

'No, no, no. Don't be happy, everything is a disaster now. Oh Rosel, you've missed so much. Raphaël, Vee's homeless dude, stole thousands of dollars' worth of clothes and ran away minutes before it all started, and so Violet locked herself in her studio and I called Benjy to help me get her out and they went crazy searching for him while I kept guard at the studio, and then they found him and he's pretending not to know Violet and I'm trying to convince Vee it's not her responsibility but she's super miserable, won't talk to me and it's not at all my fault and Benjy's gone off to photograph Raphaël, not sure how that's going to help anyone and Neera is missing, pouf! Completely vanished,' she stopped to take a breath as she built up to her climax. 'And I have solved the mystery of Monsieur Allard's death.'

Rosel didn't know how one solves an open-and-shut case of catching an all-pervading, deadly virus, so she was all ears.

Once Dasha ruled out the lightweight with the overweight bags, she became a detective possessed. The shadow of doubt that Vee's vile cabinet had cast on her *Weltanschauung*, the sullying of someone she venerated, was quickly forgotten. Blessed be the young, for they shall forever have access to selective forgetfulness! What set Dasha apart and continuously redeemed her was her acute awareness that it was okay not to be okay. Normalcy was a fallacy in her world—not one person around her had ever felt normal. After the initial blow, her discovery in Violet's apartment had only helped confirm this personal axiom: nobody was a hundred per cent complete, so it was futile to want to feel whole. Then she'd stumbled, quite literally, upon her next mission. And this time, it would not be allowed to slip away.

That awful afternoon when her father had left, she'd been too slow to comprehend the words he was uttering. The picture his words were painting was completely alien—her brain couldn't connect speech to tangible objects like another man, departure, rejection, heartbreak... If she had understood, she would've said something, *anything*. Even saying 'Papochka' might have halted him. She made a promise to herself after that: to be sharpest person in the room. Always.

It wasn't hard to find Jean-Paul Allard's agency online. They directed her to his accountant and manager, Ludovic Cohn, who refused to entertain Dasha's inexplicable inquiry into the matter of his client's whereabouts in the late March lockdown. Then she showed up at his office door. *Who'd let her into the building?*

How did she discover the digi-code to get into his wing? It very quickly became obvious, however, that he would not be the one doing the questioning.

Introducing herself as Neera's best friend and proving it with an ID card with an address as her neighbour worked like the golden ticket into Willy Wonka's highly guarded chocolate factory.

Ludovic ushered her into a café next to his office and bought her an early lunch. It was fortuitous she was here: he needed to break some complicated good news to Neera, and it had been impossible to get hold of her all week. And in any case, it was best if the news was delivered via a friend. The accountant didn't think that it was any of this girl's concern that he would do anything in the world not to see Neera. As much as he was happy that Jean-Paul had found happiness with her—and he had never seen his long-term client-turned-friend happier—he was afraid of Neera, of her unnerving presence.

It didn't bother him in the least that she had always been civil but cold towards him. He had seen enough life not to expect enthusiasm from everyone, but there was something intimidating about her. Though she showed him adequate respect, her offhand comments often made him doubt his own wisdom. She was so unwaveringly on Jean-Paul's side that anyone who didn't share the intensity of her loyalty was quietly relegated to the opposing team. Yet he knew she knew that 'Ludovic could be trusted'. She loved his friend fiercely and Jean-Paul deserved nothing less. Still, he preferred to keep a safe distance and under all circumstances avoided meeting her sans Jean-Paul, which was now impossible given the devastating situation they were all in. So, he couldn't have been gladder to be lunching with this peculiar, pushy Russian, whom he could entreat to play go-between.

'Before I hear what you have to say Monsieur Cohn, I need a few answers about where Monsieur Allard had been and who he met before he contracted the virus. Did he continue working?

Was he filming on the sly?'

Ludovic was paid to simplify complex details for his clients, so he expertly cut to the chase. Against his advice, Jean-Paul had secretly remortgaged the apartment he lived in to complete his film. He had been sure he would be able to pay back the debt in double once his film released, except hardly anyone had wanted to buy it. Then, just after the confinement had been announced, he had insisted that Ludovic draw up papers to file for bankruptcy, so that Neera wouldn't end up with his debts. He had also wanted to transfer all his existing assets, shares, life insurance and royalties—no small amount—to a small holding company, co-owned by Neera and Eric, to avoid French inheritance tax that they might be burdened with on his death. Then, he had handwritten a carefully crafted new will, ensuring that neither Eric nor Neera would ever be in want of anything.

'He didn't want to wait till after the lockdown was over. He told me to bring a witness who could oversee the signing of the documents,' explained Ludovic.

'So Neera knew he met you?' asked Dasha.

'No, she would've never let him. He snuck out under the pretext of stretching his legs. I met him at the corner of his street. We weren't really permitted to, but there is—was—no saying no to Jean-Paul, and he sounded urgent.'

'Like he'd had a premonition of his own death?'

Ludovic was taken aback at the young girl's acuity. 'Yes, precisely what I thought in retrospect.'

'So he knew he was sick?'

'Except he wasn't. He most likely got corona because of this meeting,' he clarified. 'The witness I brought along was a twenty-something-year-old who was interning in our office before the lockdown. The boy called me the same evening to tell me that he'd been volunteering with the frontliners and the test they'd made him take earlier that week had come back positive—and since none of us had worn masks and all of us had shaken hands after the paperwork, we should be careful. Of course, I was livid with him for not sharing this information before we met. But there's only so much you can say to complacent young people who are convinced of their own infallibility,' he said, not noticing that he was talking to a member of the aforementioned class. 'Also, you can't play the blame game with a determined indiscriminate virus that no one can see. He got it, I didn't, who's to say why? What's the point in trying to track who infected who when it's in the very air we're all breathing?'

This accountant's aphoristic take on the virus tallied with her own. Yet Dasha could feel an anger bubbling up. 'But why didn't you tell Neera this?' she scolded. 'She's been blaming herself.'

'I didn't know that. It's definitely not her fault—I know how careful she was with Jean-Paul's health and well-being.'

'You should've told her.'

'I couldn't tell her about the meeting because he made me swear, and with him falling sick, I didn't end up filing for bankruptcy. So I didn't see the point.'

'Does that mean Neera will lose the apartment to debt?'

Once again Ludovic was struck by how two-steps-ahead this girl's mind was.

'No, and this is the good news,' he said with a smile. 'The unfinished film started a bidding war with the channels and the platforms posthumously. Overnight, an ignored film from an archaic producer has become the last work of a legend. I've sold it for an obscene amount of money. It will be released on TF1 on Christmas. Jean-Paul is having the last laugh like he always did.'

'How much is an obscene amount of money?'

'That's none of your business, young lady. But please will you convey all this to Neera? Tell her that stubborn old Jean-Paul was the only one responsible and he'd never want her to blame herself. And could you also give her these documents?

I've put everything in order and these are copies for her records,' he requested, handing her a big manila envelope full of papers. 'She can call me when she's had a chance to go through it all. No rush,' he concluded, before he bid this timely messenger a grateful goodbye.

Chapter 7

How long could she hide with Dave? It was coming up to a week.

He had slumped down with her on the overly decorated bridge, and they had sat there in her pool of tears till her eyes had run dry. Then he had wordlessly walked her back to his boat. He didn't seem to tire of salving her wounds, and the more he nursed her, the more lesions she revealed. She gave up the booze, soaking instead in his sagacious energy. They weren't having sex or being intimate, though they hung around mostly in the buff; clothes cover little when souls are exposed. Without her having to say it, he had understood: she simply couldn't be physical with her healer. Who would have thought that the app that didn't encourage vowels was capable of delivering this floating refuge, equipped with its own naked nurse?

The only time Neera had been on a péniche before was when Ricky Garcia took her to a large under-construction vessel called the *Louise-Catherine*. It was named after a radical artist, who had a lot of firsts attached to her name. Her female companion, and possible lover, bought it as an ode to the artist after she died; none other than Corbusier was commissioned by the artist to redesign it as a Salvation Army shelter for homeless men to use. And then it was destroyed in a flood.

When she and Ricky visited, it was in the midst of being renovated by Fondation Le Corbusier into a new cultural space. The last she heard, it had been ruined again by floods. Perhaps a péniche was not an ideal pit stop for a sinking woman.

'Grief comes in waves. Let it wash over you,' repeated Dave. 'Stop fighting it. Embrace it by becoming water itself. Make little difference between the ebb and the flow. Only then will you be able to coast along with the current.'

He let her cry without comment and rant without encouragement. He stood or sat near her, a witness to her loss, to her guilt, to her self-flagellation. At some point, she too had started watching her pain without identifying with it. *Was this detachment?*

What Neera forgot was that she was built to survive murkier seas—and she not only knew how to swim, but was a long-distance swimmer. With a trainer like Dave methodically deflating the float he had dotingly put around her to save her, she was finally ready to stop drowning.

'*Fluctuat nec mergitur*,' he said. 'That's the Latin motto of the city of Paris. It means "she is tossed by the waves, but does not sink". You belong to her now. She will drag you up and down and thrash you left and right, so enjoy the ride.'

She didn't deserve to be surrounded by lifeguards like him, and yet she attracted them because their title had no meaning without someone to rescue. After losing her chief rescuer, Jannie, hadn't Violet stepped in to keep watch and throw her a lifeline each time she had been about to hit the bottom? Vee knew how to stay afloat through strong currents. No one was going to be allowed to drown under her vigilance.

A cataclysmic memory clawed at her—her friend's impassive face as she had creeped in on Neera and the kitchen scissors.

Having been denied her last goodbye—her last chance to possess, preserve and frame a precious arte-part of her husband—Neera, in all her Hindu wisdom, took matters into her own hands. Perhaps more literally than was wise.

Dressed in a pure white chanderi silk sari, she printed out her favourite portrait of Jannie, found a suitable frame in the cupboard full of unopened gifts, played mantras for the death rituals she had got her parents to compile, lit sandalwood incense, smeared turmeric paste on the image of her husband's forehead, followed by her own, garlanded the frame with the wreath that Dasha had refashioned for the occasion, folded her hands in prayer and chanted along with her mother's voice coming from the speaker—'*Om Namo Narayana, Om Namo Narayana, Om Namo Narayana, Om Namo Narayana...*'

The three other women of rue des Diablesse had wanted to be present for the homespun memorial.

'I don't need witnesses to my grief, okay?' Neera had growled, and the subject had been closed for further discussion.

But Violet, being the mama bear she was, slunk in unnoticed at the appointed hour. The repeated chanting put Neera in a trance, or so it seemed to Violet. Neera realized that the small ceremony, attended by no one, was not enough to invoke any emotion. The ceremony was inadequate. Her mother's pitch didn't match hers, the unwitnessed rituals felt hollow and it all ended before she had a chance to lament the way she had imagined—wailing and mourning like widows ought to.

In ancient Hindu societies, she remembered, widows were made to shave their heads and beg for a living. Perhaps, it was a way to make them feel ugly and helpless. She reached for the large kitchen scissors and chopped off her tresses.

'Shall I help you get the back?' asked Violet softly, not wanting to startle her friend.

'I got it,' snapped Neera, and went to the bathroom to get her dead man's clippers.

Violet had not missed a beat in all the drama that Neera had starred in over the past few months. And with that realization, she got up from the white floorboards, found her long-discarded Lure ensemble, kissed her tanned saviour and walked home.

⌒

This was not the first and not the biggest mistake Violet had made. She had to forgive herself and move on.

'You can. Raphaël has,' Violet said to herself in the mirror, wanting to peel the skin off her face, crack open the bones, pull her eyes from their sockets and make them see who looked back. The only thing that stopped her was the fact that her mother lived on in her DNA. 'Put your face on, hold up your head and strut your stuff out of this studio. You are stronger than this. The blood of your ancestors pumps in your veins, lady.'

She thought of her yaay, who, like Mohammad Ali, got up after each face-splitting punch to give it back harder, with humour and pride. When sixteen-year-old Vafi resisted getting on the boat in the dark hours of the morning, insisting he would amount to nothing in France, so there was no point in leaving, his mother quoted Ali at him: 'If they can make penicillin out of mouldy bread, they can sure make something out of you.'

Why didn't she come with him? They had enough money to pay for both their passages. Granted, there wouldn't have been much leftover, but together they would've found a way to make it work in the land of liberty. Her work, she averred, in Saint-Louis needed her. She wasn't about to abandon everything she had fought her whole life for, just to watch her son wear a dress, no matter how good she was sure he'd look in it. Vafi must have been utterly desperate to have agreed to go without her—desperate to leave his life of easily discovered falsehoods, desperate for a chance to begin anew.

The idea came from her. *She* was the one who found and contacted her distant cousin in the not-so-touristy Parisian suburb of Saint-Denis and made arrangements. Vafi's mother, the woman who gave him life was willing to sacrifice her own so that he could have a chance at another life. There was as good a chance as any that he wouldn't make it across at all, but the risk was worth taking beacuse if he didn't get on that boat, it was guaranteed that he'd have no chance at all.

He shouldn't have gone to the Saint-Louis jazz festival dressed in his mother's turban and beads. Why did he have such a need to draw attention to himself? And what had his father's pious students been doing there in the first place? If they hadn't recognized him and called the *marabout*, the mother-and-son duo might have been free to carry on living how they had been for the two years since his father's gruesome death—the cheeriest years of both their lives. It had been straight after being chased that evening for not being straight that the police had started sniffing around. Or maybe it had merely been a question of time, for the years of 'moral panic' of impure men had already begun in Senegal.

For two years, the authorities had been content to claim that Professor Dembélé's murder had been a clear-cut case of a thieving intruder, but the boy in beads had made them think again. His mother wanted him out of this country where the truth was as dangerous as any lie, depending only on whose mouth it was coming from. She knew that if discovering the truth about the murder didn't kill her son, living a lie eventually would. The way she kissed him goodbye at the port said all this and more. But no, she wasn't right, he didn't have a better chance without her. There was no logic to that. But who could argue with his mother once she'd made up her mind? Her ancestors had tried and failed.

His mother was the only female member of her clan to be a griot, and the only woman in the village to go out with her grandfather to tell mythical stories of the land, play instruments and keep the past present. Her parents educated her as best as they could, and she went to a city school on the days it was her turn to wear the shoes she shared with her brother. The rest of the time she sat with her grandfather, under a three-hundred-year-old baobab tree, waiting for her turn to play the *kora*—the long-necked, twenty-one-string lute-harp attached to a calabash.

'Look here, girl, the calabash might seem like nothing more than a smooth round fruit, but it is the resonator,' her grandfather would say to her. 'The sweetness of the sound that comes out of the kora is entirely dependent on the quality of the gourd you choose.'

The two of them would spend their afternoons walking around fields as he inspected and rejected one hanging gourd fruit after another. Tapping his knuckles on their green surface, he'd be listening for something she couldn't hear, rubbing his hands around the circumference of the sphere, feeling for something she couldn't see. Finally, he'd settle for one—not necessarily the biggest, not always the roundest. It was this mystery that made the instrument mystical.

Having found the perfect gourd to work with, they'd sit once more under a baobab tree—everything of any import invariably took place under an awkward-shaped baobab—and the old man would push his small, sharp knife just short of halfway down the fruit and cut it into two unequal hemispheres, revealing the discoloured, viscous insides. She'd be ready with a spoon-like instrument to scoop out the sticky fruit from the bigger sphere, careful not to damage the interior or waste a single seed, her grandfather watching the whole time with hawk eyes. The hollowed gourd would then be scrubbed cleaned, polished and left out to dry for a couple of days in the sun.

It was her job to bury a stiff cowhide under a shallow layer of soil, pour water on it and leave it to soak overnight. Together, they would uncover the softened hide and she would watch, her smile bigger than her face could hold, as her grandfather would smear the animal skin with powdered baobab leaves and water to make it slippery and then expertly stretch it over the dried-out sphere.

'Pay attention, girl. You must ensure there are no wrinkles on the skin,' he'd say. 'Don't be fooled by how easy I'm making it look. Not everyone can make the sweetest sounding kora.'

The older man would force his keen apprentice's ear to the earth, instructing her to listen to the music of nature: the beetle collecting dung; the sound of soil soaking up water; the roots pushing their way to find deeper ground. This was the ear that Violet had inherited from her great-grandfather without ever meeting him. Even in her urban life in Paris, she heard music in everything: the scurrying of rats; the stream of piss of a drunken refugee; the ping of the lift she lived next to; the clatter of crockery; the rotation of the turnstile. Her yaay ensured that the memories of her ancestors ran in their blood. And blood didn't seem to care if it was a son or a daughter. Long before Violet started singing out stories of her soul, her mother proved that, sometimes, to be a keeper of tradition, one has to break from it.

Chapter 8

Looking fabulous, show ready and worthy of her mother's sacrifice, Violet stepped out of her studio to compete with the sun. It was time to stop hiding, and time to be her mother's daughter.

In front of her, in the middle of the road, a taxi screeched to a halt. The driver got out and started yelling at the woman he'd nearly hit.

'*Poutain! Imbécile! Tu veux mourir ou quoi?*'

Now there was a clamour of horns and irate drivers shouting, 'Fucker! Imbecile! You want to die or what?' at the taxi guy who'd decided to stop in the middle of the road at rush hour causing a traffic jam.

Oblivious to the chaos she'd caused, the woman with nine lives revealed herself to be none other than Neera running across the street to meet her friend. Violet allowed her to hug her for an implausibly long time before detaching herself.

'Typical Neera. Now that I don't need you, you show up.'

'Yup, guilty as charged. Can I go wherever you're going? If your outfit is anything to go by, it looks like it's going to be a party I don't want to miss.'

'Yes, you can. And no, you don't,' replied Violet, offering the crook of her elbow.

They walked in silence, comforted that they'd found their way back to each other.

'Vee,' said Neera, when the silence reached a natural end, 'What was it that I was supposed to be here for anyway?'

'To help me not let my mother down.'

'Oh dear, I would've been the worst choice for that,' laughed Neera. 'I've spent the better part of my life trying not to let my mother down, only to end up wanting to kill her. Luckily, my father was the most loving partner in crime I could've asked for.'

'My mother was my partner in crime,' said Violet. 'We killed my father.'

Neera didn't have to look at her friend to know she wasn't joking.

'I was only a middle-school student when I was cast as the lead in the Annual Day musical,' said Violet. 'It was a big deal. Only the seniors got speaking parts, a few "middlers" would make it to the chorus and the rest were either trees or soldiers or scene changers.

'My school was one of the most prestigious private schools in all of Saint-Louis. It had a fancy French name—Lycée Sainte Jeanne d'Arc—kind of silly to have the name of a female saint for an all-boys school. Still, the day I got admission in it was the only time my father was proud of me. Which, now that I think about it, was weird because it was a Catholic school and he was staunchly Muslim. I suppose it had to do with appearances: it was important to be seen giving your child the best French education. And, at the time, I was just grateful not to be shipped off to a *daara*—you know, one of those Quranic schools.'

Neera resisted the urge to speed the story to get to its crux. Her friend had just dropped a bomb about the death of her father—the last thing she was interested in was the quality of education in Senegal. Yet, she controlled herself, accepting that it was finally her friend's turn to purge.

'Anyway, the Annual Day was the biggest day of the year—it was the day my school flexed its muscles and proved that it was worthy of the exorbitant fees it charged by putting on the glitziest show in Saint-Louis. I was surprised when my music teacher pushed me to audition. He said he'd already put in a word with the director and it'd be good for me and for the show. It's true, no one could hit the high notes of "Born to Love" with the ease I could. I wish you could've seen my audition, Neera—heard how I made the empty auditorium reverberate with Juliet's juvenile desire to be loved by Romeo. Even though I'd never so much as been kissed, I understood that kind of longing and was desperate for it. And then, being younger, and evidently more effeminate, than all the senior boys made me a clear choice. Openly playing a girl for the first time freed me in a way that I had never known. Neera, I was a star—nay, an entire constellation—on stage.'

'You're a born star, Vee. I've no doubt everyone loved your Juliet.'

'Yes, they did. There was barely a dry eye in the house when the star-crossed lovers died. The applause at curtain call was the best thing that had ever happened to me—till I caught my father's eye. My parents were sitting in the third row, right in the centre, and my mother was beaming at me. But my father looked like he wished the floor of the auditorium would split open and swallow him up along with his shame. He should've never married my mother whom he called a charlatan. But who could've blamed him? He had been young and blazing with beliefs on African identity and she was a daughter of the soil; he always claimed she had bewitched him with humanitarian notions of saving the souls and stomachs of the Senegalese. But then I had come along, an epicene embarrassment, and ruined his life. He told me this every day. But thanks to my mother, I learnt to gloss over what he thought, said or did. Bowing in front of the whole town, I tried to not see myself as he was seeing me—a disgrace in a wig and a frock. I focussed on my mother's smile. I focussed on how singing on that stage had made me feel. I focussed on how my future would be.

'For a few electrifying minutes, I felt like I owned the world. Then, the applause ended, the curtain came down and the bullying recommenced. I was so stupid, thinking that my stage debut, even though I was a mere "middler", would earn me respect. No, playing Juliet only gave the bullies more ammunition. Backstage, the senior boys knocked me about like a punctured ball, like every slap and kick was validating their machismo.

'It's bizarre. There are some bits about that night that I still remember like it was yesterday and some as if they never happened. I remember this boy who played Juliet's nurse started twisting lines from the play—*But soft, what light through yonder window breaks? It is the east, and Juliet is the slut who will suck my cock.* Then, he lifted the dress he was still wearing and shoved his pelvis into my face, and the other boys pinned me down and started guffawing in delight. I felt so scared, so small.'

Neera, not known for her empathy, visibly winced at the plight of little Vafi. She squeezed Violet's hand tighter.

'Luckily, my music teacher walked into the green room to congratulate us, and the boys let go of me. He had always been my protector. He'd give me extra music lessons after school for free, spend time correcting my posture, rubbing my belly to teach me to breathe from there. If I had been harassed by the other boys at lunch break, he'd let me hide with him in the anteroom he had access to. We had named it our hush-hush room and I had poured out my heart to him while he had hugged and comforted me. Sometimes he'd bring me a bowl of home-made *sombi*—do you know of it?'

Neera didn't.

'It's rice pudding with coconut milk, a Senegalese speciality. Then, one evening, after a private music lesson, as we had been sitting together in the anteroom eating *sombi*, he had done the strangest thing. He'd leaned over and licked a bit of the pudding that had dripped onto my chin. I'd flinched, obviously. And he had just laughed and laughed, giving me some excuse about not having a napkin and not wanting his hands or my chin to get sticky, and that I had been a scaredy cat. No, I hadn't been. It had been just so gross, Neera, and yes, maybe, I had been scared.'

Neera nodded, not knowing what else to do.

'After that licking, I had stopped going for the one-on-one music lessons and avoided the anteroom altogether. But I'd missed my teacher, our talks, our lessons... He had been my confidant. I guess he'd missed me too because he'd pushed for me to be cast as Juliet, erasing any possibility of bad blood between us. So, that night when he entered the green room as as my face was being pinned to his crotch, I was so grateful—an end to my misery, I thought. I was so goddamn wrong.

'Now that I think of it,' Violet looked at Neera as if realizing something for the first time. 'The music teacher was a soft-spoken, sissy man with little authority, no match for the senior boys, who were big and brusque and found safety in numbers. The presence of the teacher meant nothing. The boy dressed as the nurse had the gall to stick out his leg to trip me as were rushing to the exit. And as I was scrambling up, he pinched my balls hard, once again spouting lines from the play—*Good night, good night! Parting is such sweet sorrow, That I shall say good night till it be morrow.* And I knew this romantic line was heavy with the promise of harassment that awaited me the next day.

'The minute my teacher and I were at the end of the dark corridor was when I let out that small sob that had been stuck in my throat. I wanted to be back on that stage with a spotlight on my face—the only place I'd felt safe, where the world had finally seen me. I wept that my moment had come and gone. Putting his arm around me, wiping my tears he told me I was the brightest star and not like the other boys. In that moment, all I wanted was to be like the other boys. I hated that I was different. I couldn't stop crying.

'We heard footsteps coming our way, so we ran into the hush-hush room to hide. He wrapped me in a bear hug, told me I was special and didn't let go of me till I stopped crying. Neera, he was good to me, kind. But then he pulled me into another embrace, rubbing his groin against mine. I cannot forget how DEFCON 1 sirens went off in my head. I pushed him away, saying my parents were waiting for me, wanting him to know I wasn't alone. And he kept telling me he'd make a man out of me, make me brave again, so that my parents would be proud of me. I remember I was wearing my favourite stonewashed jeans and he was trying to unbutton them, telling me to trust him.'

Neera's body tensed, and she clenched her jaw to stop the tears from falling. It was not her turn to cry. She needed to be the strong one. She let Violet continue.

'Maybe I let my guard down, maybe I had no choice. This is where my mind goes blank, pretending that nothing happened. But I often wonder what course our lives would've taken if I'd gotten away, if I'd run and found my mother. Or if my mother had found me instead of my father.

'And do you know what my dear father did when he walked into that room?' Violet asked Neera. 'He *apologized* to my teacher. He was so ashamed or so damned sure that this scene he'd barged in on was the doing of his despicable boy that he actually apologized to the man.'

Neera couldn't bear to hear the rest but she knew that her friend needed to say it all, needed her story to finally be heard.

'My father dragged me home through back alleys. I kept asking where yaay was and he kept saying, "You're nauseating, the day you were born was the worst day of my life, now I'm going to make you pay and I'm going to make your yaay pay for producing a pansy like you." He didn't even let go of my arm when I stooped over a drain to vomit, pulling and cursing me all the way home.

'As soon as we got to our front yard, my father pulled down a nylon wire from the clothes line, dragged me inside, wrapped the wire around my neck and started choking me. I couldn't breathe. I realized he was actually going to kill me this time. I was not even fourteen. And my life was over.

'My mother, who, not an hour ago, had been bursting with pride at my performance, trailed in, wondering where we'd disappeared. She didn't stop to ask what the matter was, picked up the steel stool her face was well acquainted with and brought it down on the head of her husband with a violence fuelled by years of abuse. One blow was enough to make the hulk of a man collapse. When I could breathe again, I grabbed the heavy metal stool from my yaay and slammed my father's skull in several times. It wasn't necessary. I did it so neither could be sure who had actually done it.'

A disobedient tear rolled down Neera's face. Her heart was breaking to see how much Violet and her mother had loved each other. They'd truly been natural-born partners.

Apparently, the particulars of finding a burglar as they had entered their home after attending the Annual Day had came to both mother and son with ease and had been memorized to the minutest details. Vafi had never set foot in Lycée Sainte Jeanne d'Arc again, joined an up-and-coming jazz trio called the Roaring Moths, accompanied his mother to the slums and ghettoes, burnt the professor's beloved religious books, shredded every copy of his celebrated thesis and, with alarming speed, erased his father's imprint by expunging the written word from his life.

To their surprise, Neera and Violet found two empty deckchairs on one of the strange little sunbathing islets, created for leisure by some Paris mayor or another, along the Seine. This kind of vacancy was new. Later, it would be said that the summer of 2020 in touristy Paris had belonged to the Parisians and to no one but the Parisians. Perhaps these two women were now certified Parisians after all.

'What happened to your mother after you left?'

'She toiled harder than ever to uplift the forgotten and the abused. She always said it was the best way to forget one's own abuse,' replied Violet, who felt an ancient knot untie itself in her belly—a knot that in a bizarre twist of fate had held her together, making her strong and more resilient, giving her the determination to look out and up and never in and down. She hadn't told this story to another living soul. Not even Benjy. 'Then, a SaniAid volunteer managed to track me down to tell me that my mother had contracted yellow fever and died two months earlier. Apparently, she hadn't taken her symptoms seriously because she had been vaccinated against it, and then it had been too late. Her colleagues had buried her in her family village under her favourite baobab tree next to her grandfather, like she had wanted. I had found work handing out fliers for a cabaret at Pigalle, and my papers were close to being processed here, so I couldn't go back home. And what or who would I go back for, anyway?'

'Isn't it strange that we always think of home as the place we come from, regardless of the fact that we never want to return there?' said Neera.

'True. Once my papers came through, I left my aunt and uncle's place. They had been kind, as kind as their circumstances allowed them to be. All the same, I didn't aspire to their limited life. It wasn't enough for me to be in the free world, I wanted to *be* free.'

'You're not merely free. You are flying, my friend.'

'I thought I was done paying for that flight of freedom,' said Violet, 'but the price keeps increasing. No matter what I do, I feel soiled.'

'I'm going to help you repair things with Raphaël, if that's what it costs, okay? Besides, you know I'm a rich widow in search of a cause now.'

It was not till later that evening, however, that Neera would discover, via detective Dasha's delivery, exactly how rich a widow she really was.

PART 5
The Skin We Shed

Chapter 1

The hospital corridor's cold floor had no sympathy—it had seen too much to care—it made Rosel feel awkward and ensured she stayed alert, foiling any plans her body had of passing out. The ceaseless reapplication of gauze and pressure with Russian military rigour had coagulated some of the blood that had been flowing down her face since the unexpected encounter. The taste in her mouth was metallic, her neck was sticky and her head whooshed like a helicopter stuck in a tin blender. Perhaps if her head would stop whirring, she'd be able to piece together the whens, whats and whys of the event, though she doubted such answers existed.

Not thirty minutes ago, Neera had pulled Rosel's reluctant hand and steered her through the entrance of yet another hospital, stopping at multiple registration counters to hand over documents and collect tags. Then, the two had traversed the teeming waiting room without a word and pushed open a 'medical personnel only' door. And now they were planted in a desolate corridor, waiting for the plastic surgeon to arrive.

'We're not breathing the same air as all those people in the ER,' Neera said. 'It's bad enough your face has been split into two, I refuse to catch the virus on top of that.'

Neera was as surprised as the others at her resoluteness to not be infected. One would think, given the catastrophic events in her recent history, she would welcome, or even seek out, the bug and beg it to reunite her with her dearly departed Jannie.

Yes, for a moment, Neera had nursed the image of herself being contaminated, gasping for air and living out her last days alone as an homage to her husband's days spent without her. In her fantasy, every atom of oxygen that her lungs were denied edged her closer to the man she had been dispossessed of. By right swiping the chanciest characters, she had invited risk into her bedroom for months. And then one flippant flick of her finger had brought her to the man on the boat.

Now, after her days of drunken healing, she had done a three-sixty: it became her mission to vanquish the germ that had wrecked her life. 'The invisible devastator will win over my dead body, and I ain't dying before I squish that bug,' she would say, practically bathing in disinfectant and double-masking long before it became fashionable. What's more, she'd donated a large chunk of her widow's windfall for vaccine development in Bengaluru and Oxford.

It had taken only a few calls for her to get the woman of the moment on the phone—the woman whose father was the world's largest pharma developer. His biotech factory had halted all other production in a bid to mine gold in the times of Covid and was leading the race in bringing the entire year of absurdity to the finish line.

His daughter, the woman on the other end of the line, had many petty moons ago relegated Neera to the invisible section of society because Neera had publicly ridiculed her offer of an annual girl-gang holiday—an act akin to mocking a personal invitation to a Mediterranean cruise co-hosted by Oprah, JLo and Ariana Grande. The holiday had come with a caveat of two positive mentions a month in her column, and though Neera was not a woman of scruples, she had fought hard to be the sole boss of her words. No amber-haired jetsetter dressed in not-yet-on-the-market couture was going to control her, no matter how tempting the wildebeest migration safari in the Ngorongoro crater sounded.

Then, the had column disappeared and the columnist had reappeared on the chicest side of the world, married to a radical celebrity. It went without saying that all previous grievances had been quickly forgotten and the pharma heiress had made it a point to look Neera up for a spot of lunch whenever she had flown from Mumbai to Paris in the pre-pandemic world.

So, now she took Neera under her sequined wing, encouraged her altruistic ambitions and helped connect her with all the panaceas making the pharma rounds. If Neera was going to be a charity warrior, she was going to be on the winning team and she'd get there by liaising with the best.

This was precisely the thinking that had landed the nanny and the widow on that inhospitable hospital floor that autumn day.

Rosel was not yet thirty, and it didn't seem fair to Neera that she should, henceforth, for no fault of her own, wear a tag of 'dwarf with a scar'. By nothing else but the virtue of being in Neera's inner circle, her face had earned the right to the surgical equivalent of Michelangelo. And, as luck would have it, Neera knew just the modern-day sculptor who'd be happy to oblige—a man who could manufacture beauty without a single inherent ingredient. To the discerning eye, his masterpieces could be identified from a distance at charitable gala dinners, exclusive auctions and all over the red carpet on the night of the César Awards.

Fortunate little domestic, thought Neera. Dr Vincent Beau was still itching to get in her pants, else they would have had to wait weeks, if not months, to get a consult. And here they were, about to see him pull his enchanted thread through skin that had been split not twenty-four hours ago.

'Does it still hurt?' asked Neera. 'If the throbbing in your head gets unbearable, I suggest we step out to smoke one of my rollies. Always does the trick for me.' Then, as an afterthought, 'Uhm, maybe best not to part your lips or open your mouth, in case your face falls off.'

This was not an exaggeration. Rosel had her jaw in her hand all night and was practically holding her wee little face together, which was slashed from ear to ear just below her lips. Chunky white sinew glared at them for a frightening moment after Dasha cleaned up the blood, before it flooded in red again.

The weapon of choice was a professionally sharpened ice pick; the assailant, a mixologist about to step into aperitif prominence; the moment when Parisians and their dreams were commanded to go back and hunker down in the holes they had come from.

This tattooed cocktail-maker had perfected his art at a Prohibition-style gem of a bar called Fitzgerald in the 7th arrondissement, and the satisfied grunts of repeat customers had boosted him to liquidate his life insurance to open Dionysus' Juice at the heart of Opéra less than a year ago.

The small brewery-style bar with a Greek twist (no one knew what that meant) shared a wall with an iconic Chinese restaurant, which refused to take reservations, opting instead to hand out electronic pagers in person with a waiting number. From the very first day, Dionysus' Juice's business benefitted from the young Asian clientele who ordered drinks and nibbles while waiting for their pagers to flash.

Soon enough, thanks to its delectable nectar, Dionysus' Juice became a scheduled pit stop, bookending trips to the Chinese restaurant. The magazine given out free at airports—*Paris Vous Aime*—ran a rather flattering two-page story on the alcohol entrepreneur, with photos that made his watering-hole-in-the-wall look like an intimate speakeasy from a bygone era. He was the first in his family to move out of poverty, and he posted this article with much aplomb on the official website of Dionysus' Juice, like an auspicious horoscope. It turned out, however, to be an unforeseeable horror-scope. He had imagined building a rapport with the deep-pocketed Chinese patrons, welcoming them and their friends but not *their* virus. A month after the glorious article appeared, he lost everything, along with his mind.

Unlike his neighbour, his bar couldn't transform into a takeout. And every day that he was forced to keep the door to his dream closed to outsiders, he opened a door to the darkness inside him.

With his last fifty-euro note, he bought a bag of cocaine, parked his scooter on the pavement outside his bar and entered his party for one. He mixed, garnished and served himself one glass each of his signature cocktails, interspersing them with neat lines of coke and tunelessly belting out macho-making French resistance songs. He repeated his favourite, 'Les Chant des Partisans', till the words no longer made any sense on his lips.

When all the charlie and cocktails had been ingested, he stumbled out of his speakeasy and onto his two wheeler, flying like John Travolta in Pulp Fiction. But his grey Honda Forza was no blood red Chevy Malibu and he was definitely no Vincent Vega. At some point, he must have been too wasted to carry on riding his scooter, which somehow got him as far as the western periphery of Paris. The night curfew was still a few hours away, yet, the day was as dark as his countenance. He stumbled upon what looked like a bus stop, not knowing if buses even existed in today's world. He heard a person getting off the bus cough. *Oh, a yellow dog-eating miniature*, he thought, and the beast inside him awoke. He ripped off her mask and rummaged his jacket pocket for the exact tool he needed. *I'm going to gouge out the virus from this ching-chong's face.*

The bus drove away. It was on essential duty to protect people by getting them home, and the driver wasn't about to give in to distraction. The few who got off the bus at the same time as Rosel scattered quickly, refusing to see the violence. This was not a time to be brave and certainly not on a stranger's behalf. Besides, they had a legit excuse—the curfew was edging closer.

Did she scream or did her voice get caught in her throat? It was the acrid odour of alcohol radiating from his mouth that brought tears to her eyes. Her brain must have switched off its pain sensors because she couldn't feel anything. Had she missed this lesson at nursing school? A thing emerged from an unnoticed sleeping bag and pulled the smell off her. The thing had eyes made out of her grandmother's jade necklace. Then, Rosel passed out.

When she came to, a man with a camera was too close to her face. She found herself slumped on an orange plastic chair in a tube-lit waiting room. There were others around her, bloodied and moaning—a hospital. She could hear her brain buffering: she had been attacked. The face in front of her came into focus: Vee's boyfriend, clicking pictures of her bleeding face. *Why*, her eyes asked.

'In case the police require proof to convict the man,' replied Benjamin.

The police did not sound hopeful. There was no CCTV footage and, barring the homeless man who wasn't making much sense, no witnesses.

'You know that such cases are on the rise, the officer on late-night duty had said to Benjamin. There was more than a hint of resignation, perhaps even empathy for the perpetrator, in the officer's tone. 'People are fed up of being cooped up. Sometimes they let out their frustration in violent ways.'

'What does that have to do with this girl?' asked Benjamin.

'Nothing. Probably, nothing… I mean she's Asian, isn't she? And she could be infected, *non*?'

'She is not,' said Benjamin, shocked at where this conversation was headed. 'And even if she was, what has that got to with anything?'

'Nothing,' repeated the officer. 'I'm just saying there's not much we will be able to do. Leave your number and we'll keep you posted.'

The call never came.

Not knowing what to do, Raphaël picked up the bleeding child (it was only later he discovered that she was a fully grown half-sized woman) and took her to the hospital for refugees and outcasts, where they didn't ask too many questions.

'Is there someone you need to call?' the kind receptionist asked after Rosel had been taken in.

Raphaël had never called anyone except his mother once. Then, he remembered that at their last photo session, Benjamin had given him his number. He might know what to do better than Raphaël. 'Yes, I want to make a call. I don't have a phone.'

The world was strange and (sometimes) so small, thought Raphaël, for it turned out that Benjamin knew the girl and took charge.

Pumped up to her eyeballs with pain killers and told to wait on the orange chair till the doctor had a minute, which most likely wouldn't be till the morning, Rosel slipped in and out of dreams: little Danilo, all of four, perched on top of Ferdie's broad shoulders. The three of them running through rice fields behind her parents' hut, which was not a hut anymore; it had morphed into the Eiffel Tower, yet it is where her parents lived. 'Talk softly,' she heard herself saying to Danilo. 'You'll wake Nana and Lolo.'

'They are old,' he said in his sweet baby voice. 'I don't want to disturb them. Lolo will come after me with a stick.' This made him laugh. And then the dream-Danilo started shrieking, 'Run, run, run, mummy, he's coming, Lolo's coming.'

She held her Ferdie's hand—a hand of love, a hand that fit hers like no one else's, a hand that spelled happiness, a hand that had explored and exploded her insides, a hand that held her whole world, a hand that lay puffed and cold, refusing to bend into its final home-made box. With this hand in hers, she ran, the Eiffel Tower chasing them, trying to spear them with its pointy top and the top was a flesh-eating ice pick, moving closer and closer to their unbroken skin and then she was Simone Biles, somersaulting and straddling the tower between her legs, riding it hard and fast, away from Ferdie, away from her baby, away from all the love she had ever received.

A familiar, irate voice made Rosel open her eyes.

'Yes, yes, calm down, I know we're not supposed to be here,' Neera was saying to the nurse, 'We've only come to take our friend home, okay? You don't seem to be doing anything for her here, anyway. What kind of hospital *is* this?'

'The only one you've got right now,' said the nurse matter-of-factly. 'She needs stitches and all the night doctors are on Covid-19 duty. I've given her an injection for the pain and infection, and that's all we can do right now. A surgeon will come in the morning and deal with her. She can wait here under my watch till then but *alone*. Okay? You all need to leave. OUT. NOW. PLEASE.'

'She's going to receive no treatment till morning?' asked Dasha as politely as her incredulity allowed. 'And they say France is a First-World country. This is ridiculous.'

'Take it up with the President, Madame. Till then, that is the exit I'd like you to use,' said the nurse, who hadn't been home for more than seven hours at a stretch since March. Now, it was nearly November, and she had all but forgotten what a weekend looked like and had been performing procedures she was assigned but definitely not qualified to. She could have threaded a needle through this little woman's face and sent her packing, but the pulsating wound seemed alive and she feared it would eat up her hand. Would that be so terrible…? At least she'd finally be allowed to go home and rest. Was she insane to entertain such an idea? 'Now, can you all get out of here before I call security.'

Violet, who had been standing quietly next to Benjy and

Raphaël, letting her enraged friends handle the situation, stepped in. 'Pardon Madame, we don't want to cause you any trouble. We are leaving.'

'Come on, then,' said Neera, and dragged a dazed Rosel out of the hospital.

Benjy took Raphaël and his camera to the police station to file a report. Meanwhile, Neera got busy on her phone to wake a few doctors up, Dasha put herself on gauze duty and Mama Vee put a comforting arm around her stunned friend.

Chapter 2

'I don't suture emergencies, Neera,' Dr Vincent Beau had protested on the phone the night before.

'This is not an emergency, Doc. This is a challenge. I'm sending you a photo and you tell me if you're up to it, fine if you're not. You know I'll find someone who will be, and then the glory won't be yours for the taking.'

He knew without seeing the photo that he would end up rising to this incorrigible woman's dare. After he agreed, she refused to hang up till he said that they'd be the first ones he'd see in the morning, of course.

Waiting, however, was a prerequisite for such talent. Already impatient, Neera looked at her watch for the seventh time that morning as Rosel sat on the floor of the hospital corridor, cradling her head. Neera paced up and down—five minutes short of 10 a.m. How many hours before they would be welcomed into the magician's chamber? It would be worth the wait. The fact that the doctor was probably a pervert was neither here nor there.

∽

To be fair, it was *she* who wanted him to get in her pants first. Now, that story had no relevance to the matter at hand. Besides, she no longer recognized the Neera who wanted a G-spotplasty. Was it part of her quest to turn up the volume on thrill seeking? Had Parisian ennui dulled her peaks? Or was it simply another not-thought-through bid for adrenaline that verged on self-destruction? Who could say what thoughts propelled *that* Neera into action?

Though Dr Beau's speciality was face reconstruction, Neera's friend from the gossip-and-window-shop box couldn't stop going on about the designer vagina he'd created for her on his return from a course in LA. The very next week, Neera spread her legs on his table with her feet in stirrups, but the LA-returned surgeon told her that her spot was near perfect, that he had little to offer towards its improvement and that, in fact, if he could do some basic research, he would model some of his G-spotplasty on her anatomy. To that end, he explained that he'd like to experience its working efficacy first-hand—would she be willing? *She most certainly would not.* Such an advance would be considered criminal anywhere else in the world. But this was France, and here, it was seen as flattery. Feigning outrage, she zipped up her newly certified jewel, paid for the consult and marched out of his surgery, strutting smugly with newfound pride in her miraculous G-spot.

After the non-incident, however, she bumped into him twice: once at a Lancôme event, where he apologized for his tactlessness and insolence, though still with a charismatic twinkle in his eye, and another time at the fortieth birthday weekend of the friend who had recommended him. The weekend celebration was at the friend's ancestral chateau in Honfleur in Normandy, a twelfth-century castle that was both impressively ancient and magnificently restored. But even the fanciest French soirées felt a bit DIY to Neera, who had been spoiled irreversibly by years of overzealous Asian servitude, where a mere nod got you all that you desired, wrapped in a smile and inverse gratitude for the chance to serve.

Mercifully, France came with other charms—manicured French gardens for one. Neera had a soft spot for the rows of lollipop trees, geometrical hedges and methodically colour-coded flowers, and the garden in Chateau Honfleur was a soaring example of how man could tame nature to boost its beauty. The sky remained a beaming blue all weekend, making even the grouchiest of city-frowners relax their faces into something resembling a smile. Jean-Paul, as was customary, was surrounded by a coterie of literati that talked over one another without lending an ear to anything coming out of anyone else's mouth. And the good doctor with bad desires followed Neera into the hornbeam-hedged labyrinth and pulled out every trick from his Gladstone medical bag to charm her into letting him have a go at her spot.

She was well aware that there was a queue of refined women who would forfeit their fortunes for such a chance—a chance at any part of this doctor touching any part of theirs without the presence of a scalpel and chequebook. And as the sun cut shadows on his cheekbones and bounced off the beckoning skin he flashed by leaving more than a few shirt buttons undone, she clearly saw why. While she was hardly the type to shy away from a romp in the rose bushes, his overtures felt invasive. So she flirted her way out of the maze and back into her husband's arms.

∽

At exactly 10.53 a.m., Neera and Rosel were ushered into his surgery. *Fatigue suits Dr Beau,* Neera thought. The dark bags under his eyes adding character as he glued, sutured and stapled Rosel's face back together. He was ambidextrous—what a convenience when having to pull and push metal through damaged layers of tissue without a support staff. Those with weaker stomachs might have looked away but not Neera. The coarse and rudimentary way the curved needle pierced, punctured and darned the torn layers of skin sent waves of satisfaction through her.

'Tell me again what kind of knife it was?' asked the doctor. 'Because honestly, I've never seen a laceration like this.'

Rosel tried to speak, but he stopped her. 'Now, you are not to speak for three whole days, young lady.' He turned to Neera. 'This is some of my finest work. Normally, I prefer to do such procedures under general with a team of residents and nurses, but there's nothing normal about today and I know you don't want to be in the hospital a minute longer than you have to. When it heals, you'll finally see what my hands are capable of.'

Thirty-nine stitches and a tube of skin adhesive all neatly formed a line that would eventually disappear. The only marks left on the victim would not be visible on the surface and, in all probability, leave permanent scars. As far as the surgeon was concerned, Rosel had been rebuilt. The curative powers of modern medicine were absolute and highly addictive. How simple life was when seen through his surgical loupes. Neera felt the hallelujah of healing, right down to her painted toes. If she wasn't in hyper-cautious beat-the-virus mode, she would have hugged the doctor and kissed his fingers.

'Dr Beau, I never doubted your genius,' Neera said. 'When we are on the other side of this circus, perhaps we can...' She didn't bother completing her thought before leaving.

Chapter 3

The numbers kept climbing. From twenty-four views the previous night, they had gone up to 791,905 views by the morning. Dasha knew she had made the right choices by tagging politically active celebrities and using incendiary hashtags for the starkly provocative video. The Internet was her turf: it had always tilted unfairly in her direction. She had nevertheless been expecting the numbers to top out at twenty to fifty thousand. That was before Sandra Oh retweeted the video in the middle of the night with #StopAsianHate #itsanhonourjusttobeAsian and #JeSuisMeToo. *Sandra Oh! Dr Cristina Yang herself!*

From that minute, its reach was a forgone conclusion because that's how virality worked. Dasha resisted the urge to look at her phone every five seconds but she couldn't. The numbers were behaving like rabidly reproducing rabbits who had mistaken a jar of Viagra for their feed.

As far as Dasha could see, Fan Bingbing, Gong Li (and her new French husband), Tadao Ando, Gemma Chan and Henry Golding—*she had to google the* Crazy Rich Asian *actor; he was hot*—had all jumped on board, censuring the lack of protection for Asians in the West and praising the brave little girl. *Who cares that she's not a little girl?* Unlike Sandra Oh, these celebrities were hardly known for their political activism, and this, of course, made it all the more exciting because now that their public personas had belatedly started to echo and amplify the grief of people that looked like them, their entire entourage and LA-based PR teams had gone into overdrive to be the loudest and most concerned voice in the room. She'd be stupid to look away while history was unfolding live—a history that she, Dasha, had personally set in motion.

'One million, we hit one million,' she screamed into Astrid's ear, brandishing her phone and running out of the apartment—all the way down, out, across the courtyard, then in and all the way up again to the service floor. She was on autopilot and it was a wasted effort—she'd forgotten Rosel had moved out of her room under the roof and into Neera's guestroom.

The music video came together with such minimal effort that it felt almost unethical to be reaping these benefits. Not that there were actually any benefits to reap just yet. There would be, of course there would be! The lanky Russian Internet Tsarina could smell it.

It was little mademoiselle Blanche who had set things in motion. 'Rosel, if you're feeling scared, the best thing to do is sing it out. Your voice always makes me strong.'

So that's what they did. Blanche sprawled out on Neera's heated parquet floor and arranged sheaves of paper and coloured pencils. Her brothers slunk into Eric's unoccupied room-cum-recording-studio, which was nothing short of gadget Disneyland, and found a keyboard, bongo and some other useful-if-we-figure-out-what-they-are instruments. Before anyone could tell them differently, the boys lined up their findings in aid of their sister's grand scheme.

Paper after paper was crumpled into balls and thrown into the roaring fire in the salon. They were writing in English, which, even though the Decoste kids went to Paris's most pretentious bilingual school, was not their strong suit. Rosel was uncertain how to adequately articulate the awfulness she felt inside. But Blanche, who had just turned ten, understood more than she ought to about the world being a beastly place and had plenty she wanted to express.

Last month, her friend Isaure had stopped talking to her because she had refused to stop playing with and sitting next to Kelly, who Isaure had said was responsible for bringing corona to Paris. Kelly's grandparents, Isaure had said, eat bats and snakes and puppies in China and that's why we have to wear masks now. The ever-sensible Blanche had needed a trusted adult's opinion on the matter and asked her maman about it, who had told her that a virus does not have a nationality, which means that it doesn't belong to one country and can travel without a passport.

Before she could ask her perpetually distracted mother whether she thought it was unfair that no one wanted to sit next to Kelly or that the older boys were pushing and spitting on Nuan, her mother had kissed her on the forehead and locked herself in the bedroom to finish her call. Blanche was inured to being left to her own devices and deliberations, and had never been actively taught how to hate (which, to the surprise of civilized society, is an acquired skill). She usually tended to side with the underdog and, after careful consideration, had made it a point to become Kelly's new best friend. That had been until Kelly and her brother had stopped coming to school altogether and Isaure and her gang had found a new target in Blanche, the China-Lover and Puppy-Eater.

After much posturing, editing and rephrasing, Colette's children presented their ditty to Neera. It was a rap song with a strong melody, like the haunting creations where Eminem laments and Rihanna harmonizes, except it had an unpolished, raw and almost unhinged quality, which, in the age of home-made masterpieces, spoke more to the times than any perfectly produced studio creation ever could. Augustin banged out a beat on the bongo, Thomas pressed play on a pre-recorded riff on the synth and Blanche egged Rosel on. Neera sat stunned.

You cut my face,
And loosened my tongue,

You dug my skin,
But I'm not done.
What you want,
I won't be,
What you see,
Is not me,
I won't shed skin,
Just to fit in.

Neera marvelled at the lyrics. *How hurt do you have to be to come up with something so deep?* Rosel's voice sang on.

You call me a disease,
From overseas,
A problem in the world?
No, just another broken girl.
Living in exile,
'Cos society is hostile,
There's no place I can call home,
A victim on the road, wherever I may roam.

The kids joined in harmonizing—all the days of karaoke and singing on the way back from school were put to good use. They reached the high notes with an innocent ease that bypassed the listeners' brain and went straight to their hearts. In unison, they sang:

Why-aay-yaay
Erase a future,
Try-aay-yaay
To be a teacher
You'll see,
There's no stopping me

The song hit a crescendo and they took a dramatic pause that made you hold your breath in anticipation. Rosel's voice broke the silence with the chorus.

You see not me,
What you see is
What you see,
The reflection in your eyes,
Is all but lies,
Je suis me,
Je suis nobody but me,
Je suis me,
Je suis nobody but me.

Neera, who had never heard Rosel sing before, felt like she was slowly sliding into a womb-like cave. That left her feeling like the happy child she had never been.

The Decoste kids clapped, bursting with pride for themselves and their little nanny, and ran to hug Neera, who shocked herself by hugging them back. Earlier that week, she had been shocked at how easily she'd agreed to move Colette's three kids along with their nanny into her duplex. *Was this becoming a pattern?* Admittedly, the situation leading up to it had been insane and scarcely believable. New world, new rules. Jannie would have been proud of 'New Neera'. Thinking of him, she pulled the kids closer.

∽

Since Rosel was out of action, Colette volunteered to walk the kids to school each morning, and with every step, the grudge she held against the world grew.

Well, if someone—as in her husband—bothered to ask her, she would tell him in no uncertain terms that she simply didn't have the bandwidth to do it. On second thought, hadn't she told him exactly that, and he had chosen not to hear, leaving her with no choice?

'Oli, my work day starts hours before yours,' Colette remembered saying to him. 'You are the boss of your own time.'

'And when exactly am I supposed to go for my run if I drop them to school first?'

'Go right after!'

'What am I supposed to do with Milo?' Olivier had asked genuinely. 'The dog starts huffing and puffing after five minutes of keeping pace with me.'

'Drop him home after you drop the kids and carry on!' She had felt like she had been talking to an imbecile who needed help planning how to get the toilet paper from the holder into his hand to wipe his own arse.

'Then my breakfast time gets pushed to 9.45 a.m. I'm not supposed to have a gap of more than fourteen hours without eating. You know that.'

'Then eat your dinner slightly later, damn it, or have a snack before sleeping.' This infuriating moron was going to be the death of her. 'You are old enough to figure this out, Olivier.'

'Yeah, easy for you to say—you don't exercise.'

'I don't exercise because I don't have the fucking *time* to exercise!'

'Hon, there's no need to curse, okay?' he had said, placing a calming hand on hers, which, of course, had had the exact opposite effect. 'You need to make time to exercise. It'll make you feel less uptight.'

'I'm uptight because it all lands on me. If there's something that needs doing for the family, it's always "Maman will do it".'

The truth was, Colette loved being Superwoman, juggling family, work, kids, dog, holidays, menus, deadlines, waistline, school projects and, lately, bedtimes, a dying marriage and an undying sick father, in the most efficient, cost-effective and mutually beneficial manner. However, Superwoman got time off when not in the line of fire to recharge as a regular, mortal, flawed human, unlike supermom, who was never off-duty. But while Colette's life seemed to be speeding from one emergency to another, she couldn't openly admit that she was ready to hang up her cape. 'Why does it always have to be me? I don't see you taking any extra responsibilities around the house.'

'Don't I do the science homework with the kids?' he had asked.

'You are kidding me, right? That takes twenty minutes total per week, half the time of your *daily* run. You need to do more because I'm stretched thinner than the Lycra on your running shorts that are three sizes too small for you.'

'I would happily step in, if you would just let me and not micromanage how I'm pouring milk into Thomas's glass or how thick I'm cutting the baguette for the tartine.'

'If I didn't micromanage, we'd have to buy a new toaster every day because you don't seem to understand that you can't shove bread in there that's thicker than the slits,' she had hissed.

'See what I mean?' he had said with a smug smile. 'Everything I do, you can do better. So you might as well do it.'

Colette had centred herself, breathing in deeply. 'You're right. I'm sorry. I will let you do things your way, no matter how much they bug me. And I will try not to be bugged by them.'

He had kissed her cheek. 'And I will do more, I promise. Just tell me what you need.'

'I need you to drop the kids to school,' Colette had said, her shoulders visibly relaxed.

'That's not fair, I have to go for my run. Not a minute ago I told you that,' Olivier had replied. 'Typical Colette, listens to no one but herself.'

For the rest of the week, Colette had put her headphones on, switched her video off and taken conference calls to China while walking her kids and the dog to school.

Chapter 4

The most unimaginable thing had happened in the Decoste family. One day, not long after the attack on Rosel, Colette found that she couldn't will herself to get out of bed. Dr Olivier Decoste had known for a decade that his wife was postponing personal catastrophe for a sunny day, and it came on a frosty emotionless November morning. Colette's eyes were parched and red like the flag of People's Republic of China that had started infiltrating her daydreams. She was in the in-between space that all insomniacs get stuck in: lying in bed, wanting to do nothing but sleep and completely unable to. She had long believed insomnia was indulgent. And, in any case, the unofficial perk of being married to a doctor was access to his prescription pad. She'd been self-medicating with a pill and a moderately full glass of wine for years and never had an issue with sleep till now. When had the pills stopped working? If only her brain didn't feel like wet cotton—obtuse and inextricably entangled—she'd be able to pinpoint it. The nausea was building up again inside her. The bathroom seemed miles away. There was no way she was going to make it.

She didn't. She lay in her own sick, not able to wake up or sleep.

Never before had she realized that guilt was an incarnate entity, something that grew ever heavier—and there was no guilt like a mama's guilt. Ironically, she had never suffered from guilt when her kids had been incidental, but this was not the case anymore, not since she actually started enjoying spending time with them. Now, there was no limit to her guilt—guilt for the years she had not spent marking their first words and steps and bruises and best friends and disasters and successes. The number of firsts she'd had no interest to clear her schedule for! They couldn't be rectified by being present in the present: those firsts would never be firsts again. There'd be others, but what if she missed them too because she was on a call haggling through a translator with the Taikoo Hui Shopping Centre in Guangzhou?

And what if Guangzhou passed on her proposition altogether? Time was running out on her dreams, and suddenly, she didn't know the next steps to take to accomplish them. If China said no, would Hermès give her the golden handshake, just without any gold because this entire year had been a force majeure? What would she do without Hermès? Who was she without a job? Her kids, whom she had failed for the sake of her career, would now look at her as a failure just like she looked at her father. Was she ever going to forgive him? Was he going to acknowledge his cruelty as a parent? She still had so much unresolved anger towards him and towards her useless mother who did nothing except facilitate him, put on maroon lipstick and drink gin and tonic. This was argument enough to not feel guilt for outsourcing the duties she ought to perform as a daughter. Yet, there it was: a daughter's guilt, adding kilos to the weight on her chest.

It wasn't that she hadn't tried. With the best of intentions, she had gone to Saint-Cloud when her mother had called to tell her that her father had been lashing out again and she was at her wit's end. Despite being fully aware of the supersonic speed at which the tamest of their interactions turned sour, Colette had deluded herself into believing she could care for the dying man—that she would find peace within herself. It was true, no one else was waving a white flag, and she was adult enough to lay her fury to rest on her own.

However, within an hour of being with them, listening to them dismiss her and her life choices, she had been ready to rub her father's full diaper on his face. To distract herself, she had announced that she had been fast-tracked last month to become the international director of communications, a higher position than she had ever aimed for. Her mother had not paused for a breath before saying, 'Can you pass me the water, Colette?' and then in the same breath had carried on railing against her incontinent father. The diaper had been likely to end up on her face too if Colette had not walked out of their door that instant.

So, as penance for her identity deception, Rosel had been sent to Saint-Cloud in her stead. It had worked in everyone's best interest. That was until Rosel had been attacked at the bus stop—a bus stop she had been at only because she had been helping Colette's father. If Colette herself had been a better person, had forgiven Rosel for pretending to be Len without demanding a pound of flesh or had at least been a more dutiful daughter, the nanny's face would not have been butchered. This had been a lose-lose situation and instead of managing it, Ms Communications Manager had completely lost control.

So, her father would die, she would not have forgiven him. He'd remain a thorn in her psyche that she would indubitably prick her kids with and they theirs, and on and on it would go, generation to generation, till the end of time.

Her disciplined mind spiralled out of control in all directions, like an octopus free falling while skydiving without a parachute.

'Hey hon, what's for lunch? Oh, and is your tummy better?' she heard Olivier's voice coming from the kitchen as he walked in from his surgery. 'The kids were so excited to have Papa drop them off today. I think I'm going to do it once a week and cut short my run. It'll make them so happy.'

His foraging around the kitchen proved unfruitful. 'There's not much in the fridge, darling. I think you better do another online order today.'

A tiny sob travelled up her stomach, climbed through her oesophagus, almost got caught in her pharynx and then stumbled out of her mouth. Several small sobs followed the same course of action, till she was ululating at a volume that even her husband, with his selective hearing, couldn't ignore. Undoubtedly, he was not the world's greatest spouse. He was, however, a very gifted doctor and it didn't take him long to throw out his diagnosis from earlier that morning.

'This is not an upset tummy, Coco.' The last time he had called her that had been when Blanche was born and he had been bursting with love for his two girls. He brushed her hair away from her face. A big clump of it came off in his hands. 'You are having a burnout, my Coco.' This was not a catchphrase for him but a medically recognized health condition with ascribable symptoms. And his wife was demonstrating all of them, all at once. He sponged her and propped her upright. She didn't allow him to leave her side, screaming in fear when he turned off the lights. He switched them right back on. Her phone rang, so she smashed it against the wall. He lay down by her side in bed. She rested her head on his chest and sobbed.

They lay like that till it was time to pick up the kids from school. In spite of her exhaustion, her internal clock chimed, reminding her that one of them would have to go. He placed an anti-nausea pill on her tongue, kissed her on her forehead and rushed back as fast as he could.

'I left the kids at Neera's for the night. She'll move Rosel down with her, so they'll be fine,' he said, re-entering the bedroom. 'I'm going to take over some clothes and stuff. I'll be back before you know it.'

'Thank you,' she managed to mouth. If this is all that was needed to jolt her husband into action, she would have laid lifeless ages ago. And this made her weep some more.

Colette didn't know how long she had been staring at the wall or when exactly the wall started talking to her.

'What is the purpose of your life?' asked the wall.

To be successful. To have a perfect family. To work hard in order to play harder. To be better than my parents. To live an honourable, godly life. To be a role model for my kids. To see the bigger picture and set goals to achieve it. Every answer that would've satisfactorily defined her existence sounded inadequate today.

The wall tried again: 'Who are you?'

'I don't know anymore,' she said, defeated.

'Who do you want to be?'

She thought deeply about this. 'A person not overwhelmed by guilt.'

'Is it easier to love or be loved?'

'Neither, love is not meant to be easy.' That sounded wrong the minute she said it. 'No, I take it back,' she said, thinking of her children. 'It's easy to love. When you love someone, it fills you with love and then you become lovable.' Gosh, was it really that simple? Her eyelids gave in to gravity.

'What makes someone beautiful?' the wall went on. Colette fell into a deep unassisted sleep.

It didn't last long. When she awoke in a cold sweat gasping for air, Olivier was checking her pulse.

It had been six days, or so she was told, since she'd seen her kids or logged into work or worn shoes. Hours played mean tricks of time—stretching for interminable periods, where the seconds hand on the oversized London station clock in her room hardly moved and then zipped past, and she suddenly found that three days had gone by. The kind stranger she was married to was flitting about the room, neatly folding things into a suitcase.

'Are you going somewhere?' The quiche that her unrecognizable husband had spooned into her was not threatening to resurface, and that was sufficient cause for celebration.

'*We* are, Coco. I told you yesterday. I've booked us a mini-break to Dubai.' He had called her office a day after the collapse and, without mentioning the breakdown, had informed them, as her doctor, that it was a medical emergency. Couldn't she postpone till after the China contract was signed? Which part of emergency did they not understand? Grudgingly, they had allowed her time off.

That evening, en route to the airport, they made a pit stop to kiss the kids goodbye. Colette hugged her children close to her for as long as they would let her, inhaled their smell and didn't say much.

'You never go on holiday without us. That's not normal,' said Augustin.

'Well, my big boy, what makes you think anything about this year has been normal?' said Olivier. 'Anyway, you have school, and Rosel needs you to be the brave man of the house for now.'

'Papa, that's not fair. You always say girls and boys are equal,' said Blanche. 'And I'm older than Aug, so I want to be the brave girl—no, the woman—no, the madame of the house.'

'How about you be the empress of the house, my darling, and you can boss over the boys and make sure they behave?'

'Yes, I can be the empress,' she said happily.

'Neera, I cannot thank you enough,' said Olivier.

'You better get out of here before I change my mind,' said Neera with an honesty that made him rush out of the apartment.

With France closed and the rest of the world out of bounds, Olivier masked up, took his broken wife's hand and boarded a flight to extract her from herself. Invisible to all save himself, his macho, red cape fluttered, for the very first time, behind him.

Chapter 5

The rooftop room was flushed with light. Benjamin, who was going for 'burst of divinity', was still not satisfied and tweaked his small studio lights clipped on the ceiling, trying to make them look more like God's rays coming from the skies.

The kids assisted Queen Vee in scrunching up the puffy, bell-shaped sleeves on Rosel's sheer blouse. They'd had one of the best days of their lives rummaging through Violet's studio to fashion a traditional Filipina outfit for their nanny's next video, and had created a simple plaid wrap skirt with a butterfly blouse in all white. The plan was for Rosel to descend from the hole she called a window and then continue singing while being suspended in the air, held up by white sheets wrapped around her underarms. Benjamin, with Dasha's help, had made the miniscule room look even tinier than it was by placing an oversized painting on the wall and adding a rather bulky table and chair.

Earlier that week, Violet had sat Rosel down in front of Neera's bathroom mirror and given her a sharp blunt cut with a fringe, making her look like a doll, though a raggedy one, since her countless stitches still hadn't dissolved.

'When was the last time you cut your hair?' Vee had asked. 'The split ends are scaring me.'

'My sister cut it before I left Dasol.' The memories from that last full day at home were like gold dust in her hands: utterly precious, entirely ephemeral. When they had started fading, she'd superglued a few to her mind: the smell of Danilo's head as she had bathed him for the last time; her mother holding her face in both hands and kissing her cheeks; Ferdie's father handing her a 2,000-peseta note, which he had been saving almost all his life without knowing that it had long gone out of circulation in Spain; her own father passing her his dinner plate to eat from because it had the biggest portion of fish and rice; the practically new jeans her richer neighbour had brought her to take on the trip and the fistful of salt she had put in her pocket from the salt dunes, so she would always have a piece of home with her. She had all but forgotten about her sister sitting her down on the muddy ground outside their hut and trimming her hair.

'We should be ready to roll in fifteen minutes max,' announced Dasha. 'Rosel, we want to do it in one shot. You'll need to hang and sing the whole song in one go, okay?'

The new song called 'When Asian Angels Cry' had almost written itself, with just a little editing from Neera. It was a definitive ballad, showcasing the range of Rosel's voice, telling the story of her life as an outsider in Paris and, once again, had an unmixed, homespun appeal to it. Blanche, who hadn't understood all the lyrics (*My past I own, Down to my bone, It'll spread like a cancer, If you unleash my anger*), had nevertheless made her rehearse the song ad nauseam. Violet had worked her make-up magic to transform Rosel into a blend of seraph and raging geisha, her big, round eyes full of fury, flower-bud lips demanding answers and hollow cheeks shaded in so fiercely that it would make the blood drain from the beholder's face.

By the third take, they ironed out all the technical issues. Victor and Astrid, positioned on the roof, were responsible for Rosel's descent and for swaying her softly, as she sang mid-air. Benjy's camera was placed on the floor and angled to reveal the dark winter sky above Rosel's head while the beams of dusty yellow light camouflaged the window.

Dasha, whose idea this second song was, could hardly wait to post it. Secretly, she needed to be busy doing something to forget that she wasn't doing anything. There was also a compelling cyber urgency to get it out there ASAP to ride on the freak wave of #JeSuisME, a wave that showed no signs of plateauing.

Yes, Sandra Oh and gang helped get the initial eyeballs, but then the simplicity of the lyrics arranged around an austere rap, along with the sheer melancholy of the melody, struck a chord with all those stuck at home. And when they saw the haunting voice coming out of a dainty but horribly cut-up face, the song took on a poignancy, reflecting the listeners' own pain of disenfranchisement and isolation. The hit song, 'Je Suis Me', seemed to ask an unsettling and long-unsettled question: why do some individuals get to call a country home when others can't? What does one need to do to belong to the place they live in? What is the correct shape of eyes or shade of skin or number of zeroes in a bank account that allow a person to be accepted in a land? Rosel's blank, patched-up face in an extreme close-up, repeatedly chanting 'Je Suis Me' right into the camera, asserted— with direction from Dasha—that it was time for change.

It quickly became an anthem for Asians protesting against hate crimes and was even used in a Black Lives Matter march all the way over in NYC. Insta-posters rapidly materialized, which fittingly shifted the long line of stitches from under Rosel's lip to run over her mouth, making it look more like sinister barbed wire than the handiwork of a plastic surgeon.

It didn't take long for Len and Julie to show up with an olive branch at her apartment (nothing escaped the Filipino community, and an address for a countrywoman was the easiest blank to fill). What stumped Rosel was that they brought along the famous Mrs Rodriguez, the head of the charitable organization Pinoy in Paris, which behaved more like a gatekeeper to the community than a social network. Apparently, being attacked and singing about it was *exactly* what the community was in need of, especially with the celebrity support the song and Filipina singer had found. Rosel was hailed as the brave mascot of this movement that she had no intention of starting or starring in. Her voice permitted hundreds of people who looked different from their white neighbours to speak up. Repressed stories of racism poured in, a sickening war of words commenced online, YouTube removed the comments section and Pinoy in Paris jumped in to redirect the conversation and, more importantly, the traffic.

Some two-bit journalist with unwashed hair and a strong accent showed up and stuck a France24 English microphone under Rosel's nose. She froze. Dasha stepped in and made all the right noises, ensuring that Rosel Andal was a name no one would dare mispronounce nor forget in a hurry.

'She works long hours, pays her taxes, follows the rules, and some out-of-work, benefit-eating drunk has the right to tell her she doesn't belong. Why?' asked Dasha looking directly into the news camera's lens. 'How is this *égalité*? France cannot call itself the land of liberty, if it does this to the people who leave everything to come live here.' She pushed Rosel's scarred face in front of the camera.

'Have you filed a police complaint? Have the authorities reached out to your friend?' enquired the journalist.

'The system is skewed in favour of the white man, so, as expected, they did nothing,' answered Dasha.

Mrs Rodriguez pitched in, 'If you are not white, rich and French, you are invisible to society. It is only when you need a cleaner that you go out of your way to find us. We clean your caca and then you shit on us.'

'We foreigners have to stick together,' Dasha interrupted before Mrs Rodriguez's rage made people switch channels. 'Even celebrities like Sandra Oh identify with Rosel. She might not be able to speak for herself today because, as you can see, the assailant *tried to pull out her tongue*, but now her words fall out of every mouth that has been muzzled. And there are countless like her in the shadows—together, their voice will grow louder and louder till the hate is silenced. We love France and it's time she loves us back.' Dasha could not get over the ebullient intonation of her voice, how feverish it became without sounding shrill. She was on a roll and could have gone on forever. But she was too shrewd to be verbose. 'Love is all you need to build bridges. Thank you.'

Had Dasha known that this two-minute news clip was precisely the sign someone sitting in a damp basement flat in Liverpool was searching for, she might have tailored a line or two for him. And, as it turned out, her words reached places much, much higher than Liverpool.

∫

The music video for 'When Asian Angels Cry' didn't require much of an edit. Dasha added her final touches to the credits and worked at making the final frame, with its contact numbers for helplines, look more cheerful and less ominous. She was pondering over the colour and size of the font as Nicolas barged through the door, tripping over the three-tiered bunk bed that had been pushed to join its twin to make a double bed.

'Why are the beds blocking the door?' he cursed, rubbing his knee.

Dasha ignored him. She was in no mood to explain that it was on this joined space that Astrid and she nocturnally feasted on each other. When asked if they were a couple, they found the question obsolete and old-fashioned. Their generation defied definitions, just like the hippies had defied authority. In reality, neither of them knew nor cared how committed they were or wanted to be. In the here and now, they simply felt it was spring whilst in the other's company. Astrid, who had run away from the pressures of her confined family, held onto Dasha who, in turn, held onto the belief that the moment they were out of confinement, her father would run to her.

Alone, they were two models on the periphery of Paris struggling to make it. Together, they were *au courant* and on point, which gave them power in Paris, a city partial to creative kooks. The curious stares on the streets made them feel like gods. What more did they need?

'I've called you non-stop today,' said Nicolas. 'Where have you been?'

'Right here,' said Dasha coolly, without picking up on his hysteria. 'I have a deadline to meet for this video. My phone was on silent.'

'Where's your friend?' he asked.

'You've put on weight, Nic. Fridge too accessible?'

'Have I really?' Nicolas had replaced going out of his apartment, exercising, meeting designers, searching for clients at hotspots and everything else that made up his life with bottles of beer. 'Never mind, where is she?'

'She's at her call back for an activewear clothing company, which is crazy because they don't even make her size. Didn't you send her?'

Lately, Nicolas had been sending Astrid to all sorts of genre-busting auditions due to a delayed demand for diversity. Unfortunately, 'ugly giraffe' or 'unseemly alien' or 'too tall' didn't make the diversity cut the way plus-size and rolls of fat did, which enraged Dasha. *After all*, Dasha thought, *Astrid's version of abnormal was largely a result of free will and epicurean pleasure, while Dasha had zero control over the length of her neck or the size of her forehead or the space between her eyes.* But Dasha hadn't bothered to learn the national art of complaining, and instead nurtured the belief that soon she'd grow to a position where no one would dare give her an opportunity to complain, providing her with everything her heart desired without ever having to ask. Thus, her rage went unexpressed, making her moody and giving her indigestion. Tragically, in a city full of irate moaners, no one seemed to notice, which had a snowball effect on her temperament. By now, almost everything bugged and bloated the Russian.

'No, not Astrid, the other one,' said Nicolas. 'The one you were speaking on behalf of, the one with the cut and the song. The viral song.'

'You mean Rosel?' she asked, 'What do you want with her? Casting for Lilliputians?'

'It's not me who wants her, it's the president,' said Nicolas and waited for his words to sink in.

'The president of what?' asked Dasha dismissively. 'Asians in Paris Association? Immigration Support Society? They've all been calling, but Rosel doesn't want to get involved with any of them. They're too political, she's scared she'll get deported and first she wants—'

'The president of the Republic,' the portly agent interrupted. Then, to ensure his words didn't miss the mark and got the reaction he had come for, he added, 'Of France. The president of France.'

Chapter 6

From that moment, a scent of urgency hung in the air of Number Thirty-Six and everything moved at a frantic pace. Dasha's irritation found distraction. If she hadn't got the other women to pull up their stockings, they would not have managed to keep pace with her. Rosel had been invited—*officially invited*—to Le Palais de l'Élysée for a chat with the president in front of the press. *I am definitely more deserving of this honour* looped like a GIF in Dasha's head. Yet, she stayed mum. She wasn't sure how to reach and teach the misinformed people of France, so the next best thing she could do was to ensure that the invite was not wasted on Rosel—a person she had grown to love and respect and a person she could strangle with her bare hands right now for her reluctance.

Before the ladies of the building got carried away, Rosel wanted this incomprehensible mix-up sorted. There had obviously been a mistake. It was beyond her grasp that this might well be the authorities' way of atoning. And who could blame her? So much of her life had been spent preparing for the worst that when the best came knocking, she was completely unprepared to open the door and let it in.

Dasha grabbed her by the shoulders, shaking her, and when that didn't work, she called in Neera and Violet. They took turns scolding her like she was a toddler throwing a tantrum, chucking food at the very people trying to feed her because she was too hungry and infantile to be rational.

'What did you come to Paris for?' demanded Neera, her always limited patience becoming gossamer-thin. 'Rosel, don't sit there with your tongue in detention! Just tell me what you left your home in the Philippines for.'

'I wanted a chance at a better life. I wanted to give my son the chance his father didn't get,' said Rosel, surprising herself at how coherent her wish was.

'Exactly, you want a permanent place in France and you want your son to come join you.'

Rosel blinked wide-eyed. What could she say in the face of this impossible dream that she'd never have a shot at?

'Yes? No? Is it not what you want Rosel?' asked Neera. 'No, don't you *dare* pull that blank face on me. Honestly, I don't get your problem.' Neera, who had been brought up on a steady diet of busting your arse and seizing chances to get ahead, could hardly be expected to understand Rosel, who had been fed on the faith that a bowed head and lowered eyes improved your prospects of a decent life.

Violet stepped in to fill the silence. 'Honey, you made it this far on your own. Now an opportunity has flown in out of nowhere and landed on your doorstep. Are you going to welcome it or shoo it away because it's a stranger? This can be everything you want. You have nothing to lose.'

'What if they kick me out of France? What if they find out about my lies? I can't go to this meeting. I have to hide.'

'Dasha, do you want to shake her up again? Because if you don't, I will,' said Neera.

'The lies you speak of no longer exist. Colette employs you with your real name and even Len has forgiven you,' Violet said.

'There's been a mistake. Why would the president call me? I'm nobody. Why is this happening to me? With cameras there, everyone will see me. What if my Kuwaiti Madame finds me?' Rosel was freewheeling straight into a panic attack.

Neera rolled her eyes and Dasha took over. 'Do you remember when the President called in that Malian migrant Spiderman who saved a kid dangling from the fourth floor of a social housing block and gave him a medal of honour along with citizenship in front of the country's press?'

This had happened a few years before the virus—the perfect story of a person who happened to be at the right place at the right time being captured on a smartphone. Seeing the hits it had been getting on the Internet, the languishing traditional press had bought the footage and put in their twenty-four-hour news cycle till no demographic had missed seeing it. The popular President, who was now no longer popular, had hoped that rewarding Spiderman would divert his people from the assault of the *gilets jaunes* and make him loved again. It hadn't. There had been public frustration at the President bypassing the system on a whim. Why had the Malian got to jump the queue to Frenchdom when there had been tens of thousands of French drowning in daily bureaucracy, waiting their whole lives to make it to the other side of something or the other? This incident not only made the President unpopular but also come across as a confirmed egoist. It did, however, make excellent television. A downtrodden, muscular black superhero standing next to a leader with movie-star good looks: you couldn't look away, and it was worth it just for that.

'Yes, I do.' Rosel remembered it well. 'God really works in mysterious ways. That freak accident entirely changed the refugee's life.' Neera reeled under Rosel's rectitude. Too soon, because Rosel's doubt had not ended. 'But what has the refugee boy from Mali got to do with me?'

Perhaps, the ability to see beyond the obvious was not universal. It was obvious to the Russian, the Indian and the Senegalese that the unfortunate attack was fortune belatedly smiling at the Filipina, that the gash on the face was Rosel's dangling child and, like the Malian, she merely had to grab it and haul herself into visibility.

Neera picked up the mantle of breaking this down for Rosel.

'In times of national crisis, when public sentiment turns nasty, all leaders need to distract their citizens. And you, Madame, happen to be the good news story the President has chosen to ride on.'

'How do you know that? What if he only—'

'We don't know that, my dear. It's true we don't and can't know for sure,' said Violet. 'But tell me: what have you got to lose?'

'Nothing,' said Neera, 'because you *have* nothing. So now, sit up straight and pay attention.'

They had a day and a half to prep and dress Rosel suitably. Her scar, as Dr Beau had promised, was healing without a trace, which wasn't ideal for the upcoming meeting, in which the cut was the pièce de résistance, but they made do.

'The King of France, I think it was Louis XV, bought the palace as a residence for his whore,' exclaimed Dasha, one nod away from happily swapping places with Rosel, which would've made both the girls happy. 'It has over 365 rooms. You will probably meet him in his golden study, the Salon Doré, except this office is just for show and is not where he actually works from. So, don't be overwhelmed by all the personal photos and artefacts; they're just there for effect.'

Neera shushed this irrelevant history lesson and started going over the topics that might come up. Once Rosel stopped resisting her chance at redemption, she proved to be an eager student, diligently memorizing all the key phrases that Neera and Violet spun for her: the need for State-led inclusion on the basis of taxes paid; the inherent systemic racism in the West that makes immigrant nurses work as maids and a constitutional flaw where you are allowed to work but not be seen, which proves a bias towards money as a valued entity and not those who generate it.

Armed with her well-rehearsed answers and looking appropriately Asian, she was ushered by the security guards feigning casualness through the Cockerel Gate, which opened out into the garden at the back of the palace. Dasha hadn't mentioned anything about the garden because this entrance was hardly ever used.

The gilded rooster on top of the iron gate spread its wings, flaunting his French-ness. Rosel looked the cock straight in the eye. *I will be as French as you when I walk back out. You wait and see. I will be.* Her assurance no longer amazed her—the women had not messed about while drilling this into her. They had reminded her in her bones that she had escaped from a four-storey prison tower and was now an online sensation with celebrity following.

'A sensation. A silly YouTube sensation,' her son had accused her of choosing fame over him. 'Yes, why don't you completely forget about us and fly high, Mummy? Go ahead, be the cheap star you left us to be. Know that when it all collapses, your online fans won't be there to catch you. You will have to come running back to us and we will turn our backs on you like you did on us.'

It had hurt her deeply. It had also convinced her that if she wanted Danilo to love his mother, they could no longer live apart. As well-meaning as her family was, she could hear the words of her envious sister coming out of her child's mouth, as if being attacked had been something she had willed on herself.

There was no point in defending herself to him. He only had the image of the fabled West, where overweight kids in fancy shoes wasted food and no context of how she really lived or all that she had survived without their support.

'You would rather be mother to three strangers who have everything while I have no father and a mother who might as well be dead,' was how the last call with him had gone.

She had changed the topic by asking about school, which had been a mistake.

'They tease me for being a bastard. I am not going back to school, and you can't make me. You are too far way, so don't even try,' Danilo had said and hung up.

When had her sweet little baby turned into such a rude, angry boy? She feared that unless she went back home, he would follow the illicit footsteps of a father he had never met. No, she had walked too far for too long to turn back now. The rooster she was passing under had better defy the natural order of things and lay her a couple of golden eggs.

Chapter 7

The city lay in silence, the sodden pigeons shivering rather than making their usual ruckus. The heavy November rain dampened everything. Everything, that is, except the mood in Number Thirty-Six, rue des Diablesse, for tonight, they had ample cause to celebrate and no cloudburst was going to change that.

The disco ball reflected myriad, multicoloured solar systems on Neera's ceiling. She looked up, mesmerized by the mirrored galaxy of lights. With her eyes, she picked, followed and lost one revolving planet after another. There was a definite pattern, but it didn't seem to obey any rules. Was there a simile for life to be drawn from this? Her introspection yielded nothing today. Admittedly, she was bombed, even though the party was still a few hours from starting.

Violet scanned the room, putting final touches to her French and Foreign–themed party. Neera's apartment had been transformed: African animal prints, Soviet iconography, Indian lotus-and-marigold garlands, Chinese paper dragons and a photo booth with twenty kilos of real sand and two fake palm trees to represent the Philippines. The drapes, balloons, streamers and lights were all blue, white and red, symbolizing the country that had granted Rosel citizenship last Friday. Violet had been shocked when Neera had blithely agreed to the sacks of sand being dumped in her pristine apartment. Violet walked over to her friend, who was chasing fairy lights.

'Thank you,' Violet said, planting a kiss on Neera's cheek, her gratitude extending way beyond the sand and the jamboree she was hosting.

∽

It all started on the night of the day Neera went to film her blink-and-you-miss-it part for *Le Grand Gourmand* at Château de Charmant, about fifty kilometres west of Paris. The producers found an insignificant but status-loaded role for Neera to fulfil in the show as a guest judge for their episode showcasing India. Apart from the fact that she kept messing up her French lines, it was a pleasurable day.

Lucas, charming as ever, was a darling. First, he bigged her up to the contestants and the crew and then took her by the arm for a tour of the hidden gems of the historically listed manor they were filming in, which came with its own three-tier theatre with red and blue velvet curtains and a mysterious Chinese pagoda in the garden. In spite of the embarrassing number of retakes on her account, the filming didn't take more than a few hours, and, by seven in the evening, she barged into Violet's studio, charged and bursting with a plan, which seemed to happen every few days lately.

Not one to do things by halves, the raging widow had transmogrified into a beacon of positivity. Cynicism had simply bounced off her shiny new exterior. It was unbearable for those who knew her. So, the pessimism coming full pelt at Neera from the very person she had vowed to rescue was no match for her resolve. If anything, each attack reinvigorated her. She had sworn to Violet that she'd find a way to her salvation—that she was willing to die (or, more accurately, kill) to live up to that promise.

'This soup kitchen is going to feed our souls, Vee,' said Neera, beaming dementedly.

'I hate to break it you, but there are as many soup kitchen charities in Paris as there are homeless people. The poor scoff at these meagre attempts to bandage their wretchedness.' This was neither true nor what Violet truly believed. On the contrary, free hot meals had seen her through many a rough night in the days after she'd left the paltry comfort of her aunt's place.

Neera ignored her. As far as she was concerned, Vee was suffering from an amygdala hijack, where her neurons were constantly in alarm mode and every response tapped into the stock of negativity stored in her brain. She was not making this up or trying to give it a clever gloss and was, by no means, the sole recipient of Violet's enduring funk.

Neera was in her studio when Benjamin walked in with his fresh prints of Raphaël. Politesse demanded that she excuse herself. But while a tigress can be tamed, befriended and even taught to smile, she is never going to rid herself of her stripes. And so, the widow stayed put.

She had no idea that trouble was brewing in paradise—not that that would've made her leave. From the few occasions Neera had observed Benjamin and Violet, she had inferred that they were bound together like Bonnie and Clyde. On closer reflection, not a pleasant parallel, seeing as that love story ended in blood and bullets. And in that moment, theirs seemed to be headed the same way. Vee spoke to her lover with thinly veiled contempt. *I should not be here*, thought Neera, reeling under the awkwardness of the situation. And yet, it was exactly what made her stay: confirmation that there were other loved ones that Violet was lashing out at.

Neera was moderately impressed with the photo essay that Benjy had done with Dasha, but now she could plainly see that those pictures were no indication of his real talent. He laid out his prints on the floor, wanting Vee to help him choose two or three. He had captured the beautiful beggar going about his daily routine: holding an 'I'm hungry' sign; brushing his teeth; waking up in his sleeping bag; eating a sandwich; buying a beer; talking to other homeless men… Nothing out of the ordinary. So, what made these images so exquisite?

The eyes in the images looked up at Neera, taunting her, daring her to look away. She couldn't. Her hand trembled slightly as she lifted a print off the floor, brought it close to her face and shuddered. Raphaël was shifting, coming closer, his hand reaching out, asking for something. He was asking her to lean in, to go deeper into his world. Benjamin's image had only one man and somehow, there was another behind him and then another and another. She blinked once, twice, allowed her eyes to settle. Almost indiscernible multiple exposures were moving the beggar towards her. *Genius!* The sheer starkness of the image compelled her to notice the absences. She found herself looking down at the monochromatic man's face from high above and felt like she was pushing him away as he was approaching. This odd placement of the camera at an extreme angle was a clever trick. It skewed the boundary between subject and observer. Instantly, it made her not only a voyeur but actually a *contributor* to the fate that would befall the man. She recoiled. The image fell to the floor like a drunk butterfly.

One by one, however, Violet tore into the banality of Benjamin's photograph, detailing its flaws and ordinariness.

'You've done nothing with his handsome form. It's lazy work. You've captured him as he is, put some filters on, cleaned up the background—and you want applause for it!'

'He doesn't need anything done with his form or otherwise,' said Benjamin. 'That's what I've been trying to explain to you all along, Vee. Raphaël doesn't need a fairy godmother to change his life. He's made his choice, whether society thinks it is the right one or not.'

'Society didn't give him a choice,' Violet spat back. 'I tried to.'

'That may be so, my love, but from what I've observed, he can't help who he is, or rather who he has been forced to become. It is too upsetting for him to be told that he must now be someone he can't. He is happy for you or anyone to be part of his life on his terms, to witness his life but not to—'

'Don't you know it all, *Doctor* Benjamin Vidal. Listen to you talk!' she said. 'You think by taking a few mundane pictures of a man *I* spotted, you'll catapult into art house fame? Well, let me break it to you, clear and simple: you are not going anywhere except down. These photos are shoddy at best.'

When Neera tried to rise to defend the photographs (she didn't much care about the photographer himself), she was brusquely told to leave.

It was only later through Dasha that Neera found out that Violet felt betrayed by her boyfriend for using her discovery as a muse. If Neera didn't have personal experience of the irrational bile that spewed out of a jilted woman, she would've said that Vee was being nonsensically petty and claiming proprietorship where she had none. But this was complicated terrain, involving an unresponsive beneficiary and an overenthusiastic boyfriend, and Neera knew that unless Violet was restored to her role as benevolent Mama Vee, her wrath would continue to spiral out of control.

'In the final round, when I was judging with Lucas—can you hear me out before dissing my soul kitchen?' Neera continued from where she'd been cut off. 'Anyway, there was this young unassuming chef; she couldn't have been more than twenty years old. She presented this complex structure of a dessert and called it "Mirrored Palace of India". It had the most unusual combination of flavours—honeyed dates with *amchur* masala and clove oil.'

'I've never heard of amchur masala.'

'That's exactly the *point*,' said Neera, trying to get the story out as quickly as she could. 'This timid chef grew up moving from one French orphanage to another. Often, her duty was to help the Christian sisters in the kitchen. One day, a nun on an exchange from Calcutta cooked Bengali sour fish curry, using dried mango powder that she had brought with her—this powder is amchur. The orphan had never so much as seen a mango, yet that smell triggered her imagination, taking her to places she'd barely heard of. Of course, the curry was served solely to the sisters while the children inhaled the foreign aroma and ate their sausage and pasta. But that scent changed the orphan's life.'

Violet understood better than Neera ever could. When you sleep in rat-infested tunnels marinated in urine and semen and are subjected to the most outlandish forms of deprivation, you are simultaneously blessed with an essential survival tool: the most vivid inner life. Violet had often escaped into a wonderous imaginary life, where kings and queens rhapsodized over her dancing, copied her costumes and commissioned songs for her to perform. So, when a real-life version of her invented life came to pass, Violet moved through it with a been-there-done-that ease.

'It's a touching story, Neera,' said Violet. 'Not sure what it has to do with your soup charity baloney.'

By the time Neera was halfway through her grand plan of cooking and doling out free gourmet fair for the poor to take them on an exotic journey through their stomachs, Violet's dull eyes were beginning to narrow and sparkle.

The time to shed her old skin had arrived. For weeks, she had been rubbing against the abrasive surface of her own sullenness. She was ready to rid herself of this battered and baggage-heavy layer that no longer served her and glisten once more like Shahmaran, the mother of serpents, who she was born to be.

Chapter 8

Voluntarily back. *I'm here because I'm choosing to be.* It was the first time Violet had gone there since Benjamin and she had managed to make it out of that part of Paris. The memories came in enhanced technicolour, like digitally restored scenes from an old silent film. She hadn't forgotten a moment, even though, over the years, she'd trained herself not to think about any of it.

Bafflingly, the area of La Petite Ceinture was being romanticized by more than a handful of Parisians who belonged to the age of recycling, post-capitalism, sporadic-earning gigs and universal despair. Evidently, this long-disused circular railway, which wound around the waist of Paris and now was a green wasteland, had been gentrified since Violet had left. Yet it didn't warrant the glorifying blogs and cyber-poetry. According to their sentimental drivel, the area served as a haven of biodiversity in an overcrowded city. *A haven of crackheads, more like.* The bloggers and poets only came for nature walks or to paint graffiti or score substances and human flesh, and they disregarded what didn't fit with the narrative they were knitting. They glossed over the thieves, misfits and lowlifes that had erected permanent homes out of garbage; they bypassed the druggie tunnels, teeming with rodents and abuse, and focussed on the beauty of the wild vines, creepers and the occasional fox crossing the tracks. Their herb-hued version would have had a very different tint had they slept rough on those rail lines, as she had.

'No, no, no please stop. The boxes will spill open if you pile them in like that,' Violet cried out.

Neera was an Uber call away from bidding her project

adieu, particularly after the previous day's disaster. So, Violet had taken over.

A team of six fidgety volunteers—who would've just as eagerly scraped hardened chewing gum off the streets if it meant leaving the isolation of their cramped homes and having something legitimate to do—had followed Neera's directions to cook up the gorgeously creamy split-lentil and coconut chicken soup-curry, topped with fried mustard and coriander seeds, served over caramelized aubergine and lemongrass rice. The owner of the pub *La Folie Douce* in the 19th arrondissement had been persuaded to let them use his large vacant concert venue as their charity kitchen. So, there they were, surrounded by gas cylinders, Excel sheets and containers. Everything had gone according to plan until the appointed hour, when no one showed up save two sheepish characters, tempted by the aroma, who insisted on paying for the meal, and thus had to be turned away. Today, however, Violet had a new plan in place.

'Why can't we set up like yesterday?' asked Neera. 'I think it's absurd—this going to *find* the hungry and the homeless. They should come find us. We've put up signs! Once they see poor people like themselves lining up, they'll follow suit, right?'

'If you are ready to waste all your efforts one more time and watch Astrid and Victor gobble down boxes, fine let's stay put. No? I didn't think you were. Okay, look, here's how you pack a caddy so nothing spills.'

'Everything is going to be cold and taste disgusting,' grumbled Neera.

'The caddy is insulated, it'll stay at its current temperature for at least three hours, and we will be done with the stash long before that. Then we can walk back and refill it. If it goes well, we can look into buying a few more of these caddies. But for now, let's make do with what we have.'

Violet could see that Neera had not signed up for this labour-intensive humanitarian work. All she had wanted was to see the light switch on in the deprived eyes of the needy as she served them steaming spoonfuls of soup—to be bathed in the warm saintly glow of their gratitude as each bite took them closer to a foreign paradise. And she wanted to achieve this *without* leaving her bougie quartier. It was Violet who had insisted on this dodgy area because of some unresolved past ties and was now compelling her to pull a trolley around these disagreeable streets, looking for disagreeable people to feed. None of this had been part of her plan. She was prickling to throw a princess strop. But luckily, she knew she was being watched by friends, family and the gods-that-be, and her ego would not allow her to walk away from her own genius idea. *Suck it up and stick it out. I have made a promise to help my friend and this is helping my friend.* The princess forced herself to focus on the long, warm bath that awaited her when it was all over.

Violet paraded over to a group of ageing Kurds near a roundabout, parked the caddy, and asked if they'd like a hot, home-made meal.

'Do you have toothpaste?' one bearded man asked.

The others crowded around peering into the trolley, looking for any little treasures they could lay their hands on.

'Soap? No soap? Razor?'

'We have only soup curry, and it's delicious. Take it, you'd be lucky to have some, especially for free,' said Neera. 'Do you want some or not? If you don't want it, please move along.'

Grudgingly they took the boxes.

'Bread? Some bread? Bread is nice with soup,' one asked.

'There's rice underneath, try it.'

They did. Neera searched their faces and didn't get the reaction she was certain of. Violet laughed, making Neera laugh and they walked on. One old lady came running after them.

'One more,' she demanded, 'For my boy. Give.'

Next, they stopped near the metro, where a large group of people of all ages were lolling around the hot air vents on the ground. Empty beer cans, fragments of foil and wrappers were scattered all around. Neera saw one of the older ones shoot up and make devil-like eye contact with her before retreating into a chemically induced ecstasy. Neera's altered humour was past caring.

A bony, toothless young man, dressed in mangy leather, strode up to them. 'Man, this is the best shit I have ever tasted. Fuck me, the flavours are out of this world. *Putain! Putain!* I don't know what I'm eating, whatever it is, it's like a fluffy gunshot to the head! The way the textures melt together, Jesus fucking Christ.' A tear rolled down his eye and before he could control it, he was weeping, but he kept eating.

He wept into his soup, asked for another and then walked away from the rest of the gang to sit under a tree with his food, quietly and slowly journeying somewhere he had never been. He came back three more times, each time less able to speak, overcome with happiness.

Neera caught Vee dabbing her eyes. She knew the taste of this moment and that the memory of being transported would see the boy through many rough nights. The two women put their arms around each other and exhaled. When the skinny man was done, he made his way over to them, thanking them profusely and awkwardly tried to give Neera a hug. She backed away, horrified.

'Covid,' she said, faking a smile behind her mask, hoping that it was explanation enough.

'Do you have tampons?' a leather-clad woman asked.

'Next time,' replied Neera.

And, true to her word, the following week, along with the ingredients, Neera packed tampons, sanitary napkins, soap, shower gel, everyday toiletries and at least a dozen unopened, in-flight toilet bags that her Jannie had amassed on his business class trips around the world.

La Petite Ceinture ceased to be a sordid place in Violet's past, becoming instead a weekly hajj to where her journey had begun, a reminder of all that she had overcome. It also became a pilgrimage to the memory of her mother, whom she could hear saying: *Vafi, you know what all the prophets say: no one has ever become poor by giving. Open your heart, my son, and listen to me. If you want something, give it first.*

It made her happy that Neera didn't skimp on the flavours or pare down her creations despite the erratic reception. With every aromatic box that Violet handed out, she understood more clearly that her mother had given so much of herself not because she had much to give but because she knew exactly what it felt like to have nothing.

Chapter 9

It wasn't jealousy that Dasha was feeling. She had been resistant to that emotion her whole life, so why would she be jealous now? She was living the dream in the capital of fashion (even if fashion felt futile) as a ramp model (*surely* she'd be hired again). Nah, her twin was wrong. She couldn't possibly be jealous. Of whom? An obese girlfriend? A half-sized friend? No, it had all happened too fast and caught her by surprise, that's all. But how had she not foreseen any of this? By not being ahead, she was likely to be left out, and there was nothing she loathed more than that.

Overnight, Astrid had gone from never-been-cast-before to the face of Xanadu, a multinational e-commerce company based out of the Netherlands. Dasha adored Astrid, but she was a realist—*in the real world, girls like Astrid only became ambassadors of clothing companies as a joke or, at best, as an experiment.* It was pity, not envy, she felt for her lover, and this was not a sentiment you share with the person who inspire it.

Queuing with Astrid, waiting to pay for the quickly melting bags of ice that Neera had sent them to get for the party, she felt the pang again.

It was a party for Rosel, whom she was personally responsible for making a citizen. Rosel had always shown her gratitude, even on occasions when she had no reason to. Right now, that didn't feel enough. Nothing felt enough. Dasha was done helping others. *Who is helping me?*

She'd solved a mystery for Neera to help absolve her guilt and then assisted her in becoming mega-rich again. She'd got Violet's boyfriend to rescue her from herself. She got the boyfriend to do his best work photographing her, a House of Lure model no less, for free. She'd tugged and squeezed Astrid's thighs into the impossibly tight yoga onesie for the Xanadu casting. She'd devised and posted Rosel's music video. Now everyone else's life was on track and she was an out-of-work model peddling sleaze. How was this fair?

'You are used to your plans falling into place,' Andrei had said to her on the phone a few days earlier. 'You are falling apart because, for once, they aren't.' He had become increasingly concerned about her; he'd noticed that she'd become emotionally unavailable and, more often than not, had to urgently run off to take care of a disaster.

'Dasha-the-doer does not fall apart, Andryusha,' she said, without enthusiasm.

She hadn't built up to telling Andrei about the men she was entertaining through Violet's Internet connection, and it was eating her up, making her excrete the little she did eat more than usual. They talked often, but now, never deeply. And though she shared endless details of the women who had become her kin, she had not come out to him about *the* girl in her life. She wanted to feel good and sure of who she was before blabbing to him, and that feeling had come and gone with her as she had walked the Lure catwalk many months ago.

She was done keeping up with everyone else when no one could be bothered to keep up with her. Not even her twin. It was *his* fault that she hadn't been able tell him. She'd always protected him because she knew he needed her to be more than she ever was—she couldn't bear to let him down with the way he looked up to her. It was exhausting. He'd never actually said the words, but she knew. She was his twin, after all.

'Maybe, it's okay not to be the doer all the time,' he said.

She laughed bitterly. 'If I don't do it, who will? Things don't just get done, little brother. Someone has to do it.' If she could just hug her twin right now, smell his hair full of gel and sweat, everything would be okay. This emotional distance between them that she would never openly admit to being solely responsible for was doing her no good. 'I think I'm owed something too. I deserve more, right?'

'You know you've always been at the centre of the action, and almost everyone loves you for it. Just sometimes, you have to make room for others to shine. Let your friends have their moment. You have nothing to be jealous of.'

'Don't be ridiculous, you know I don't get jealous.'

'Which is why I'm surprised. Those closest to you seem to be riling you up all the time,' he said. 'How many times have you told me that they're family—your "chosen" family?'

She flinched at those words. Did her brother forget that, at another time, in another world, she had not been chosen? *You were not chosen, Andrei. We were not the chosen ones*, she wanted to scream. Instead she said, 'Yes, yes, and I'm happy for them. All I want to know is: when does my time come?'

'I'll ask the mermaid on the cactus tree, I owe her a visit. You know she's been drinking moonshine with the grasshoppers again. I'll need to soften her. What shall I use—butterfly jam or ladybird lotion?'

Dasha's mood wouldn't allow her to engage in the fantasy.

'Sis, is your head full of him again?' He knew her better than the lines on his own palm and he knew she was not telling him everything.

His sister was the star of their family and community. Born forty-one minutes before him, she combined the confidence of a firstborn with a constitutional commitment to be special. His whole life, he'd happily taken a backseat so that his twin could shine. As much as he'd wanted to be part of the Saturday sojourns with their father, he'd feigned fatigue so Dasha could spend solo time with the man who made her world go round. It was enough simply to enjoy the experience second-hand because the sparkle in his sister's stories made *his* world go around. No one bathed him in tenderness like she did. What she gave and got from their father, every bit of joy and adoration, she multiplied and passed on to him. 'He loved us. He loved you. You loved—you *love* him. Isn't that enough? It wasn't like *you* were going to stick around in Vyborg forever, anyway.'

'Tell me, honestly, doesn't it kill you that he's having this wonderful life without us?'

'Honestly, no,' he said, and that was the truth. 'How do you know he's having a wonderful life? Maybe he's struggling and ashamed. Maybe he's dead! Maybe the Russian authorities found him and killed him for running off with a man. That labels him as mentally ill here, don't forget.'

'Stop! How can you even think that?'

'It makes no real difference one way or the other, sis. He's not in our lives, we have no way of finding him because he doesn't want to be found. So, dead, alive, it's all the same to me. Cherish the past and move on.'

'You're jealous that he chose me and not you. That he loved me more than anyone else in the family, that you were not as important to him.' She had never been this cruel to Andrei before.

'Ouch,' said Andrei.

She heard him breathe down the phone for a few seconds in silence. She'd hurt him. Intentionally. *Why?*

'I'm sorry, I'm so sorry,' said Dasha, her face reddening with shame. 'I don't know what's come over me lately. I don't know how to stop being so angry all the time. I'm not this person, I'm hating on everyone.'

'It'll pass, Dasha. Focus on the family around you, be grateful for them. And stop being jealous.'

Andrei was right. Not about the jealousy—that was a minor blip, easily fixable. She had to relearn to live in the now or she'd have no future. Colouring her present with the past had made her a walking advertisement for therapy. *Let's look at where this anger/guilt/self-hate is stemming from*. Or worse: *can you remember a time when and why you first felt this emotion?* Was she falsely reconstructing her past with how today was making her feel?

Besides, hadn't the selfish action of this human propelled her to the city of chic, given her membership to Number Thirty-Six and allowed her to explore her own sexuality? This ought to change how she felt towards that human and his departure. Why was she still harping on about the past? If she couldn't be present in her present for whatever pressing reason, she wouldn't be present even if her desired future unfolded as, technically, she'd be hardwired to either taint the present with the past or permanently plan for the future.

It was absurd that she hadn't been able to move past him after all that had happened to her: becoming the face of Lure (no need to split hairs on accuracy), finding her own girl gang (none of them would agree to the nomenclature, but still), earning big money (okay, irrespective of the source), owning her sexuality (one day soon, openly), painting Paris pink (yes, that one time when she'd lost her shoe and almost her best friend) and the pandemic (the end of the world and he still hadn't reached out). Maybe it was time to let him go.

Never.

People born in the extreme conditions of Vyborg could endure much more. He had ingrained that in her.

The melting ice soaking her hands brought her back to the here and now. Without a word, Astrid took the dripping bags from Dasha and let her lover wipe her wet hands on the loose end of her T-shirt, so that Dasha's hands would be free and ready to pay. It was a casual gesture and one that made Dasha think: *this is my family*.

Chapter 10

The guests started arriving around 8.30 p.m., half an hour before curfew kicked in. It had been implicit in the invite that this was going to be a sleepover or 'risk the night police for a spot of fun' kind of night. Though the air was frosty and wet, Neera—who had changed into a blue-and-red handwoven patola sari, wrapped strategically around white sequins leggings—was busy flinging open all the windows. After all, the world was still full of the virus and she had no intention of aiding its spread. And with the number of people who had jumped on her invitation, like she was offering the last seats on a flight promising to get you out of hell for a few minutes, the apartment would warm up soon enough.

Vee made her way back up, dressed in blue and green, her mother's favourite colours. She'd cut an African wax-print kaftan to flaunt her long torso and was sporting a turban. Later in the night, the turban would unravel as part of an unannounced dance performance depicting Rosel's great escape. Another surprise was hidden up her sleeve for Benjy, with whom she knew she had behaved despicably. But now she had to wait for Nic the sleaze to arrive to right the wrongs. The thought of seeing her boyfriend's stunned face made Violet all fuzzy for the future, like an expectant mother waiting to break the news to her partner that their fifth and final round of IVF had worked.

The attack on Rosel had made the pair a team again, although Violet had softened towards her lover a short while before that. Specifically, after The Curry Caddy had become an intrinsic part of Neera and her lives. He'd been right about Raphaël; she could see that now. It had been selfish to try and change his path to bring him into a life she had believed would be better for him. Benjy had accepted the homeless hunk for who he was, had become part of his life without intrusion, and she was learning to do the same.

In spite of Neera having drawn a line at inviting the homeless man everyone seemed obsessed with, Violet had gone ahead and done it anyway. Fortunately for everyone involved, he would not be attending tonight's festivities. A long time ago, a celebration had ended life as he'd known it, and even though his fragile mind had been completely shattered after that, the memory itself was a stubborn one and refused to leave.

∫

Raphaël's father had a humble job as a receptionist at the equally humble two-star Hôtel de l'Europe in Rennes, up north in Brittany. He sweet-talked the housekeeping manager into giving his wife regular temporary jobs. With Raphaël's unpredictable behaviour at school and bouts of self-harm, it wasn't possible for her to take on a more permanent position. She didn't mind: from the moment she had looked into the forest-green eyes of her first born, she had loved him more than anything else in the world, even if there was a gentle, slow sadness about him from a young age. Both parents tried to get professional help for their son, but the highly specialized diagnosis, prognosis and treatment plans only led to more confusion, waiting and frustration. And with the arrival of Raphaël's more 'normal' sister, they compensated him with love for overlooking his little quirks.

For his wife's fortieth birthday, Raphaël's father managed to book a heavily discounted long weekend at the hotel's far fancier sister branch at the seaside village of Perros-Guirec in Côtes d'Armor. Of course, the family of four took vacation trips almost every summer—they were French after all. It would always be a modest couple of weeks: either an all-inclusive, everything-communal camping trip or renting a basic, self-service holiday apartment from Saturday to Saturday. They never stayed in a hotel, certainly not one with an en-suite bathroom with its own hairdryer and bidet, daily housekeeping and an all-you-can-eat breakfast buffet.

The father had shelled out for two rooms side by side. His wife deserved this weekend: the last few years with their teenage son, who was unlikely to complete school or ever leave home, had been harder than ever. He was guilty of dropping the ball while his uncomplaining wife had kept it rolling all by herself. This weekend belonged to her.

A cold, salty breeze sauntered in through their open windows to wake them earlier than usual. Hôtel l'Oceania wasn't high enough to have a view of the water, but the ocean was hardly a kilometre away. Raphaël and his sister ate three soggy pains au chocolat and a bowl of non-branded cereal, drank two glasses of canned juice and one of Nesquik and licked clean two mini containers of Nutella each. They would have found room in their bellies for more had the beach not been beckoning them. They shed their clothes as they ran straight into the ocean. On the shore, their mother pulled a shawl around her shivery shoulders and waved from her mat—how lovely, she thought, still to be the age where your body could ignore the cold if there was fun to be had.

When they returned to their hotel room, their mother filled the rather large bathroom sink with soapy water and asked for their salty wet bathing suits. She hadn't learnt to stop babying them, and it was not in their interest to make her. Their father urged them to go get dressed—he had made birthday bookings at a recommended brasserie; tonight, the family would celebrate the woman they all loved in style.

Raphaël snuck back into the bathroom to surprise his mother, the only person who didn't ask him confusing questions, with a shell necklace he had made for her at the beach. She was still wet from the shower, wrapped in a towel, blow-drying her hair. The dryer was not the greatest piece of equipment—old and noisy. She didn't hear or see him in the fogged-up mirror. And so, when he moved to place the shells around her neck, she jumped in fright. Her hand, along with the dryer, fell into the full sink and he wasn't sure what was happening to her, all he remembered was her unseeing eyes staring at him.

The hotel said that their dryer, which had an EFCI protection certificate, was not to blame. It was the salt in the water, compounded with her bare feet, wet skin and amount of fat insulation, which allowed the relatively small current to flow directly through her central nervous system and kill her. A freak accident. They were sorrier than was possible, but not responsible. His father never went back to the hotel he worked at or any other. A year later, his sister was taken into foster care and Raphaël found himself, penniless and confused, on a train to Paris.

∽

In spite of all the French windows being open, the apartment was already smoky. Neera recognized barely more than half the guests, who were all drinking with the determination of prisoners on parole. That model friend of Dasha's walked in looking pretty as a big, fat button. *If she lost weight, she'd be stunning. No, I'm not allowed to think that these days, am I?*

'Where's Dasha, my dear?' Neera never could remember her name, invariably forgetting it as quickly as she was told it.

'She'll be up in a bit,' said Astrid. 'She needed the room to make a few calls in private.'

'To whom?'

Astrid squinted at Neera, baffled. 'I don't know. It's private?'

Neera couldn't bear this generation. They all took themselves and the rules of conduct far too seriously. *No wonder they were all suicidal or bulimic,* she thought. *This girl could do with a bout of bulimia. Wait—you are not allowed to think that these days.*

Chapter 11

How had he got her number? But of course, he'd managed it. Dasha herself had never not found a way when she wanted something. *Girl, who do you think you learnt that from?*

Why today? Just when she was almost ready to stop feeling the lack of him. *He heard me. Of course, he heard me. Why now? Then again, why not?*

Dasha FaceTimed Andrei on autopilot. 'He got in touch with me.'

Andrei did not need to be told who. 'Where is he? How is he?'

'I don't know yet, I called you first,' she said, calm spreading over her by simply seeing her twin's face on the screen.

'But why now?' he asked.

'Right?! Why now!' She knew he'd have the right words for her, that he'd mirror her exact emotion. She missed him in her life. For a while, she hadn't been telling him the whole truth but that didn't mean she loved him any less. They were twins: without the other, neither was whole.

'He must have seen your TV interview about the hate crime— it was everywhere.' Dasha had sent Andrei the clip, and later he had also caught it on RVTV. Seeing his Russian sister dubbed in Russian had been comical. The national news channels around the world had cheerfully picked up the story as an opportunity to belittle France, the self-appointed champion of liberty. 'Send me his message.'

```
My darling Darya, the light of my eyes.
I have been unfair in my silence. I was
```

scared. It was not possible for me to find happiness in my new life if I held onto the pain of leaving my old. It's only now I realize you can't leave something that is inside you. My kroshka, you were always my clever one; you are making me extremely proud. I will wait as long as it takes for you to get in touch. Your papochka.

'Don't tell mother,' Dasha said. 'It'll just reopen the wound.'
'Of course, I won't. Are you still angry with him?'
'I was never angry with him, Andryusha.'
'No, you never were.'
'Isn't that the strangest?' she said, more to herself than to him. 'He left us with no money, no goodbyes... He must've heard our mother was sick and still remained silent. And yet, somehow, I don't hate him. He filled me with so much love for myself, for the world, Andryusha. I'm who I am because of him.'

'You were always daddy's little girl,' he said without an iota of jealousy.

Take that, you imperious therapists. I loved my father, he left me, I bled, I never stopped loving him and the power of that brought him back. Nothing more, nothing less. No letting go of the past or future needed here.

She looked at her twin's sunshine face and took a deep breath.
'Promise me you won't be angry with me.'
'What have you done now?' he asked, bracing himself for the worst.
'First, promise me.'

He promised her, and she told him all about her lockdown goings-on, the details about touching her body for business and touching Astrid's for pleasure. Confusion was written all over his face, and yet it felt good to get it off her chest. Making him a compulsory witness to her choices validated them for her. Andrei was not angry, although, to say that he fully understood would be a lie.

'I will need time to process this, okay? You have to allow me that,' he said. 'Now, you promise me that you are going to be safe. I mean it, sis. Promise me. There are a lot of crazy creeps out there and this isolation is making the world all the more aggressive and violent.'

'Those creeps will never touch your sister, I promise. I'm a Queen of the Screen: I use it as I please and command it to protect me from all my enemies,' she said playfully, feeling lighter than she had in months.

'That you are, Dasha, that you truly are: Queen of the Screen,' he laughed.

'And when the world opens up, Andryusha, you are headed straight to LSE and you will live and eat like a Russian Tsar, because your queen decrees it.'

When they hung up, she realized it was the first time they had spoken without either indulging in their nonsensical code talk. Sitting on her bunk bed, she took a moment to mourn the fact that she and her twin were all grown up now before dialling her juvenile father.

∽

By the time Dasha made her way up, dressed in a Prada mink *ushanka* hat with furry ear flaps that she'd borrowed from Violet, the party was in full swing. A dense cloud of smoke hung low in the high-ceilinged salon. The palatial apartment was decked out to impress, and the costumes were ingenious, inviting outlandish behaviour. It'd been so long that people had forgotten how to socialize: they were dancing and acting like they were characters in an impromptu film audition for a Gatsby party that was being directly beamed, along with all its bloopers and middling performances, onto a 75 mm screen, magnified and heightened. Dasha felt obligated to assume her part or risk being relegated to the spectators' gallery. And speaking to *him* again had confirmed that she was born to take centre stage, not sit in the audience.

Dr Beau turned to Rosel, who no longer looked as meek as he remembered. But that could well be because she was now a fleetingly famous news item, and he—like everyone else who had seen her—was projecting on her.

'Look at you, Mademoiselle Andal! You look great. They tried, didn't they, to deface you?' said the doctor, half-shouting over the din of the party. 'They couldn't have imagined that removing that skin would reveal such strength. I'm proud to have helped you in my own little way. You are a marvel, young lady and *that* is your revenge.'

Rosel turned red and mute as a beetroot. She still didn't know how to own her space and compliments like these, which came way too often nowadays, invariably made her want to retreat to her roof.

Singing her songs in front of a camera, with Dasha telling her when to blink and when to nod, was controlled, intimate even. The world on the other side of that camera, however, was far too daunting. She had begged them not to have this party, had said again and again that there was nothing she hated more than being the centre of attention. Then, realizing that she was in no such danger given the three women who were throwing her this party, she acquiesced. Besides, there wasn't a person in Paris who wasn't desperate for a big boozy boogie in this age of social distancing, and she happened to be the one with a certified reason to celebrate.

It still felt like a dream that the rooster's egg had landed without cracking in her lap. Soon, she had been officially promised, she could begin the process to apply for Danilo's visa. And if that was not reason to rejoice then she was doomed to die a miserable woman or so she had been told repeatedly by Dasha.

She smiled uncomfortably, excusing herself from the doctor and started to collect discarded glasses, taking them to the kitchen, till Dasha cautioned her for being a server for life and made her do two tequila shots in a row as penance.

The lights went off, the disco ball continued to cast its magic. A song pierced through the darkness, and the revellers turned to the voices. Blanche, Augustin and Thomas made their way down the grand stairway in the lobby of Neera's apartment, singing a song they had written for their nanny, set to the tune of 'So Long, Farewell' from *The Sound of Music*. The choice had Violet's stamp all over it.

The staircase, along with the five chimneys, was one of the original features that Ricky Garcia had insisted on preserving in the duplex apartment. Jean-Paul had always thought it too grandiose, and he'd finally had a chance to demolish it when they had renovated—but Neera and Ricky had oohed and aahed at the black railing with its gold accents and the burgundy-carpeted stairs. They had accused him of being a philistine for not cherishing the swirls that signalled the beginning of the Belle Époque. The double-height circular lobby had added volume and intimidation, making first-time guests think they had the wrong address—that they'd mistakenly entered a new boutique hotel. Neera had loved it from the get-go. The apartment was so much better than the dream home that had been planted in her head, first by her mother and subsequently cultivated and finessed by her obnoxiously loaded cohorts.

The children held torches like spotlights under their cute little faces as they sang, going through the choreography they had spent two days practising. Colette—who, as of yesterday, was unemployed and, twenty whole hours later, still unpredictably happy—beamed at them from the bottom of the stairs.

Blanche signalled to the other two and they held up the torches to reveal Violet at the top of the stairs. Vee's voice boomed and the song began to pick up pace. Her turban unravelled, transforming into a rope attached to the railing, which she was sliding down—an ode to Rosel's prison break. The lyrics became clearer as Violet continued—*We say 'Felicitation', You are one of us, Done is the mission, After much fuss, You are one of us...*

Dasha bristled at the words. This was the root of the problem: creating divisive lines between an 'us' and 'them'. The premise that everyone wanted to be 'us' is how seeds of prejudice were sown. These kids would grow up believing in the advantage and virtue of white privilege. *Stop it, they are just kids and they love their nounou.* No one else seemed to have picked up on the potential offence. Was Dasha the only woke person in the room?

She was aware she was white and, as far as shades go, probably the whitest person in the room. But having escaped small-town Russia, she could see the errors and the exclusiveness of the arrogant Western world, and she wasn't afraid to call it out. When had she become so political? Did having a platform make her so? It was a chicken-and-egg and a Catch-22 rolled into one: after all, she wasn't foolish enough to waste the voice that was finally being heard. Tonight, however, she would let it go. It was Rosel's night and the night that she had finally spoken to the very person for whom she had set all this in motion. Tonight was a night to drink and let drink.

The song was over, Violet twirled and landed in the lobby, the kids bowed, the drunken guests cheered, and this was Neera's cue to turn the lights back on and return to the playlist. But she was nowhere to be seen.

Chapter 12

The marble floor cooled the fire that was emanating from deep within her. Neera surrendered the weight of her body to the floor, just as her yoga teacher in Mumbai had taught her, till the ground pushed back up and she was weightless, floating in Shavasna or, fittingly called, corpse pose.

The sound of the party filtered into the bathroom. The surprise performance had just ended; it didn't matter that she'd missed it. She wasn't yet ready to rejoin them. She lay there, shielding her eyes from the hidden spotlights in the ceiling. The not-quite yellow lights always made her skin look flawless in the mirror. It was such a pity she couldn't take these lights wherever she went—no other mirror made her look the same. She'd decided never to look at her reflection anywhere except here, which kept her confidence intact while time was bent on destroying it.

The printout of the booking she'd chanced upon, along with the brochure, rested on her belly. She stroked the sheaf of glossy paper and exhaled smoke from crudely made joint number—oh, who knew what number it was anymore. The ticking of the seconds hand on the quartz clock above the toilet was a hammer on a metal surface reverberating in her ears. Another spasm in her stomach made her contract in pain. She might need to get up and make her way to sit on the pot. Or was it better to throw up? For the moment, she couldn't move. This happened every time she overdid weed. She could recognize when one more drag would tip her over, and yet she was adamant about inhaling anyway. At forty-something she was still behaving like a teenage delinquent. She was close to a white-out. Well, at least, she was in her own bathroom.

It passed. And then she was flying and the world was exciting once again. She turned her head, saw the unbearable clock reflected in the mirror and the exact time she had her epiphany (a realization so obvious to the others that only she dared to call it an epiphany): 10.45 p.m.

The sensation she was feeling, which she'd been chasing for decades, was not what it seemed to be. She had been confusing sinking with soaring. The cannabis gave her an out-of-body experience, true. But it wasn't flying—far from it. She was instead drowning in the depths of despair, where her brain protected her from itself by switching off. She had mistaken her inability to string a thought together with having no extraneous thoughts in her head, mistaken being brain dead with being entirely at peace with the moment. *This* was not the epiphany. It was the realization, which arrived like a three-ton truck ramming into her cotton-candy head, that if she stopped sinking into this self-inflicted space, she would no longer need a saviour.

So, that was that: 10.48 p.m., starting now, she was going to stop seeking escape through herbs. It was simple: no smoking equalled no flying, which really meant no falling, no sinking and, therefore, no need to be saved. *Voilà!* Epiphany!

There had been a time when drugs had invigorated her and helped her live the life she wanted to live. Had she been fooling herself back then, too? No, she was definitely more functional and engaging high than when sober. In the absence of regulation, though, her herbal habit had started controlling her. It wasn't that rare now for her to have to lie down, no matter where she was, before she could carry on.

The worst incident had been when she and Jannie had walked into his premiere party for *The Scientist's Apparition*. She had literally legged it down the red carpet, her legs feeling like jelly, in search of a toilet to be horizontal in. The cubicles hadn't been large enough, so she'd simply sprawled out, in her gold Zuhair

Murad gown, under the row of sinks, hoping that no one would enter. Many had. She had pretended to have knocked her back out, and through clenched teeth and tightly shut eyes, had told them that because she didn't want to ruin her husband's big night, she had been hiding here till the pill she'd taken started showing some effect. They'd bought the lie, and in less than thirty minutes, she'd gone from flatlining to being the life of the party.

Enough. It was time to be her own man. The minute she could get off the floor, she was going to quit. Or at least not get high all the time. And definitely not in this bottomless quantity. Somehow, she suspected, she'd always be synonymous with weed. She'd never be ready to kiss goodbye to her most cherished image of her future: as an old granny, on a rocking chair on the veranda of her beach house, saluting the setting sun with a fat joint in her wrinkled fingers. It was strange: she never thought of herself as an old lady but always as an old *granny*, even though there was no possibility of her ever having or wanting grandkids.

10.54 p.m. Eckhart Tolle's voice in her head was telling her to take one slow breath in and let a slower breath out. The human body was made to be entirely self-sufficient. It was a wonder how blind most were to this miracle. Lately, she had discovered the bliss one could access by merely breathing in and out. Focussing solely on the oxygen that filled her, she managed to lift the gloom that had hurtled her to this floor. She made her way up on to her feet. The brochure of the house on the hill fell from her belly, along with the itinerary carefully planned by Jannie.

She hadn't been looking for it. She hadn't even known of its existence till she had stumbled upon it in Jean-Paul's desk drawer.

All these people, most of them Jannie's friends, in their apartment, marvelling at the home she had created, made her ache for him. As much as he dreaded stepping too far from his home, he absolutely loved entertaining people, indulging in food, wine and a good laugh. Why had they constantly gone out and not done more of it in their elegant, extravagant home? It had never been the right time or the right occasion, mainly because Neera had not entirely understood what pleased Parisians—whether she should pull out all the stops or stop at the basics. They seemed to curl up their lips no matter what was doled out for them, and she had no desire to put herself voluntarily on the receiving end of criticism in her own house. Now that she didn't give a damn, it was too late.

He'd have treasured tonight. They'd have talked about every detail, every conversation, every faux pas for days on end. They had a rule that in any social gathering: he would bring Neera her first drink and they would seek each other across the room or table to make eye contact every hour or so to check that neither needed rescuing. They would kiss and hold hands a lot in public because they couldn't resist it. Often, he'd imperceptibly slip his hand under her backless dress to find a breast or caress her lower back. Tonight, she would have given anything to feel him touch her.

She had escaped into his office, normally a forbidden territory for her. It was where she felt his presence the most. Everything had been as he'd left it. She had sat on his leather chair, with its McKenzie backrest and spun around. Closing her eyes, she had let herself imagine she had been sitting on his lap. Comforted, she had carelessly opened his drawers, hoping for a portal to him. Smiling back, as if waiting to be found had been his last act of love for her: a fully planned and paid for Christmas holiday at the near-impossible-to-reserve house on the hill in the mountain forest of Bois-d'Amont.

The snow-covered photos of the place had made it look like a winter wonderland—the kind of place that made Neera believe they were living in a story. This one could have been Narnia or the Northern Lights. Caressing the brochure had made her feel like she was touching her dead husband. He had been the last person to hold it and hide it, had been patiently waiting for the perfect moment to surprise the wife he had loved travelling with.

Neera splashed water on her face, brushed her teeth, scraped her tongue, which, for anyone searching, was a key give-away of all indulgences committed. Worse, the lumpy organ was a reminder from within her own mouth, in more ways than taste, of all the lies she had told; she cleaned till no traces were left. She reapplied her lipstick and admired how flawless and young she looked. This mirror saw her the way her husband had.

Chapter 13

Standing by the bar with Benjamin, Nicolas had to raise his voice to be heard over the beat of the music. 'Monsieur Baptiste de Beauchamp has taken over Manko for the moment and wants to use the nightclub as a private gallery, which, strangely, are the only places allowed to stay open. Do you remember him? Do you know who I'm talking about?' he asked Benjamin.

'Uhm, not sure, I think so.'

In fact, he more than remembered him—he hated that entitled bastard. Two years ago, Benjy had helped Violet dress up as a kinky geisha to go entertain Japanese guests at Beauchamp's countryside chateau. One of them had peed all over her and her fancy, rented kimono, rendering it unreturnable. Violet hadn't dared to make a fuss—she had needed the money of these perverted patrons. Benjy didn't mind that Vee funded her rich tastes by servicing the fetishes of richer men.

Actually, as a matter of fact, he did mind. He minded very much, but he had never felt he had a right to tell her. How could he? They'd been in it together, facilitating and guarding each other in turn, else they'd never have made it out. And in their new life on the west side of Paris, not once had they discussed putting an end to this sordid source of income. Well, it had been years since he'd peddled his body but only because his needs were different. Benjamin didn't want Fendi bags and Gucci shoes like Vee did. Something about their status and price made her feel worthy and valued. Then again, didn't he turn to her every time he was short, knowing where the money was coming from? He loved her, but they needed a way to put their past to bed. They needed to rid their lives of all the de Beauchamps. 'Is he the one who combs his hair forward to hide his baldness?' Benjy asked, pretending not to have noticed every vile detail of the offensive aristofart.

Violet watched Nic and Benjy from the corner of her eyes. Her timing had to be perfect or the surprise wouldn't go as planned.

'Anyway, Beauchamp and his moneyed friends, who've miraculously got wealthier as the rest of us have been furloughed, are bored. They have nowhere to go, nothing to spend their money on, no reason to dress up,' said Nicolas, taking his time to get to the point. 'This pandemic has made online collectors of them all. They believe that as taste-shapers they must champion the arts because that's what the world needs right now.'

'Obviously, and not vaccines and ventilators,' Benjamin said, unable to hide his contempt.

'I thought you'd be pleased to hear this, being an artist.'

'There's a time and place for everything, Nic.'

'Well, would you say it was the right time for you to exhibit your photographs at Manko? An exclusive month-long silent auction with the who's who as patrons, lining up in their designer heels, eager to get in to drink bubbly and spend a small fortune on one of your pieces?'

'What are you blabbering about?'

'Vee showed me. I've seen some of your collection, what do you call it, *Les Invisibles*? As a wedding present, I've convinced Monsieur de Beauchamp to make it his opening show,' said Nicolas and tipped his head in a smug bow.

Benjamin was lost. 'Whose wedding?'

In answer to his question, Violet was kneeling on one knee in front of him. When had she appeared? What was going on?

Dasha had lowered the volume of the music at the exact time, and a fresh-faced Neera had reappeared with a champagne flute in her hand. All eyes were now on Benjamin and Violet.

'Will you, Benjamin Vidal, make me the happiest girl in the world?' Violet's voice trembled with a rare vulnerability. Benjamin fought back tears. It took awfully long before he joined Violet on his knees. 'Nothing would make me happier.' Then, they were kissing and crying and laughing, and the party was roaring back to life around them, the guests were dancing wherever they stood and the night was full of a fresh lease of madness.

A few early peakers, who no longer had any idea how to pace themselves around drinks and human interaction, gave in to exhaustion. They lay expunged on the couch, the rugs, the chaise lounge, the grand staircase—wherever space was to be found. Neera had the foresight to lock the bedrooms: she knew that the more illustrious the crowd, the more entitled they felt and she didn't fancy any of this lot in her private quarters.

Some of the more Catholic guests, who Neera had invited for amusement value, reached the threshold of their tolerance. They thanked Neera, who artfully dodged their goodbye kisses, and ambled out of her apartment shaking their heads. The melange of eccentrics had mystified them. *Who puts a guest list like this together except a classless, grieving widow from a faraway land?*

They couldn't get away fast enough. They needed the familiarity of their god-fearing homes and had stayed this long because, at first, they'd been shell-shocked and didn't know if they were coming or going. And after their shock had worn off, they'd persevered in the misplaced hope that the soirée would start taking some sort of shape that made sense. *Who hosts a grand party like this for a domestic?*

They'd reached their absolute limit soon after. *That sinful proposal of that African man-girl to the pansy boy with the strange face was pushing it,* they whispered. *It was one thing to support gay rights, or the rights of the LGBT+ weirdos or whatever they called themselves these days—that didn't mean they had to be* invited to one's living room and become a part of one's life. This kind of behaviour is best if it remained foreign and not French.

The remainers, made of sterner stuff, yawned, rubbed their eyes and kept going, ingesting, inhaling and drinking whatever was on offer.

The marriage proposal, which Neera had known nothing about, had cheered her to the bone. It had also given a purpose to Jannie's gift of love: the ladies of Number Thirty-Six would be staying in the snowy house on the hill for Violet's bachelorette. It would be perfect. Her dear Jannie would smile down at Neera's new collection of friends, laughing at their antics from wherever he was. And maybe, as a wedding present, she would offer Vee the snip from Dr Beau! He was, after all, the best in the business. Then again, she wasn't entirely certain if Violet wanted the full transition or not... *I have to stop getting ahead of myself. New mantra: learn to ask and listen.*

'You seem pleased with yourself.'

Neera would recognize the voice of her naked messiah anywhere, even if she wasn't entirely sure of his name.

'I am! And all the more pleased to see you.' She wrapped him in a bear hug. Had he become more toned since the last time she'd seen him? Definitely more tanned. 'I'm sorry I've not been in touch. How's your péniche?'

'Still there,' said Dave. 'You look really well, Neera.'

'You have no idea how much of it has to do with you.'

He smiled his sunlit vegan smile, and she kicked herself for not having had sex with him when she had a chance. He was more than cute—he was wise. *You don't have to bed everyone you like.* 'I'd like us to be friends,' she blurted out.

'That we are, my dear. Aren't I here?' he said looking at her with all the time and care in the world.

'In that case, I'd like to see more of you.'

'It's a deal.' He pecked her on the cheek platonically and she felt the love. Just a different kind than the one she had come to expect from men.

Colette quietly crept out of the room that Neera had set aside for the kids, carefully shutting the door behind her. She had, after a lot of bribing, managed to peel them away from Rosel and into bed. She had kept waiting for dread or regret or shame or some cousin of that emotion to sweep over her all day. But the lightness she had felt when she'd finished her call with the HR had given way to elation. There was no other word for it—she could've literally cartwheeled down the stairs in glee.

It wasn't merely that they had agreed to let her go without insisting on a notice period or that they had proposed to make her part of the generous PSE scheme the French government was offering, the purpose of which was to avoid redundancies by providing financial support to an employee who was looking to branch out. She hadn't been fully listening and told them she'd think about it. It had been more that for the time being, for the first time that she could remember, she had no schemes up her sleeve, no plans in her usually overcrowded head.

She found her husband, who had never been more handsome to her, talking to Lucas, the chef. Now she'd finally have the time to try out some of his recipes or take an online cooking class or two. The thought made her jaw hurt from smiling too widely.

'Olivier tells me you gave good old Hermès the boot. I guess the shoe no longer fit?' Lucas laughed at his own bad joke.

Olivier tensed. He'd shared the news with Lucas expecting some discretion and had been on red alert since the call. His workaholic wife could go off her rocker at any moment, and he needed to be on full superman guard duty to pick up the pieces. She slipped her hand into Olivier's, interlacing her fingers with his. Though their hands felt rougher, drier somehow, it was a perfect fit. It always had been.

'Are you still doing your online classes? I'd like to sign up,' she said.

'I see Dubai knocked some sense into you,' said Lucas.

'Actually, fighting with my husband in the fancy hotel over who gets three pillows and who has to make do with one was all I needed to set my priorities straight.'

'She's not even joking,' said Olivier. 'On our honeymoon, many many moons ago, Coco taught me to love pillows, especially fluffy hotel pillows, and now she tortures me by hogging them all.'

'I have no idea what you two are on about. All I know is that women are born to drive you crazy: the good crazy and the *crazy* crazy.'

'I'll take that any day over my wife going crazy,' said Olivier, laughing a little too loudly, letting out weeks of pent up tension from when he had thought he'd lose Colette if she didn't allow him to help her. She had welcomed his intervention and he was proud that he had risen to the challenge. Yet it didn't seem real to have a mild, almost cheerful, slightly rudderless wife. He wasn't used to captaining their ship and these were some stormy seas.

What her husband couldn't see, however, was that though the crash had derailed her, it had also set her on a new path. She hadn't lost her drive. Her ambition had found new direction: to be happy, to have a happy family. Goals that she would have gawked at a few weeks ago had become motivators. Of course, she would eventually go back to earning a living and being a high-achieving bitch at work, but it would not be her lifeblood anymore. And that difference meant everything. Slowly, she moved her interlocked fingers, circling the inside of Olivier's palm purposefully—a signal he knew all too well. He followed her wordlessly to the guest toilet with the Venetian mirrors and snazzy wallpaper.

He locked the door. She lifted her skirt. *What had happened to her panty? Had she gone commando all night?* He pulled his pants down, his erection hard and needy. They stood a few inches apart, eyeballing each other. She leaned back on the counter. They kept their hands to themselves. He let his eager penis brush against her. All foreplay was limited to their eyes, played out in the precincts of their minds. They didn't kiss or touch or speak. She moved her feet wider and lifted a knee. He entered her and they rode each other straight into a new beginning.

This was turning out to be the best night of Benjamin's life and Dasha wanted to ensure that she was included. Cheering from the sidelines was no longer a game she was happy to play.

They were in the kitchen waiting for the kettle to boil. It was so much later than late that it was almost early, and for an hour now, all of them had been on fizzy water or cola, none brave enough to go near the alcohol that was in any case wafting off their hair, nails and breath.

'Who wants camomile and who wants ginseng?' asked Rosel.

Victor was the first to state his preference. When he'd finally stopped drinking for the evening, he'd intended to climb up the spiral staircase at the back of the building to call it a night. The thought of leaving this opulence for his grey cubbyhole of a room, however, had engulfed him in misery. Eventually, he knew he'd have to head back to his own life of endless nothingness and soiled common WCs, but there was no hurry. He wished he shared Rosel's optimism about their living conditions. He needed to tap into his neighbour's secret. She was utterly blind to the bleakness of their quarters, to the point of being cheery about it. Had she come from even less? It was important to remember that one person's nothing could be another's plenty. He was pleased he had a resident membership, by default, to the motley crew of Number Thirty-Six.

Benjamin, who hadn't stopped shrieking from the minute he had said 'yes', said, 'Dasha, can you talk some sense into this girl? She's refusing to let me use her image for my exhibition.'

In his mind, he had played out the opening night at the gallery, which had been confirmed for mid-December, to its last detail. Of course, he'd allowed himself to imagine the rave reviews and the cash he'd legitimately earn from doing what he loved. There was another reel playing simultaneously in his mind: Violet dressed as the sassiest bride in white, dancing her way to him, confetti and tears all around them. His glee knew no bounds tonight.

'I'll convince her only if I'm in the exhibition too,' said Dasha pointedly. 'Don't think you're leaving me out of your big moment.'

'As if! You started it all.'

'I did start it all, didn't I?' she reiterated, looking for confirmation.

'You certainly did,' he agreed, pulling out his phone to show her the very first image he'd secretly taken of her, when she had jumped on the table in her lingerie with all the casting lot looking up at her. She had clicked a selfie from above, looking down at them, and he had managed to capture her from below in the split second she took to review and admire her handy work, before bouncing off the table. Benjy had already worked on the image, adding his signature now-you-see-it-now-you-don't magic with exposure and graphics.

'You can't tell if I'm coming or going, whether I'm jumping on or off the table... You can't see my face, either. I mean you can, it's like *you* get to decide if I'm there or I'm not there. If I'm laughing or weeping. *I love it*.' He was a true artist: she could see that more than ever now. Glad he was going to get his moment, Dasha was gladder still that she was going to be part of it. 'Rosel, stop being a fool, you have to be part of this,' said Dasha, blowing into the tea that Rosel handed her. The rising steam from her ginseng swept aside the miasma of tequila, cheese samosa and unbrushed teeth in her mouth. It was nearly morning. Soon, she would curl up against Astrid and plot and dream of the reunion with her father.

'My son is already angry with me for my YouTube songs. I don't want to upset him further.'

'That is beyond ridiculous. If you hadn't done the songs, you would not have become a symbol, the President would not have called you, and then Danilo would not be coming to Paris. He has no right to be angry, ungrateful child,' said Dasha. 'He should be celebrating that you sang those songs and got him a visa.'

'Actually, I haven't told him yet. I want to be sure, like *sure* sure, that they'll bring him here before getting his hopes up.'

This time, Victor jumped in. 'You can't get surer than the President himself publicly ordering the process to be fast-tracked. Of course, your little Danilo is coming. This is your time, Rosel, you have to know that. You have to believe that. You made it.'

Rosel let herself be infected by his positivity, not realizing that he was only giving back what he'd got from her. She had to believe. Jesus had finally found the time to look in her direction. She had been put through His tests. She had never abandoned His ways—not when He took Ferdie, not when she left Danilo and not through those lonely nights in Kuwait. She had remained forever committed to Him. When she had stumbled from His path, even when she'd lied or stolen or revoked Him, she had been sure to repent for her sins, if not immediately then eventually for certain. And now, she would feel His mercy. She would. If she believed it, if she kept the faith, she would.

'Let your wife-to-be decide,' said Violet, sashaying in and hijacking the attention. 'Show me, Benj, it's the only one I haven't seen.'

The image was from the night that Rosel's face had been ripped open. He had removed the background and the orange plastic chair she had been sitting on. 'Icy' was the word that popped in Violet's head at first glance. The hospital tiles were all arctic and neon-lit blues, and a chill radiated from the image, sending a shiver through Violet at first glance. It was as if she was being prepared for what she was about to behold. She tried for as long as possible to not look directly at Rosel's bleeding face, but there was no resisting Benjy's mastery—it pulled her in. She braced herself. There was nothing horrific about her slaughtered face. *How? How had he achieved that?* Around her head, a yellowish light brought the only warmth to the picture, making Rosel look angelic, the wound poetic.

Yet, the image itself told a story of untold horrors. Violet squinted and stared—yes, there was a phantom being behind the injured girl, there and not there, depending on the angle. Was it gearing up to attack her or was it walking away from having fulfilled its savage feat? There was definitely a hand assuring violence, and when Violet blinked, it disappeared, only to reappear again. The effect was chilling, playing on everyone's greatest fear of being violated by the bogeyman hiding around the corner, an invisible creature intent on defiling you and devouring your hope. Yet, if you pointed him out, he was no longer there. If she looked long enough, and the photo definitely invited her to, she began to see a glimmer of victory. The phantom looked like the walking wounded, and Rosel looked flushed with peace.

Her lover's photograph embodied an appalling universal experience, a sickening emotion, and given it voice. Violet was speechless. It was as if her own encounter with evil had found expression.

Neera, who was peering over Violet's arm, said, 'Aaah, I guess that's the moment you went from being an immigrant to a Parisian.'

Acknowledgements

This book, much like my life since the age of 11, has Shalini Malik's finger prints all over it. You help me think my thoughts, form my words, read my books and get through this crazy wonderful thing we call our I lives. I don't say it often enough (next to never)—I love you and here's to a 100 more years of pure friendship.

John Ash, I couldn't be happier that you loved and cared for my characters as much as I did. You instinctively knew how to shape them and helped bring this book to life.

Chiki Sarkar, I'll be forever grateful to you for being one of my earliest readers. Without your encouragement this book would have remained a few chapters.

My team at Rupa—Kapish Mehra, Nishtha Kapil, Smita Mathur, Bena Sareen, Amrita Chakravorty, Vasundhara Raj Baigra and all the invisible minds who worked on this—you rock for always giving me yeses. You have given this book a more supportive home than I could've ever dreamed of—*did I get the tense wrong, again?*

Shahrukh Sheikh, I love the way you restructured the rap. You understood, without explanation, the emotion I wanted to convey through song. Now can you make it a hit song, please?

Lipika Bhushan, you went out of your way to help me just when I needed it the most. Thank you.

Priti Paul, you pushed me to write a book, any book, so that *'Your daughter will be proud of you, KP, and you'll be proud of you'*. I did and it's true.

Kalli Purie, I'm thankful for all the dots you connect. You always see and paint the real picture when I get stuck in irrelevant details.

Ankoor Purie, you always have the sanest words to douse my fires and, till date, have never refused me anything (please don't start anytime soon).

Rekha and Aroon Purie, I am the person I am (the good, the bad and the weepy) thanks to the both of you. I wouldn't be me without the education, experiences, opportunities and love you have gifted me.

Thank you, family and friends, for continually putting up with my mood swings (you know who you are), especially when I'm trying to do too much while sleeping too little. You are my most annoying but necessary reality check. You keep me grounded so I can fly.

Viviane Bossina, Sufia Lambrou, Marlow (and his owners) and my Tchoopsie, thank you for stepping in and strutting your stuff on the cover. I owe you big time.

Laurent Rinchet, you make my life that much more possible, my choices that much easier. Thank you for the adventures and the space that have all furnished my writing.

This book is an amalgamation of hundreds of stories that incredible women (friends and strangers) have sometimes intentionally, and often inadvertently shared with me. If you find resonance with a line, a chapter, a moment—know that I'm indebted to your experiences.

I write this book for all those who at some point or another have felt unseen. I see you. Your struggles may be invisible, but your courage to carry on is not.